BODIES
AND
SOULS

Other Works by John Rechy

Novels:
    CITY OF NIGHT
    NUMBERS
    THIS DAY'S DEATH
    THE FOURTH ANGEL
    THE VAMPIRES
    RUSHES

Non-fiction:
    THE SEXUAL OUTLAW: A Documentary

Plays:
    MOMMA AS SHE BECAME—BUT NOT
           AS SHE WAS (one act)
    RUSHES

BODIES
AND
SOULS

A novel by

John Rechy

CARROLL & GRAF PUBLISHERS, INC.
New York

First Edition 1983
First Printing 1983

ISBN: 0-88184-003-3
Library of Congress Catalog Number:
PS3568.E28B6 1983 813'.54 83-7192

An excerpt from Bodies and Souls has appeared in *Oui* magazine.

Manufactured in the U.S.A.

Distributed by Publishers Group West

Carroll & Graf Publishers, Inc.
260 Fifth Avenue
New York, N.Y. 10001

For Michael Earl Snyder . . .

. . . and for the memory
of my mother
and of *tía* Ana

Acknowledgments

I would like to thank Nicolas Bautista for his friendship and help in arriving at the title of this book; Kent Carroll, for his invaluable encouragement, trust, and superb suggestions; Beverle Houston, for a singularly cherished friendship and years of supportive, abundant kindness; Melodie Johnson, for a unique, stimulating friendship; Marsha Kinder, for her astute observations and a special friendship; Barney Rosset, for his continuing support and courage; Floriano Vecchi, for years of affection; and Michael Earl Snyder, for his sustaining love and his creative comments, a major contribution from the inception of this book to its end.

Contents

"And I heard a great voice out of
heaven saying, Behold . . . God
shall wipe away all tears from their
eyes; and there shall be no more
death, neither sorrow, nor crying,
neither shall there be any more pain;
for the former things are passed
away."
                        —*Revelation* 21:3–4.

"Doom! Something seems to whisper
it in the very dark trees of America.
Doom!"
                        —D. H. Lawrence.

"I see your body,
Show me your soul,
And I'll believe ya,
I'll believe ya!
Where's your soul?"
                        —Revolver.

Bodies and Souls

There is a section in Los Angeles where all its freeways or their extensions converge into a twisted concrete star connecting all the parts of the city, its varied lives and destinations.

Above this point of intricate connection—of sweeping cement arcs—land furry with grass and thick with pine trees rises into an uncultivated hill—an incongruous patch of forest in the midst of the vast city, its tall steel and glass buildings just blocks away.

In the surrounding area of vacant lots, where pretty yellow weeds creep through tenacious remains of dusty foundations of houses long ago cleared away, fragments of streets, unused, remain. One, desolate and wide, separates the high hill from the grassy slope that borders the freeways here. Lavender-dotted vines dip to the very edge of concrete lanes.

Orin, Jesse, and Lisa stood on that viny decline. About them, tiny white flowers erupted like miniature sparklers. Nearby, on another truncated street, Orin's indigo Cadillac—a classic of the finned models—waited next to crushed fields.

Palm trees everywhere fringed the sky cleansed by new wind shoving away the dying heat of days and nights. Fires that had seared the distant canyons were contained at last. Only a slender glowing band rimmed an arc of the horizon.

Jesse lean and tanned, Lisa golden and beautiful, Orin boyish and handsome—the two youngmen and the teenage girl laughed joyously as they stood over the clot of freeways. The chrome of automobiles captured the white sun in flashing silver blades.

It was almost noon.

Jesse held his shirt over one shoulder, Lisa held a frayed doll, and Orin held the rifle.

John Rechy

Jesse pointed to a car on the freeway, and Lisa looked down at the blue automobile slowing as if to pull away from the flowing traffic. Ambushing wind plucked at their sudden words. With a cry, Orin raised the rifle. His finger touched its trigger.

In one deadly instant, multiple bursts of fire spat into the freeways.

PART ONE

Lost Angels: 1

Ten days before the slaughter on the freeways, and on an afternoon in late spring, early summer, Orin, Lisa, and Jesse James stood before the gates of an abandoned mansion on Sunset Boulevard in Beverly Hills. Many tourists milled about the notorious house. From behind the elaborate gates, burly guards stared at the gathered spectators.

Although unpredictable, June is often murky, even cool; but a Southern California day can go through a mild version of the four seasons—the blue coolness of morning moving to sweaty warmth. Today in that seasonless month, a breeze containing a hint of heat kept the smog against the watery horizon of an azure sky.

"It reminds me of Tara in *Gone with the Wind*," Lisa said. She had just turned eighteen. She had a prettiness saved from cuteness and nudged toward beauty by a full, sensual mouth. She had cultivated a crooked half-smile like Lauren Bacall's in *To Have and Have Not*.

"You're crazy," Jesse James laughed. The jagged angles of his twenty-one-year-old face gave him a composite handsomeness his individual features did not possess. Under his cowboy hat, darkish hair licked his forehead. He opened another button of his shirt, exposing his chest to more sun. "*Gone with the Wind* had tall columns, and it sure didn't have *those* statues."

Beyond the iron-grill fencing of intricate fleurs-de-lis looping over stone-embossed walls, the mansion is painted green, smeared now by buried smoke. A large tree, killed by fire, lies over a long veranda. Statues of naked bodies line the cracked balustrade, muscular figures of men, curved bodies of women, almost life-size, once painted in flesh tones, with rosy lips and cheeks

3

and eyelashed tinted eyes, and pubic hair, drawn black and realistic. Now the colored bodies are faded; only the painted hair over exposed genitals remains bold and dark. Defiantly the mansion faces the strip of coiffed grass that divides the wide boulevard as it curves and swerves along miles of green, flowered wealth and stops far away in Malibu at the frothing edge of the Pacific Ocean.

Jesse James grasped the iron bars of the main gate, as if looking into an opulent prison. A guard approached, and he let go. In substitute defiance, he pushed his cowboy hat forward, squinting up. His brown eyes fixed on the crotch of one of the female statues; he felt a stirring between his long, lean legs.

"I didn't say it *looks* like the house in *Gone with the Wind,* I said it *reminds* me," Lisa upheld. She took another delicious lick, close to the last, of a Baskin-Robbins ice-cream cone, flavor of the week, vanilla-pistachio. Some of it dripped onto her chest; she captured the melting sweetness with a finger and poked it into her mouth. Her breasts were becoming roundly full; because she was slender, and shorter than the five-foot-six she claimed, they appeared lush. She was blessed with truly violet eyes—and thick dark eyelashes, although her hair, worn loose and to her shoulders, was brown, auburn in spring, streaked blond by summer. In Mundelein, Illinois, she had wanted to be a movie star; she no longer cared about that, or about anything else. "Doesn't it remind *you* of *Gone with the Wind?*" she asked Orin.

Orin stood very straight glaring at the gutted mansion—as close as he could come to it from the sidewalk. There were times when he looked like a grown Huckleberry Finn—reddish blond hair, mischievous blue eyes, lanky angular body neither short nor tall, just slightly too thin, a fair, almost translucent complexion unmarred by freckles. Then unexpectedly a somber look might push away the boyish smile, extend the tilt of his eyes—suddenly haunted eyes—and dark semicircles would deepen under them; a moody beauty would emerge, along with the impression of darkness—despite the glowing hair, the clear eyes so moistly blue at times they seemed to weep without tears. Approaching twenty-five, he aged or grew younger in alternating moods. Now he stared intensely at the naked statues on the aging lawn. His fair eyebrows knotted. In answer to Lisa's question, he shrugged and shook his head.

"My *God,* you didn't *see* it?" Lisa said. "I thought *everybody* had." She took the last bite of her cone, not swallowing it, letting the cream thaw slowly in her mouth, preserving the wonderful flavor. When it was gone, she said, "I'd like to go through *all* thirty-one Baskin-Robbins flavors." She tasted her lips for any lingering sweetness. "Wouldn't it be something to change names, like the ice-cream flavor of the week? Could I change my name each day, Orin?" she asked.

"Sure," Orin said. His eyes were just slightly too large for his lean face, but the square jaw compensated for that disparity. Often when he smiled, his whole face was radiant with life. Other times only his lips smiled. He smiled fully now.

"Thank you," Lisa said. She lowered the white-embroidered blouse at the shoulders. Her young breasts vied favorably with those of the sculpted women on the lawn of the rich mansion.

Jesse felt a smarting resentment. They had been together two days and one night since Orin had stopped the old, beautiful Cadillac—one of the first of the finned models—to pick him up in the Texas–New Mexico desert. He'd jumped in next to Lisa, delighted by her prettiness. Jesse learned Orin had stopped for Lisa—her brand-new suitcase beside her—just outside Chicago only a few days before that. In their time together, Lisa had never asked Jesse for an opinion. But she asked Orin for permission sometimes. What would Cagney—Cody, Cody Jerrett—what would he do in such a situation? Jesse had discovered Cagney, Cody, and *White Heat* on television; he saw the movie once again, in a theater, and would have gone back again and again but it played only that day, once.

A nervous breeze was becoming warmer. Jesse felt moisture grow under his arms. He opened another button. He wasn't sure what Orin's reaction would be if he took off his shirt.

There was not a trace of perspiration on Orin, although he wore a light, gray jacket over his white shirt—one button open. His eyes seemed to bore into the mansion, as if to perceive its essence within the scorched gaudy grandeur, the meaning in its disorder.

The original house was white. Then a few years ago an

Arabian sheik bought it for his pretty teenage bride. He paid two and a half million dollars for it and spent several million more to convert it into the assaulting palace. It was painted the color of ripe limes. The nude-colored statues were mounted on the sweeping balustrade. Intrusive trees were cleared so that the house was brazenly open in a section of Los Angeles where other luxurious mansions hide behind walls of dark tall trees. The sheik's name was engraved on ebony slabs under round mirrors like clashing shields at the gates. Intricate paths and the outlining walls were embedded with brown, amber, ecru stones, smooth and swarthy as the sheik's skin; iron gray stones, the sheen of burnished silver; and green and purple tiles, dazzling as a peacock's tail. Under a gleaming copper dome which blazed at sunset, the thirty-eight rooms of the mansion curved in two wings facing iron posts holding lanterns which glowed like haloes of green fire at night. Concrete urns topped the many ledges.

Now, Los Angeles is a city of scarred beauty. But for miles and miles throughout its stretching horizon, its flowered, verdant beauty, as grand as that of any other city in the world, is unmarred. In this city of grass and trees perennially green, layered in shades of amber green, rusted green, silver green; of flowers that flash out of shrubs in crimson and gold flames; a city overlooked by palm trees that transform long streets into corridors to distant hills; a city where blood-red bougainvillea pours over walls, balconies, sidewalks, streets, even the edges of the freeways; a city in which giant hibiscuses open into sparklers, scarlet orangy leaves form proud paradisaical birds, and Joshua trees clutch torches of white blossoms; a city of roses pale as the sky or garish as an open wound; of jacaranda trees veiling the ground in lilac filigree; of enormous blossoms with color-saturated hearts draining, through pastel veins, to white at their curled edges; of rampant flowers deep pink just before they turn red, azure this side of indigo, lavender that is almost violent; a city of flowers whose clashing colors and shapes assume a paradoxical harmony in recurrent discordance—in such a city, the young sheik filled his concrete urns with plastic yellow and white flowers and waxy artificial leaves.

Hundreds of people came to stare in awe, disbelief, derision, admiration, envy, resentment at the ostentatious palace that dared to flaunt ancient foreign wealth in an area of somewhat less strident, newer—and concealed—excess.

Scandal and outrage—bruitings of bigamy and assault—soon swirled about the house. The young sheik and his wife moved out, and the mansion was left in vague judgment. Then fire burst from the heart of the house, its arced windows and doors exploding in pieces of colored glass and mosaic. During the night of probable arson, a tarnished glow captured the mansion.

After the fire—quickly extinguished—burlier guards inherited the vacated palace. Unnoticed at first because they sputtered with small yellow buds, weeds made incursions into the lawns, then exposed leprous patches of dirt. Tourists ripped pieces off the black-stoned walls and left white, gashed scars.

Grime has settled on the plastic flowers. Windows and doors are barricaded. A blackened pine tree accepts rot from its roots. The pale statues linger amid the ruins of the mansion like desultory traumatized inmates of a decaying asylum accessible only to the very beautiful, the very rich.

"I could be Scarlett O'Hara for a day," Lisa pondered, her voice tinged with an unsure accent. From behind the iron fence a guard stared at her. She flipped her hair saucily at his bold gaze and looked away from the house. They had been on their way to the beach when they saw the mansion and the people lingering; Orin parked immediately on a side street. "Remember when Scarlett swore she'd never be hungry again? That's my favorite scene, everything ruined and burned behind her—everyone so mean to her—and her, so brave, swearing she'd never be hungry again even if she had to lie, cheat, steal, or kill."

"Or fuck!" Jesse added. Some tourists glared at him. He tipped his hat sheepishly. His semihard-on was growing pleasurably. To enhance it, he put his long bony fingers on Lisa's shoulder, just above her pert breasts.

"Oh, *you!*" Lisa tried not to flirt. "She didn't swear *that!*" She shrugged just slightly so that the hand would touch the part that tingled.

Orin turned his back on the gouged house. His eyes deepened on Jesse and Lisa. Jesse removed his hand—but he opened the

last button of his shirt. Lisa averted Orin's unnerving stare.
When it occurred, it might remain for a long time.

Himself avoiding facing Orin and a possible forbidding reaction,
Jesse removed his moist shirt. He'd lost weight since he'd left
Kentucky (and Indiana nearby), but he liked the carved leanness
of his torso. He had to be careful to remember he had told Orin
and Lisa he was from Texas. Kentucky. People always said,
Oh, yes, the Blue Mountains—sometimes they said green, even
black. He was from Morganfield, Kentucky, mostly reddish
dust in summer, gray dust in winter, stretches of flat land.
Evansville—in Indiana—was a city of white houses. That's
where he'd begun hitching from, tote bag over his shoulder.
Five or more dull, tiring rides—and then he'd met Orin and Lisa
in a steaming limbo of desert. He would never forget the finned
beauty of a car pulling up to the side of the road! And then there
was the instant pleasure of Lisa's pretty, crooked-smiling face—
which tempered Orin's studying gaze.

"Would you three like me to take your picture—you're such
a good-looking threesome!" an older white-haired man said.
His thin wife smiled reedy encouragement at them. "Grandchildren," the man indicated a boy and a girl trying to climb the
barred wall, backing off each time a guard approached. Another
child, the youngest, a dark, slender boy, stood sullenly apart.

"Sure would!" Jesse looked eagerly at Orin.

Lisa arranged herself prettily for the picture; then she glanced
unsurely at Orin. She hoped the children would stay away.
She'd learned Orin didn't like children at all, wouldn't even sit
near them in a restaurant, or even glance at them in the motel.

The energetic, chubby boy asked Jesse James if he was a real
cowboy—"with yer hat 'n boots 'n all."

"Might be a stunt man in the movies," Jesse said, deliberately vague, thinking that for the first time.

"Whass-*at*?" said the round-faced girl.

"Well, *I'm* not going to be a movie star," Lisa asserted
haughtily.

"Why did *you* come to Los Angeles?" the thin woman asked
Orin, who was facing the quiet boy staying away.

"Cause I had to," Orin said.

"Oh," the woman said.

Orin talked like that often—you couldn't always understand him. At first, riding with him before they met Jesse James, Lisa would ask him what he meant, and his answer would be even more unclear. "Depends—. . ." he'd start. At times now, she *thought* she understood him, sometimes.

"How about it—your picture?" the man reminded.

Secretly—hands behind her—Lisa shooed the bouncing children away because she could see Orin's annoyance growing toward them and she wanted the picture. "Oh, *please,* Orin," she pled.

"Okay, Orin?" Jesse resented asking, but he didn't want to anger Orin, who could be moody in a moment. Jesse was riding along with them—with Orin—and he didn't have much money left. Neither did Lisa, he suspected, from the way she had hedged about paying for her flavor of the week but did anyhow. Orin paid for all the gasoline. Jesse had the impression Orin had more money than they did. They were all sharing so far—not equally, Orin always paying more—for food and the motel, which was very pretty, in Hollywood. It had a pool and looked like a Spanish hacienda. Last night, when they arrived—a whisper of coolness in the misty air—it glowed with mothy blue, green, and red lights hidden among trimmed hedges. The wood-beamed room had a large color television set. Orin had asked the clerk about that immediately, and several times, and about which channels they received and how clearly. He even checked it before they actually registered.

Orin smiled the full-faced smile that made him look like a kid. "Don't mind a-*tall,*" he agreed to the photograph.

Jesse draped his shirt discreetly over his shoulder, Lisa did her half-smile, Orin stood straight and formal. The dark child remained apart from the clustered others.

The man clicked the camera. "Part of the fun is watching the picture appear."

In the developing photograph, their ghostly figures became flesh-colored, undefined tinted shadows, outlines; then a grayness coated the paper and evaporated. The photograph appeared sharply. In it, the statues lingered like phantoms behind them.

"Bodies." Orin turned away from the picture.

That was all he said. Lisa thought he would go on—about how sacred bodies are. That was one of the many subjects he talked to her about, in those days and nights of hills and desert and driving. There would be times of silence, too, and times when he searched the radio from one preacher station to another— all there was along the desolate stretches—especially at night.

Jesse and Lisa admired the photograph. Lisa took it from him. They *did* make a good threesome—as if they had set out on their trips to Los Angeles together.

"Come see the pichur, you!" the girl called to the reclusive boy. The boy turned his head away.

"You *know* he won't," the other frenetic child imitated an impatient adult—resigned hands crossed on his round chest.

"Just leave him alone to sulk," the woman said. "Moody the whole trip," she mused. "Wanted to stay with his mother instead of come with *us,* and *we're* having *such* a good time!"

"He'll grow out of it," the grandfather said automatically, indulgently battling the two loud children.

"Howdee," Orin called to the somber boy.

Lisa was startled.

"Hi!" "Hi!" The romping children started to rush at Orin. He looked down sternly at them, his hand raised in a thwarting gesture. The children backed away. "Wanna fly?" Orin addressed the quiet boy, who did not respond.

"We've *all* given up on him," the thin woman warned with exasper ated acceptance.

"He'll grow out of it," the grandfather said.

Orin spread out his arms like airplane wings. "Wanna fly *away?*" he asked the boy. The boy looked at him. "*Want* to?" Orin insisted. The boy nodded. Orin swayed his outstretched arms. The boy rushed to him. With a strength belied by his slender frame, Orin whirled him about, the boy stretched his own arms, flying, and almost laughed.

"Can you believe that?" the woman said.

Lisa couldn't.

The boy struggled to be put down. Orin lowered him. The boy retreated to the fence.

"Home of an Ay-rab sheik," an amplified voice boomed. A tourist bus paused before the mansion. "Fire destroyed parts of—. . ." Behind it, a regular bus stopped to allow the straining heads of tourists to gape at the statues and the awesome house. In the second bus, the outraged face of a black woman looked out—and quickly away in disgust. Orin saw her.

Now from his pants pocket he brought out his round, elaborate watch, gold and shiny. He looked up at the sun, back at the watch. He said to the man and woman, "Thank you for the picture, ma'am, sir."

"Sir, ma'am, thankya both," Jesse echoed.

The slender boy inched closer.

In a strong voice Orin said to him, "You *learn* to fly!—wherever you want!—and then you don't have to *be*—anywhere!"

That strange talk. Lisa still marveled at Orin.

He marched away from the house. Jesse and Lisa followed him.

A fat, past-middle-aged woman and her tired husband were walking up to the gates of the mansion. The woman gasped ecstatically, "*Well!*—that's what *I* call a beautiful home!" She waved happily at Orin, Jesse, and Lisa, who glanced back.

Each time Jesse saw Orin's long Cadillac, he beamed, proud to know he'd be riding in it. A beauty, a real beauty, a 1953 Eldorado convertible, one of the most expensive ever made, a classic now—and it was like new! Orin always raised the top when they parked. In the daylight the car was indigo, at night it was black. On Sunset Strip—as they drove through the neon portion of the boulevard—gaudy elaborate billboards screaming about great rock albums, great movies, great Las Vegas shows—young people called out compliments to the car. That pleased Jesse. Orin just drove on in the car with Massachusetts license plates.

When Orin lowered the roof of the car now, warmer wind flowed in. Lisa stared about her in delight. Along the streets everywhere, delicate blossoms floated like purple mist over jacaranda trees. "The most beautiful trees in the world!" she pronounced—but even those had rivals in this unbelievable city.

"You sure the car's yours, Orin?" Jesse blurted the question he had asked silently over and over in the last two days.

From the beginning of their coming together, there had been an understanding, tacitly but strongly asserted by Orin, welcomed easily by them, that they would not inquire about each other's past life. Each had left behind an ending. Now Jesse had violated that rule clumsily. Instantly he felt threatened—and so did Lisa.

Orin said in a voice that gave no hint of his feelings, "Yes, it is mine. Now. Longest it's ever been driven's from Salem to here. I got papers for it. You wanna see them, Jesse?"

"Hell, no, Orin," Jesse withdrew. "Just joking."

"It was willed to me by an old woman. Died just a short time back," Orin spoke those words in a voice that still buried—or controlled tightly—any emotion. "Why I'm here, now." Then he fired at Jesse: "You sure your name is Jesse James?"

It was clear that Orin's anger was a warning to Jesse—and to Lisa—of what such questioning might provoke, a dredging of their lives. Was she next? No, he was sealing their pasts from inquiry. Lisa was all too willing to discard her past.

Jesse's face crimsoned. "Yeah," he said. "Except it's really James Jesse." He regretted his probing. No more serious questions!—that was that!—no matter how many he collected in his mind.

Orin laughed. "Just joking, Jesse, just joking!"

About *all* of it? Which part? It was true that sometimes in a clueless voice, Orin would say something that sounded very serious, and then he'd laugh, for having put something off on them. Lisa preferred to move away quickly from this mined territory: "Tyrone Power played Jesse James in the movies," she informed Jesse. "Linda Darnell could've died when they shot him, she loved him so—and *then* he was so mean to her in *Blood and Sand*."

Jesse said dejectedly: "Cagney should've played Jesse James." He was genuinely saddened that Cagney hadn't.

Lisa slipped the snapshot into a small wallet she carried. She sat in the middle of the front seat. Her skirt rose slightly. Her thigh connected with Jesse's. Sometimes—but she cautioned herself increasingly—she *still* let it touch Orin's briefly.

Orin drove expertly. Several times Jesse prepared to offer to "help" with the driving, then didn't, reluctant to get a "No" from Orin. The engine purred, as if throughout the many years of its existence the car had lived sheltered.

Orin maneuvered into the still light, early afternoon traffic on Sunset. Heat was throwing away the coolness in the rising breeze. Lisa liked to describe the various flowers she spotted, constantly thrilled by the city's beauty. "Pink stars with red hearts! Orange orchids!" She was enjoying the growing pressure of Jesse's thigh against hers.

She didn't prefer Jesse to Orin, no; she liked both, a lot, equally. Before Jesse joined them—just standing there so tall in the pale desert—she would slide tentatively toward Orin so that their bodies would touch if the car lurched. At times he seemed to welcome the sensual contact; she would feel an answering pressure; and then—and now more often than not—he pulled away from the touch. Sometimes he'd actually wince. The first night they stopped at a motel, Orin got a room for her, a room for him. At first Lisa had felt hurt, rejected; but the old movies she cherished had saved her. From them she borrowed explanations for Orin's contradictory reactions—he was being faithful to some *one;* hurt by a powerful love; or "saving" himself for the *exact one.* Eventually those conjectures satisfied her less: It was the abandoned women of those romantic movies who pined for true love that way. And, too, Orin reacted to a lengthened touch as if it hurt him, really *hurt* him. Then he'd be quiet, and the murmuring of the Cadillac would be like unformed whispers. When those silent periods had stretched and pulled along the miles to Los Angeles, Lisa told him about the movies she had seen—"only the old great ones," she emphasized.

She had seen them all in a theater in Chicago that showed only those cherished "all-time favorites," as its marquee proclaimed. It changed movies three times, sometimes four, each week, double-feature each day. Running away—from Mundelein—about two hours and several worlds' distance away—to the dark ecstasy of that theater, she would sit through the movies over and over, repeating lines to herself.

And so as she had traveled with Orin through the sun-misted forests and then vaporous deserts—and later with Jesse, who

would listen enthralled one moment, then tease her the next
while Orin listened, just listened—Lisa told about Pearl Chavez,
the half-breed in *Duel in the Sun;* mounted on her horse, Pearl
moved determinedly under a bleeding sky to her inevitable
assignation with her lover, Lewt—"so mean to her, so mean."
Lisa would shift easily to tell about Roberto—"Ro-*ber*-tow,"
she emphasized the correct pronunciation—and his betrayal of
"beautiful Maria" in *For Whom the Bell Tolls*—forced by her
lover to leave him, wounded, though she longed to die with
him. "You told us and *told* us," Jesse would disguise his
eagerness to hear it all again as she moved on to tell about
Scarlett O'Hara. Scarlett!—among the blackened stones of
Tara—"swearing to survive no matter what!" That scene didn't
exactly fit with the others, but she loved it. Her voice became
strong with Scarlett's conviction then, but as the Cadillac glided
on the heated concrete, the tone of lament for the doomed
heroines buried in the darkness of that old theater would resume,
and she evoked the ghost of Cathy, cursed by Heathcliff—"so
mean"—to wander the desolate moors of Wuthering Heights
until he, too—. . .

"Flaming birds!" she named another flower now, now in this
city of blossoms and dead movie stars. Her own words jarred a
sad memory—of a bird that had crashed against the windshield
of the car before they picked up Jesse. The bird splashed blood
and feathers. Orin cried out. He stopped the car. He got out and
gathered the crushed bird carefully in his handkerchief. She saw
him carry the small bleeding bundle to a side of the bare
highway. He searched until he found a bush to bury the bird in
soothing shade.

Jesse restrained himself from turning the radio on. Earlier,
propped by evoking the image of Cody, he *had* suggested
another station—the news bombarding him; and Orin agreed.
Jesse felt good about that. "We going to the beach?" He tried
to make it a statement, but it came out a question. That occurred
often. "Sure," Orin said—but Jesse wasn't sure he'd even
heard his words.

They passed a sign that said "Bel Air." Carefully tended
pools of orange, purple, and yellow flowers gather there be-

tween white portals. Paved tributaries off Sunset Boulevard dash into the depths of the locked verdure where other mansions flee to haughty seclusion. Dark brown arms crossed impatiently over her white-uniformed bosom, a black woman waited for a tardy employer to pick her up.

"Broken hearts, bleeding," Lisa named another cluster of flowers—and quickly changed the name: "Red valentines!"

They drove past a grotto of green vines surrounding a white statue of Christ, in splendid, festive white robes. Several long blocks farther, they passed another statue of Jesus, on the lawn of a church. That figure was crucified, its bloodied forehead haloed by thick thorns. "I wonder which one he looks like now—real happy, or *still* real sad," Orin said.

Both Lisa and Jesse were becoming used to the way Orin seemed to collect his thoughts, then connect them aloud.

"Just depends, I guess," Orin answered himself.

"On what?" Lisa queried. These were the moments—when his voice was so soft, a sigh—that Lisa longed to touch him, just to touch him.

"On what people do," Orin said.

Past the exits and entrances of the San Diego Freeway in a rich area called Brentwood, a giant American flag over a slick hotel flapped erratically in the undecided wind.

Lisa moved her leg away from Jesse's, Orin's sad sigh lingering.

Last night, the first night the three spent together, Jesse hadn't known what would happen, whether Lisa and Orin would sleep together. Orin had been flicking television channels off and on; it was late and several stations were off the air. In a short nightgown, Lisa slipped into one bed. Jesse, lanky in his boxer shorts, stood between the two beds. Orin nodded toward the vacant one. Then in his own shorts and t-shirt, he got into the bed with Jesse and lay on his back—all night and hardly moving, as far as Jesse could tell—on the extreme opposite side of the bed. The whole incident had surprised Jesse; he hadn't been sure whether to be disappointed or encouraged; all depended on whether the situation made Lisa more or less available to him. Orin clarified that soon enough—this very morning when Jesse touched Lisa's bare shoulder. Orin's look froze on him. And yet, Jesse noticed, Orin often stared at Lisa himself— maybe wasn't even aware he was doing it, his blue eyes fixed on her breasts, or on her exposed thighs when she moved into the car. Orin's stares contained desire, Jesse recognized *that*. But then his gaze, darkening, would pull away from Lisa's flesh.

Lisa pointed out the window at saffron-tipped flowers: "Exploding stars— . . ."

Orin braked. Lisa's head jerked. Jesse's pulled back, then forward. "What the hell!" Jesse said. The Cadillac almost skidded into a car that had stopped just as abruptly. Ahead of it, another car had, too. There was the gathered scream of brakes. Traffic froze. Nearing sirens shrieked, gasped, shrieked. Approaching red lights swirled just ahead.

Orin guided the finned convertible along the shoulder of the boulevard. On a side road, he parked near a velvet-grassed incline. He jumped out, running up the short mound.

The sirens were throttled into silence. The red lights swirled within a contained radius now.

Jesse followed Orin up the incline.

At first Lisa decided she'd stay in the car. An accident had occurred, that was obvious. She didn't like the sight of blood, not real blood, anyway—only "romantic blood," like in the last scene of *Duel in the Sun,* when Pearl Chavez climbs the desert rocks to die with— . . . But it was too hot to stay in the unmoving car. She blew into her blouse, cooling her breasts as she walked toward Orin and Jesse. She still didn't want to look, afraid of what she might see.

Sounds of panic came from nearby, exacerbated voices. Then there were sustained screams. The red eye of police-car lights tainted the area in a bleeding glow. Orin and Jesse were looking down into a schoolyard.

A few terrified men and women—teachers—were herding and rushing more than a dozen children away from a large tree on the grounds. The children balked, looking back. Two or three policemen and some men in white uniforms dashed toward the tree.

Lisa looked away from the schoolyard—she had caught a glimpse of what was there. Turning away, she saw cars backed up on the street. Heads leaned out of open windows to gape. Lisa looked away from that, too. She felt hot, caught in a sudden fierce darkness.

"*Jesus Christ!*" Jesse James said.

In the schoolyard, the body of a man was hanging from the branch of a jacaranda tree. The strap that held his strangled neck was partially obscured by pretty, dainty lavender flowers. The head, tilted to one side, was covered with a black hood.

Amber: "Meat"

Deliriously, vibrant red hair flailing like a whip, Amber Haze rode the man's cock. Her hand held one breast like an offering, a firm, round, pink offering, nipple hard as the tip of a finger. Spreading her perfect legs, she lowered her torso, raised it, lowered it, her red-furred cunt clinging to the full round cock inside her. Lying on the lavender sheets, the man shoved his hips up, farther up, pushing harder, his long legs propped in order to penetrate her more deeply, into the farthest depth. Amber opened her eyes widely—gold-flecked eyes, heavily lashed, darkly outlined—and looked up in an expression of delirium. She moaned, groaned, sighed, moaned. The hand not stroking the proffered breast reached back, behind her arched buttocks, as if to double the sensation of the lunging cock—in her, and sliding on her eager finger tips. Now the man tumbled over her roughly and mounted her thrusting body.

He was a slender man in his thirties, tall, just slightly better-looking than plain—hair brown, features as regular as those of anyone walking any street. Still, he was extraordinary. He was Jimmy Steed, the man reputed to have the largest cock in the country, perhaps the world. Again he manipulated Amber's body over, his large hands pulling her up from the stomach, so that her buttocks were toward his waiting cock. She was on all fours, kneeling. One of his hands still grasped her flat stomach and slid toward the pink breasts, his other hand clutched his inflated organ, and he shoved it into her cunt.

She groaned, red hair glorious, luxuriant over her face. She pushed the cascading hair away. Her head turned from side to side. Her gorgeous face, tongue licking her scarlet lips hungrily, seemed to be about to accept the ultimate in sexual grace as

18

Jimmy Steed fucked her. Even in that position, her breasts, large and sculpted, retained their firm hardness, although he pushed forcefully against her in hard, jerking shoves.

Again in one tough motion, Jimmy Steed turned Amber over, face-up on the pillow. Her lips parted, moistened wine red, and her tilted nose flared as if to allow for the increased quickening of her ecstatic gasps. He fucked her from the front now, separating her legs with his hands, allowing his penis to display its full, round length before entering her again. Proudly, Jimmy Steed looked down at his organ, not at Amber. As if in a state of pained bliss, her beautiful face turned toward the pink pillow, biting it as if to contain the spilling ecstasy, to extend it. Quickly, Jimmy pulled out his cock, and pumping forward from his hips, he came in a jetting arc. Holding the sputtering cock like a shooting gun, he aimed the cum at Amber's magnificent breasts. When the sputtering diminished, he rubbed the sticky thickness on her nipples. He moved his dripping cock in an arc over her breasts and made a whistling sound with half-smiling lips.

Amber stood. The mound of red pubic hair shocked the creamy flesh into greater nudity. In the bathroom now, she stretched her resplendent body in a sunken tub. Following her there, Jimmy turned the shower on. Water streamed onto Amber's breasts. Leaning her head back, eyes closed, lips licking at random drops, she rubbed the water on her breasts, between them, on her nipples. Spread-legged, Jimmy stood over her in the shower. The intercepted water ran down his shoulders, his chest, his stomach, his cock—and from there it jetted down over her breasts. Then he turned the shower off. He stood over her again. The liquid flow continued—now only from his cock. "Rub it on good, babe!" his twangy voice commanded. "Drink that— . . ."

"*Goddamn that son of a bitch!*"

"Shhh."

"Shut up!"

"*Shhhhhh!*"

The irritated admonitions came from the darkness of the theater. In a row toward the back, Amber Haze turned away from her reflection on the movie screen. As if anticipating that moment in the film, waiting for it, a man in front of her gasped, then surrendered into the velvet seat. Amber was aware of at least two other men nearby—concealing convulsed movements.

This was the time of day, just after lunchtime, when there were the fewest people in the Pussy Cat Theater on Hollywood Boulevard, where *Meat,* starring Amber Haze and Jimmy Steed, was breaking attendance records. She had waited for this early day in the week, this hour of the day, to see the film for the first time.

In the theater now, she wore a bandanna to hide her famous, identifying mane of red hair—its real color; and she had changed her makeup. *That son of a bitch!* Anger stabbed more deeply. For a few moments she did not move, still facing away from the screen, hearing her recorded voice reciting stupid lines, silly double *entendres,* which Jimmy Steed—the worst "actor" in the world—was trying to answer in his slow drawl: "Wanna eat th' sweet candy, li'l girl, while I eat—. . . ?"

Until she heard the man's whimpered, smothered sounds, she did not realize she had been looking in the direction of a man sitting in the same row but across the aisle from her. Having waited too long, he was coming now, during one of the few unsexual moments in the film. Amber thought she should want to laugh. She wondered why she didn't, didn't want to.

Removing the concealing bandanna, she stood up, releasing the red crown of her hair. She walked out of the theater. Nobody even glanced at her—eyes fixed on the flickering garishly colored figures on the screen. Another man, in a back row, was choosing his moment to masturbate. Amber glanced back at the screen and saw a full shot of her nude body exposed. She had always loved that, the knowledge that men would fantasize about her, her body, long after the movie was over.

The lobby of this theater is carefully decorated—mirrored, gold and red, pseudo-neo-"Victorian." Because Amber Haze was one of the three top female stars—perhaps *the* top female star—in pornographic films, her movies did not play in the rancid, crouched, stenchy, black-squashed theaters along the lower part of the boulevard.

Standing in the bright light of the lobby, Amber frowned. She was staring at her own reflection in a mosaic of mirrors that decorated one whole wall. Her reflection was chopped into glass blocks, individual body parts separated by the partitions between the small mirrors. Spread apart in the reflection, her breasts seemed extracted from the rest of her body, which appeared distorted. She turned away from the fragments of herself in the silver mirrors. The usher—wearing white gloves—recognized her; she knew that look. He was about to speak, but already she was outside in the sweating heat of Hollywood Boulevard.

The trashy street shimmered in the heat—or perhaps it was the assault of afternoon brightness that made it seem so. The sweetish odor of smog tinged the unseasonably warm air. A chilly night had become a coolish morning, which was giving way to a sudden warmth, shoved in by the desert winds.

Amber pushed the bandanna off her neck, releasing her hair freely—her pride, yes, as much as her breasts. The blowup outside the theater and behind glass exhibited them fully—her hair, her chest; longish scarlet hair over creamy white breasts. STEED MEETS AMBER IN "MEAT" AND IT SIZZLES! The tips of the *M* in the title pointed to her exposed nipples. Behind her, the thin body of Jimmy Steed was rendered full-length, the lower portion of the *T* in the title concealing yet emphasizing—and exaggerating—his famous cock.

Wearing a gray jacket in the hot weather, a red-haired youngman faced her. Nearby, an extremely pretty girl revealing freckled shoulders over a white-embroidered blouse stood next to a tall youngman with a cowboy hat, shirt open. the two were looking from the poster to her. The other youngman frowned at her, and the frown transformed his face entirely; moody, angered.

Automatically, Amber shook her hair in defiant abandon, and her lips parted as she moistened them—that was her automatic reaction when she sensed a verbal assault about to be unleashed. But the man, still staring, said nothing. The "cowboy's" eyes shifted from her to the poster, as if to intensify the feeling of radiating sexuality.

"Did you get your name from *Forever Amber?*" the girl asked her in a voice that was not unkind, not at all.

"Partly—but also from the color of my eyes," Amber said. She looks like me, in a *new* way, she thought, feeling instantly close to the girl. "But my real name is Barbara, Barbara Leighton." It was the first time she had told anyone her real name in— . . . How long! Years. Years. This girl was so young, so unaffected; she made Amber feel old, at twenty-nine.

"Bodies," came the voice of the man Amber had expected to hear speak first. Though the single word was uttered softly, it left a disturbing echo.

She turned away from it. She strode away in the loose, leggy style she had made her own—her proud gait, both bold and shy, sexual and elegant. It began, her walk, in preparation, with a quick toss of her head, her hair brushing her cheek as she turned her face just barely to the right, her chin raised for a second, then back as if in qualification of its overt assurance. Her left shoulder and hand swung slightly back, and her right leg extended in a long assertive step against the always-adoring fabric of her dress, which shifted to greet the advance of her left leg—now the right shoulder swung back in opposite complement. It was an assertive, joyful, sexual walk—which might pause uncertainly for only a moment before it resumed with the quick toss of her head again.

She had parked in a lot near Max Factor's on Highland Avenue. She had to journey through the shattered spectacle of Hollywood Boulevard. Rows of ignored bronzed stars, bearing the names of famous and not-so-famous movie people—hers would never be among them—are embedded into the concrete of the sidewalks; shabby, tacky reminders of one of myriad attempts to restore "glamor" to this vanquished street of squeezed game arcades—machines pinging, tiny electric colors measuring out tiny victories; oniony food stands; frothing fruity-drink counters; army surplus stores with limbless manikins; and, at intervals, grand atavistic theaters, temples, now triplexes, fragments of their Art Deco heritage assaulted by flat plastic additions, partitions. Along the blocks, people waited for buses; others just waited. And there were hustlers of all kinds, all sexes, all types—pushing sex and cheap dope.

On hot days there is much nudity on this street—young girls in cutoffs that show the crescents of their buttocks; squads of shirtless, sinewy youngmen. Lounging, moving away, coming back, moving away. A mobile indolence.

Amber passed the pale lavender building on that strip: Frederick's of Hollywood. In the windows, pretty pouting manikins are dressed in the type of clothes she often wore in her movies—lacy black corsets designed not to close in the middle, frilled brassieres through which nipples peek out, nightgowns that open strategically in cut-out heart shapes to reveal flesh, bikinis that part at the lower tip of the wider V. In attitudes that are meant to be sexually provocative, the giant sex-dolls behind the polished glass looked crazily desperate to Amber today, all bunched together, coy hands meant to flutter but paralyzed in alarm. It was as if these frozen creatures were wandering through a pretty disaster. The head of one sultry manikin was tilted too far to one side. The neck looked twisted under the see-through pinkish peach material of the open-striped creation she wore.

Disturbed all at once by the odd conglomeration of fantasy bodies, Amber retreated from the window. On it, her own reflection was ghostly. Pulling back farther, she bumped into a meek man emerging nervously out of the store. He clutched a large box to himself as if to hide it. "Excuse me," he apologized. "That's all right," Amber said quickly, "that's really all right." "Thank you," he said. The man looked so mild, so lost, like the man who had waited too long to masturbate in the theater earlier.

Walking slightly faster, avoiding the tarnished copper stars on the sidewalks, Amber passed an army surplus store. In combat uniforms, the manikins there were truncated torsos with featureless faces.

She stopped for a red light. Across the street, near the shiny kaleidoscope of pulpy colors—magazines lined in outdoor racks next to a yellowish coffee shop—young male hustlers gathered. Cheap odors wafted from the cafe, like rancid perfume. Many shirtless, some skinny, masculine youngmen loitered among pretty, androgynous boys. Both groups stared invitingly at cars that drove circling the block. Some of the youngmen motioned hopefully at the drivers, then flung resigned middle fingers at them when they didn't stop.

Crossing the street, Amber almost ran into a muscular shirtless youngman in his late teens. With him—leaning lovingly on his bare brown shoulder—was a youngman of extraordinary blond beauty. He had golden long hair. He wore denim cutoffs, a short shirt cropped just below his nipples. The more masculine of the two pretended—obviously pretended—indifference, loving indifference. Their open closeness pleased Amber. "Hi," she said. "Hi," they echoed.

By the time she reached the parking lot, the walk had stilled Amber's rage. She had gathered strength from this wounded but defiant street. The courage she had come to search in the theater showing *Meat* asserted itself. Next to a liquor store was a series of exposed phone booths. The first one swallowed her coins without connecting her to anyone, anything. "Damn!" She wanted to avoid becoming anxious, nervous. The receiver in the next naked booth had been torn, the coiled wire like a silver cut vein. She moved away quickly. The third phone worked.

"Landers'," the woman's voice answered.

"Theodore, please," Amber said. She had been about to greet the familiar receptionist, but her breathing became instantly irregular.

"Mr. Landers is not— . . ."

"It's Amber; tell him I have to talk to him."

"Oh, Amber," said the receptionist, "you sound so different. Theodore's talking to Jimmy. He tried to call you earlier, to tell you that— . . . Well, I'll let him tell you."

"Amber?" came the steady voice of Theodore Landers. "I just tried to telephone you earlier, darling. What a coincidence. Jimmy's here. He brought me the *Reporter*. It confirms that *Meat* has already surpassed *The Devil in Miss Jones* in gross profits. A few more weeks and we'll go after *Deep Throat*."

Jimmy's voice called out: "Tell her what they called us!"

"Jimmy wants me to tell you," Theodore Landers said, his voice cool as always, "that the *Reporter* called you and Jimmy the Jeannette MacDonald and Nelson Eddy of the erotic film circuit." He never said "sex films," never said "porn" or "porno" or even "pornography."

"Who's supposed to be who?" Amber attempted to release at least one coil of tension. She heard Theodore tell Jimmy Steed what she'd said.

"You cummon over and I'll show you!" Jimmy yelled at the phone.

"Darling," Theodore said, "I've got the ideal script for your next film—you and Jimmy again—and it's better than *Meat*."

Script! "I have to see you—tomorrow, Theodore," Amber emphasized. "It's important."

"Of course, darling, let's have lunch," he said. No questions; that cunning, easy "acceptance."

He knew it was about *Meat*, Amber was sure; she had told him last week she was seeing it today. "And I'd like Jimmy to be there," she said. She looked away and saw that the street where the ruined phones were was lined with rows of extremely tall, skinny palm trees; they all tilted slightly toward the same side. Toward the ocean? Away? A gusty wind was rising, shaking the dried leaves drooping under green branches that open like fans. She heard Theodore's voice, then Jimmy's.

"Jimmy says the pleasure is his," Theodore Landers said. "And mine."

Amber took a deep breath and then said, "At Chez Toi." She had chosen the most flagrantly—showily—"exclusive" restaurant in the city. It was where Theodore took the wealthy backers and bankers who made his "quality erotic films" possible. But he had never taken her there.

Hardly a second of silence, then the cool voice said "Chez Toi it is, darling." His tone was a riddle. "How's twelve-thirty?. . . You, me, and Jimmy—and whatever you want to tell me. . . . *Ciao,* darling." Before he hung up, Jimmy Steed's voice pushed into the receiver. "Chow, sweet!"

As she drove up into the wind-scrimmed distance off Sunset Boulevard to her home in Laurel Canyon, she felt the air, not cool at all, rush at her in her small, shiny new red MG. Often, with nothing to do, she would drive about the city—into the freeways—going nowhere, and then she would feel exhilarated by the wind brushing her flesh. Now she did not feel triumphant. Was it that Theodore had agreed so easily and that, expecting some resistance and therefore geared for battle, she had not had to fight? This unfought battle might render the war itself savage.

She entered the area that meanders into the Hollywood Hills. She lived off Lookout Mountain. Wild with trees and flowers, Laurel Canyon has gone through several vicissitudes in the last years. In the Sixties, rock stars pretending gypsy poverty and offering weekly smorgasbords of expensive drugs clogged the area with dazzling sports cars. In the Seventies, the new "hip" film-makers and the "new" serious actors and actresses asserted their need for "space" and wore expensive working-class clothes. Many of them remained, along with the newer tenants, stars and demistars of nervous television series.

This area, not inexpensive, is seasonally threatened by torrential rains. When soaked soil moves, houses fold into rivers of mud. During thirsty spells, the threat of fire is a constant reminder with the ashy odor of smog. Still, the area—constantly rebuilt and reinforced after every disaster—survives, desirable.

Amber parked her MG in the small garage under her sunning porch. Her house clutched more deeply into the soil, and so it resisted the crawling mud. A handsome structure of glass and wood, it was shoved against a mottled-green hill. That protected it from the sheets of water in the rainy season; rocks blocked the flowing rain and sent it in an arc over the house. Flowers grew wild. Amber liked the crash of bright colors, the jagged forms and varied heights.

Inside, the house was sparingly furnished. She preferred uncluttered, open rooms. She sat on the dark brown leather falcon chair she preferred. She felt sad, tired. But her body seemed charged with inner energy. The erotic film circuit! How she hated Theodore's phrase. Circuit, like electricity. An electric circle.

Standing up, she removed her clothes, almost as she did before the camera, slowly, sexually—but this time for herself, enjoying her own private sensuality. She walked naked onto the porch, which perched over the hill. Sometimes deer came to the edge of the house. She had tried to feed one once, but it had fled. They always stood so proud and free, lithe, almost delicate. Then impulsively they'd rush into the crackling brush.

Amber never attempted to get a tan. Her fair skin warred with the sun; and, too, it was the creamy whiteness of her body that emphasized the copper of her hair, especially between her legs. In her films, it was tinged with a dot of brilliantine. She touched her body with both hands, and felt aroused in the naked warmth. It was spring, but like summer. She would have welcomed skipping over the cruelty of spring, the end of winter's hope.

The next morning, the heat had abated—but it was edging in—as Amber drove into Sunset. She wanted to be just slightly late, let Theodore—and Jimmy—be waiting for her as she walked into Chez Toi.

The main appeal of Chez Toi is not its food—it is sometimes good—but its vaunted, expensive snobbishness and exclusivity. Its telephone number is listed in the name of the maitre d'hotel. Only those chosen by wealth or extreme fame, or those who can purchase attention, are welcome into what looks at first like a plain, smallish house over which a huge plastic parachute has fallen and been reinflated. The translucent plastic distorts the reflections of the entering guests into melting figures. Fat, overfed shrubs squat along the narrow walk.

It is the ambience of restriction that makes Chez Toi exclusive, sought after, craved, courted—and a source of despair to many, and that despair renders it even more desirable for those who do not have to feel it. In this city of shaky wealth and status, the maitre d'hotel of Chez Toi has been allowed the papal power to bless or excommunicate the anxious courtiers who pay to see who else will be allowed, who turned away—a salubrious, regular ritual. Telephone-accepted reservations may be denied—if a name or reference is not recognized at the door. Dress at lunch may range from expensive—always expensive—tennis shorts and shoes, armies of sewn, tiny green alligators proclaiming the correct label displayed like combat badges—to the outrageous—one round producer holding often daily court in draped caftans of tangled spectrums—to the doggedly chic—original dresses and suits purchased just moments earlier on Rodeo Drive, for this one lunch, this one entrance—and exit—this one trip to the restroom, which can become a journey through a mined warfield of appraising eyes, meanly strained necks. But anything is acceptable if there is enough wealth, enough power behind it.

Like everything else about it, the inside of the restaurant is at best ordinary. Beyond the plastic-sheeted patio, there is a tiny bar and, upstairs, a room for sealed parties. Within a certain imperfect social circle, one's reception at Chez Toi is an essential component in determining status.

Outside, the squat house recedes a few feet from the street. In a small dirt lot before it, uniformed attendants park only Rolls

Royces, Corniches—free advertisements for the restaurant. Lesser cars—the fleets of ordinary Mercedeses ubiquitous in this city—are rushed to hidden lots surrounding the restaurant.

Inside, the tables are arranged to allow exposure to the important and obscurity to the candidates, who may graduate into prime visibility, or its orbit, through larger tips and contacts, if they are willing to wait.

Amber parked in the lot. A young Mexican attendant ran to open the door. She stepped out and dazzled him into momentary disfunction. She wore a sleeveless dress of diaphanous white silk. No jewelry. A swirl of wind wrapped the silk about her legs, outlining them lovingly. Barely kissing her nipples, the soft touch of silk hardened them so that her breasts asserted themselves with subtle daring. Her copper hair emphasized the exposed portions of skin. Sexual, glamorous—refined.

The attendant drove off to hide her car.

She was not sure whether or not she wanted to be recognized. Certainly being a "sex star" carried an amount of fame, awesome to some, tarnished for others. She knew she wanted to be admired, yes, and would be. Her stark beauty commanded that, always—even in a city of beautiful women. Again the wind wrapped the silk about her legs, carving the long limbs.

"Wow!"

She turned.

Leaning against a silver gray limousine parked in the place of honor with other powerful, impervious cars basking in their wealth was a chauffeur in a gray uniform, the color of the car. He was good-looking, yes, a man beginning to show—and to attempt to disguise—his age; early forties, tanned, broad-shouldered, brown-haired; he had a blondish moustache, perhaps brushed with bleach to conceal white obtruding hairs.

Amber remembered Rhett Butler eyeing Scarlett O'Hara on the steps of Twelve Oaks—that look that still made audiences sigh, just as Amber had when she first saw that film she loved. This man, this chauffeur— . . .

"Wow! Sweet! Suh-*weet!*"

Those words—the kind she was used to, expected, and welcomed at other times—sent stabs of panic through her now, because she knew he would not have dared utter them to any of the other women here, no matter how beautiful, alone or unescorted.

Without having been to Chez Toi, Amber had always detested it, all the rancidity it stood for. Its brutal hauteur had a radiating power. It could extend to contaminate even those who did not go—care to go—there. She had chosen it as the site for confronting Theodore because of what she knew it represented to *him*. It was here that he came with the people he took seriously, his "equals." She chose it as her battleground.

She looked away from the chauffeur. The bone-colored heels of her shoes clicked assertively as—in her inimitable, impossibly elegant, sensual style, her long legs thrusting against the clinging silk—Amber Haze strode into Chez Toi.

At the entrance to the square plastic patio were two men in tuxedos, one of them a step behind the other. Amber recognized the man in front—often photographed, a powerful man simply because as maitre d'hotel he reigned over Chez Toi. He looked like a failed gigolo. "Madame?" His voice pounced on the last syllable. For a second she felt her beauty being drained by the chilled voice.

"With Mr. Landers," Amber said. Eyes in the patio were already on her. For now, her extravagant beauty would be her passport, even if her identity, known, might restrict its terms. The tuxedoed man in front nodded to the man slightly behind him—small, pudgy, all scrapes and bows. Amber knew she was being relegated to the assistant. She wondered whether Theodore, with Jimmy, had been. No, not Theodore.

"This way, madame." The squat man led her in.

A drone of voices that remains at one level is constant at Chez Toi. Faces turn quickly, eyes shift slyly—then away. All here have learned how to look just slightly, to appraise in one glance—and even to stare in accusation, even opportunistic admiration.

Passing a long table, Amber saw a woman she recognized from photographs—Margaret Manfred. One of the richest women in the world, she appeared constantly in society photographs—and on the front pages of trashy scandal sheets. Sitting like an empress and surrounded by two suited men and three women, the rich woman was looking so overtly at her that Amber paused near the table. Margaret Manfred had a pallid white face that seemed to have been ironed, the wrinkles pulled away, the skin cut, sewn behind the scattered strands of brown hair. Dressed in a high-necked gray dress even in this day of whitening heat, she sat stiffly as if the clasped skin had been traded for any expression indicating emotion. In its severe lineless agelessness, the face became ancient. Amber turned away from the stare of the woman, just as one of the men leaning toward the rigid face whispered: ". . . woman in that thing called *Meat*."

Near them, laughter erupted in high, false peals. A stumpy, fat man in a ridiculous oriental robe waved his long sleeves like colored ribbons. Bits of crushed caviar tinted the edges of his fleshy mouth. He was entertaining a clutch of strident men and women—who leaned toward him and automatically echoed his laughter—a second or two after each burst. Never on him, their eyes constantly ricocheted about the room.

Amber saw Theodore Landis—and Jimmy. They had not been shoved into the shaded purgatory in back. Although she had never really liked him, she felt a sigh of warmth at the sight of Jimmy Steed, at ease anywhere.

The assistant maitre d'hotel pulled out a chair for Amber. Theodore Landis stood up. He had resplendent, old-fashioned manners. Beaming, Jimmy Steed tipped his chair—he loved being seen with beautiful women. The only thing better was being seen with beautiful rich women. Theodore Landis placed cool lips on Amber's cheek: "Darling." Amber sat down, aware of the looks swirling about her, the buzzes perhaps identifying her. Jimmy leaned over and kissed her on the mouth; his tongue automatically attacked her throat.

"Theodore . . . Jimmy," she said. Jimmy! So well dressed, his hair so lovingly styled, his shirt open one button past acceptable daring. A man under forty—how far under, or how near, was a matter for conjecture; that he was tall was apparent even when he was sitting down. Despite the careful grooming, he was still ordinary. Not threateningly handsome, he did not alienate the heterosexual men who saw all his movies. That near-plainness—and his enormous cock, which men fantasized was theirs—made Jimmy Steed the top male sex star in films. He was also an expensive prostitute. His fan mail was impressive.

It came from men—whom he always turned down, Jimmy announced periodically—and from women, who would offer to pay his fare for bought assignations. Usually in a happy, loose mood, Jimmy could be brought down deeply by any aspersions on his penis—which he took with profound seriousness. "It looks bigger on screen" sent him into a serious sulk.

"You look smashing, darling," Theodore approved of Amber.

"Good enough to eat, yum-yum," came Jimmy's expected remark.

The captain filled her glass with wine—good wine, Amber knew, and as cool as Theodore.

Theodore Landers was not fat, he did not sweat, he never huffed, his tie never became loose or askew, he did not have a balding spot, and he never chewed cigars or used profanity. No, the most successful producer-director-manager in the production of "erotic films" looked and acted like the high-paid legal advisor of an international, powerful corporation. In his middle fifties, with neatly cut graying hair, he wore conservative but fashionable suits. Producing "erotic films of quality" was his business. "Quality" meant big budgets, careful sets, audible dialogue, clear, focused, imaginative shots—and bookings only in the best theaters available. "Russ Meyer," he was quoted as having said, "is a very vulgar man."

"Sorry I'm late," Amber called attention to the fact.

"That's all right, darling," came Theodore's cultured, modulated voice. "Jimmy and I were enjoying this excellent wine—isn't it?—and Jimmy's been recognizing some of the women he's been with— . . ."

"That's that rich millionaire woman," Jimmy Steed indicated Margaret Manfred in tones meant to suggest he had been with her. But Jimmy was not subtle. If he had been with her, nothing would have stopped him from announcing the details of the encounter. "Must've fucked half the women at this Shay Too, and that's the truth," he drawled in his shanty tone.

"You're lying, Jimmy," Amber challenged. Oh, yes, the wine was fine—and self-assured.

"Well, at least a dozen," Jimmy reduced the number of his conquests.

"You're still lying, Jimmy," Amber said.

"Okay, then, two—and that's for sure. That woman over there with those two others? She don't—doesn't—know I know who she is, but she's the wife of a very powerful politician or judge, something like that. I saw her picture in *Beverly Hills People*."

"You read that?" Amber asked in amusement. That was the "house organ" of the chic restaurants and social affairs in the city.

"Sure. Get to know my rich ladies." Jimmy winked.

Amber's eyes glided toward the woman Jimmy had just indicated. She had an anxious face, which she kept touching at the edges of her hair. She caught Amber's look—merely another in the constant magnetized trajectory of glances that sometimes become stares. She almost smiled, absently.

The captain was bowing at Theodore's table; the waiter stood next to him. A cute busboy was fussing unduly with the silver, napkins, water at their table, flinging entranced glances at Jimmy. Amber ordered poached salmon. Theodore chose the mixed grill. Jimmy said, "A large, blood-rare steak, and some A-1— . . ."

"Monsieur?" the captain stopped him, in premature accusation; his eyebrows collided.

"A-1 Sauce. With the steak," Jimmy said easily. "Never have meat without it."

"If monsieur— . . ." the captain began.

Theodore said, "The gentleman would like a New York–cut steak please—very rare—and some A-1 sauce. Kindly bring that to him."

"Of course." The captain was in full retreat.

Amber couldn't help admiring Theodore. He had frosted the captain. Yet it would be that same ability which he might use against her, his controlled performance warned her. He could give—seem to give—in abundance, and then take more, much more—all.

Margaret Manfred's eyes were on Amber again. The lips had managed the slightest smirk, harsh tilts at the tips.

"Darling, I have great news," Theodore began. He frowned in annoyance because his wine glass was empty. Filled! "I have the largest budget ever for your new film. It will be pure quality.''

"Is that the title?'' Amber said. She wanted Theodore to perceive more of her purpose in her sarcasm.

He cleared his throat, as if for words he was already gathering.

"Dynamite.'' Jimmy was enthusiastic. "You're married to this middle-aged guy, Amber—this is the story. And the only way he can get it up—listen to this—is by showing movies of this big sex star *before* he fucks you. Guess who plays the sex star *and* the wife? You! See, you *are* the star, moonlighting, but he doesn't know it. I play your partner in all the movies he watches before he fucks his wife, who's really the star—he just has to pretend he's fucking a whore. In one skit in the movie, I play an electrician fixing your electric oven, and I'm carrying this long, long wrapped wire.''

"And it unwinds,'' Amber said.

"Yeah. It's supposed to represent my cock.'' He let his hand drop into his lap, and the busboy gaped.

Over his wineglass, Theodore's eyes locked on Amber.

Amber said casually, "Have you heard, Jimmy, that there's a new . . . star . . . who's bigger than you? Young kid, too; got a movie coming out, talk of the town.''

Ambushed, Jimmy Steed needed emergency reassurance. He sought the awed busboy and deliberately dropped his fork. The busboy leapt for it. Finally, he handed Jimmy a clean one.

The boy said quickly, "Hello, Mr. Steed, it's a pleasure to meet you.'' Jimmy flashed what came as close to being a dazzling smile as he could muster. "Thanks.''

"Real cute kid,'' Amber said.

"You're bullshitting about that other guy,'' Jimmy recovered. "I'm the biggest—and in this country *big* is best, right, Theodore?'' He felt flushed with patriotism; he knew Theodore was very patriotic. "Hey, babe,'' he said to Amber, "what the hell's eating you? It's not me—at least, not *this* moment,'' he laughed, satisfied.

Amber faced Theodore. "I saw *Meat* yesterday.''

Theodore did not stop his wineglass on its trek to his lips. But when he put it down, he twisted it in a full circle, his fingers sliding on the skinny stem.

"You never saw it?" Jimmy Steed marveled. He was still basking in the busboy's awed attention. "Was everyone jerking off in the theater, Amber?" Jimmy asked her. "At night you get the better clientele—the hip young swingers, the women and the men. The early part of the day, that's when the guys come alone, or come back, alone. You get off on people jerking off watching you fuck, Amber? I sure do!"

"Yes," Amber said. "I do."

"Those guys imagine they're me," Jimmy Steed said, "that *they* got the big ding-dong, and they're fucking this gorgeous whore— . . ."

"That's the second time you've called me that, Jimmy," Amber said calmly, not wanting to spend any of her stored anger on him, not now. "Just for the record, I have nothing against prostitutes, but I've chosen not to be one. *You're* the famous prostitute, Jimmy."

"Shit," Jimmy gave the word three syllables. "Men can't be prostitutes." He glanced at the woman he had pointed out earlier; their glances collided. The wife of the famous man touched her hair again. She said something to another of the three women with her, and they all looked at Margaret Manfred, who faced Amber. "Hey! Get this. Somebody sent me this little bottle in the mail—well, it wasn't really *little*—and guess what they wanted me to shoot in it?"

The waiters arrived, the captain began serving. The A-1 Sauce was in a small peaked vial. With a flourish, the waiter placed it next to Jimmy, who devoured the meat with his eyes. The busboy rushed over, about to pour more water into the filled glass. He retreated just in time, but Jimmy granted him another smile.

In the moments of the serving, the noise of Chez Toi asserted itself in broken cacophony. Jimmy poured all the sauce over his steak, coating it. A waiter looked wounded. Theodore began cutting the varied cold meats, neatly, tasting the chicken first, then the liver. Now he cut a piece of lamb and held it up between his plate and his mouth. The piece of meat was impaled on the fork, slightly away from him—almost as if he were going to toast Amber with it.

"All right, Amber," he said, the meat still in mid-journey, "Tell me what you're playing so I can play, too."

Afraid her words would drown in anger, she looked down at the salmon, a slab of pink flesh. She put down her fork, her appetite gone.

"So! You saw *Meat* today—and you didn't like— . . ." Theodore paused like a judge about to pronounce sentence ". . . —yourself."

"I love seeing myself naked," Amber asserted. "I like sex, sometimes I love it, and it excites me that men masturbate looking at me."

"You like other women's bodies?" Jimmy asked absently.

"Yes," Amber said.

"You're not a lez?" Jimmy felt stung—somehow.

"No—but I can still admire other women's bodies. What about you, Jimmy? You like other men's bodies?"

"Hell, no," Jimmy protested. "I'm no fag, you know that. Hell, I turn down— . . ."

Theodore interrupted. "You're very serious, Amber—but you don't seem to know about what."

That strategy, that strategy! It allowed him to win without even fighting. "I am serious, very serious," Amber said, "and I do know about what. And so do you."

"Tell me, tell me, tell me," Theodore fired the words at her—but still softly. He said, "You didn't like how you *looked* fellating Jimmy?" Nothing sounded sexual coming from him, he rendered everything neuter. "We light you splendidly, you know. The best!—everything to display your beauty."

"I didn't care how *I* looked eating *your* pussy, yummy," Jimmy said. "*Meat*—that's a great title, isn't it? . . . Hell, I love being a hunk of meat—a great big prime salami."

"Why are you suddenly ashamed of showing your body?" Theodore thrust at Amber.

"You're doing it, Theodore, you're doing it—trying to confuse before anyone even explains."

"Then explain!" he said.

Amber placed her hands on her lap, to contain her premature rage; he wanted to dissipate it, she knew. She glanced at Margaret Manfred. The woman ate carefully, tiny pieces on her fork, brought into her mouth, which hardly opened, her movements almost like those of a puppet, careful, guarded. When someone spoke to her, she merely leaned, slightly, in that direction.

"I'm proud of my body," Amber said, and then she formed the words: "You tricked me, Theodore."

"How did I trick you?" came the controlled words. "You get very well paid—the highest!—and more for this new film. You get well treated—always! You thought I wouldn't bring you to Chez Toi—oh, I knew that—but here you are. And just look at how that Manfred woman is looking at you. She hasn't taken her eyes off you. You know why? Because she'd give all her millions to look like you. Think of that. And have I ever even asked you to meet the people who make the big budgets possible—who want an introduction to you as a contingency? I tell them no, I won't stoop to that, I'm not a procurer, you're not a harlot— . . ."

"Hell," Jimmy said.

"Did I ever force you to do anything?"

"No," Amber conceded. "I'm not ashamed of any of it."

"Damright." Jimmy shaved at a strip of fat on his plate.

Theodore lowered the fork with the stabbed meat, releasing the lamb onto the plate. He cut the liver. His appetite seemed aroused.

"That scene where you had Jimmy hold his cock over my breasts while he made that hissing sound— . . ." Amber started.

"Hot scene," Jimmy enthused. "That's the one guys come back to see—alone—that one, but mostly the one it sets up."

"Which one?" Amber thrust. In his clumsy way, Jimmy would lead her into the territory where she was faltering.

"Golden showers," he said easily. "That's probably the main reason the movie's such a big hit."

Amber breathed in audibly. "You created the impression that Jimmy was pissing on my breasts, Theodore. And in my— . . ."

"I was," Jimmy said casually. He ate the stripped fat.

The owner of Chez Toi was making his late lunch rounds now. Faces strained eagerly for his benediction. He chose those to honor, shaking a man's hand, kissing a woman's. Those passed over were shrouded in gloom. He approached Theodore's table. He glanced at Jimmy, quickly away; then at Amber, slowly, coolly. "Monsieur," he touched Theodore's hand—more lightly than at other times, Amber knew, from Theodore's slight frown. Because of that perhaps, the owner reached to kiss Amber's hand. She dropped it to her lap. He glided away to dance about Margaret Manfred's table.

"You're lying, Jimmy," Amber said softly. "That scene was faked."

"Yeah. And no." Jimmy chewed on the red, red meat.

"It was *water* I rubbed on my breasts!" She faced Theodore's unblinking gaze. "You shot Jimmy pissing alone into the bathtub, then you spliced the film so it looked like he was doing it on me, and you inserted his line telling me to drink— . . ."

"Some of it *was* piss—on your breasts," Jimmy said easily. "When I stood under the shower with you in the tub, remember? Theodore told me to get a few drops in the water, make the fake golden showers look even realer."

Amber felt cold, hot, cold.

Theodore fired: "I don't understand you, Amber. The camera has been almost inside you; you've been sodomized, you've fellated, you've had cunnilingus performed. And whether you pretend or not, you're the most convincing actress in erotic films. Everybody feels you love it—all."

"Goddammit, Theodore, what the hell was *sexual* about that scene—which you had to *fake!*" Despair echoed in her voice.

Theodore's words were softer than ever, every word modulated, precise—the expensive corporate adviser explaining the most intricate transaction in the simplest terms. "You *really* don't understand, Amber. You're not just *a* woman on the screen. You're *the* beautiful woman. And you are—a perfect face, a beautiful body, the most famous breasts. When those men see Jimmy urinating— . . . pretending to urinate— . . ."

"I did piss, you told me," Jimmy emphasized.

". . .—on you," Theodore continued without a break in his words, "they can pay you back for all the times they've wanted you—the beautiful woman they've longed for, long for, without being able to have. You. They come to see you turned into raw meat. It's revenge, Amber—that's what you don't understand."

The buzzing in the restaurant drilled into Amber's ears. She saw the fat man in the oriental robe wave wildly at a woman in tight jeans, boots, t-shirt. Black oily liquid smeared the man's lips.

"*Did* Jim piss on me?" Amber asked Theodore.

"Yes," Theodore's lips sealed the word with a forkful of cold lamb. "Just what do you want, Amber?" he asked her.

"Not piss," Amber said.

"You want to be a serious actress?" It was the only time Theodore had allowed overt derision to sweep his voice "If you do, reduce your breasts. Have breast reduction. That's the only way anyone will take you seriously."

"*Repeat that!*" Amber commanded. Her hands were wet on the white silk.

Theodore chewed on a piece of chicken. Jimmy basked in the attention of the people looking toward them.

"That's what you've been doing all along," Amber said, "reducing my body, my breasts, my sex—until no sex was left. Just revenge. What did you have planned for the next film?" She stood up.

"Sit down, Amber. Everyone is watching," Theodore said.

Amber looked down at him: "I know why you are always so cool, Theodore, because you're always sweating and panting *inside*."

She walked away. Margaret Manfred's eyes seized her. The undisguised look wrenched at her even when, standing very near her, Amber challenged it. The maitre d'hotel froze, the captains stopped their movements about the room, all eyes in the restaurant swiveled. The two women stared into each other, deeply. It was Margaret Manfred who withdrew—looked away. Flustered, the captain snapped his fingers at all the waiters. In the rare silence of Chez Toi his *Snap!* was like the crack of a bullet. Margaret Manfred winced.

Then Amber walked out of Chez Toi, hearing, behind her, like the hurried breathy prayers of commiseration at a spontaneous wake, the urgent whispering around Margaret Manfred.

Outside, the young Mexican attendant ran to get Amber's car. She stood in the small lot, isolated—thinking she was isolated, until she heard the man's whistle and knew it was the same chauffeur.

He took a step away from the haughty silver gray limousine. "Hey, Amber," the chauffeur drawled, "you really come that good all the time? Or you just fake it, huh?"

No, that wasn't how Rhett had looked at Scarlett in that scene she loved, Amber realized. Rhett's look had contained desire, sexual desire, not hatred disguised. How many times had she seen this man's look, even—yes, she faced it—courted it without knowing it, because she expected it, that look that had nothing to do with sex, like the scene in the tub?

Words of rage formed inside her. She sought exact ones to hurl out. But what *were* the words, how exactly was that look of contempt formed? She didn't know the vocabulary or what went with it.

She could learn! She closed her eyes for a moment, as if to contain everything in an ordering bright darkness. The cherished sensual lightness of the silk asserted itself on her breasts. She felt a delicate flush there. She opened her eyes onto the shimmering day, and she thought, Do I want to? Do I *want* to learn that ugly, cruel vocabulary?

No.

Like an anxious private, the chauffeur came to attention. He moved back to the limousine. Margaret Manfred and her entourage were emerging. This time the frozen woman did not turn in the direction of Amber—but the others did, quietly. The chauffeur opened and closed doors. Margaret Manfred and her court entered the limousine. The chauffeur moved briskly into the driver's seat. Behind the tinted windows of the brutal car, Margaret Manfred's face looked dead.

Amber shook her red hair against the rising whirls of wind. The heat hugged her. Then the wind swirled the silk about her body, pushing the material to outline the *V* at her thighs. She welcomed that, the pleasurable, sensual warmth there.

Even in the ugly wavering plastic that forms the enclosure of Chez Toi, even in that distorted reflection, her magnificent hair glowed—gloriously—in the light of the fascinated sun.

Lost Angels: 2

"I wonder why he did that? Why would anybody do anything like that?" Jesse James pondered the matter deeply.

The Cadillac purred into the tawdry streets of Hollywood, past an abandoned movie lot, gray and aging; long stretches of oleanders reigning before clusters of stucco or wooden bungalow courts; a discarded jail, still emanating gray anger; a TV studio with lines of undaunted tourists awaiting possible entry; purple-leafed trees, silver when they face a sunless light; shabby and neat shops of every variety, featuring everything from tents to statues of David. And everywhere are sprinkles—showers—of blue-starred flowers. Colors, natural and artificial, are bright on these streets, like smashed crayons.

Heat was charging sweeps of wind.

"Who?" Lisa asked Jesse. "Oh, have you *ever* seen leaves that big?" She was looking at a spilling tree whose leaves were like green blossoms.

"That guy who hanged himself in that schoolyard. Weird. Why there? And that black hood!" Jesse clarified.

"I wish you'd stop bringing that up," Lisa protested; she wanted to forget about it. The memory made her both sad and frightened.

"Wonder why," Jesse continued musing. "The news'll tell."

"Depends," Orin pronounced. "Maybe they will tell, maybe they won't. They might. Depends. But sometimes you *never* know why—get no answers. Sometimes you do. Sometimes you just *feel* why, and that's the time you know best." He never struggled with words. Though vague to others, they always managed to convey his certainty of their clarity.

Jesse James looked at Lisa, to see whether she was confused.

"You can make ugly things sound pretty sometimes, Orin," Lisa said.

That's the truth, Jesse thought. He had slept a lot on their way to Los Angeles. One time when he woke—in Arizona— craggy rocks looked like a herd of huge animals advancing toward them. He'd yelled. Orin didn't swerve; he said, "I bet you had a hallucination. Lots of people do with rocks like those—see tigers, dinosaurs." That's what Jesse had seen. Other times, he awakened to hear Orin talking to Lisa, once about how the bugs on the windshield *wanted* to crash against the glass—and Lisa said, "But it's invisible." "No, they know it's there." Orin had sounded sure. "Yeah," Jesse said now, "you can make things sound pretty, Orin. Sometimes," he qualified. He didn't know exactly when he had begun feeling important, being with Orin. Of course that was partly because of the car; he beamed when he saw people cluster around it. Sometimes he'd walk to the driver's side of the parked car, hoping to create the momentary illusion that it was his.

" 'The Mortuary with a Heart,' " Lisa read the wording on a bus bench as they drove by. Many of those benches throughout the city advertised interment. "A mortuary with *lots* of hearts." The slogan had struck her as very funny. "Look—a Baskin-Robbins ice-cream parlor!" she blurted, as if she had witnessed a miracle. "Can we stop, Orin?" She couldn't predict what his answer would be. Sometimes when he was about to say no, he would smile as if he was about to say yes, or make her believe he was going to say yes. Other times he would frown and then say yes.

"If you want another one," he said.

"Awright, kid," Jesse used Cagney's phrase in *White Heat* and pretended that Lisa had asked his opinion, too.

Orin stopped, and Lisa skipped out into the candy-painted parlor. Jesse started to ponder further about the strangled man, but Orin was looking straight ahead in that way that announced his silence. All Jesse could see ahead were the fringes of palm trees, and they bobbed all over the city. Pushed away by the wind, smog crouched on the horizon in a dark gray layer.

Lisa burst out of the ice-cream store. "Peach!" she announced her new flavor. She licked the cone, waiting for its taste to settle on her palate. With enormous disappointment she realized that this flavor did not begin to compare with the earlier one. She offered Jesse a lick. He took a tongue-scooping one. To her amazement, Orin accepted a taste. He even said, "Ummm, it's good!" and he turned into the cute red-haired boy!

Emboldened, Lisa said, "Okay—I've definitely decided; I'm going to change my name whenever I want to, and today I'm not Lisa any more. I'm— . . ." The first name that occurred to her was Scarlett, but she decided against it. "Maria," she chose, giving the name its "ee" sound in the middle. "From *For Whom the Bell Tolls*," she reminded them—again. She remembered, as always: Maria pulled away by horses from her dying lover. "He tricked her," she told Jesse and Orin insistently, as if she needed to convince them. "That Gary Cooper—Ro-*ber*-tow—he had to to blow up a bridge so the enemy soldiers wouldn't win the war in Spain. And the only way he could make Maria run away with the gypsies, on that horse, was to trick her—he was so mean— . . ."

Jesse was ready to say, You told us, you told us! so she'd embellish, but— . . .

"How did he trick her?" Orin surprised them with his question. Usually he was just silent.

"Yeah—*how?*" Jesse revised his prepared words.

Lisa said evenly, "They were going to go to America, together, after the war—Roberto and Maria; but he got wounded at the bridge he had to blow up and he lied to her that he'd meet her afterwards, now she had to go with the gypsies—but *he* knew, and *she* knew, he was going to die and she wanted to stay with him, die with him, but he kept lying that she would live for *both* of them, his *soul* would go with her, always be with her. He *tricked* her," she asserted with what she hoped was finality.

It wasn't. "Makes good sense to me, that she didn't stay," Jesse said, "if he was going to die anyhow." He was proud that his opinion sounded so intelligent; he turned to Orin for affirmation that it was.

Lisa felt a strong anger—a disturbing questioning, unexpressed. "You think Roberto was right?" She was aghast at Jesse. "Orin?" She, too, turned to him for support.

Orin seemed to ponder the question deeply. Moments passed.

"Depends on *if* you *can* live for other people, or if you *have* to," he said finally.

Jesse didn't know whom he'd agreed with.

Lisa breathed annoyance. Maria was loyal—like Pearl Chavez—to the very end. Loyal! *And* betrayed!

Look at her. Prettier every moment, even when she was mad. Like now, Jesse thought. Her breasts seemed actually to have grown in two days—but it was more probable that she was just exposing more of them, the blouse moved lower and lower as the day got hotter. Each time the car bumped, Jesse peered over to see whether maybe at least the deeper-hued part around the nipples might show, but it didn't—or hadn't, so far.

"There aren't any real movie stars anymore," Lisa said as they drove past a billboard announcing a silly new comedy; there were cartoons of the actors and actresses in it, dressed in caveman costumes! "The real stars all died when Marilyn Monroe did." Her voice faded. She gave Orin the rest of the cone and he ate it. "Would you really like to be a stunt man, Jesse?" she asked him.

Jesse had just made that up, when those kids outside that green mansion were pestering him. Now he said, "Uh, yeah, I guess. Maybe, yeah! I used to be real good at gymnastics and stuff; that's how I got my body."

"Oh, you!" Lisa giggled.

"In Westerns and pictures like that, they use stunt men. Even in gangster movies. It's never the star. Except sometimes. *Cagney* did all his own, I bet. In *White Heat*— . . ."

"You and Lisa with those old movies." Orin shook his head.

Jesse felt accused. "*I* saw only the Cagney ones—and some Bogart and Robinson—the *tough* ones. They had this all-gangster-movie week on TV . . . Just wasting time, Jesse," he echoed from somewhere in his past, "just wasting time . . . And then I saw *White Heat* again, without all those commercials. They had one of those old-movies-only places in Evansville, too, in Indiana, Lisa, and that's where I— . . ." He stopped too late. All along he'd known he would slip.

"Oh, oh," Lisa caught it immediately. "You're not from Texas, Jesse!"

It was a relief, actually, to confess—not worry about it

anymore. "I'm from Morganfield, Kentucky," Jesse revised soberly. "Near Evansville, Indiana. Ugly damn towns!"

"Doesn't matter, Jesse," Orin reminded him. "We all left things back there, things we don't want with us anymore—even if they keep wanting more of *us*."

Lisa sighed. Yes, that was true. "Sorry, Jesse," she apologized.

Jesse still wondered what Orin really thought about his lying. He didn't like Orin having anything on him. "Anyhow, this *White Heat* I'm telling you about," Jesse rushed on. "Cagney—Cody—Cody Jerrett—he learns in prison his father just died— . . ."

Lisa had not seen all of that one, an odd second feature with *Dark Victory,* with one of her top favorites—Bette Davis. A woman is beautiful only when she's loved, she remembered that line, but that was from another movie. Don't ask for the moon when we have— . . . "It wasn't his *father,* Jesse; it was his mother, and she was mean— . . ."

Jesse was puzzled. But he defended anyhow: "She wasn't mean, she saw how good he really was—and then Cody went up on this water tank or something and before they shot him he yelled— . . . yelled— . . ." The last line garbled. He shifted: "I bet that wasn't a stunt man! But if it was, he was lucky—to be Cody, or near him, just for a while." Misunderstood Cody, so misunderstood.

"Farmers' Market!" Lisa read the giant sign.

They parked on the street and got out. Jesse and Lisa admitted they had never seen anything like it. The Farmers' Market in Hollywood is a huge beehive of a building—across the street from the sterile whiteness of CBS Television Studios. Parts of the market are in the open, parts of it enclosed. It contains dozens and dozens of other smaller enclosures, some shops are more like booths—all different colors. Immediately, just standing at one of the many entryways, you saw: clothes! crystal! fruit! donuts! souvenirs! candy! toys!

"Go in and buy it, Lisa," Orin said.

Lisa was staring longingly into the window of a toy store; the bakery shop next to it looked like an extension of it. She was looking at a doll, less than a foot tall, dressed in blue ruffles, perhaps a bridesmaid's dress, long. Over blondish curled hair, she wore a lacy hat. Her eyes were blue speckled marbles outlined with thick black eyelashes. "Almost violet," Lisa said. "She's staring at *me!*"

"They're meant to look like they're staring at everyone," Jesse derided.

"No," Orin said. "She's looking at Lisa."

"You see it, too, Orin." Lisa didn't remove her eyes from the doll. Now the doll's eyes *were* violet.

Jesse didn't like this moment between Orin and Lisa. He admonished Lisa, "You're going to run out of money. Then what?" He looked at Orin. He liked the pretty motel with the big television Orin had chosen, but it would eat up a lot of his money. They had paid last night's and today's rent. "Then what?" he repeated.

"Depends," Orin said, and laughed.

Jesse James was relieved by the laughter. Money wasn't worrying Orin, he'd made that clear. "Makes sense," Jesse was glad to say.

"I'll buy you the doll, Lisa," Orin said. He took out money from his wallet.

Jesse was puzzled. Orin really wanted Lisa to have that doll—a grown woman, well, almost— . . .

Lisa emerged out of the store hugging the doll to her. She tilted her, so that the heavy eyelashes draped the gleaming blue—*violet*—eyes. She kissed the doll. "I love her, Orin! Thank you." She wanted to kiss him—but she didn't dare. Lowering her head, she said, "Orin, you gave me a baby."

Jesse laughed. "When you have a baby, you got to grow up—that's just a doll."

Orin was studying a display in another window—cubes, spheres, cones; inside the tinted plastic were other perfect shapes.

Abruptly Lisa turned to the doll and said, "Don't turn ugly!" It didn't sound like her voice. Even she reacted to its harsh, strange tone; she smothered the doll with kisses.

Jesse peeked at her cleavage. Still, the nipples didn't show. It was weeks since he'd fucked a girl—and she hadn't been that pretty, the last one, in Evansville. Pangs of recurrent rivalry pricked at him, because Lisa seemed to take Orin much more seriously than him. "Lisa, you're dumb, you know, talking to that doll like that," he shot his anger at Lisa.

Orin turned and frowned.

The aroused rivalry pushed Jesse to remove his shirt again; he'd seen other shirtless youngmen here.

"I'm not so sure I'm dumb, Jesse," Lisa said. "I don't think so. I've never had a chance to find out."

"I never had a chance," Jesse did Cagney. Then another line pushed forward: "I could've been a *contender*." Where was that from?

Orin leaned away slightly from the window with the plastic geometric models. He tilted his head as if to perceive their shapes from another angle.

Suddenly dreamy, "I'll call you— . . ." Lisa said to the doll. "I'll call you— . . . Pearl! Pearl Chavez!" She often thought *Duel in the Sun* might be her favorite movie, but then that would change when she remembered another favorite; it was certainly *one* of her favorite "all-times." "The real Pearl was a half-breed," she explained the doll's name from the movie. "Her father killed her Indian mother—*he* was the good one, but they hanged *him* . . . Pearl. She really loved that mean Lewt," she said with enormous emotion. "But he wouldn't marry her, took her away from his good brother. So mean, that Lewt!" She remembered the gory last scene in the movie: Pearl Chavez drenched in blood and perspiration claws her way up the barren desert rocks to confront her wounded lover, Lewt. "She *had* to shoot him because he was so mean to her and she couldn't live without him—and he shot back at her, so mean. She loved him so much she climbed that mountain, *bleeding,* just to die with him. And then," she sighed, "years later, a beautiful flower would grow there, from their blood."

Jesse said, "She should've let him die and she could have lived for both of them."

"Oh, you! You got that from what I told you about Maria and Roberto in *For Whom the Bell Tolls!* I *don't* agree! . . . Pearl Chavez," she repeated as they explored one of the many walks within the giant market. She moved before the window of a flower shop. Behind glass, red roses burst out of green leaves.

There, she baptized the doll with a disguised stroke of her hand: Pearl.

"You must've seen those same movies over and over," Jesse grumbled, "the way you remember everything about them."

"Some I saw just once, but I *still* remember," Lisa said.

Jesse felt even more chagrined.

They wandered among the mixture of odors—candy and meat—and sounds—recorded music and the excited comments of swarming tourists; past "international shops carrying imported objects from all over the globe," Lisa read. Jesse James bought a *Guide to Places of Interest in Los Angeles and Environs*." They stopped at one of the food shops, featuring "Swedish delicacies." Leaning against the ribbon-colored counter, they ate hot dogs with melted Swiss cheese. They were having a great time, both Jesse and Lisa basking in Orin's surprising, silly mood—he took off his gray jacket in front of the Spanish Delicacy Shop and pretended to be a bullfighter, the coat a cape!

As they walked back to the Cadillac, Lisa announced she was through being Maria. "They were *too* mean to her."

"Maybe some people do have to die so others can live," Orin said. "Grant you—it's hard to know when, sometimes." He stared away, pensive.

Was he actually thinking about *Maria!* Lisa broke the sad silence as they approached the car. "My name now is Tondelayo," she said in a husky voice. She slinked about a traffic light, lowered one side of her blouse just slightly more. "Hedy Lamarr, in *White Cargo*."

Jesse approved: "You just keep right on being that Tandy-whatever. Sure looks good on you—doesn't it look good on her?" he ventured at Orin, noticing him staring, too.

"Yes," Orin said, but he looked away from her.

The smog had retreated but thickened as the afternoon declined. Against the horizon it assumed an orange glow, like exhausted fire. Inside the car, heat had coagulated. Orin lowered the roof, and two waves of hot air collided.

"Where now?" Jesse asked.

Sometimes Orin answered; sometimes he didn't—like now.

For the first time, Jesse reached out defiantly and turned the radio on. He felt his heart pound. He'd done it! Classical music—but he left it on that station, not wanting to reemphasize his daring gesture.

Without reaction, Orin steered the car onto a freeway. Peak traffic was thinning, and so they were able to flow. As they rode on, the drivers and passengers in most of the cars were either Mexicans or Negroes.

IMPERIAL BLVD, the sign on the off-ramp read.

The indigo car, topless, floated imperviously into a section of stunted buildings, short houses. Mexicans and Negroes roamed a busy business area. Now there were mostly Negroes.

It was dusk. Streetlights sighed on. The graceful snobbish music—Pachelbel, the announcer had intoned—was eerie along the black-teeming streets.

"Looking for a house," Orin announced belatedly.

They came to an old warehouse on this wide street. Huge cylindrical tanks lay rusting. An American flag waved over a western-clothes factory, locked now, across the street from a junkyard coated with dark steel ashes. Orin made a right turn.

As if leaving one world and entering another—Jesse impulsively clicked off the radio—they were driving along a long stretch of dead houses, a graveyard of deserted houses in varying degrees of collapse, some totally demolished. Only the walls of others stood, pastel green, yellow, pink plaster crumbling into colored dust. Others remained almost intact, except for smashed windows covered over by crossed boards. Large red numbers had been painted on the houses still standing. The red paint had dripped in long streaks and dots; the numbers gave the houses the appearance of marked graves, or dwellings hit by a deadly plague.

"It's scary," Lisa protested.

Jesse James was silent. He didn't want to admit that he too was frightened to be in this area. There was nobody else anywhere, no one; and no car except theirs—the obvious arrogant car, uncovered—and the plucked frames of discarded others.

On bare fields dried palm leaves formed piles, fallen, scratching wearily at the erratic wind. Weeds clutched struggling grass and persistent wild flowers. Many still alive, brave trees, just beginning to mourn, surrendered enormous white and red blossoms to the blemished ground. Farther ahead, an urgent crush of bougainvillea splashed dazzling color into the desolation.

The long, wide street ended in a field of dirt, wind-shoved dried vines entangled like tumbleweeds and huge clumps of concrete like overturned tombstones.

Years ago, the city had decided to build a freeway through this area; it was to stretch to the outlying beaches. People were evacuated into already crowded areas nearby. Grass, trees, and flowers were allowed to die. The demolition of houses began. Then the freeway project was abandoned, and the miles-long area exists like an unhealing wound.

The streetlights remain—on, as dusk fell into night; but most have been shattered, not replaced, so that darkness saturates the wasted area.

"There's no one around," Jesse said. But he thought he had seen a straggling shadow—a branch bending in the abrupt wind?

"Pearl's scared," Lisa said. "Don't cry," she soothed the doll anxiously.

Muted music floated from somewhere within the isolation of the slaughtered buildings. One note, another, three; then the fragment of a phrase—from a guitar. Through a small partition in one of the scarred structures and seeping out into the night from an opening unstopped by the crossed wooden boards, a dull light flickered.

Orin stopped the Cadillac under weeping black trees. He raised the top.

"Is that the house you're looking for?" Lisa asked.

"No," Orin said. But he got out anyway. Jesse was quickly behind him. Orin locked the car. Jesse looked in panic at it, so vulnerable out here. Then the three moved across a weedy path toward the faltering light, the smothered sounds. The building which contained them had once boasted windows with colored glass. Shards like painted fangs remained on the frames. "Bet it was a church once," Orin identified.

A muffled male voice sang:

Ya say you gotta soul— . . .

Orin found the door—boards had been pushed apart, nails pulled out from the bottom, then the boards swiveled back into place. The wind had pushed one slab of wood to allow the sliver of light to escape.

> I say if I can shoot a hole
> In ya, I won't see no soul— . . .

Orin entered the wrecked church. Only the remains of one or two benches had been left, like brown bones. Jesse stood behind Orin. Holding Pearl carefully, Lisa worked her way in through the sliding boards.

> Ya say ya got a body in the image
>   of a lord?
> I say all ya got is meat, bones,
>   filthy flesh and dirty blood.
> Ya say— . . .

At the extreme end of the abandoned church, a corner was lighted with candles. One was flickering, about to go out, darkness waited to enclose it. Several young bodies bunched in that one area. A youngman plucked on a guitar again, only once. He was skinny, almost bony. His hair was straight, oiled to gleam black. Around his neck, he wore a leather strap dangling halfway to his stomach. A skull over a cross hung from it onto a sleeveless black t-shirt. About him were two other thin youngmen, also with cutoff shirts, one a combat green fatigue jacket, with a large swastika painted on it. Their hair was shaved, except for one long carefully level patch in the middle—like a Moh-hawk Indian's. A girl sat on the floor near the singer. Her hair was dyed green and frizzled, her eyes were black tadpoles. Another girl with purple and yellow hair huddled over a candle as she heated a can of food. Other open cans rested on the floor. Male or female, another body lay on a mattress.

The girl with green hair squinted lazily at Orin, Lisa, Jesse James. One side of her face was painted in various colors, the other was chalk white. In the light of the few candles, all the faces seemed to float. The singer turned away, unconcerned, from the three, caught in the flicker of dim flames. Plunk! A loud note on the guitar. His hand quickly muffled it. He sang softly:

> Ya say ya got a soul?
> Well, I say fuck it,
> Fuck your soul cause
> All ya got's a filthy body— . . .

He stopped. "You like that, Fever?" he asked the girl sitting near him.

"I guess," she shrugged. She dipped a spoon in the warming can, ate from it, and placed it on the floor.

"Needs more shove, Revolver," said one of the youngmen with the Mohawk haircut.

The girl warming the open cans said to Orin, Lisa, and Jesse, "You better find another place of your own—like toward the end of the strip. Pigs come around and too many people fuck up for everyone."

Outside, Orin replaced the boards carefully across the door. Jesse made sure they were in place. The three moved back through the weeds to the Cadillac; it looked somber in the assaulted area.

At night, car lights on opposing sides of the freeway shoot like tracer bullets—white lights hurtle along the darkness. The top left up, the windows of the speeding car all open, the moving air stirred heat. Usually the nights are cool in Southern California; but tonight, heat did not release the city.

They got off the freeway, moving across Western Avenue, a shabby street of bars, restaurants, pornographic arcades. At the intersection of Sunset, black and Mexican prostitutes gather outside an all-night food shop. Cars drive through an intersecting alley, appraising the shiny women.

Before they left the motel this morning, Orin had checked the television several times, to make sure it was all right. Even so, he elicited reassurance from the man at the desk that they would be able to provide a replacement if anything went wrong with the present set. Now back at the motel, they parked in the allotted space before their unit. Hidden lights smeared colors in the pool.

The room was very pretty, and large, with wooden beams, dark brown, and pictures of the ocean, and several elaborate lamps, one looped to a chain over a round table, on which the telephone rested. There were various comfortable chairs. And the two double beds.

"We sure do live in a pretty place." Lisa admired the room again. She lay Pearl gently on one bed. She was so *beautiful!* The doll's eyelids shut the agate blue eyes.

Bootless instantly, his body moist in the sudden coolness of the room, Jesse looked at Lisa and thought, She gets prettier and prettier. *Damn!* He stared annoyed at Orin.

Orin consulted his pocket watch. He turned the television on. He seemed impatient for the picture to coagulate on the screen. "It's working real good," he said, clearly pleased. He shifted channels.

". . .—in a schoolyard, with a black hood over his head. Authorities say he— . . ."

"They're talking about that guy who hanged himself!" Jesse leaned over to listen and watch attentively.

On the screen a pretty woman with light-brown hair was continuing in a tone of grave concern: ". . .—was an ordinary twenty-one-year-old man, a good student; he had no known connection to the school." "You wouldn't have expected him to do anything of the kind," an old woman, hair carefully sculpted for the cameras, was talking into a microphone as the scene shifted from the television studio to the dead-man's neighborhood. The first woman's voice-over continued over the newsclip of a fat bald man wearing a tie: "Another neighbor, Mr. Albert Silbert, said— . . ." The man's voice took over: "That boy was just like anybody else—just like you and me and everyone else, as far as I knew; and he sure laughed a lot, always laughing." The picture faded back to the pretty woman in the studio. "No one seems to know why he hanged himself in that grisly way—or how he managed in the early afternoon to make his way into the schoolyard, drape the black hood over his head— . . ." The voice continued over a film of the deserted playground, the deadly flowered jacaranda, then the victim's placid dwelling—curtains drawn, silent. ". . .—loop a strap, and hang himself from a branch." The picture returned to the woman, sitting at an oval table in the slick television studio. Beside her was a well-dressed gray-haired man. "Nobody knows why he did it, Kenneth, or what the black hood was meant to signify, or why he went there," the throbbing voice of the woman said.

The man she was addressing shook his head. "What about the rumors circulating, Mandy, that he was the Viet Nam veteran who escaped earlier today from the army psychiatric facility in West Los Angeles?"

"No connection. Just a rumor, Kenneth," the woman said earnestly. "And about the disturbed veteran, police received several calls from people reporting to have seen a man matching his description; some of the callers even claimed he had a rifle. Sightings were reported—simultaneously—in Westwood, Hollywood, Venice Beach, several at the Griffith Park Observatory. Police ruled them all out as crank calls. They attributed the embellishment of a rifle to the fact that the veteran has been described as having been suffering from so-called 'flashbacks'—. . ."

"Believing he's still at war," the gray-haired man clarified. The camera closed in on him, shoving the brown-haired woman away. There was a very subdued but deliberate smile on the man's face as he continued: "On another front—no pun intended! —both camps claim it is pure coincidence that *both* Senator Thom Hutchens and Cardinal Unger are scheduled to speak—*on the same night*—at the same Beverly Hills hotel. In different rooms—I hope." His voice became serious. "As you know, Mandy, Senator Hutchens is known for his—this is a quote— 'extreme left views'—and Cardinal Unger—again a quote—has been called 'one of the most reactionary men in the established religious hierarchy in the country.' While both— . . ."

"Fuck *them*!" Jesse said irritably. "More on the guy in the schoolyard!"

"That's all there'll be," Orin said. "Won't be any more. And nobody'll ever know why he did it."

Lisa had retreated quickly into the bathroom. Now Jesse heard the shower running. He imagined her naked body, her hands soaping it lovingly, under her breasts first, bubbles bursting right at her nipples, and then the soap would drip down her stomach, to her legs, and then the water would wash *all* the bubbles away, and she'd stand there naked and wet and— . . .

"This is Kenneth Manning with the latest news," the white-haired man on the screen was saying. "We'll be back—after these announcements—with Mandy Lang-Jones, substituting tonight for Eleanor Cavendish, who's a little under the weather."

"And we'll have a full report on *that*—the weather," Mandy Lang-Jones said with the slightest smile, "when we return with a full report on the Santa Ana condition that has caused unseasonal soaring temperatures all over the southland, with winds rising up to— . . ."

Again, Orin consulted his watch. Now he brought it to his ear—as if he were deliberately stretching time. In apprehension? To prolong anticipation? Both? He shifted channels. One. Two. Three— . . .

In azure hues, the television screen revealed a woman sitting on a high-backed, gold-gilded chair like a throne. With her in a similar chair but located facing hers at an angle so that his did not seem as imposing, was a man in a handsome, subdued suit.

Orin removed his hand from the dial. He sat on the edge of the bed and watched.

Against a cyclorama of peaceful blue artificial sky, the slender woman had light, light, delicate blond hair that at times appeared almost silver; it fell in soft white-yellowish clouds on her shoulders. Her eyes were coal dark, or appeared so because they were outlined black and heavily into the terribly white skin of her face. Her lips were painted a very dark red. She was ageless, she could have been forty or sixty, older, younger. She wore a long, flowing azure dress, a misty robe, which covered her neck, her arms. Now and then a sigh of a created breeze lifted the chiffon, barely. Her private breeze.

"She gave her soul to Satan," she said to the camera.

The man with her had ashen hair. Almost as ageless as she, he resembled her. "She told you that?" he said sadly.

"Yes," the woman answered. Her words were breaths, like puffs of the softest cotton. Her hypnotic voice issued from the gashed dark lips. "One of our operators for Jesus took down her words while I spoke to her, and this is what she said." In awed words—distinctly pronounced whispers—the woman read from a paper. " 'And I played with him and he caused me to do all manner of vileness, and caused me to mock Jesus.' ' "

"The unspeakable adversary!" the man denounced.

" 'Until the Lord led me to you,' " the woman finished reading. Then she looked into the camera. Her face radiated power. "No." She shook her head. No!" Her voice and hands rose. "Not to me. To *him!* To the blood! The blood of the Lamb! . . . Jesus." She pulled out the word, longer, longer, as if to possess it.

There was a telephone number on the bottom of the screen.

The camera enclosed the woman as she knelt. Her sleeves flowed onto the floor, the long skirt spilled in a sheer pool of blue about her.

Coming out of the shower, Lisa saw the woman. Fiercely, she turned away. She pulled Pearl from the bed, clutching her as if to protect her from an unleashed memory.

In fascination, Jesse James watched Orin; his blue eyes looked haunted by the presence radiating from the screen.

There, the hand of the kneeling woman glided out, upward, higher, slowly, more slowly—higher—and then it clenched into a strangled fist. Her eyes opened wide—black on white. She smashed down with the fist. The ghostly echoes of her earlier tones crashed: "*Crush the Evil Prince!*" Her raised fist remained frozen in an attitude of violent prayer.

Orin said, "That's Sister Woman. She's why I'm here."

Manny Gomez: "The Frontal Christ"

Manny Gomez was eighteen and living in East Los Angeles when he became aware that he wanted a naked Christ tattooed on his chest, a Christ with cock and balls.

The thought must have been there, unshaped, as far back as five years—when he was in Juvenile Detention Home in El Paso, Texas—because with a knife and a pen he had carved into the webbed part of his hand a "burning cross." But that was a borrowed symbol of a rough Mexican gang; wavy lines created the impression of smoking flames. The blood-inked drawing was almost gone now, replaced by smooth pinkish scar tissue from a severe burn.

He didn't look at that part of his hand, to avoid the memory not of the tattoo, but of the singed flesh. When the memory threatened, he drowned it with others, ugly but less so, fragments from the same time: his mother sobbing, two red-faced men shoving him into a wired wagon with three other Mexican boys—all wearing crucifixes around their necks, like him; the iron-barred windows of the long, flat building where they were incarcerated; on the floor the blanket-thin urine-tainted mattresses they slept on; police dogs barking outside; bugs that crept and flew; cans instead of toilets in the small cubicles. And voices, sounds, sights out of the limbo of nights of constant fear and loneliness; a guard pinioning him against a wall: "How'd you get that tattoo on your hand, boy? Means you're tough, huh?''—and the fist in his stomach; the voice of another guard bolting out of a distant room: "I'm tired of your shit, punk! ''—and the sound of feet thrusting against flesh; "Slit your throat next time''—and a guard—they all had reddish white angered faces—pulling a boy along by the hair, the boy's wrists flaring with blood, slashed with a broken light bulb. And the terrified voice that kept screaming throughout that first night: "*Mamaaaaaa!*"

Manny didn't know exactly why he was sent to the detention home. There were many mysteries already gathering in his young life. He didn't even go to court. True, he had stolen a kit of tools from a hardware store. Yolanda—his mother—had come home to find him dismantling a small television set piece" by piece, looking at each part carefully, holding it up to the grimy light. The set belonged to the man who was living with his mother at the time.

When he got out of detention, Manny returned with the tattooed cross on his hand to the two-room apartment—full of crucifixes and candle-lit Virgin Mary's, black-draped Mothers of Sorrows. The apartment was on the second storey of the sagging tenement where they lived in South El Paso. Manny was fourteen, just turned fourteen.

After that, Manny became an intimate stranger to Yolanda, someone who watched her very closely at times, at times didn't seem to see her even when she talked to him.

Yolanda preferred for her children to call her by her first name. After all, it was a pretty name, and she was young, her hair lustrous and dark, and even when she was a few pounds heavier than she might have been, she looked good, lush—some said she looked better a little heavy. She had married at sixteen, to get out of an infested tenement in the "Second Ward"—where only Mexicans live—up to ten people, more, different generations, occupying two dark rooms without running water; the bathroom outside, frigid in winter.

As it turned out, Yolanda merely exchanged one tenement for another—and a brutal husband. The "son of a bitch"—the only way she referred to the father of Manny and his two sisters—she told them he was the father of all three, but not of Paco, whose father was also a "son of a bitch"—disappeared after a fight that left her bruised for more than a week. Manny remembered that: he was six and kept pounding with his fists at the man's legs. Later, Manny kissed the bruises on Yolanda's face, thinking his saliva would heal them. The events of all those years often ran out of sequence in Manny's cramped memories. Several times in detention, and returns home, often fused into one endless time.

When Manny was fifteen, Yolanda decided that they would go to Los Angeles "to make a new life." They traveled, with many bandaged boxes, by Greyhound bus. A distant relative helped them locate a soiled pink bungalow, one of several in a ratty, squeezed stucco unit off Brooklyn Avenue in that clutch of small communities cemented by gray concrete streets and known as "East L.A.," populated almost exclusively by Mexicans.

Each summer, heat clenches these bungalows and won't let go until the rains thrust it off as steam. In the heat-clasped house, Yolanda slept in the bedroom, with Margarita, then almost a teenager. Manny, the oldest, Ernestina, younger by three years than Margarita, and Paco, the "baby," slept in what would have been a dining room. There would be an occasional other occupant—a man, not necessarily the same one, who stayed over for a few days, even a few weeks, and contributed a week's, even a month's groceries. Then Margarita slept in a fold-out bed in the "front room." Not that Yolanda was a prostitute—no, absolutely not. She was a religious woman. Having a boarder merely made things easier for them all.

Even the poorest sections of East Los Angeles have an impressionistic prettiness that camouflages the poverty. Flowers seem pasted on crumbling walls; vines splash color on rotting porches. In wrecked-automobile yards—which are everywhere— enormous yellow-leafed sunflowers with brown velvet centers peer at twisted chrome veins on mangled metal bodies. And green, green trees are everywhere. On far-off flowered hills up Atlantic Boulevard, pretty homes, some almost elaborate, keep a measured distance.

Murals decorate walls in the poor sections: A squad of jubilant, muslin-clothed brown-faced Zapatistas—triumphant agrarian revolutionaries! A noble Aztec prince, amber gold-faced, in lordly feathers! Muscular Indians conquered by pale *conquistadores* armed with guns and blessed by a livid Spanish priest—at the edge of the fresco, a specter of a victorious Villista emerges out of the colored vicissitudes of oppression. It is often under these murals, in abandoned, spottily green parks, that young Mexican men—often gangs—bunch together, expecting nothing.

There are many other areas where Mexicans live in Los Angeles—in the central city, downtown. In fists of blackened tenements, families live in shifts, in the same ugly apartment, sleeping in the same beds, eating at the same tables—at different, designated times. And so Yolanda was proud that she "managed" in "East L.A."

Manny was lean and sinewy, not tall. He had dark brown hair, smooth brown skin, liquidy dark eyes, thick black eyebrows, a straight nose like those of the Aztecs in the murals. He worked unpacking boxes, arranging their contents on shelves, and keeping clean a grocery store that featured, in a bold sign on its window, a "Mexican-style" butcher shop—slabs of cheap meat on melting ice.

Near the store is the Church of *Nuestra Señora de la Soledad,* Our Lady of Solitude. Atop the yellowish church, Our Lady stands with hands outstretched welcoming those who walk up its iron-grilled steps. Manny moved slowly when he passed it, and then he began to pause before it. Once he even stopped.

Yolanda paid two dollars—though not every day—to an old woman in the court to look in on the children while she was gone. She worked in a clothes factory in downtown Los Angeles— "sweatshops," a woman doing a television story on the terrible conditions in the city's garment district called them; Yolanda hated that designation. Rows of Mexican women sewed endlessly in shops owned by "Anglos" who came in once a day to hear the constant pick-pick-picking of the machines. The pay was low; hired knowingly, "illegals" from across the border were willing to work for anything. The immigration authorities made periodic raids—almost always before the women had been paid. The illegal women just surrendered. Yolanda detested it when the hatchet-faced immigration men would demand to see *her* birth certificate, even though she would speak in her best English to them. So she began dressing more "Anglo"—a lower-cut dress, more modish shoes, more makeup, shorter hair. But they still asked her for her papers.

With his background—tough credentials from detention homes—Manny would have been a leader in any of the gangs in the *barrios* of "East Ellay." Idle, jobless, restive factions of young Mexicans war against each other, from neighborhood, to neighborhood, into Central Los Angeles, brandishing bats, knives, guns. They are united only in their detestation of "the man" —the white cops—and when occasional incursions occur from "*gringo* surfers" along the coast—or, more often, from "redneck" gangs in the Valley. Then the grandsons of the exploited Okies tangle bloodily with the descendants of the conquered warriors.

Once a week, the young Mexican charioteers parade "customized" cars along Whittier Boulevard—prized Fifties' "Cheveez" with silver-sprinkled red, green, blue, purple birds or fiery flames painted on the hoods and sides of the growling machines. Girls, flaunting their budding sexuality, root for the best cars, the best-looking or most daring drivers, the members of their favorite gang, or the lowest "low-riders," cars that seem almost to touch the street.

Police helicopters hover over it all. Lights pour onto the street carving a pit of daylight. Surly squad cars with agitated blue and yellow lights swirling rush to perform rehearsed assaults. The very next day, resentment burrowing, gangs turn more ferociously against each other.

Always a loner, Manny did not join a gang. His proven credentials for "toughness" made that possible. His only friend was El Indio, and he encouraged Manny to stay away from the gangs, no matter how tight they tried to squeeze him to join. El Indio was a very dark youngman with long hair so black it looked blue; he had a scar that began at the tip of his right ear and ended at the edge of his left shoulder—carved by one switch of a sharp blade. He wanted no part of the gangs anymore. "Fighting your own people instead of the pigs, man," he told Manny, "that's what the pigs want, to keep us killing each other." It was afternoon, and they were sitting in the shade of the wall with the triumphant brown-faced revolutionaries painted on it.

A black and white squad car cruised by. Hands on their holsters, two white cops swaggered toward the youngmen. "Got any tattoos?" one of the cops asked them.

Manny knew the question meant, Do you have any needle

marks, do you shoot up? "No. Gonna get one, though," he said.

"Let me see your arms," the cop said in that soft tone that meant he would turn mean.

Manny held out his right arm.

"The other one," the cop said.

Hesitating, Manny held it out.

"What's that ugly scar on your hand?" the cop asked.

"A burn." Manny clenched his fingers and pulled his hand away.

One cop shoved Indio against the wall, the other spread-eagled Manny. They kicked at the ankles of the two youngmen so that their bodies were rendered helpless. Laughing, the cops walked away, leaving the two in that position against the mural.

"Pigs," El Indio spat as the cops drove away.

Manny rubbed the scar tissue on his hand, as he did often, especially when he was agitated. He heard a car drive by. *Ping!* Blood crawled over Indio's chest. Manny thought he himself was screaming, but it was sirens.

When he learned Indio was dead, Manny went to the bathroom of the stucco bungalow. With a knife, he drew a long line from the middle of his chest and down almost to his navel. He thought he was imitating El Indio's diagonal scar. But now he drew another line from one nipple to the other. He didn't cut into the skin, just scratched it deeply. It flared dark-pink. Only one drop of blood gathered at one edge of the horizontal line. Manny watched it trickle down and didn't try to stop its flow.

The next day he didn't go to work. He hung around the streets. Finally he walked to the yellowish church. The front doors were locked. He went into the side courtyard that separates the church from the rectory. That side door was open. He walked into the church, past the blaze of supplicants' candles lighted to the Virgin of Guadalupe, brown-faced, robed in tawdry gold-starred blue and red—the way she was supposed to have appeared in Mexico to the Indian Juan Diego, stamping her gaudy image on his peasant's smock to prove her miraculous presence to the doubting priests.

The church was empty. There is no railing before the altar, just a step. Over the ornate altar is the statue of Christ. Especially on the right side, the loincloth is brief enough to reveal sharp muscles in a *U* over the groin. Two mosaicked windows flank the crucified figure. Light flowed from one side now and splashed deep hues on the tortured body.

Manny walked up to the altar, where only priests and altar boys are allowed. "Why aren't you ever naked? Why don't you ever really reveal yourself?" he asked the figure.

At the entrance to the church, in the growing darkness, the flames of the candles before the Virgin of Guadalupe rose fiercely as he passed the statue. He raised the scarred hand over one, almost allowing the flames to burn it away into another scar. Then he withdrew.

He went to work and drew the owner's ire: "Convict!" Manny demanded, in mean tones, and got his twice-a-month pay. "Fuck you," he said to the man.

At dinner Yolanda introduced a new "boarder," a not-unattractive dark man. Manny didn't even look at him. Instead, he studied Paco, his five-year-old brother—he was getting thinner, listless; he never smiled. Manny made a face at him, to get him to laugh; but Paco didn't even smile.

Margarita sat next to Paco. She was fourteen now. She would be an exotic beauty before long; already she was the proud "old lady" of one of the leaders of a ruling gang. She was cool to Manny, maybe because he'd seen her put something like cotton between her legs, or, more likely, because he refused to join her "old man's" gang. Next to him, Ernestina—eleven years old and plain as an olive—couldn't sit still, fidgeting; the opposite of Paco, she oozed nerves.

Still avoiding the new boarder, Manny stared at his mother. She was looking especially pretty for the new man. She wore a shiny, watery dress that shoved her breasts together and showed off the ripe round ovals.

Yolanda caught Manny studying her. She never wondered what the other children thought of her "boarders," but she wondered what Manny thought. He was grown. When he kissed her—now and then, and always impulsively—when she left for work or when he did—she began to turn her lips instead of her cheek. He looked moodier to her today, his eyes steady on her; she smiled at him, but he didn't smile back. She raised her dress just slightly at her bosom, then lowered it again. Was it because of this new man he kept staring at her, or was he remembering— . . . ? No, *that* was forgotten!

Manny jerked up suddenly, almost overturning the table.

"What the hell!" the man said.

Manny had just seen it: Hanging on the wall—probably to conceal a new crack—was a garish drawing of Jesus, with long concealing robes. Yolanda kept old religious calendars. Each time a crack developed or plaster peeled, she went through them, chose one, and pasted it over the scar. Usually it was a picture of the Madonna.

El Indio was dead, gunned down by one of his own people, one of a rival gang or the gang he had abandoned—dead, just like that: *Ping!* —and there *he* was, Jesus, in his white fucking robes! "Fuckin' bastard!" Manny shouted at the picture—and then his eyes sliced over to see the new "boarder" for the first time. "Fuckin' bastard!" he repeated.

"*Please!*" Yolanda hit the table.

"What the hell," the man said.

Paco pushed his plate away. It broke on the floor with a loud crash. Gratefully, Ernestina slid off her chair to gather the pieces—it gave her a chance to hide.

Manny walked out into the starless night. He moved on to Brooklyn Avenue, the wide street that fades for a few blocks, enters a tunnel, and then emerges as Sunset Boulevard—the beginning of one of the longest streets anywhere, beginning here before it flees from the poverty of East L.A., the spill of Skid Row, the dinginess of downtown Los Angeles—and curves along the strip of electric posters announcing hit records, then sweeps into Beverly Hills, Bel Air, mansions, lofty houses perched like wide-winged birds on the purple cliffs of Malibu over the ocean.

Manny was on Main Street, in downtown Los Angeles. He had hitched a ride, so pensive he hardly remembered the driver, remembered only the man kept asking, "What's the matter, kid, what's the matter?"

It was a Los Angeles night, both hot and cold; moisture chilled the hot air.

Along that squalid street are porno shops, with colored close-ups of squashed organs on magazine covers like slabs of meat in the butcher shop; smelly fried chicken counters; cheap black and Mexican whores in tiny pants; mean bars with men who look like convicts—and fussy older men out of place—and, like giants, on platform shoes, men as rough as the convicts but painted and dressed like women.

And tattoo parlors.

Manny stood outside the largest one. Its walls were illustrated with every conceivable design—flowers, naked women, hearts, ships, panthers—the intricate map of an exotic world. And decorated crosses. And heads of Jesus.

Manny walked in.

"You gotta be eighteen," the tattooer, a thin man, said.

"I am," Manny told him.

"What's the matter with you?" the man asked him.

"I want a tattoo of a naked Christ on my chest," Manny said. He heard his voice; it sounded strange. He opened his shirt, revealing the scratch, which had healed into a vague scar on his dark brown skin. "I already got the cross, now I want a Christ, with cock and balls." What was the matter with his voice? It hurt him to speak.

"Get out of here," the man barked.

"Fuckin'-ass hypocrite," Manny shot back. "Look at all the naked bodies you do."

"I'll call the cops, punk."

"Shove the needle up your ass," Manny said.

He walked into the rancid street. Angry black and brown faces—he'd seen them before but not with so much rage on them. He remembered the boys in the detention home in El Paso, the one who had sliced his wrists with the broken light bulb. He saw roaming tramps. He thought of Paco and began to feel then what he would know later. Drunks sleeping in their own piss on filthy sidewalks. He heard the wounded laughter of desperate whores. Black-uniformed cops, cruising slowly—mean faces. He thought he saw Indio standing on a corner. Only when warming wind blowing against his face evaporated the moisture did Manny realize he was crying, had been crying from the moment he had left the house in East Los Angeles.

When Manny returned home, everyone was asleep and the

house was beginning to sweat in darkness. Manny went to the kitchen, to the drawer where his mother kept semiused candles. She lit one occasionally before a crucifix or a framed picture of the Virgin—but she never let any run down entirely, snuffing each out halfway, saving it in case of a power failure—or an unpaid electric bill. Manny took one—and the pencil she used to write the notes she left when she went out, telling them she'd be late.

He went to the new picture of the robed Christ. He was right, Yolanda had used it to patch a crack growing behind it like a heavy spider web. He lit the candle and placed it on a chair so he could see the picture clearly. He drew dark swirls of pubic hair on the lower torso of the figure.

In the room where he slept, Paco and Ernestina were lying soundlessly in their cots. Manny went to a corner of the room covered with a floor-length remnant of cloth; it was draped over a wire nailed from a wall to one adjoining it. Behind the small triangle creating a makeshift closet, there was another wire. On it hung their clothes. Now he took most of his, not that many, and knotted them into a roll. He tied it with two belts so that he could loop it over his shoulder. He went to Paco's bed and sat next to the little boy, deliberately to rouse him.

Even suddenly awakened, Paco did not register surprise. He just looked with odd eyes at his brother.

"Good-bye," Manny said.

"Goo'bye," Paco imitated the sound. He sat up. His head lolled to one side. He kept it in that position. He's retarded—Manny faced what he had suspected—Paco's retarded. He kissed his brother and eased him gently back into his cot. Paco closed his eyes.

Outside, Manny looked at his hand under a streetlight. The scar looked like a mangled flower. The avoided memory thrust powerfully: His hand forced over the lit burner of the stove, the odor of scorched flesh—or was it burnt blood? Too much of the drowned memory had floated up. He pushed the palms of his hands against his eyes. Exploding colors scattered the fragmented memory.

He welcomed the moisture of his own sweat as he walked all the way back to Main Street. Now past midnight, the ugly street was uglier—more broken bodies staggering around, some as young as himself. The tattoo shop was lit but closed, a barred iron gate spread before it. Through the bars, Manny looked into the jungle of inked contorted bodies among flowers and trees and animals and crosses. He noticed a ragged old woman sobbing beside him.

He took the bus to Hollywood. Sunset Boulevard. The section known as the Strip.

*Z*O*O*M*

An electric poster blazed. The letters of the word lighted up one by one in a rush, and then all four pulsed the word, the name of a new album. Under the electric word was a picture of three youngmen and a girl—all in shiny vinyl, more watery than black leather, but almost as menacing, the look of leather and steel. All had very short hair, bleached bright yellow; all held long black dangling belts from their hands and seemed to menace the street. Under the picture was the name of the group: REVELATION.

A few feet away, a photograph of a woman in lavender feathers—real feathers fluttering sequined in the nervous breeze—invited all to LAS VEGAS LAS VEGAS LAS VEGAS. A barnlike building with a nude plaster statue of a woman guaranteed naked female bodies in performance or money back.

Across the street, many youngmen and girls gathered before a band-club there. SALVATION was playing, the black letters on the hospital white marquee announced. Manny walked past the groups of young people sitting on the street waiting for the next show. Several resembled the girl and men in the ZOOM poster. Some had bright red hair, streaked green or yellow; many of them were in black—several of the thin youngmen had shaved heads and wore sleeveless shirts, tattoos on their skinny arms. Tattoos. Manny noticed one particularly: A skull; out of one eye, the bare torso of a woman crawled out, and out of the other, the bare torso of a man. It was on a youngman's bare chest. "Where'd you get that tattoo?" The youngman hardly glanced at Manny. "Down the street," he muttered.

Yes, there it was—large, brightly lit. And closed. A long, long tattoo parlor. Manny peered in. There were even more figures here than downtown. Inside, someone moved. It was a tall, skinny man, about sixty years old. Manny knocked insistently on the glass. The man turned around. Manny knocked again. The man mimed the word "Closed." Manny knocked urgently. The man shook his head, pointed to his watch, and flashed ten fingers plus two. "Open. At. Noon." He formed the words slowly with his lips. Manny took off his shirt, revealing the wavy cross he had carved there after Indio's murder. The old man came closer to the window. With his finger, Manny outlined roughly the figure he wanted drawn there. In large movements he drew the cock and balls; to clarify, he touched his own. Only the glass separated Manny and the man, the man had moved that close. Now he nodded his head. Manny nodded back, and then moved away.

His shirt on again, Manny followed the loose flow of people. He was now on Santa Monica Boulevard in West Hollywood. Many homosexual men cruised the streets.

In a triangle of green and concrete, youngmen and youngwomen lingered before the West-Sky Club. They resembled those outside the club on Sunset—but these looked tougher. Many wore black vinyl, some leather—and swastikas, chains, torn shirts and blouses, ragged uniforms—like an army of deserters from different, causeless wars. Yet, Manny noticed immediately, they looked healthy—some deliberately skinny, the skinniness that comes from choice, not hunger—and Manny knew the difference. They smoked dope freely, but it didn't seem to mellow them—no, it etched anger. That, too, he recognized easily. Loud music blasted its way into the night.

Carrying the bundle of clothes as unobtrusively as he could—though nobody seemed to notice it—Manny slid past the burly guard at the door. He entered a large room that contained smaller ones united by green corridors. In one corner pinball machines exploded in colored lights, ricocheting against lit squares. Everywhere were frizzle-haired girls with anger painted on their white faces—and youngmen in slick, new ripped clothes. Many looked like surfers, more of them like rednecks, and they all drank freely. Through a long tunnel, Manny walked into the restroom. The walls in the dirty room were smeared with words. Pissing, Manny read:

WASTED YOUTH KILL REVOLUTION EVOLU-
TION A PROCESS TO SLOW TO WORRY SAVE
MY SOUL JESUS HATE YOU ITS ALL SHIT
DESTROY EVERYTHING BODIES IN THE STREET
COMMIE FASCISTS GO AWAY COME BACK FEEL
POWERFUL I HATE SWEET COMMUNION ZOOM

Several youngmen, doped and drunk—or pretending to be—
swerved over the urinal. Manny had the impression of deliberate
posing.

He followed the loud music into a large room. Electric guitars
crashed against screaming voices blaring unintelligible words.
Four or five youngmen were making sounds and motions on the
platform draped in light.

Before them on a circular clearing, bodies churned and jumped
in a violent dance, shoving each other as if fighting, hitting each
other, bodies toppling, sometimes laughing, sometimes angered.
Some pushed themselves against the walls. Manny stood in this
pit of flamboyant rage.

Over a balcony, leaning heads floated out of candelight enclosed in bulbed glasses on the tables; spectators, for now. A
few similar tables outlined the extreme back of the first floor.
Throughout, several of the young figures snorted white powder.
Manny stared at the urgent, determined, writhing bodies in
studiedly trashy clothes. The white adorned faces all glared in
frozen anger.

Now the group called Unholy Communion came on. There
were two youngmen with Mohawk haircuts—narrow swatches
of hair forming a straight line from the tip of the hairline to the
nape of the neck; another had shaved his hair totally. The lead
singer had dark, impossibly black hair—black dyed blacker—
and white skin. His eyes were outlined in black paint. He wore
a black vinyl vest and black vinyl pants—and coarse engineer
boots.

Unlike the singer in the earlier group—and most other like
groups—the singer of Unholy Communion could be heard; the
words deliberately clear, the music of bass guitars and drums
allowing them clarity. Manny listened.

If you believe in angels,
Ya been smokin' angel dust
In the land of the cops
And the home of the jerks.

Manny made his way past the thrusting, bobbing bodies. He stood near the stage and stared at the singer until the singer looked down at him. He seemed to address his words at Manny:

Tell us no lies
And we'll ask you no questions.

He was different from the others, Manny told himself. Was it only the dark dark hair—so dark it gleamed silver blue—that reminded him of El Indio?

After the club closed, Manny lingered outside with many of the others, who stood there as if unwilling to relinquish the close ritual. Occasionally a reference slid out revealing a daylight reality—"school," "draggy job"—beyond the night's mask of assumed names.

It was clear the cops hated *them,* too. In brown uniforms across the street, they dared *them* to give them an excuse to move in. It came—someone threw a bottle into the street. Because it had come from his direction, Manny ran into an alley behind the West-Sky. On the other side were the backs of short houses and apartment buildings.

The singer of Unholy Communion was pissing in the alley. Nearby, a girl with green frizzled hair waited, smoking grass. Manny stopped running. "Pigs," he said.

"Yeah," the girl said, "we hear them."

Manny stared hard at her. She would have been much prettier without that strange blazing hair and those black-painted lips.

"You gonna be much longer, Revolver?" she called out to the youngman in the shiny vinyl pants and vest. In the night his hair was black without tones or shades.

A fat man rushed out of one of the houses. "You're a puke," he said to Revolver, "and you're a slut," he said to the girl.

Finished pissing, Revolver shook his cock at the man. A cop shoved him on the dirt before he could even raise his pants.

Another pushed the girl against the back wall of the West-Sky Club. There were only two cops, and so they didn't grab Manny, who stood frozen. The raging fat man said to the cops, "Kill the sons of bitches, kill 'em all."

"Fuckin' germs," one cop said.

The other said to the girl, "Your mother should've aborted you."

"Yeah—right down the toilet," the fat man said.

Lashed by waves of anger and nausea, Manny saw a bottle in the alley; he grabbed it and flung it against another wall, the glass smashing loudly. The cops whirled around, releasing the youngman and the girl—who ran—and Manny ran, too, zigzagging, knowing the cops had drawn their revolvers. He made his way through the alley and back to Santa Monica Boulevard. Although it was after two in the morning, squads of people lingered near a bookstore—OPEN 24 HOURS—that sells paperback books and pornographic magazines.

In the alleys behind and beyond it, staring men lingered. Cars cruised very slowly along dark garages. Many of the men were shirtless, others wore shorts; one youngman wore shorts so high on his legs his genitals showed.

Manny walked into the alley. Eyes. The light of a car startled a man kneeling before another in a garage. Shadows. The sweaty air soaked Manny's shirt. He walked beyond the sex arena. Near an apartment building not yet finished—its wooden bones covered here and there with thin walls—there was a series of large dark green trash bins, filled. On top of one was a discarded mattress. It was thicker and cleaner than the ones Manny had slept in at the detention home. He pulled it off and dragged it as far as he could from the trash bins without coming too close to the unfinished apartment building. There might be a guard, even a dog trained to attack.

He placed the bundle of his clothes beside him. He was tired, he didn't know how exhausted until he lay on the rank mattress and fell asleep in the heating darkness.

A gurgling noise awakened him. He felt unfocused fear. The noise had come from the closest bin. The garbage stirred—scratching noises. Dazed from heavy sleep and heavier fatigue, Manny staggered toward the bin, drawn to it. Mewling. A cat—

. . . He drew back in electrified horror. He saw flailing little hands—an abandoned baby among the garbage! He ran! Santa Monica Boulevard was still alive with night and sexual energy. Manny stopped. The streetlights revised his reality. Had there really been a baby back there? Imagined, dreamt as he ran? He had to go back; his clothes were there, and he had to find out. The perspiration turned chill as he approached the bin.

Nothing. There was nothing moving there.

He pulled the mattress and his clothes farther from the bins. He woke to a smeared sky. He ate breakfast at an open counter and put coins into a gas station bathroom to clean up. He washed himself urgently, changed his clothes, putting the dirty ones in paper towels and shoving them into the strapped bundle.

He went back to Sunset Boulevard. The tattoo parlor was open. He was sure that the man had been waiting for him. Their glances intersected.

Again on the main strip, Manny saw a new poster going up. Whatever it was, torches of electric fire would be spewing from it.

"Hi," Revolver said. "You're the guy in the alley last night when Scarlett and me got rousted by the pigs." He looked just like he had last night—black vinyl, vest. Manny noticed, this time, that he wore one earring. He had a face that seemed to have been carved—but delicately, formed by soft pain.

"You got away?"

"Yeah, thanks," Revolver said. They were standing outside a liquor store. The girl with him last night came out. "They won't sell me the booze," she said.

"She's Scarlett Fever," Revolver introduced, "I'm Revolver."

"Manny."

"Hi, Money," Scarlett Fever said. "Thanks for helping us out last night." Wearing less makeup, she looked prettier today and, Manny was relieved to see, the dye on her hair was not permanent. Where the green coloring was wearing off quickly, her hair was blond, pretty; soft where it was unfrizzling. But she still had the ugly black lipstick, like Revolver about his eyes.

Revolver looked at Manny's bundle. "Don't live anywhere, huh?"

Manny shook his head.

"Come around the club tonight, Money," Revolver said. "We might have a place. And thanks again."

Manny went to a cheap movie, ate a hamburger, hung around the boulevard, reclaimed, in the afternoons only, by the original inhabitants ambushed in periodic cop raids. Then he was on Sunset, standing before the tattoo shop again. The artist was tattooing a man, but again he glanced clearly at Manny through the window. Manny remained there for moments. The man stopped the movement of his needles until Manny walked away.

That night he went back to the West-Sky, late, not wanting to pay five bucks to go in. Apparently looking for him, "You wanna come in or hang around?" Scarlett Fever asked him.

"Hang around." He had thought she was older than him, but he realized now she was about his age—just tried to look older—a few years, Revolver's age.

They walked off Santa Monica Boulevard, north half a block into the edge of a residential district. They sat on the back sheltered portion of a lawn. Trees bunched. Wind rustled the leaves. Manny and Scarlett felt a breeze without coolness. Enclosed by trees and shadows, they sat on the grass. Manny rubbed his left hand.

"The scar hurt?" Scarlett Fever said. "It looks old. Is it new, Money?"

Manny pulled his hand away.

"Sorry," Scarlett Fever said.

"My mother burned me," Manny said. Spoken for the first time ever, the words didn't surprise him. Before, there had been no one to speak them to; and now, away from her, from Yolanda—forever—he could let the memory flow out; "I was just out of the detention home." *Another kid's father picked me up and took me to the tenement apartment, which looked out on a pile of gargage like the one I slept close to last night. My sisters were in school; Paco wasn't born yet. I had my key and I let myself in.*

Manny entered the house into what was both kitchen and living room. He called out, "Mama, mama." Nothing. The bedroom door was closed. "Mama!" he called again. Yolanda emerged out of the bedroom and closed the door behind her.

"Manny! I didn't know you were getting out, not till— . . ." *I wanted to run to her, hug her, kiss her, cry in her long hair.* Yolanda was barefoot, in a short slip he could see through: brown round breasts, a heavy black shadow between her legs. Her long hair was loose, black. She seemed angry, or nervous. "You wanna go buy yourself something to eat?" She looked around for some money, then toward the closed door; her purse was in there. "You got money?" she asked him. *I wanted her to fix something for me, just for me, and sit down with me and ask me if it had been awful, as awful as it was, I wanted—* . . .

"I'm not hungry." He reached out to touch her. *She jerked away from me.*

"What is that thing on your hand?"

"A tattoo," he said. "The burning cross." *I held it out to her.*

"That's a bad sign; it's blasphemous, and it belongs to that awful gang," she said, the anger there already.

"It just means you're tough."

"No! It's ugly! How dare you defile the cross of Jesus like that. Bring it in here. How dare you!" *She was coming at me. I backed away from her anger, not believing it; I leaned against the gas stove. She grabbed my wrist. My hand went limp.* Emotions were crashing inside him, he simply surrendered his hand to her. He was so numbed by the combustion of emotions that he saw Yolanda turn on the burner of the stove and saw her pushing his hand over the circle of fire to scorch away the tattoo—saw all this before he felt the searing pain and smelled the burnt flesh. *But in my head! I felt it first in my head—that's where the fire was!*

He saw his other hand reach out for her. The strap of her slip tore. One breast showed large, brown, red-tipped. Then the bedroom door opened. *I saw a naked slender man there.* The man seemed to have been awakened, still groggy. Yolanda yelled at him to go back in the bedroom, but he just stood there, dazed. Manny looked down at his own hand, saw or imagined he saw, the flesh smoking, *and then at the same time I saw her giant exposed breast and behind her the naked man.* The naked man leaned against the door, his arms outstretched, hands propped on the wooden frame, three heavy dark patches of hair on his body. *Then I saw only blackness*. When the blackness cleared, the man was gone. Dressed, Yolanda was tending the wound on Manny's hand, kissing it every few seconds—*kissing it the way I had kissed her bruises*—licking it, holding the hand to her breasts. Manny's head burrowed into her chest. "Mama, mama," he cried, and recognized the voice that had screamed that word over and over his first night in detention.

"She held my hand over the stove and burned it," Manny told Scarlett Fever. "And she was the one who called the pigs to come for me when I took apart a television that belonged to her boyfriend." *And she got the cops to take me each time she had a new man*. He knew that—hidden in the mire of the rest. "And that's how I got the scar."

"Bummer," Scarlett said. She kissed him with her tongue. He pushed his into the moisture of her mouth—the first time he had kissed anyone other than Yolanda. *"You wanna fuck me?" she said. He looked around—at darkened windows beyond flanked trees. "Nobody can see, nobody cares, either—they're used to it," she said. She moved farther into shadows, away from phantoms of distant lights. She leaned back on the grass and pulled up her dress; she wasn't wearing pants. He looked fascinated at the dark hairs there; brown? black? He coaxed her to move, into ashen light, to see better. "Go ahead," she said. He felt his whole body breathe with excitement, heard it—or the wind? He leaned over, studying her intently, closely—something forbidden suddenly so easily allowed.

He lay diagonally on the grass, pressing his stiff cock against the sweating earth, to contain this hint of explosion. He stared at her cunt, his face just inches from it. A triangle of dark short hairs, a slight protrusion of flesh, an opening parting it. His fingers touched the hairs, separating them carefully. He blew on them, seeing, in the increasingly lightening darkness, the exposed flesh. His finger probed the opening. Flesh so smooth it wasn't even like skin. So smooth and moist. He wished for more light, wished he could search *into* this mysterious partition. He pushed his finger into the furry lips, which became as moist as her mouth when he kissed her. Her body quivered. Her odor, the odor of a warm sea, blended with the scent of night flowers, sweet, heavy, inviting, threatening.

"Put another finger in," she said. But he didn't want to dissipate the sensation. The one finger inside her connected him to her in a current that rushed back and forth from there to his own groin, pausing there, then rushing back. He didn't want to risk anything that might change that. He felt her clitoris hardening, growing wetter, the moisture thicker. He lowered his head to look even closer.

Across the grass, the wind slid with a sensual sigh like a distant voice, stirring the grass and an unformed memory of Manny's, only a part of it abandoned, never to be forgotten, mixed now with the intense fragments of these new moments.

With a finger of his other hand, he spread the soft vaginal lips wider, allowing them to close, spreading them again, delicately. At his touch they loosened, became fuller. He continued staring, as close as he could come before it would blur—he wanted to *see* what he *felt*.

Scarlett Fever reached over, under his body, to hold his engorged cock. When she touched it, he pulled away. He would erupt! He wanted to extend this exploration, this sensation of heat and desire and fear that lodged in his throat, his groin, then radiated outward from the touch of his fingers througout his whole body. He kept one finger exploring inside her.

The other hand raised her dress so that only one breast was uncovered. *It was small!* He felt angry, betrayed. He wanted to pull down that part of her dress, cover the offensive smallness. But fascination tugged. He touched it. The sensation of coursing heat—which had hinted of withdrawing—extended from his finger inside her legs to his finger on her nipple, on through his tightening, drying throat and into his groin. His finger outlined first the nipple—which grew!—then the outer circle, slightly rougher flesh, and then the breast itself, its roundness. Now he could look at it closely. Touching it had made it seem much larger. His tongue darted out—once—on the nipple. He withdrew to see what he had moistened.

"Fuck me, Money, cummon," she said. She opened her legs wide. He didn't want to stop feeling her. She pushed up her hips. He allowed another finger to enter the incredible smoothness. Her hand grasped his hard cock, trying to pull it out. It pulsed at her touch. He pulled his pants down and pushed his body onto hers and buried his cock into her. He came in that one shove, cum drained out of every part of him—his limbs, his muscles, his bones, his veins—in a moment he wished would last forever. She raised her hips to receive the erupting rush and offer hers. When it ended, he rolled back onto the grass, leaving his pants down.

Scarlett Fever arranged her dress and sat up. She adjusted his pants, buckling his belt. "You wanna go to the West-Sky now?" she asked him.

"Yes!" Manny wanted noise, sights—anything that would thwart his feelings; he did not know how he felt now, had felt—and he didn't want to know, didn't want to feel. He was contained in heat, his body steaming, his— . . .

"You fags get the hell away from down there or I'll call the cops!"

Manny welcomed even that voice, a man's harsh voice, coming from a window above the trees. It helped to blot out all knowledge of what he had experienced.

Scarlett Fever called up at the voice, "We're not fags, motherfucker!"

A pause. Then the man's voice said, "Oh, you're a girl—well—uh—why don't you and— . . .?"

"Fuckin' pervert!" Scarlett yelled back as they walked back to Santa Monica toward the West-Sky. "You ever make it with fags?" Scarlett asked Manny casually.

"No," Manny said. He didn't care what they talked about, as long as it would ebb his feelings.

"Revolver does," Scarlett said. "Just once a week. Tuesdays or Thursdays, I forget which."

In the courtyard, the familiar figures milled—the youngmen and girls with color-streaked hair, carefully torn clothes, vinyl and leather, swastikas and crosses. Manny looked at them with intense attention.

"We really mean it," Scarlett said absently, looking at the crowd shoving restively.

"What?" Manny asked her.

She said, "Oh, you know—nothing."

Inside the West-Sky, Manny welcomed the obliterating burst of noise. Young male and female bodies prowled from room to room, looking at each other in mock challenge that might erupt into laughter or become bloody. Scarlett and Manny walked into the main room.

Revolver was ending a song. He saw Manny and he finished slowly:

> . . . louder! louder! louder . . .
> than the sound of pain.

Bodies in the oval clearing were shoving, pushing, wrestling ritualistically. Revolver grabbed his guitar and pretended it was a machine gun. He aimed at the audience, moving the guitar in a jerking arc:

"Rat-a-tat, rat-a-tat, rat-a-tat!" he fired at them.

Manny knew: Yes, Revolver was different from the others.

Three or four youngmen rushed the stage, to assault Revolver. Four guard-bouncers pulled them back toughly. One of the youngmen spat at Revolver, who dodged, avoiding the spittle. As the bouncers shoved them out, another of the youngmen spat—this time at no one, anyone. Then all around, the audience began to imitate the sound of spitting—laughing, making a hissing sound without moisture. Manny watched and watched and watched. Almost as if he were crossing himself, he outlined the intersecting lines he had scratched onto his chest.

Late that night in Revolver's battered car, Manny, Scarlett Fever, Revolver, and Razor, one of the three others in the band—a small youngman with enormous eyes and a Mohawk-style swatch of hair—drove to an abandoned church in an area of demolished and partially demolished houses left deserted for a freeway never built.

"Some black guys collect rent," Revolver laughed. "They're our landlords, man. They say they own the area. We give them whatever we can, and they keep it cool for us, warn us about pigs."

They entered the gutted church through loose boards at an entrance. Ahead, a candle was burning on a table. A girl with frizzled hair colored in different shades was there. They called her X. Crash—another of the four in the Unholy Communion—was already there, too; he too had a Mohawk cut. Manny put down the bundle of his clothes. X lit another candle and began heating up some cans of food.

"This Friday night we'll do the 'Filthy Bodies' song," Revolver said. "It's our last day—gotta do a piece they'll remember. Really remember—and understand." Looking at Manny, he plucked at a guitar, muffling its sounds. He sang softly.

The boards at the door parted. If they were cops, it was too late; so Revolver just went on:

> Ya say you got a body in the image
> of a lord— . . .

The three at the door were not cops; they moved in—a girl, two men—one looked like a cowboy. There were others who lived in this area. But if too many moved into one place, there would be raids.

Manny stared at the three new people.

X told them they had to find their own place. They left.

Revolver slept with Scarlett Fever, Manny slept alone on the floor, the others scattered about the darkness.

In the morning they drove the hidden car back into Los Angeles, and they all separated. Manny went to the tattoo shop on Sunset. The man knew him by now. Soon Manny would approach him. Manny felt the tall man was waiting for that.

He spent another night in the abandoned church with the others; he met them at the West-Sky. It was always the same there—always a fight, sometimes shocked blood—reaction to violence. Manny watched it. The rage in East L.A., in El Indio, on Main Street—even in his sister when she added another layer of paint to her face—that was real rage containing a thousand clear angers and needs. Here, anger *decorated* the faces. Violence without its reasons, indifferent anger forced into visibility, violence protesting . . . itself. That's how Manny was viewing it now.

He thought Revolver must see the West-Sky that way, too—but Manny wasn't sure. Unlike most of the others who were born with new identities and costumes at night, Revolver was Revolver night and day; he lived the life others pretended. No, it was not just the black, black hair that reminded Manny of El

Indio. Just as Indio had belonged to and escaped from only to be slaughtered by the gangs he knew so intimately, so, too, Revolver seemed at times to sneer at the shell of anger, the sketches of rage; he expressed contempt for it but welcomed being accepted as one of its symbols. Yet his songs, most times, had a direct defiance none of those of the other groups did.

That night in the abandoned church they sat eating from the candle-heated cans, passing them around. The boards at the door parted. Three tall black men stood in the darkness. One of them said, "Pigs comin'," and then the "landlords" disappeared beyond the loosened boards.

X blew out the candles. The church collapsed under darkness. Not even whispers—until it was safe. Razor lit a match, then a candle. Manny had been sitting with Revolver. They were talking softly now. When Razor lighted another candle, Revolver got up from the floor and said to Manny, "Okay, Money, yeah."

That night Manny slept with Scarlett Fever.

Again in the morning, they drove into Los Angeles and scattered.

This time Manny waited across the street until he saw the man come in. He dashed into the traffic, hearing screeching brakes, flung curses. Manny walked into the tattoo parlor. The illustrated tattoos wound like red and blue veins on the walls.

The tall thin man listened to Manny, leaning one ear toward him like a priest hearing confession. Then he said nothing.

"Please."

"Why?"

"I have to. *Please!*"

"It'll take at least two sessions, maybe three—hour or more each time. I've got to draw the design; you're lucky I'm an artist. And there's a week between each time, for the scabs to form— . . ." He went on.

Three weeks! "No," Manny said. "Tonight."

"Impossible," the man said. But he did not turn away.

Manny felt sucked into his eyes.

He kept remembering the man's eyes as he walked into the courtyard of the West-Sky that night. Scarlett Fever got him in.

Revolver was singing in the blue and red light; Razor, Crash, and the other youngman were behind him. The audience quivered within the coiled energy.

A girl whirled around in the pit of male bodies. She was very beautiful, wearing black pants and a black top. She took off the top, and whoever could get near her fondled and licked her breasts, her thighs. A fat guard rushed to them, as if to join the sexual frenzy; instead, he seized her, pulling her away, while another guard shoved the gathering youngmen. The girl kicked and screamed.

"Fuckin' fascist commie pigs!"

Manny moved away from Scarlett Fever, who stared at him, then at Revolver, again at Manny. Manny waited at the edge of the stage, the edge of the light.

Revolver began the "Filthy Bodies" song:

> Ya say ya got a soul!
> Well, if I cut ya with a knife,
> Show me your breathing soul,
> Your bleeding soul.
> An' I'll believe ya.

Manny walked up the few steps to the stage.

> I see your body,
> Now show me your soul,
> An' I'll believe ya.

Manny entered the lighted shadows. The jumping of the audience decreased. Silence grew, to receive Revolver's words:

> Ya say ya got a soul an' a body in
>   the image of some lord,
> But if ya ever had a soul— . . .

Manny stood within the light. The writhing of bodies faded toward the pantomime of action. Revolver shouted into the spreading silence before them:

> An' if you ever had a soul, you
>   let them carve it out
> An' didn't even care!
> Now all ya got is filthy meat
>   an' filthy bones!
> Filthy flesh. An' rotten blood!
> *Now* show me your goddam soul!

Manny began opening the buttons of his shirt. Revolver smiled, nodded. Manny remembered the burrowing gaze of the tattoo artist. Revolver's eyes were like that. Revolver screamed at the crowd:

> Ya got a filthy body
>   an' that's all!
> An if it's in anybody's image
> It's your rotting own!

Manny stood next to Revolver. Scarlett Fever walked to the lap of the stage and looked up at the two like an innocent supplicant.

Silence clamped the rough audience.

Revolver sang fiercely:

> I can cut
> Your gut
> With a knife.
> Plunge an' slice
> Ya up an' down,
> An' then I'll ask you,
> Where's your fuckin' soul?

Sharp buzzing ripped the silence. Revolver thrust ferociously:

> All I see's a bleeding filthy wound!
> An' ya lettem do it,
> Ya lettem do it to ya!

Manny took off his shirt. The naked Christ was on his chest. It had pubic hair over full genitals. The thorned head was tilted between Manny's pectorals. The feet were nailed at his navel. The pinioned hands touched each of Manny's nipples. The figure was drawn with black ink, the careful lines coated with colodion—to keep it intact. The varnished sheen gleamed like nail polish. The body radiated in the one funnel of light enclosed by darkness.

"He's got a naked Jesus!" someone loosed the ready frenzy. They pushed to look at it, those in front telling those in back what they saw; the ones in back fighting to get in front—bodies massing.

Revolver screamed with urgent rage.

Where's your holy soul!
AN' WHAT THE FUCK D'YA DO TO *MINE!*

Manny froze before the surging mob. Even the girls rushed into the squashed throng. Pushing, the guards unleashed more chaos.

Manny felt the spittle. They were spitting on his chest, on his chest and on the naked, really naked Christ. He felt the spittle running down his flesh, and at last he felt relief from the years'-long burning on his hand. It had to be here in a sea of indifferent anger. The more they spat, the more the spittle ran down his shining flesh, the more relief he felt. He raised his arms out, and he leaned his head, sideways.

Lost Angels: 3

"That's where they burned her?" Lisa saw the weedy vacant lot framed by two small wooden houses not even smudged by smoke. Leaves of trees clasped yellow flowers.

"I saw it on TV!" Jesse said excitedly, remembering the ring of tear-gas-masked cops like giant ants, the helicopters like giant mosquitoes. "They surrounded the house, and they threw one of those grenades that light up! And she and the others tried to escape through the crawl space under the house, but the smoke was— . . ." His mind shifted to Cody, challenging bullets. *Alone*.

Orin studied the lot where he was sure the house he had been searching for last night had stood. No trace of it now—the fire, the smoke, the bullets, the screams; not even the ashes of the charred structure. The slabs of plaster that had survived must have been smashed to dust.

The lot is in the meandering outskirts of Watts, which is the core of the black ghetto. Its boundaries widened when the Watts riots occurred in 1965. Rebelling against ubiquitous white cop faces and store owners—on a hot, hot night, and goaded by a confrontation between a black man and a white cop—protesting crowds gathered. In surrogate anger, captive frustration, Negroes set fire to anything—buildings, houses; flames leaping to their own homes and stores. They flung rocks and bottles, sent bullets zinging at anything—soon at the invading tanks and jeeps of the National Guard. A black-smoked sky hovered close over the wail of sirens. Sniping and looting jumped from neighborhood to neighborhood, as far away as 50th Street. Some Negroes, Mexicans, and the few other white people who still lived in those areas fled. With guns and helicopters and expert fire, police conquered the battlefield.

Negroes inherited the surrendered areas. It is in that wide fringe of Watts that the ragged Symbionese Liberation Army was scorched on live television by cops who hated niggers and Patricia Hearst even more for being with them.

"Patty burned to death shouting at the cops." Jesse James was thinking about Cody. Today Jesse had decided to abandon his cowboy hat, to get more of the tanning sun, which seemed to slide off Orin's fair skin.

"She didn't die," Orin said. "She wasn't in this house. She had left. She watched it all on television, like everyone did. They caught her later, she did time, she's free now—but I just wonder how *free*." He pondered that. "Depends."

"Man, was her family rich," Jesse said.

"They were so *mean* to her." Lisa was too young to remember, but she substituted Ingrid Bergman, brave-eyed on the scaffold, burning as Joan of Arc. Bergman was Maria, too. Lisa held Pearl to her chest, to protect her from evoked fire. "And she was so good."

Orin pronounced in that tone that announced he was "teaching": "Maybe she was good, maybe she wasn't. She could have been right, and she could have been wrong when she joined the rebels."

"But, Orin"—Lisa remembered the rich girl—"what if she joined them because there was nowhere else to go, and no one else to go with?"

"All depends," Orin reasoned. "Depends on what they told her and what she heard. What she heard's just as important as what she said, see? And what if her parents told her wrong? Or the rebels? What she listened to, how she heard it—that's what matters. Sometimes good is bad—*seems*."

From his tightened lips, Jesse and Lisa knew any further question risked his bolted silence. Like last night when they had asked him how that woman on television had brought him here. "I told you," was all he said. There were those times when he invited questions, though, and he did it with a look. He could "speak" with his eyes—Jesse was beginning to think that and he was beginning to understand that mixed language. "How you gonna know when right's wrong?'' Jesse risked, sounding casual.

"You look around, like for evidence—and *then* you'll know if you're right.''

"Yeah,'' Jesse pondered.

That way of saying that something was so, and it *was* so— and if it wasn't, he made it so. Like now. Lisa wasn't even convinced this was the site of the house Orin had been looking for since yesterday evening. He'd just driven past the lot and said, "That's it!'' It all looked too peaceful for the terrible things they were describing—and besides, there was nothing about it in Jesse's guidebook. Lisa looked down at Pearl Chavez and warned, "You've got to mind—and stay pretty!''

Orin sniffed in the direction of the barren lot, as if at the long-ago fire, flames, terror. "There's people who would be unhappy in heaven because they belong in hell; maybe hell *is* the right place, sometimes. Like the angels that fell—they didn't *want* to be with God.''

"And *he* didn't want *them!*'' Lisa surprised Jesse by asserting.

"That's right,'' Orin nodded.

As if her own strong words had surprised her, Lisa complained, "This isn't where you told us we were going, Orin; this isn't the What's-their-name Towers.'' She should have suspected Orin was up to something this morning, when he left her and Jesse and went to talk to the clerk at the motel. Orin's absence *had* given Jesse an opportunity to pretend his hand just accidentally touched her breasts—too slowly for an accident. She had welcomed the tingling touch. Lisa had lied to Orin in the car, driving to Los Angeles, when she told him she had never "been'' with a man. She had, twice, each time with boys about her age, a little older. Both times had been clumsy, awkward, hurried; she did not know *what* to feel—or what she felt. The old films didn't have sex, except when you *sensed* it, underneath, hidden. She had lied to Orin because she thought that's what he wanted to hear then.

Angrily—at times his anger had no discernible focus—Orin stalked back to the Cadillac, across the street. A tiny old black woman had been peering at them. Seeing Orin walking toward her, she tried to move quickly, but she had trouble placing her feet off the curb. Orin rushed over to her. She panicked, almost fell; Orin grabbed her in time.

"Just trying to help you across the street, ma'am," he assumed a strange Southern tone. "I believe you're havin' trouble, ma'am."

The black woman extended her hand tentatively. Orin took her arm gently and he crossed with her. "Be happy to drive you where you're goin'."

"Just live next door," the old lady said. "Thank you." She looked at Lisa and Jesse James. "Nice to see kind young people, courteous," she thanked Orin.

"Pleased to be of help, ma'am," Orin said. "Excuse my askin', ma'am, but were you livin' here when they burned that house with— . . .?"

"Those commu-nits?" the black woman spat. "Good riddance." She hobbled along the street, and entered a decrepit house.

As they drove past the corner, a group of black men stared with deep resentment at the white invaders in the indigo Cadillac. It drove through blocks and blocks of black faces; gleaming brown bodies, accusing eyes. Now they were in Watts. Everywhere was the sense of a city in quiet siege, some buildings and houses not rebuilt since the fires; they remain as monuments. Trees and flowers tint the poverty and rage. More glaring dark eyes.

"They look so angry," Lisa whispered.

Jesse muttered, "Mean, black nig— . . ."

Orin chopped off Jesse's word. "You would be, too, if you were them. But," he hurried, "that doesn't mean it's right, all of it; depends on what you do, and when."

"Yeah." Jesse was confused because he'd never seen Cagney with any black people. Black people were tough, but not in the gangster movies he'd seen, with Cagney, Bogart, Robinson.

"Well, it's sad," Lisa sighed, remembering how close Claudette Colbert and the black woman had been in *Imitation of Life*.

There it was!—the crazily beautiful structure known as "the Watts Towers"—thousands of pieces of broken bottles, dishes, beads, embedded into concrete in spontaneous designs; coils, layered flats, spires shaped into a boat three storeys high, higher. Simon de Rodia, an Italian peasant, made it, and died without knowledge of the eventual, grudging celebration of his crude masterpiece. After years of being considered an "eyesore," more years of indifference and decay, and even an attempt to topple the "dangerous flimsy structure"—and to prove its weakness, sinews of young cables were attached to one of its tallest spires and pulled tautly, but the structure released only one tiny loose glass, which tinkled mockingly on the street before the haughty engineers—after all that, the structure was taken over by the city, for renovation. Now propped pipes, wooden scaffolds, tied wires create a giant collapsed skeleton over the spectacular glassy structure, which waits for funds to save it.

Jesse's guidebook had recommended the Watts Towers highly "God *damn!*" Jesse admired. "It's *so* beautiful," Lisa praised. By locating themselves exactly right, they could see the spectacular creation under the flung skeleton. "Reminds me of that tower Cody stood on," Jesse exulted. "It's nothing like it," Lisa said. "*Without* the glass and things," Jesse insisted.

Orin moved back to look at the Towers from a distance, as if to perceive the whole of them; then he advanced closer, stopping, looking up, tilting his head, as if now to see its components. He often gave complex structures careful attention—the various on-ramps and off-ramps of the freeways seemed to fascinate him; sometimes he'd drive off, to get back on, and stare back at the swirls of concrete. He would pause before buildings throughout the city, especially the ones made of pieces of glass—blue, clear, even black. It was as if in his mind that helped him to construct something highly intricate of his own.

And Los Angeles is a city of vast intricacies, subtle vicissitudes. The facade of passivity, of ease—of life flowing effortlessly to congregate at the beaches—a city of bodies adoring and being adored by the sun—is deceptive. Under the tanned facade are constant intimations of massive violence. In one moment's shrug, earthquakes, fire, flood, murder may ravage. Seeming to reject death, this city asserts it: in happy billboards offering burial and cremation and in intimations of eternal spring, a promise withdrawn almost nightly in the seasons of chill, fog, thrashing rain and wind.

"You happy now, Lisa," Orin asked her, "now you've seen it?"

"Yes," she said, "and thank you very much."

They were on the Harbor Freeway. It was crowding but not yet enough to slow or stop traffic. Recurrently, windshields and the chrome streaks of cars shot bolts of white reflected light into their eyes. In Los Angeles, at peak times, the freeways become the clogged arteries of an enormous body, affecting a wide radius of the city. One accident, one stalled car creates stoppages on virtually every other main street as cars scurry to find alternate routes.

There had been a false cooling this morning, the heat resting to thrust in with greater force. Waves of it entered the topless car now. Lisa sat in back with Pearl, to get more wind. Even along the freeways, she noticed, grounded vines produced tiny blue flowers. Should she dye Pearl Chavez's hair darker, so she'd look more like the passionate half-breed who killed and kissed her lover? Certainly, the bridesmaid dress was not appropriate, although there *was* that scene where Pearl dresses up for the dance, to entice mean Lewt— . . . "Bad girl," she said to Pearl, the doll, but in a soft, loving voice.

"Just look at Lisa, Orin, playing with her dolly," Jesse chided.

"Stop talking about me like I'm dumb, or not here," Lisa said. "I *am* here."

Suddenly Orin's face was a mask of dark moods. "What did you say?"

"I just said, 'I *am* here.' "

Orin brushed his face with his hand, as if to thwart a turbulence aroused by Lisa's words. His breathing broke in a harsh sound, a withdrawn gasp. He seemed pulled into a trance.

How could her ordinary words have trapped him in such a strange mood? I am here—that's all she had said. She saw both his hands clench the steering wheel, tightly. "Orin!" she called to him. He did not look at her, his eyes fixed as if on a far, far distance. "*Orin!*"

He stared at her, through her, then his eyes focused on her.

Slowly a vague smile overtook the disturbed look. Now there was a real smile on his face. The black moments were over.

"And I *am* here," Lisa asserted. She longed to ask— . . . But there was too much risk in any question now.

"You sure are!" Jesse whistled and shook his head admiringly.

Lisa looked down at her breasts. Yes, they were becoming fuller. That's where Jesse was looking. But not Orin. Not now. And yes, he too, now and then—but it wasn't exactly clear, like when Jesse looked at her. "And Jesse, Pearl's *not* a 'dolly.' You don't understand."

"Want to change your name again?" Orin asked her.

She didn't like his tone. It went with the disturbed motion he had made just earlier. But he was smiling. And Orin could understand things right away—maybe that Jesse had offended her—and that she'd been moody since earlier—that talk about those people burned in that house, and then those sad black faces. She would welcome a game: "Yes! I'll change my name to— . . ."

"Cassandra," Orin chose.

"*Kings Row!*" Lisa welcomed the choice. "But they called her Cassy, Orin. Her father was so mean. He poisoned her because she was going to go away with that doctor." She remembered the dark black and white night, with thunder, and Cassy's terrified face livid in the lashing lightning. Take me with you, she pled, but Parris Mitchell had to go to Vienna, to be a doctor. Cassy. Tortured even as a child when nobody came to her party— . . .

"There was another Cassandra before her," Orin said. "Some people thought she was a witch. She had powers of prophecy. She could see into the future. Play *that* Cassandra, Lisa. Look into the future and tell us what you see."

He was serious. The smile on his face worried her now; it had abandoned all his features, except his lips. The orangy eyebrows furrowed.

"Tell us what you see, Cassandra," Orin insisted.

Not just anything would do, Lisa knew. She squinted her eyes so that everything blurred. She'd describe whatever she saw through squeezed eyelids. *Smears of grayish green, a dirty ocean.* "An angry ocean," she said. She shifted her filtered gaze. "Silver and black." She opened her eyes to see what that really was: a high building in downtown Los Angeles; it was formed by three cylinders of black reflecting glass. "You're crazy, Orin," Lisa wiped away the game with laughter. But now she was pensive. Orin could be kind, kinder than anyone, ever. He had bought her Pearl, knowing she longed for her, and he was beginning to pay more and more of their expenses. But he could also be— . . . She avoided "mean"—because he seemed to have a good reason for everything he did, said—even if the reason emerged much later. "It just occurred to me—we don't know much about each other." But of course it hadn't "just occurred."

"Don't know much about ourselves," Jesse was profound.

"Don't need to," Orin asserted.

Lisa didn't know whether he meant her or Jesse's observation. "I know this, though," she said. "Now I have you, Orin, and you, Jesse, and this beautiful city—and Pearl." You gave her to me, Orin, she said silently.

"Yeah!" Jesse wanted to assert the closeness.

To fill the long silence that followed, Jesse idled with the radio; once he'd done it, it was easier—but he still glanced at Orin. Orin didn't shake his head. But he said, "The news."

Jesse found the news station they listened to.

". . .—continues her series on 'The Lower Depths,' " the male announcer said. "Hidden worlds—prostitution, pornography, lost souls on Skid Row. You may be shocked, but you won't be the same again. Tonight, on television!" Then the news resumed: "Police checked out still another of the escalating false reports on the whereabouts of the veteran who escaped the psychiatric ward of the Veterans Hospital. We received an anonymous call that a hiker had seen a man in jungle combat fatigues wandering near the Observatory in Griffith Park— . . ."

After last night's report, Jesse had looked that up in his guidebook. "That's where James Dean was killed in *Rebel Without a Cause*! Wow!" He didn't identify his source.

"Other reported sightings reached the Los Angeles Police Department, but Officer William Gaddis dismissed them as crank calls. He emphasized without clarifying further that police have definite information about the whereabouts of the man and that no threat exists. The officer strongly implied the veteran is no longer in the Los Angeles area. He could not account for the way this incident has seized the public's imagination, inciting a rash of pranks. A fraternity student dressed in combat fatigues and armed with what turned out to be a toy rifle appeared outside Mann's Chinese Theater in Hollywood and caused panic among toruists there.''

A woman's voice took over: "What many have called the party of the year occurred in Beverly Hills last night when Claude Ester celebrated the first anniversary of his posh boutique— Amadeo's—by lavishing seventy pounds of caviar at a cost of four hundred dollars a pound on two hundred exclusive guests.''

The man's voice resumed: "Continuing high winds and heat—. . .''

Orin snapped off the radio.

Jesse knew: Now there would follow the sealed silence. He fumed quietly. More and more he felt "attached" to Orin.. He didn't know how tightly, or exactly how. Sure, he liked him. And Lisa. A lot. Though differently, of course. That festered, too: Jesse would get a hard-on just hearing her in the shower. Yet Orin didn't like them to be even in underclothes till they got to bed. He'd made it clear—with a frown. This morning—when Orin went to the motel desk—Jesse had pretended it was accidentally that he'd touched Lisa's full breasts. He wanted then to push his lean body against hers and he felt she would have let him. Yet he was afraid Orin would come in then! That bothered him a lot, especially since he was bigger than Orin, who sometimes looked like a lost boy. But there were those powerful— yet sad—eyes. And his strange talk, which was at the same time so pretty, good to hear, like nothing Jesse had ever heard before. Also, Jesse had checked his money, and he was running lower than he had thought. He contributed some to this morning's motel rent—and Lisa less, he noticed. And Orin didn't mind, never worried about running out. And they were having a good time touring the city. Jesse had just run a circle: Everything was just *fine!*

On the Santa Monica Freeway the traffic was coming to a stop, cars merely inching along. Maneuvering on the shoulder of the freeway, Orin rode off. To their left was a veterans' cemetery—endless rows of identical white gravestones on monotonous green grass. The sun had begun to set. When the wind pushes the smog against the edge of the sky, like now, the sun looms like a phosphorescent red ball before the ocean pulls it down.

At the fork where Wilshire and Santa Monica boulevards form an *X*, Orin took Santa Monica into West Hollywood, the prettiest of all the ghettos in Los Angeles—the stylish homosexual ghetto. A series of clothes shops contain overtly masculine manikins in poses of sexual indifference, dressed in chic, expensive versions of work clothes, undefined uniforms, athletic outfits. On warm afternoons, bronzed homosexuals, many shirtless and in shorts or trunks—most with cropped moustaches and short hair—show off bodies constructed by exercise machines; they look very much alike, as if molded from one desirable pattern, masculine in a studied, dogged way—at times to the point of caricature—as if they are imitating the figures in the windows. Orin looked away from the cruising men.

"You don't like queers, huh, Orin?" Jesse inquired. "I coulda guessed it." He didn't know how *he* felt. Here and there, he *had* noticed some very *pretty* youngmen, he had to admit—but most were as masculine as he and Orin were.

"God hates only *sin!*" Orin said forcefully.

Jesse looked over to see how serious he was. Very. Actually, Orin didn't talk about God or Jesus that much, but at times he seemed to create the impression that he *was* doing so, constantly!

"They're all so cute," Lisa said, looking at the men on the streets. "How come they don't like girls, Orin?" she asked him.

Orin was silent.

"Cause they're *gay,* that's why," Jesse settled it for Lisa.

They drove past blocks and blocks of male sexhunters. Then, after a brief limbo, there occurs another stretch on Santa Monica Boulevard, distinct from the other. Here, malehustlers linger for the length of several blocks, perhaps a mile. Some of them are very young, in their teens, runaways; others are older, harder, clearly more knowledgable, in their twenties. The hot afternoon sun had brought them out in squads—dozens of them mingling on corners—waiting to be picked up. Several wore only swim trunks. Some very masculine, others almost girlish, several thin, skinny, others well-built, they lined the ragged strip. They stared eagerly into passing cars, drivers eyeing them—but not nearly as many as there were hustlers.

In one corner, a television film crew gathered. A woman and a man were interviewing a very beautiful youngman in a cutoff shirt. Other youngmen stood around eager to be filmed. Artificial lights waited to replace the dimming sun.

Orin remained silent. He kept looking at the people on the street the way he had studied the Towers today, the way he studied the freeways—a part of the same structure he seemed to be attempting to find, define. His intense look was the same on Sunset Boulevard, where female prostitutes clustered for the afternoon trade, the more stylish—some outrageously beautiful and flagrant—congregating closer to Beverly Hills; others— shabbier, more desperate—nearer Western. Many wore tiny shorts, high heels, tied bandannas as tops. "Wow!" Jesse kept saying. "Wow! Wow!" But he didn't see one nearly as pretty as Lisa, not one. He didn't tell her.

As if he had seen enough, Orin turned into Franklin Avenue, along its intermittent soft-lawned graceful houses among increasingly decrepit others.

"A *purple* tree!" Lisa couldn't believe it. The tree had leaves that were violet on their undersides. The wind exposed a crinkled sheet of purple. "Can you believe it! A purple tree. And, oh, *look!*"

Surrounded by birds of paradise—purple and yellow-beaked flowers—a sign next to a brick-columned entrance said, "Magic Castle," and pointed up a curled dirt road to a hill topped by a weirdly steepled house—gables, spires, turrets.

"A castle!" Lisa gasped.

Jesse James found it in his guide. "It's just a restaurant," he said. "You gotta be a member and you gotta wear a tie, 'no slacks for ladies, please,' and gorillas and monsters roam throughout the room at dinner, and they got live magic acts."

"You're making that up about gorillas and monsters." Lisa refused to be deflated. "Imagine! A magic castle! And a purple tree!'' She closed her eyes deliriously. "And the *real* movie-star homes, somewhere! It's just like it's supposed to be. Just like I knew it would be. *Hollywood!*"

They had dinner at Denny's Restaurant, one of many of a purple and orange chain. "Meal's on me," Orin announced, in sudden high spirits after the reflective mood, the intent journey. Lisa ordered roast beef. Jesse had steak with onion rings. Orin had chicken. The boy's-smile of delight gracing his face, Orin asked how they would like to be treated to a movie?

"A great *old* one, yes!" Lisa craved, finishing her apple pie. No ice cream; she decided to be loyal to Baskin-Robbins, realizing she hadn't had one today.

Outside, from a row of propped, beaten plastic containers on skinny metal stilts, they got a paper by dropping coins into a rain-rusted slot. Several theaters in the city, and nearby, showed only old movies—two different ones each night. Lisa was in ecstasy. Her soaring happiness alighted, slightly, when Orin chose two movies none of them had ever heard of—but he liked the titles: *Blow-up* and *The Conformist.*

Her face tortured, hands pressing against the car window while a man inside looks away stoically, a woman screams soundlessly. Then she runs through a snow-blanketed forest, trees as stark as dark lines. Men are chasing her. They shoot at her. Blood colors the snow. Then there is an abrupt change in place and time. A man is propositioning another. The man who sat in the car, listens to them, listens.

It was not a "great old movie," but Lisa watched carefully. So different from anything she'd ever seen.

Jesse had been impatient, and he groaned when Orin said, "We'll stay to see the beginning."

Jesse began to doze, would wake up, doze again. *Green, green grass, so green it looks dyed, a breeze is blowing through the trees, a woman fights with a man or coaxes him to make love—she leads him—* . . . *A series of photographs, each larger, larger, larger. A hand holding a gun, a man lurking. Larger. The "man" has become an opening within the dark trees, the "gun" is a protrusion from them. Larger. The close scrutiny has destroyed the clarity of the photograph, creating totally new*

*forms. . . . Against white steps on which sit abandoned figures
as a cold wind rampages scattered newspapers, a man flings his
arms about himself, inviting a strait jacket.*

"I *much* prefer the all-times!" Outside, Lisa had to assert her
fidelity to the old movies. It had been jostled as she watched the
new films intently, fascinated by the complicated characters, the
bold situations. "*Much* more!" she reaffirmed. "I bet *you* liked
the part where the two girls come in and the photographer takes
off their clothes— . . ."

"I missed that!" Jesse was annoyed.

"Those movies are *not* great all-times!" Lisa further forced
away the strange new characters in the films they had just seen.
In the car, she held Pearl, who had waited there. Lisa hardly
ever carried the doll with her anymore—people didn't understand that Pearl wasn't just *a* doll.

"The man couldn't make up his mind which side he was
on," Orin said, without identifying which film he was talking
about. "He was really on both—and that's why he couldn't
act—and then he didn't know what was real, so he didn't know
where he belonged."

At the motel, Lisa took a shower first. Orin touched the
television, but didn't turn it on. He looked out the window. He
seemed nervous to Jesse; did he really try to *avoid* turning the
television on, the way it sometimes seemed? The water from the
shower . . . Jesse heard it. Lisa would be naked under it. Again
he imagined the firm body, her pubic hair the color of her
nipples—yes! He let his hands drop between his legs. The soap
would make bubbles between her thighs, and her fingers would
touch, just inside. Then she'd bend to wash— . . . He removed
his hands from his groin quickly. He "felt" Orin's eyes. But
when he looked, Orin was staring out into the night.

In her light robe, Lisa came out in a cloud of steam, which
was shoved back immediately by the cool artificial air. She was
glad the television wasn't on.

Jesse could smell Lisa's clean bathed body. "Gonna take my
shower," he said. In the bathroom, he locked the door, careful
not to allow a sound. He breathed deeply, to gather Lisa's
intimate sexual scent where she'd stood naked, right here; he

detected a slight, arousing odor, like clean perspiration. He touched the wet towel, running his hands along it so he would be sure to touch the part that had dried her breasts, the part that had rubbed between her legs, the— . . . Then he noticed she had left her half-slip neatly hanging on the rod of the shower curtains. It was dry! She hadn't washed it when she changed into another one. His hard-on chafed against his jeans, and he opened them. Had she left the half-slip there deliberately?—for him—sensing his growing want, asserting hers? He touched the slip where it would have slid between her legs as she walked all day. Yes, she *had* left it for him. He moved the flimsy material over his own groin, connecting with hers. He could smell the sex, and he was *very* sure she had left this for him.

Or for Orin?

Orin could just as easily have come in next—but he hadn't. Jesse put the slip neatly on a shelf—and then he showered, forcing his hands away from his eager cock. He dried with Lisa's wet towel and moistened another, to leave as his, on the floor. Then he folded the dry slip carefully and replaced it where she had put it. He would leave it for Orin, extending to him the touch of Lisa's flesh—the sexual woman.

"Pretty mothers don't have ugly babies—and pretty babies stay pretty only if they don't make their mommies ugly and old, because a woman is beautiful only when she's loved. That's what Mrs. Skeffington said in one of the *real* all-times. . . . Now go to sleep, pretty Pearl."

Lisa's childish voice jarred Jesse. There she was, a little girl again! The television set was still not on. "Your turn, Orin," Jesse said. Orin seemed to welcome another excuse for leaving the television dormant. He walked into the bathroom. Jesse heard the water running. He wanted to ask Lisa about the slip, but if she claimed she'd left it there accidentally, that would disappoint him a lot. The water stopped in the shower.

Reddish hair dampened darker, Orin came out. He looked at the television set, still gray, silent.

"Forgot to brush my teeth." Jesse returned to the bathroom. The half-slip was folded on top of a stack of fresh towels. And so Orin had at least touched it—and carefully! Jesse felt proud of his smart maneuver. But what had he proved? He puzzled. Later he'd figure it all out. When he came out, he heard Lisa's angered voice: "*She's* that other Cassandra!" She pointed to the screen.

Now Jesse wished he had masturbated. Wafted by the currents of sexuality, he had hoped that "it" would happen tonight with Lisa. But watching Orin staring at the forbidding woman on the screen made him doubt it. He felt awfully frustrated, and he sat dejectedly on a chair.

Sister Woman's hands rose, sighing material floated; the hands wove invisible pictures, seen only by her. Her gliding fingers provided shades and hues. The chiffon fainted onto her lap, her hands folded.

"You had a vision," Brother Man said. Even in his suit, he was like a fleshed shadow of her, her echo.

The willowy hands of the woman rested like birds. "Something awesome," she said. She widened her eyes, as if the vision were so enormous she must enlarge her sight to encompass it. "Something awesome is coming," she breathed. Her eyes closed, and her arms rose, the blue chiffon spreading like frail wings. "Prepare now to be a part of it. Praise Jesus!" the gashed lips whispered, echoing the breath of the chiffon. "Prepare!" the rising voice ordered. "Bring me your sins—*and theirs!*—to burn in hell; your tears of salvation will quench the fires."

The telephone number appeared on the screen. The camera pulled back on the bowed head of Sister Woman. Brother Man bowed his head, too, and imitated the placement of her hands. As the camera pulled back on the figures praying, now kneeling in the attitude of supplication, farther back to reveal a crowded traumatized audience of men and women, young and old, many with their eyes shut, quivering hands raised toward the woman's pulling presence—a solemn male voice intoned: "If you have a problem, call us; share with us; witness with us for Jesus. Send love, send a love donation to aid in his holy mission; help the blessed mission of our blessed Sister Woman." Against the blue backdrop, the kneeling figures diminished, fading, faded. The screen blazed blue. Across it, unfurled, was the American flag—and, over it, the white shadow of a luminous cross.

Orin turned off the screen, his eyes fixed on the pinpoint of shining light that remains there for seconds. He said, "She knows I'm here."

He stood up. The reddish blond features seemed shaded. He closed his eyes. His hands covered his face, for seconds, a minute, longer.

Lisa watched him, terrified. Jesse moved toward him. Orin seemed to have stopped breathing. Then they saw him release the pressure of his fingers on his face. His hands slid down the somber face they had covered, unmasking another one. The little boy smiled. A fragment of laughter issued.

Lisa breathed in relief. She got into her bed, with Pearl beside her. "Now don't you fuss and wake me so I look a wreck," she admonished Pearl.

"We're sleeping together," Orin said.

"You mean it!" Jesse stood up. Lisa's slip! That's what had done it! he congratulated himself. It had worked! And *that's* what he'd intended, and why he hadn't masturbated then! He understood it all now, proudly, what he'd done, and why.

"Leave Pearl there, Lisa," Orin said softly. "She'll grow up in her sleep."

"She's not supposed to grow up!" a childish voice answered Orin.

Orin nodded, yes.

Lisa covered the doll. Barefoot, and gladly now, feeling desire stirred instantly, she got up and lay in the other bed. She heard her heart thumping, but even that was a good sensation, warm, good, expectant—better than all that. Jesse sat on the bed and removed his pants. The light was still on; he moved slowly, half expecting—dreading—Orin would forbid. Jesse slid naked into the bed. Orin stood before them. Lisa moved to the middle, Jesse beside her; his leg didn't dare touch hers, not yet.

"Take off all your clothes, Lisa, please," Orin said.

Naked, Lisa felt the warmth grow. She raised the sheet up to her and Jesse's necks. She smiled, the way she remembered Scarlett smiled in that scene in bed after— . . .

Orin turned off the light, but bright night flowed in through drawn drapes, filling the room with dark whiteness. Orin took off all his clothes. His body was thin, chiseled, translucent in that bright darkness as he stood before them. Lisa and Jesse watched him. His thick cock was aroused, firm.

Lisa moved closer to the middle, to make room for him beside her. She felt Jesse, hard. Orin lay in bed next to her. Then in one violent thrashing, he turned away from them, his face buried into his pillow. In a moment, the pillow was wet with smothered tears.

Hester Washington: "Purified Fire"

Hester Washington looked back at her house in Watts and wondered whether it would be intact when she returned. It was a neat white house in a tidy block of small houses on Grape Street—she liked the name—lawns carefully tended, flowers like parrots. Curled wrought iron, camouflaging as decoration, bolted the windows. No matter how pretty or viny the design, the iron bars were there for one nagging purpose, to attempt to protect from pillage and violence; everyone who could afford them had them. As she looked back, the iron-barred houses assumed the appearance of pretty fortresses.

Hester was a small, handsome woman, smaller than she looked because her bones were big, and she was well-proportioned. She was a healthy fifty-five years old, and had kept her weight intact for twenty-five years, 130 sturdy pounds. Her hair was solidly black—not one single devil-white hair! She dressed well and always wore a hat; white gloves in summer, dark ones in winter. She carried her maid's uniform in her bag, and she folded it neatly so that it would not crease. In Arkansas, her mother had taught her manners. Not only had she kept them, she had refined them. A proud woman, she walked with her chin held slightly up. Her eyes—the source of her one self-allowed vanity—were the color of chocolate mints.

Some other Negro, and Mexican, maids, whom the bus would collect at the various stops throughout Watts and its outskirts, assumed the authority of their employers—basking, but only in the bus, in the borrowed shadow of someone famous, rich, powerful. Not Hester; no one knew whom she worked for. That she worked in Bel Air—perhaps the thickest concentration of wealth in the country—she could not conceal from the others who transferred to the Sunset Boulevard bus, but she herself never mentioned it. She preferred to carry her own authority.

As she began her trek to Bel Air this mid-morning—her employer had called to tell her to be late—Hester looked back at the bars on her window. As soon as she could, she would get prettier ones—the flowery ones; these looked too much like stark jail bars.

People marveled—especially if they came from other big cities—at how pretty Los Angeles's black ghetto is, especially what Hester considered its "front part." But even there, trees are not as lush, not as many, as in other sections of the city. Lawns come much closer to the streets than elsewhere. Even the flowers here grow more desperate, in splashed colors, and die more quickly—with one exception, giant-headed, ordinary sunflowers. It is always hotter in Watts, because the houses are shoved together, miles from a soothing ocean breeze.

Beyond the deceptive prettiness—which continues, lingers, never completely disappears—and into the belly of Watts—are sweaty two-storey tenements, then rows and rows of time-scarred houses, walls reinforced with sheets of corrugated, aging aluminum. Deeper in, the area resembles poor urban pockets in the black South; wooden shanties huddle among tall yellow grass. Oxidized pieces of cars that refused to budge lie dead among blades of yellowing grass. Increasingly shoving out of the thinning prettiness, the desolation and poverty become more visible through screenless windows: barren rooms, bedless bedrooms, cardboard-patched walls, houses without electricity or gas.

There are recurrent remains of houses, left abandoned, with boarded-up windows next to which half-burned trucks or cars decompose in lots choked by weeds clutching at debris; walls—slabs of former buildings—lashed by smoke; gutted houses; patched ones—these are reminders of the fierce Watts riots. These remains convey a sense of a battle fought and lost and—those unhealed scars retained as monuments decorated only with angry slogans—of a war still to rage, inevitable even if also inevitably to be lost.

Hester had long arranged her almost daily journey from Grape Street to the bus stop in such a way that she avoided the sights she hated most, encountered the ones she liked, or tolerated. It was difficult to accomplish that entirely, since aspects of one intrude into the other. Hester would walk an extra block in order to avoid a wounded area. She also had alternate routes, depending on her mood, her tolerance of one view as opposed to another.

Several sights she could not avoid, no matter what the route: the grubby loan shops, their windows guarded at night by chained, iron spider webs; the liquor stores flooded with dirty light; the gnarled junkyards; and the Coors Beer signs with what she knew were white models colored brown—no Negro man *ever* looked that silly, with a tiny moustache, short-cropped straight hair! Intertwined throughout, however, were the usually white churches with names Hester read aloud like a prayer: "Straight Way Baptist Church," "Fountain of Life Church," "Mount Calvary Assembly."

Unavoidable ambushes were the outdoor furniture "stores" and outdoor clothes "shops"; they sprouted overnight on the edges of abandoned dusty lots—ugly clothes and ugly furniture offered at outrageous "bargain prices" by white—and black— "distributors." Hester concentrated on the open fruit and vegetable stands—healthy squash and golden corn, fat strawberries.

There were other sights and presences no one in Watts could avoid: the constant spectacle of dark men pushed against walls by white policemen; handcuffed men and women lying helplessly on the ground. In their cruising or speeding black and white cars, the white policemen with hate-spattered faces and ready derision rode like impervious lords. One of them had killed a friend of Hester's—a woman, on her own lawn—claiming she had been about to assault him, while she was lying facedown on the ground. The demanded investigation about to be completed would merely uphold the policeman, she knew. Now and then there was a Negro in the despised uniform, and he would try to prove he was just as mean as the white ones.

Hester looked beyond frayed trees toward the scaffolded Watts Towers. Before the city had begun—and quickly stopped— renovating the structure, Hester had been able to see the glimmering tip of the highest glass spire.

She had often walked to the Towers, delighting in the shards of patterned plates she located embedded in the cement. They reminded her of her mother's careful selection of Sunday china, much of which she had inherited. Until the scaffolding had gone up, a visit to the Towers had been part of the soft rituals that defined Hester's life. Evenings, she watered her careful garden. Each Sunday she prayed—in *church,* not with those television evangelists who claimed to be holy but were on the side of the devil, just draining the poor. She watched television only infrequently, with one exception, when she had followed every moment of "Roots." It had convinced her that her heritage intersected with one or another of those great ancient African kings. Nightly, she read from the Bible, usually from her favorite book, *Ezekiel;* she memorized passages from it. And there were the regular visits she paid the poor, the sick, the elderly in her neighborhood, always bringing an appropriate sweet or other food. She would have made a good nurse, she knew—she enjoyed ministering to the needy; but she had married very early in Arkansas a man who brought her here and died in a car crash on the freeway only a few weeks later; and there was nothing Hester could do but become a maid.

Today Hester was taking the "flower route," because a warm June—and it was certainly that this year!—pulls out flowers in abundant colors. Unfortunately, taking that route meant she had to pass a sun- and fire-seared lot. Four teenage Negroes were idling at that corner, near an abandoned building, still a few blocks away from where she caught the bus five days a week, sometimes six, even seven—when one of the regular staff was sick or absent and she was called to please, *please* "come and help us out please."

The boys were squatting near the building, which had once been a small Baptist church. Part of its name was still on it—Ch ch f ohn the aptist—but the name was further obscured by red letters: KILLER BLOOD.

"Mawnin," one of the boys said to her.

She smelled his breath. Liquor. "Morning," she said curtly. She was no prude, but she disapproved of their getting drunk, and it was very early; so she disapproved mightily. Trouble. She saw a black and white squad car moving along the street. Alerted, the boys threw a bottle into the debris in the field.

Hester waited. The white policemen drove by slowly, eyeing the youngmen. Hester had seen this countless times. They would look, their pallid faces staring out. They'd pretend to be about to drive away, and, instead, braking, they'd rush out and corner whomever they wanted.

They did that now. They shoved the boys against the wall, palms pressed against it. Then one of the two—while the other drew his gun—went from boy to boy and kicked his ankles out, away from the wall, so that their bodies were all at a sharp incline.

Their guns alert, the police frisked the boys. Finding nothing of interest, they left them in that surrendered position. When they heard the car moving, the boys spun around, screaming. "Fuck you!" "Fuckin' white pigs!" "Motherfuckers!" Another boy struck a match and threw it on a pile of debris—crushed papers, dried weeds.

Flames rose!

Not here! Hester's silent anger shouted. Why always here?

Unfed, the small fire died.

There were often random fires in Watts. All here lived with the scream of sirens. It erupted in instant fury—from police cars, ambulances, fire engines. It was not rare for rampaging youths to throw rocks at firemen—because they had the same faces, the same look of contempt, as the police.

The policemen who had frisked the scattering youngmen swerved back. Stopping the car with a deafening screech, they jumped out with guns drawn.

Murderers, ready murderers! Hester thought. She echoed the warning of the Lord: *I will scatter your bones round about your altars.*

She decided to change her route, although it meant passing the loan shops and liquor stores. She reached the bus stop. She adjusted her hat to shade her face from what threatened to be a hot sun. It was that heat that comes with wind, she knew—those awful Santa Anas.

Fire.

She looked back but could not see the field where the brief flames had danced.

Why *here?* Why the iron bars on *our* windows?

She sat on the bench and waited for the bus. The advertisement on it had been changed. A mortuary. There were mortuary signs and posters all over the city. The big mortuary, the famous one—that one didn't advertise on the benches here. Segregated death. And anger.

Segregated anger!

Fire! In her mind, the dead flames leapt alive.

Now is the end come upon thee, and I will send mine anger upon thee, God's words reassured her.

The bus came, and she got on.

Usually she knew several of the other maids who journeyed into the wealthy parts of the city. She would sit and even chat pleasantly if she knew the person next to her well enough. But today's changed time rendered her anonymous among the scattering of black faces. The bus had not yet collected the Mexicans in their own isolated stations a few miles away.

The morning scrim of haze had already lifted. Distant, spectral palm trees outlined the city in imperfect designs. Many of the freeways were bordered by green knolls; there, even weeds grow pretty flowers. Bluish stars. Orange-flamed tips like lit matches.

Flames. The word glued itself to her mind.

She transferred to the Sunset Boulevard bus so automatically that she didn't realize it fully until she saw that horrible green mansion with those naked statues on the lawn and those devil-ram heads on the vases full of *artificial* flowers. She'd look out periodically, hoping the statues would be gone; other times she just turned to the other side of the street. Today she looked, because yesterday she had noticed that one of the statues had toppled over near the burned tree. Yes, fire had attacked the wasteful house. *I am against thee and will execute judgments in the midst of thee in the sight of the nations.* Look at all those silly tourists having their pictures taken before that outrage!

At the first gate to Bel Air, its twin white columns proclaiming guarded exclusivity, Hester got out. She stood to one side of the familiar white concrete pond of concentric circles of orange, lavender, and yellow flowers, perfectly kept. At her regular time, there would be other maids waiting to be picked up by their employers. Black and brown faces, white uniforms. They would get into one of the cars that had just descended the velvety hills beyond the gates: "Mawnin, ma'am." "Good morning, Agnes." Or whatever name.

Hester always hated to wait, preferring *they* be waiting for *her*. But that didn't happen often. Like those in "Roots," her African descendants had been raped, their kindly wealth stolen by white men. She didn't believe other Negroes had cooperated in trapping the slaves, no, the television sponsors had demanded that lie in exchange for showing the glorious saga.

Yes, she liked to see the car waiting for her because then it was easier to imagine, as she did now and then, that she—a princess—was being driven up to the tall house on the top of the hill. Too, she hated to wait because she didn't know who would be picking her up. Only once had it been that judge. He had hardly seen her, and she had returned the favor. Usually, it was Mrs. Stephens who picked her up—and talked all the way into the house. Once or twice it was Mark, the college boy, whom she didn't mind, might even get to like. The oldest daughter, Tessa, whom she didn't mind either, had just disappeared. Once Hester had asked about continuing to clean the unused bedroom of Miss Tessa, and Mrs. Stephens put her finger to her mouth and shushed even the name, as if not wanting that lurking hateful younger daughter—Hester deliberately forgot her name—to hear her. Hester had seen that ugly commercial on television where a girl exhibits herself lewdly in denim pants, and she had thought it was the Stephens creature, but the Stephenses were millionaires and that judge wouldn't have allowed his daughter to work, although Mark sometimes referred to his "job."

She saw the car and Mrs. Stephens in it, saw the carefully dyed hair—very natural looking, Hester had to admit—brownish hazel. She wouldn't have known it was dyed if she hadn't heard her make an appointment one day on the telephone.

"Good morning, Hester," Mrs. Stephens called out of the creamy brown Mercedes.

"Morning, Mrs. Stephens," Hester said, and got in.

"I'm sorry I'm late," Mrs. Stephens began to rattle on. "It's been an unnerving day; that's why I called and asked you to come later—you can leave at the same time, of course. Tessa is back! Don't say anything to her, *please!* And yesterday at lunch

I saw the last person I thought to see again in the whole universe, I'm just about to come undone— . . .''

Do! Hester hated to be converted into a concerned mammy like in that terrible *Gone with the Wind* she'd walked out on with all those Negroes silly-happy and just loving to be slaves.

They drove into Bel Air, past manicured lawns and flowers that grow only for the very rich, past houses that dash behind trees or sink into private hills to avoid uninvited contact. Everything perfect, beautiful, rich.

"I'm so unnerved." Mrs. Stephens had a way of repeating or forgetting what she'd said. She touched the edges of her temples, tenderly.

What unnerved her, Hester didn't know. She had everything.

Mrs. Stephens went on. "And I may as well tell you before you hear it on the news: The judge upheld the death sentence of that poor black man. Yes, Hester, he cast the decisive vote for death. And you know I'm against capital punishment; I hate it! I haven't spoken to him since—my little way of protesting. He *knows* I oppose capital punishment, it's so unfair, you know— mainly minorities and the poor—it's so unfair. *You* know how I feel about all that.''

No. Hester pressed her lips shut. *Fire.* The word itself flared into flames. She looked out at birds of paradise on the lawn as they drove past the portals at the gate; the ledges were trimmed like some of those silly quivering poodles maids in the area had to walk. Her gaze returned to the birds of paradise. Orange. Flames. Fire. *So will I stretch out my hand upon them, and make the land desolate, yea, more desolate than the wilderness,* Hester remembered.

Mrs. Stephens parked the car, which made no noise at all. Hester came five days a week "to tidy up." "And don't you dare do one more thing!" Mrs. Stephens would admonish her periodically. They had a regular maid, but she had other chores, and there was a housekeeper—that Helga or Inga or Heidi— Hester refused to remember her name; in her mind, she called the white housekeeper the "head maid" or "that imported servant." It took that many people, and others who came periodically, to keep the house, which was enormous, two and a half storeys tall. *Like the palace my great, great, great grandfa-*

ther shared his wealth from, Hester would think, *but his was grander!*

Ahead, like a snake on a rock, the hated Linda sunbathed by the pool; yes, Hester could remember the name of the younger Stephens daughter on occasion. The girl's top lay loosely and unstrapped across her breasts—no, her nipples. The top was almost briefer than her sunglasses. She was brown, dark brown, the tanned body oiled, blond hair streaked. She crooked one leg, the other stretched out, extending her bare foot, the nails manicured.

"Poor Linda," Mrs. Stephens said absently. "She does need to relax; she had a dreadful experience last night at one of those awful punk places or whatever; the guard claimed she— . . . So don't say a word to her. You know how the judge dotes on her. Well, can you believe they actually said she took off her— . . . It's too awful!"

Linda removed the sunglasses and glanced at her mother, and then at Hester.

Whatever they said she did, she *did!* Hester thought.

Linda put the sunglasses back on and straightened out both legs, raised both hands and placed them under her blond head, her shaved underarms exposed, whiter than the rest of her. The strip of her top slid off one nipple.

Hester inhaled audibly.

Linda responded to the powerful gaze. "Hi!"

"Morning," Hester said. Under the white-hot sun, wavy, barely perceptible smoke seemed to rise from Linda's burned-brown flesh. Oh, vapor from the pool— . . . Hester continued to watch the rising smoky steam.

In the garden hibiscuses grew in various colors. Trashy flowers, Hester thought. Mrs. Stephens referred to them as "rose mallows." In Hester's mind, the sweaty vapor leapt as smoke from Linda's body and turned one of the lush bushes brown.

Hester followed Mrs. Stephens into the house. Mark was coming out of the breakfast room. "Morning, Miz Washington," he said.

She stretched to her full stature. He didn't always call her that, but he did increasingly—called her Miss, although she was Mrs.—or maybe he was calling her that new "Miz." She had tried at first to find a pattern to the times he addressed her formally—so courteous—but she hadn't been able to, just as she wasn't able to figure out when he would be wearing the black-rimmed glasses, when not. She supposed he called her "Miss" when her royal blood "showed through" most clearly.

"Morning, Mr. Mark," she said. He was a good-looking white man. Serious, too.

"Where are you going, dear?" Mrs. Stephens asked casually. Again she touched the sides of her face, right by the ears—a curious nervous reaction she had. Hester knew she was fifty, perhaps a little older; she had a slender figure, guarded carefully by hours at a "body shop" every other day and by careful green lunches—except now and then when, she would "confess," she had eaten more than she ought at some place called Shaytoo.

"To a lecture at school," Mark said.

"Learn a lot!" Mrs. Stephens exhorted. She looked up the stairs. "Tessa's back," she told Hester again.

"*Yes,* Mrs. Stephens."

Square as a white domino, the white housekeeper appeared. "Gut mornung," she snapped at Hester.

Hester nodded. She was, after all, no matter what they called her, just another maid, even if she wore a different uniform and lived in her own "quarters" here and could tell her what to do. So important, that Hilde—and just because she'd worked for that judge's father, who brought her here—*imported* her from Europe.

"Hilde will tell you what needs doing today, dear." Mrs. Stephens turned Hester over to the square woman.

Mrs. Stephens took a step away, another. Then she just stood there as if paralyzed, looking bewildered into her own magnificent house. Hester saw her staring at the paintings on the walls, some very strange ones, some very beautiful. One was just lines bunched in one corner; another a sphere filled with silver chrome, which dripped into different shapes as the day wore on; others, the beautiful ones, of grand ladies and gentlemen—all white, of course; paintings like tiled linoleum; and there were peaceful landscapes— . . .

Mrs. Stephens's stare shifted toward the stairway, which branched into a graceful *Y*; she stared about the room filled with vases of freshly cut, carefully arranged flowers; at drapes that swept the floor like a bride's gown. She seemed to study the high arched windows. Sunlight drowning in the pool flooded the room in a reflection of blazing light.

The light that will expose them! Hester looked at Mrs. Stephen Stephens III just standing there as if wondering where to go, frowning into her own palatial house as if it owned her. "Hester," she said, without turning around.

"Ma'am?"

"I'm sorry." She reached back, as if to touch her.

"Ma'am?"

"I mean I'm *really* sorry. About the judge. He affirmed the death sentence of a man of your color. And I'm sorry, really *sincerely* sorry."

Hester said nothing. She turned to look outside, where the judge's favorite child lay in the sun. Let *her* body roast! Flames rose and jumped to the trees, and trees fell into the pool, which bubbled and boiled over.

". . .—dosting wery vell."

"What?"

"Dat you don't been dosting wery vell," Heidi or Helga or Whoever said.

"Where?" Hester challenged.

"Everyvere," the white woman said.

Hester went to the maids' quarters and changed into her uniform. Then she went and got the cleaning equipment and began to vacuum. The Persian carpet. She had never noticed the buried orange in it. Buried fire. The vacuum cleaner would pull out the contained flames. They would curl toward the ceiling, swirl there, dancing—fire crawling over the floor and then reaching out, jumping to another house, then another—to the very portals of Bel Air—the way it had done in Watts when the police invaded!

The judge affirmed the death of a man of your color! Each word lashed at her, shouted itself over the sound of the vacuum cleaner. Her great, great, great grandfather struggled against the white hunters. The conquerers were not braver, no, just more cunning, meaner, crueler; they assaulted by surprise; they caged him, broke him. She saw the great man with beautiful exotic feathers from birds that flew freely only in Africa. The humming of the vacuum cleaner droned on so loudly, and her images flared so vividly that she did not notice, until the vacuum cleaner almost touched the bare feet, that a woman stood there, a strange youngwoman with strange dark eyes staring at her.

Hester pulled back the vacuum cleaner, halting its sound. She looked at the woman. It was Tessa. "Miss Tessa."

"Hes-ter." The youngwoman seemed to have trouble pronouncing the name.

Where have you— . . .? Oh, no. "Morning, Miss Tessa," Hester said.

Tessa frowned. Her eyes seemed outlined in blackness, but not with paint. Pain. She stood there, just stood there barefooted.

The way her mother had stood earlier, Hester thought.

Hilde was standing like a prison guard before the girl, forbidding her to move farther. Tessa looked lost.

"Mrs. Stephens!" Hilde called.

"Don't," Tessa pled. "Please." She put her finger to her lips, to soften the voice.

"Mrs. Stephens!"

Tessa covered her ears.

Mrs. Stephens appeared. "Tessa, darling. Where were you going, darling?"

The woman and her older daughter stared at each other.

"Nowhere."

"Where are your shoes, dear?"

"Oh—uh—I don't— . . . Upstairs! I'll get them."

"Where were you going, darling!"

"Just outside."

"Linda's out there."

"Oh!" Tessa began to retreat.

And so *she* can't go out because that harlot is out there. Hester pulled her lips in.

"Got on vith your cleanung!" Hilde told Hester.

Get—not *got*! Hester turned the vacuum on to the highest level, deliberately devouring the raised voices. She saw Mrs. Stephens's mouth moving. Tessa stood before her. Then the youngwoman walked barefooted into the patio and stood staring at her sister. Linda removed the sunglasses and sat up, looking back at the dark girl. The two sisters and their mother formed a triangle overlooked by Hilde.

Lowering her head as if to charge, but also to disguise the deliberateness of her act, Hester roared the vacuum cleaner toward Hilde. She cleaned and cleaned and cleaned there until she had managed to raise a cloud of dust or smoke right at Hilde's feet. Flames, fire, flames! Hilde backed off, aghast. Hester sailed away in a curve with the vacuum cleaner. Hilde marched into the depths of the house.

Mrs. Stephens rushed to the telephone ringing in a small sitting room. She sat there, one ear covered, talking—screaming—into the telephone, yelling to be heard over the machine's roar. Hester chopped the noise off, and Mrs. Stephens's raised voice shouted, ". . .—a lark, but I did love your act—you in your marine uniform and— . . ." Shocked to hear her words roar into the sudden silence, she looked imploringly at Hester. Her tone of voice changed; she said into the telephone, "Just a moment, Mr. Maxwell, I'm putting the telephone on hold and taking it on another extension." She avoided even glancing at Hester.

Hester looked outside. Tessa had disappeared. Only the tanned snake remained there.

Hester dusted fiercely.

The phone rang again. Answered.

Mrs. Stephens appeared a few moments later. "Hester, darling, I have a huge favor to ask you, but you must promise to say no if you can't or I won't even ask you. Now promise. A friend of mine is in desperate need of a— . . . of help. Do you mind if he borrows you? I mean, would you mind helping him? Of course, he'll pay you double. He's a wonderful friend, and he's just despondent because he's having a show—a fashion show—and a small important dinner tonight and his own— . . . Well, the woman who helps him out didn't turn up today. Only if you agree, of course. And of course, if you do, I'll drive you, and he'll pay your cabfare to East Los Angeles."

"Watts," Hester corrected.

"Oh, Hester, forgive me, please! Of course I know you live in Watts. I know that, of course. I've driven you there myself, remember?'' she pled urgently. "Once during the taxi strike, and another time when— . . . Do you mind helping him out just this once?''

"No, ma'am,'' Hester said. Fire arced over Mrs. Stephens and rushed up the stairs.

When they walked back to the Mercedes, Linda was no longer by the pool. Mrs. Stephens was already babbling. "I just have to get it out of my mind, that's all!'' She didn't identify what. They drove down the perfect roads. "It is true, though, that crime is spilling out of the inner city— . . .''

Hester remembered the fires that had lit up Watts in a smoky orange halo. *Spilling out of the inner city! Segregated rage! Yes! Yes!*

". . . —all know, of course,'' Mrs. Stephens pushed on, "what the real crime is: poverty!'' They sailed past the white columns of Bel Air, the concentric layers of flowers. "And I feel so *helpless!*''

I have set the point of the sword against all their gates. Flames rising up the white portals would form columns of fire. Hester clenched her bag on her lap.

"I myself refuse to join one of those awful self-defense places. Can you imagine? The man who owns that new one wants to have a rooftop patio resembling Chez Toi's! Indecent! It's all becoming so— . . . so— . . . Oh, I don't know.''

No, you don't know, you can't know. Don't know anything about violence, woman. *Thou shalt burn with fire, a third part in the midst of the city when the days of the siege are fulfilled.*

At the house where she was to be borrowed, Hester got out. Mrs. Stephens blurted, "Hester, I promise I'll make this favor up to you. Next time we need you on Sunday, I'll go pick you up, myself. In Watts. I have some things for you—clothes, *things*; I'll bring them to you; and— . . .'' Her hands flew to her temples. ". . . —and tell Brian—*please* tell Brian I love him but I can't stop, I'm in a rush—but I'll call him soon, and I'll be at his showing, and I'm dying to know what he's hiding, and thank you, Hester, *thank you*, we'd all be lost without you.''

Yes!

The creamy Mercedes purred away.

The house seemed a series of white cubes somehow located over a cliff. Hester pushed a square black button. "Come in," a man's voice said. Hester walked in.

Black and white.

That's all she saw. Paintings: black and white stripes, squares. The floor: black and white swirls. Mushroom sofas and couches: black and white. And chrome and glass and crystal everywhere. Hester reacted as if someone had run a fingernail along glass. Through an invisible window, the azure of the pool was a shock.

Talking into a square telephone—bone white—a man sat on a black chair that looked like a humped hawk. The man was blond, thirtyish; maybe older but looking younger; short hair, a moustache. Barefoot, his legs curled under him, he was wearing a combination of pajamas and robe—calf-length, loose-sleeved, tied at the waist, open on a hairy *V*, and the sheer material was white. He waved at Hester and mimed words at her: You. Are. An Angel. Then he continued into the telephone: "No, no, no—*no!* You don't understand, Vera. Darling, my fashions are not of *today!*" He mimed more words at Hester and pointed to the telephone: New York. "I said *not* of today. Today is passé! . . . Wait a minute, darling." He covered the mouthpiece and said to Hester, "Tandy, you're a darling for letting me borrow you from Alana."

"Hester," Hester said.

"Of course. *Tandy* didn't show up. A cold." He looked about the cubed rooms. "*Do* something with it all, will you, angel?" He blew her a kiss. "Whatever you need is straight through the hall and into the kitchen, out, then right, and right again." He returned to the telephone. "Vera, it's what everything is about now, darling!"

Hester marched past black and white squares, mirrors, and chrome. Behind, the man's voice continued: "*Tomorrow* is when it's *all* going to happen, you see; and so, yes, how to address yourself to *then*, but *now*."

Hester paused, listening. A twisted piece of plastic sculpture caught a blade of sun. Hester willed it to melt, heated by approaching fire, twisting the plastic into even uglier forms.

"Violence. Injustice," the man's voice continued. He stopped and sighed. "Well, we have to accept it. And that's what tomorrow *is*. . . . *Of course* today is the same, but that's not the point! . . . Yes, yes! . . . *No!* Violence *and* injustice, yes! The spirit of tomorrow's revolution. . . . No, darling! Do we have a bad connection, Vera, or do you need a— . . .? Not *e*volution, I said *re*volution. Don't you see? The rich will be wearing messages of— . . . of— . . . I'll say it: oppression! . . . *Op! Op! Op*pression! Really, darling, you do have a— . . . Don't you see how *tomorrow* that is?"

Before the implements of her profession—the tubes for gathering dust, the claws for dredging out clean dirt, the white cleaning rags—Hester closed her eyes, tight, more tightly, willing a hot, orange darkness. Borrow *me*? *Then shall ye know that I am the Lord, when their slain men shall be among their idols round about their altars, upon every high hill, in all the tops of the mountains, and under every green tree, and under every thick oak, the place where they did offer sweet savor to all their idols. So I will stretch out my hand upon them, and make the land desolate, yea, more desolate than the wilderness. . . .* Borrow *me*?

"Well, Vera, all I can say is this: You'll see when you show up," the voice of the man still talked on the telephone when Hester opened her eyes again, feeling flushed. The man was saying, "And don't send that bitch who works for you; he knows nothing about style. . . . Of course you can bring *him,* darling—I may even forgive her for what she wrote last time. . . . Yes, it *is* true! . . . No exclusives, darling; if so, I'd give it to you, you know I adore you—but it has to remain a secret. It will be *très sen-sa-tionnel, je, vous, promette!* I'll make everybody gasp. . . . I really can't; you have to come to the showing to see it for yourself!"

Hester was wiping a glass top when she saw Brian's reflection. It disturbed her to have anyone stand over her. She rose quickly. He kissed her on the cheek. "You're an angel, Esther. . . . Tandy couldn't come—she gets these torturing backaches!—and tonight I'm having a very important dinner, the night before tomorrow's opening—and this place is a hovel. I won't tell you what to do; just dazzle me, won't you, darling?" He moved into another room.

Hester wiped, dusted, vacuumed. She heard the shower. She walked into another room, another cube. There was a drawing board here perched on a stand before a tall stool. Hester looked at the drawing. It depicted a long slender woman wearing a cocked cap, a jacket with epaulets, pants bloused over brown boots strapped with several small buckles. The material of the jacket and the pants was brown, orange, green, each color swirling, like soldiers wore in the news. An expensive combat uniform! And the woman in the drawing held a rifle at a diagonal across her chest, the barrel pointed as if soon to be aimed.

Hester turned away. Like a huge green spider, a fern hung by a window. She hated those pampered ugly plants! With one hand, she pushed its limp leaves away, and some fell on the white floor. A white-tufted dog came into the room and stood yelping feebly at her. She hated their plants *and* their ridiculous nervous dogs—better fed than Negro babies. The fire she had ignited to the gates of Bel Air grew long fingers that grasped toward this black and white monstrosity of a house.

". . . —and I'll leave you the— . . ."

Brian was wearing dark blue jeans, an open bluish jacket, no shirt, tennis shoes, no socks. The dog continued to yip.

"Stop it, Zsa-Zsa," he ordered. "My God, Esther, I just realized I don't have any money with me—I never carry any—and Alana warned me that I must pay you cash and cabfare and double, but I never carry a cent. . . . I'll call my— . . . roommate. He works just down the hill; he'll come and pay you. I'm sorry, but I have to dash—I'll call Stuart now."

The dog quivered after Brian.

Hester heard the man's voice on the telephone: "Stuart, be a prince, come home, will you? I don't have a cent to pay Esther, and— . . . Esther! Tandy didn't show up and Alana loaned me her— . . . Alana Stephens, the judge's wife. He's up for an appointment to the Supreme Court. . . . Yes, her! . . . I told you Tandy didn't show up again. . . . Yes, I'm sure that's what it is—she does it here, too; I'm going to have to lock the— . . . Which reminds me, we need more Scotch. Nobody's drinking wine anymore. Can you believe I offered that New York bitch Scotch the other day—Chivas Regal—and he said, 'Don't you have anything cheaper?' . . . I *know*—but you can leave now. I had an interview; that bitch Vera talked forever. . . . Yes, yes, the one from New York, and she's bringing that awful closet case who wrote those vile things about me. . . . Of course I didn't tell her about the sniper design. That's the surprise! And I've decided definitely: the model *will* carry a real rifle. And she'll pretend to shoot at the audience! . . . Yes, isn't it? . . . Anyway, come right away and pay Esther and bring lots and lots of cash for cabfare. . . . Yes, I did say cabfare. . . . Alana said Watts—. . .''

Hester was wiping a lamp that looked like a skinned cobra.

Brian mimed the words: Where? Is? Watts? Darling?

Hester pretended not to understand.

"I don't know *where* it is *exactly* either, Stuart!'' he said to the telephone. "But she'll tell you. . . . Yes, and double whatever we pay Tandy. . . . Just for today, don't worry, just for today! . . . Lorenzo will be here to cook. . . . Yes, yes, yes, yes, yes, no, *ciao!*''

He returned to Hester. "Tara is saved!'' he said. "My roommate will bring the money to pay you, Esther, and thank you, darling, thank you, you can leave the door open, we have total security, and you're an angel, but of course you know that, and I love your uniform. . . .'' He started to move out of the black and white cubes, and then he stopped. He turned to face her. "Can you *believe* me? I called Stuart my roommate! My God, I called my *lover* my roommate! My God, how closet Fifties! I called my lover my *roommate*! It's all the tension— . . .'' He was gone.

Sodomites! Hester's mind screamed. White sodomites!

She cleaned and cleaned and cleaned, ferociously. Borrow *me*?

Exhausted, she leaned on a chair and forced back tears, which nevertheless brimmed on the lids of her chocolate-mint-colored eyes.

The door opened. Footsteps.

Her proud chin shot up. She wiped her eyes.

"Hello, Esther,'' said the man. "I'm Stuart, Brian's lover.''

Hester stared at the man standing there, his hair cut carefully short, his moustache trimmed exactly. A man of Brian's age and build, a man who looked very much like Brian—except that he was black, black like her.

"I'll put the money here." Stuart glanced away from her. "I hope this covers your taxi—I called up the cab company to get an estimate." He placed the money on a clear plastic rectangle enclosing a black sphere. He moved away, turned back. "Oh, and, darling, thanks for helping us out." The door closed.

Hester shut her eyes. She leaned against a glazed wall. The memory flowed over her. She remembered watering her house on Grape Street during the Watts riots, which became police riots; remembered standing on a chair and holding a hose soaking her roof in water so that the flames—set by her own people first, and then by the police, their flares, their bullets—would not destroy her home, her mother's inherited, precious, beloved bone china, her own carefully tended garden.

She sighed now.

The roiling flames of purifying fire sweeping down the luxurious hills, roaring past the gates of Bel Air, raging at Beverly Hills, engulfing the green mansion on Sunset Boulevard, slowed their blazing avalanche—slowed, slowed. Slowed. Stopped. Hester pushed the hungry flames back, dousing, drenching them, smothering them—until she had put the fire out entirely.

Lost Angels: 4

"Where's Orin!" Jesse James sat up startled. The place at the opposite end of the bed was vacant.

In the other bed, Lisa wiped troubled sleep from her eyes. She looked at Jesse. "I dunno where . . . he— . . ."

Jesse dashed to the closet, to check whether Orin's clothes were still there.

Lisa jumped up and drew the drapes. Was the Cadillac parked in its usual place?

Last night, when Orin's sobs subsided, Lisa and Jesse James remained unmoving, not daring to touch. After a few minutes, she rose, put on her underclothes, and got into the other bed, with Pearl Chavez. Jesse put on his shorts. Orin lay huddled, naked. Lisa and Jesse fell into disturbed, heavy sleep.

Now Orin was gone.

"His clothes're still here!" Jesse James discovered; that only partially relieved the rising apprehension. Was Orin rash enough to walk out and leave everything behind?

"The car's still there," Lisa said.

That assuaged Jesse further.

Orin was at the door. "Morning," he smiled.

"Orin, you *worried* us!" Lisa said.

"Yeah," Jesse sulked in a crush of emotions. "Where'd you go?"

"Woke up early, got up—paid today's rent," Orin said.

His way of shutting out last night? Jesse resented having panicked at Orin's absence. Now the mixture of feelings was further complicated by Orin's having paid the rent. That meant Jesse's—and Lisa's—money would last longer. At the same time that having their own money made them feel "independent,"

119

they were increasingly aware of "owing" Orin. His purpose?
No, he never made them feel indebted. Just like Orin to create
opposite situations at the same time! Jesse didn't know exactly
what to feel. So he evoked Cagney as Cody: "Awright, kid,"
he said, ending his sulk.

"We missed you, Orin," Lisa said, going to take her turn in
the bathroom.

"Shouldn't miss anyone," Orin said.

And so last night's occurrence would be sealed, an invisible
presence. Lisa took her clothes with her, to dress in the bathroom.

Realizing he was still in his shorts as he walked to the table
for his guidebook, Jesse quickly put on his pants. He noticed
that Orin was separating or counting some bills in his wallet—
each day's increasing expenses? Orin must have *lots* of money!
Jesse realized Orin had been staring at him.

Glowing freshly in a light, yellowish dress whose material
kissed her in the sexiest places, Lisa came out of the bathroom.
Jesse James took his turn immediately after. Inside, "smelling"
her naked body, he came in his hands.

Back in the room, avoiding looking at Orin, he sat down at
the table and started leafing through his guidebook. He determined to have a strong say in today's trek.

Lisa was preparing Pearl Chavez for this day's outing.

" 'The park sprawls over four thousand forty-three and seven-
tenths acres of lush land! It was donated to the city by Colonel
Griffith J. Griffith! It is reputed to be the largest city park in the
world! It has been kept in as natural a state as possible, while
rendering it easily accessible to motorists and hikers!' " Jesse
was reading—and adding emphases to—an entry in "Places Not
to Miss." " 'Among its many features which make it a visitor's
delight are the famous Observatory and Planetarium (see separate entries); a miniature 'Travel Town' with train rides; the
Greek Theater, an outdoor theater where some of the greatest
entertainment in the world is presented under the stars; natural
mineral wells; and one of the finest zoos— . . .' "

"I *hate* zoos!" Lisa said. She put a drop of cream on the
doll's hair, to brighten it.

Jesse glared at Lisa and continued. "In *this* zoo, 'Animals are allowed to roam freely in areas resembling their natural habitat while still being contained for the safety of visitors.' ''

"Oh, *sure*," Lisa persisted. "They're *still* not free."

Jesse continued intrepidly. " 'Golf courses and tennis courts provide athletic recreation. A playground with rides, including a merry-go-round, is a popular attraction. Picnic areas and hiking paths are everywhere. Visitors can take advantage of the many bridle trails by renting a horse at the stables. Rare flowers, trees, and birds add to the delights of the park. Some animals are allowed to roam wild,' '' he flung the words triumphantly at Lisa, " 'including deer and squirrels. With its many green coves and trails, the park is a hiker's delight.' ''

Orin had not reacted, just lay on the bed staring at the ceiling.

Jesse tried another marked place in his guide: " 'A million-aire wanted to duplicate the old Italian city, to reconstruct one just like it in Los Angeles. He began with the canals, a charm-ing pizza, and— . . .' Pizza? P-i-a-z-z-a," he spelled out the word.

"Piazza. Like a courtyard," Orin said.

"That," Jesse continued. "One of those 'was built and still remains although the pee-at-za has gone through several changes in recent years. Today the City of Venice West is a quaint combination of canals, Venetian rest-stops along the beach, and old Victorian-style houses.' '' Jesse looked up to see whether he'd captured Orin's interest. Nothing. He skipped to another part. "Universal Studios Movie Tour!" He counted on Lisa's support on this one.

Excited, she peered over his shoulder and read: " 'See Los Angeles Destroyed Hourly!' Ugh! Who'd want to see *that*!"

"Just special effects," Jesse said. "I thought you loved movies."

"The all-times, yes, but who wants to be right there and see Los Angeles destroyed? *You* go, Jesse, not me!" she said.

Jesse trudged on through his guide. " 'Last Supper window, Hall of the Crucifixion and Resurrection, the Mystery of Life brook— . . .''

Orin said, "Where's that?"

"Forest Lawn. A cemetery, real famous."

"No, no, *no*!" Lisa protested. Earthquakes! *Now* a cemetery!

Jesse shot at her: "It's also got a Swiss Village, and Wee Kirk o' the Heather, and it's *free*!"

Heather. Cathy and Heathcliff gathered heather on the craggy rocks they converted into their castle. Just before she died, Cathy asked him to get her some heather. Lisa stroked Pearl's glossy hair. Two or three strands came out. She shoved them away in horror; one clung to her finger, and she rubbed it urgently against the bed.

"It's got a Court of David, the Great Mausoleum, and the Court of Freedom for the patriotic dead. And the Little Church of Flowers, where you can sit on two stone chairs and make a wish— . . ."

"In a *cemetery*?" Lisa went over to see whether Jesse was making all this up. He wasn't.

"It's more than just a cemetery," Jesse said. "It says here the builder's dream was to have a resting place for the departed where it wouldn't feel like death— . . . There's God's Garden, too, where you can meditate— . . ."

They drove along Los Feliz Boulevard, a graceful area of pines, palm trees, carpets of grass, splashes of flowers, old Spanish-style apartment buildings with terraces showered by bougainvillea. From the hills, elegant houses glance at the surrounding greenery. Nearby, the sprawling acres of Griffith Park are commanded by the green dome of the Observatory.

Jesse decided not to point out their proximity to the park— although he saw Orin look at it. Jesse had insisted to himself that *he'd* chosen their destination today. Cody was shrewd, like that.

Orin punched the radio on. The news station: ". . . —rising hot winds an increasing danger of fire— . . ."

"Aw, Orin, not the news right now," Jesse pled. "We know it's hot."

Orin shrugged.

Delighted by his own assertiveness, Jesse tuned in the station he had barely flirted with once—the country and Western one. The moany music invaded the classy Cadillac. The singer was pining over aches, deep hurts "in this old heart." Jesse leaned back, tapped his booted feet—but he didn't want to touch Lisa's thigh with his leg. Last night festered too mysteriously.

"I think Orin likes Western music—look how cute he's shaking his head," Lisa teased. She liked the sounds, too; a woman singer was now bemoaning love unsustained, "driven out of town, being around."

Orin stopped his slight movement.

"It was real cute," Lisa said regretfully."You didn't have to stop, Orin."

Orin returned the dial to the news. Jesse shot a mean look at Lisa. Lisa adjusted Pearl again on the back seat.

". . . —the controversial cardinal said," the radio announcer spoke. "Senator Hutchens accused the cardinal of arousing the—quote— 'worst— . . . "

Orin silenced the radio as the Cadillac drove past the portals of Forest Lawn Cemetery.

At its entrance was the Swiss Village, where arrangements for interment are made in a chalet. Paved roads swirl into low green hills. At regular intervals large open books made of cement offer directions to: The Crucifixion/Resurrection, Museum and Memento Shop, Church of the Recessional, Court of the Christus, Mystery of Life Garden, Court of David, Wee Kirk o' the Heather, The Last Supper, the Great Mausoleum, Court of Freedom, and the Garden of Memories.

In perfect rows on the green hills, square white tombstones are decorated here and there with fresh flowers or brave little fluttering American flags. The tombstones are presided over at irregular intervals by large statues of briefly attired, clinging-clothed bodies, muscular men, soft women.

As they drove up higher, an enormous statue of David, perhaps seventeen feet tall, loomed ahead.

They parked, got out. "My God, his *thing's* uncovered," Lisa giggled.

Tourists roamed everywhere, chattering, taking pictures. Orin, Lisa, and Jesse stood looking up at the reproduction of Michelangelo's athletic youth, the pubic hair swirling over the nestling uncircumcised penis.

"It's so sexy!" Lisa said. She wandered about the figure, looking up at his firm white buttocks. "And look at those muscles right at his waist."

"I got those," Jesse said. And opened another button of his shirt.

"Oh, you!" Lisa said. "Jealous of a statue. I *know* you have them, and Orin has them, too— . . ." She turned to confront Orin's wrath; aghast, she realized she had evoked last night. But Orin did not react.

To David's right is the entrance to his court. In the square courtyard, the radiating eroticism of bodies carved in stone— nude male wrestlers in a position of proximate penetration, languorously veiled girl-women, romping buxom children, round-breasted mothers—is recurrently contradicted by soft titles—"The Dream of Peace," "The Good Night Statue."

Jesse was getting aroused by the bare breasts and thighs; he felt guilty because this was, after all, a cemetery, bodies buried all over the place. But he was getting hornier and hornier these days.

Hands knotted behind him, Orin stood before a carved pageant called "The Mystery of Life." A message on a metal box instructed visitors to punch a red button and hear a recorded description of the sculpture. Orin pushed the button.

The strong voice of a man pointed out that there are eighteen figures about a brook, which represents the flow of life, its mystery: a youngish dreamer, a boy, a scientist, a grandmother, a family, a philosopher, lovers, a monk, an artist, a stoic, a fool. "The mystic stream flows from an unseen source toward an unseen destination . . . the meaning of that mysterious force we call life."

"Forest Lawn has found the answer to the Mystery of Life," a carved stone announces.

"Gentle reader, what is your interpretation?"

Orin read that aloud from the carved words. Then he stared up at the sun, his eyes open, unblinking.

"Orin, stop that!" Lisa said. "You'll go blind!"

The blue haunted eyes looked at her, and he nodded.

Trapped in Orin's silence, they drove past the Court of Freedom—soldiers buried amid twenty-five patriotic scenes, flags.

Above the beautifully combed green hills, a museum and gift shop offers slides, photographs, postcards, and small reproductions of the cemetery's art. The museum is adjacent to the Hall of the Crucifixion.

Lisa, Jesse, and Orin entered the large hall, like a theater. A hush hovered like a balloon over the collected tourists as the block-long painting was unveiled: Christ stands in a white robe, ready for the cross. About him colored figures prepare their anguish.

Orin drove to the building that houses the Last Supper Window. Again they sat with solemn tourists while a voice vaunted the economic advantages of burial at Forest Lawn. To the piped music of "Going Home," a glass mosaic version of Da Vinci's "Last Supper" revealed a glowing blond Christ among fading apostles.

On their way out, they passed the statue of a cold white angel.

Outside they read "The Builder's Creed." Statues of two chubby children stand looking up at the carved stone explaining that this—"God's Acre"—banishes death from the site of burial.

The Cadillac floated down the hills again.

"Orin, the heather! Let's find the heather," Lisa said.

At the Wee Kirk o' the Heather, next to the Church of the Recessional—for weddings and funerals—Lisa was disappointed. There was no heather. She had expected to offer some up to Cathy on the moors. But there were two stone chairs for a bride and a groom to sit on and make a wish. Lisa sat there. "Come on!" she called to Orin and Jesse. "Sit with me!" There was a place for only one groom. As upright as real, nervous grooms, Orin and Jesse flanked Lisa. Impulsively, she reached out for their hands, Jesse's hot, Orin's cold.

The Cadillac flowed to the exit of the park. Next to it was a lake. Swans floated like white question marks. "Please!" Lisa pled, and Orin parked.

Pulling Pearl along, Lisa ran toward the lake. Jesse and Orin followed her. At the edge of the water are statues of naked children and a young girl just sprouting breasts. Lisa touched the girl.

"Children die," Lisa said. She lay back on the grass, ar-

ranged Pearl in the curve of her belly, and closed her eyes—
dead with her child, no, with her mother, no— . . .

Orin asked her, "Are you dead or is Pearl dead?"

Lisa sat up. "I'm not sure."

In the car as they drove out, Orin unleashed his gathered
judgment of the cemetery: *"Fake!"* He clutched the steering
wheel as they rode away from the site of decorated, denied
death.

It was just after noon. Freeway traffic flowed easily. They
drove for more than half an hour. In the somber mood, Jesse did
not risk turning on the radio. "Going to Venice," Orin finally
announced. Jesse had become an expert at finding their
destinations. He consulted his map. "Off here . . . left . . .
right." And there it was: Venice Beach.

" 'The Venice of America,' " Jesse refreshed their memories
from the description in his guide: " 'Canals, gondolas.' The
man who built it planned to include it all: 'Sixteen miles of
waterways were dredged and he commissioned structures in the
style of the Italian . . . Rey-nay-sense to be on the site. He
intended to import singing gon-doll-eers, set up an Oriental Art
Gallery, sponsor a scientific aquarium.' Wow! Then they found
oil."

Orin parked in a lot near palm trees hugging each other
before giving up to miles of sand, more miles of ocean stretching to the end of the world. Reckless waves challenged the hot
whipping wind.

Along concrete walks bordering the beach—and despite the
gasps of wind—teenaged skaters glided by, their ears covered
with enormous rubber "muffs" connected to portable radios,
silent for everyone else; private music. Here and there—lingering
from a time long gone—the skinny bodies of men and women,
black and white, gather to smoke marijuana, drink wine under
green-benched, wrought iron shelters, vestiges of the original
plan to create a replica of the Italian city. The beat of a bongo
drum was funereal as a youngwoman danced to the rhythm of
her inner frenzy. Old Jewish delicatessens feature cured meats,
soda pop. On more green benches sit old people with skins like
crinkled brown paper. Bodies are everywhere, going nowhere,
slowly frenetic, as if idleness had found its own motion.

It was becoming so hot that Orin no longer wore his light jacket—but only one shirt button remained open. Whenever he could, Jesse would remove his shirt, like now. Lisa lowered her blouse as the three walked along the white horizon. Birds gathering in strange hypnotized bands on the sand faced the frothing ocean. Cautiously, before they scattered into shifting air, Orin approached the birds. He studied them, and then he looked out at the ocean, as if following their mesmerized stare to its hidden origin beyond the water.

On the sand, brown bodies, male and female, seminude, lay like sacrifices to the sun; casualties of a luxurious catastrophe, scattered at different angles as if a dazzling centrifugal force had flung them out, beautifully.

"Bodies," Orin said.

The three sat on a portion of beach sparser than others. Everywhere else, people congregated in tight protection in the same areas. Jesse leaned back on the sand. He was so aware of Lisa, so aware, of the fresh, sexual smell of her body. Damn Orin! Quickly he pulled back his curse.

Lisa hugged her knees. Orin still stood before the water, in that way he had of looking, as if to locate an essence, a mystery.

"Does the ocean talk to you, Orin?" Lisa said dreamily.

"To everybody," Orin said lightly.

The ocean thundered incoherently against the wind.

"I thought it might talk to you," Lisa said. I . . . love . . . you and Jesse, Orin, she tested the words—the one word—in her mind. She had never "loved" anyone before, and even now she couldn't be entirely sure because she really didn't know what "loving" felt like, what it *was*. How she felt about the all-times and their movie heroines, yes, that had to be "love." But for anyone real? I love you, Orin, I love you, Jesse, she tested again more easily; yes, I love you both. If she *really* tested it—by saying it aloud—Orin would probably turn his back and say, You shouldn't, and then she would be even more confused, not knowing whether he was right or not.

They walked away from the beach. The moist heat clung to them. Along the piazza, a phantom of what it had been, a phantom of what it had wanted to be, columns are splashed with gaudy purple, the remains of buildings left to collapse. The area looks like a mixture of sets from different movies.

They walked across the expiring piazza and into an area of ordinary houses—and then to the canals. There are several, each bearing the name of a *via* in Venice. Small bridges jump over murky strips of water. At the sides of the canals, houses remain, weathered. They walked along the periphery of a canal.

"I forgot Pearl; I left her in the car," Lisa remembered with remorse.

"Leave her to herself now and then," Orin soothed.

"*Shhh!* Don't talk so loud. My mommie tried to kill herself again yesterday and she's resting now," a skinny little boy, eight or nine years old, admonished them. He was shirtless, barefoot. His ribs showed like fingers on his sides.

"What!" Orin seemed to push the boy's words away.

"My mommie—I said she's sleeping; she tried to kill herself again yesterday." He made a stiff finger and sliced it across the wrist of his other hand; then he did the same with that one and sliced across the other.

"No," Lisa winced.

"What's your name?" Orin lifted the boy easily.

"Teddy."

"You want some ice cream, Teddy?" Orin asked.

"I guess," Teddy said without much enthusiasm. He looked back at the house. Then he skipped along as the three walked back to the main section of Venice. Lisa hoped for a Baskin-Robbins—it puzzled her that she had not remembered to have one—*again*—but there wasn't any. No matter; the outdoor shop they went to—with red tables like peppermint—had ice cream just as good, perhaps better.

Eating his ice cream, Teddy shook his head. "She shouldn't of, my father told her and told her: Don't ever do that again, we live with your death, he told her—that's the third time she's tried. Cuts weren't deep, though—they never are. We live with death, that's what he says to her. Wanna see Venice?" he asked them.

"We already— . . ." Jesse started. He felt sorry for the kid, but he couldn't help it—he made Jesse uncomfortable.

"Yeah! Show it to us, Teddy," Orin said.

Teddy became an expert guide. "A crazy old guy wanted to make this like a foreign city, but see over there— . . ." He pointed to oil drills, which looked like dinosaurs plundering the land. "Oil. Everything stopped for the oil."

He darted into Speedway, a long stretch that is part alley, part street paralleling the beach. In the ashen orange glow of the aging sun, bodies wandered along the accumulating garbage. "You know what hippies are?" Teddy asked.

"Sure," Jesse said. "I remember 'em."

"We still got them," Teddy said. "That house over there? Full of them. A long time ago they used to call them flower children."

"The cops killed them off," Jesse James said.

"Just some," Teddy said. "Some're still around." He spoke as if they were the same ones, transported from that time to this time.

Orin maneuvered toward the house the boy pointed to. It was wooden, two-storeyed; panes were missing from its glass-walled porch. Orin walked up the stairs. He tried the door. Open. Teddy peered in.

From the steps, Lisa and Jesse waited apprehensively as Orin disappeared with Teddy into the house.

Inside, the house was broken up into units, rooms. A door along the hall was open. Teddy at his side, Orin walked in. Within a determinedly bright room, they were assaulted fiercely by colors; rugs, pillows on the floor, cloth draped in loose arcs from the ceiling, flowers—some, most, wilted. A giant poster of an old East Indian man with flowing grayish hair was mounted on a beaded drape against a wall. The benign smile on the man's face was relentlessly blissful. Before the picture, like offerings at an altar, were stones, shells, trinkets, pieces of broken glass, a piece of fruit. The fruit—a pear or an apple— was rotting. Greedy cockroaches fed on it.

Orin walked out, with Teddy.

"What you see?" Jesse asked.

"Decay," Orin said.

They wandered along the beach. The sun was surrendering, leaving behind dark heat. Only a few bodies remained on the sand, abandoned corpses after the major cleanup. On Westwind, near Speedway, two men were squashed into a cramped doorway. "Shootin' up," Teddy announced knowledgeably. One man tightened a handkerchief about his arm, the other plunged a needle into it. "We live with death," Teddy echoed his father and shook his head. "Gotta get back!" he said abruptly. "If she wakes up alone— . . ." He sliced at his wrist with a finger.

They walked back with him. Before the door of the canal house and against smothered lights from inside, a woman stood, her wrists wrapped with fresh stark-white bandages. Teddy ran to her and hugged her legs. "Mommie." She didn't move. She held up her wrists, as if they were precious trophies she must protect. "Mommie." Teddy buried himself into her.

Orin walked to the woman. As if bending to hold Teddy tenderly, he put his hands over the boy's ears, and simultaneously he looked up at the woman and said:

"Why don't you really kill yourself and leave him be?"

Orin uncovered Teddy's ears. The woman wrapped her bandaged hands about the boy's neck, fingers interlocked.

They drove along the craggy Malibu Coast, into the sinuous road along the forested hills of Topanga Canyon. Bands of aging young people remain like abandoned gypsies from an ancient time of protest.

"Mildred Pierce was such a good mother." Lisa wanted to cry, Teddy's presence lingered. "She actually confessed to a crime her daughter committed, can you imagine loving your daughter that much?" In the movies, yes, there, she recognized "love" and devotion. "And Joan Crawford was *not* a bad mother!" she said with some franticness, sitting Pearl up peremptorily. "Look what she had to do in *Rain*—because that preacher was so mean to her he raped her! And in *A Woman's Face!* Sacrificed, sacrificed! *She wasn't a bad mother!*"

From the crest of the road, the night city smashed into bits of lighted glass below and away.

At a market on Franklin Avenue, they stopped to buy a barbecued chicken, potato salad, cold drinks. This time at the checkout stand, Orin waited for Jesse's and Lisa's equal share of the cost.

What had become distanced in their minds throughout the cluttered day assaulted them as they entered the motel room: the events of last night. At least they seized Jesse and Lisa, who felt suddenly awkward. Orin just turned on the television. Then he spread the chicken on paper plates on the round table. Orin always ate very formally, as if he had been carefully taught to do so. At the beginning of each meal, Jesse and Lisa would try to match his formality, but by the end they always gave up. Now they all ate hungrily.

". . . —controversial visitors,'' Kenneth Manning was saying. The dark woman next to him said, "I understand, Ken, that Cardinal Unger was heckled by a group chanting, 'Our Bodies Belong to Us.' '' ''Yes, Eleanor,'' Kenneth Manning said, "and later in the program we'll have footage on that. After this brief message, I'll be back with Eleanor Cavendish and more on the—. . .''

"How did it feel when you pretended to be dead, Lisa?'' Orin asked her.

Lisa frowned. "I just pretended.''

"What did Pearl feel?''

"I just *pretended*, Orin!'' Lisa said.

"Tell us, Lisa,'' Orin said gently.

"Pearl Chavez felt relief that her mother was dead,'' Lisa said—just to end this, "but *she* only pretended to die.''

Jesse was annoyed by the confusing moment—which Lisa and Orin seemed to understand. "Sometimes you talk like ole Pearl's *you*!'' he aimed carelessly.

Lisa looked quickly at Orin, actually expecting that he would answer Jesse, and then ask her a very important question, about Pearl, about herself. Who *is* she, Lisa? she expected his words. But his eyes were on the screen again. "Oh, you, Orin!'' Lisa broke her own mood, a child again. "All morbid and everything, Orin!''

There was a new look now and then on Lisa's face, Jesse was beginning to notice. She seemed to be changing—really changing. And the cuteness was firming into beauty. But that wasn't all. Hard to believe they'd been together only a few days.

". . . —reaction to last night's segment on the sleazy world of pornography in Mandy Lang-Jones's continuing investigation into *'The Lower Depths'*,'' said Eleanor Cavendish. The camera pulled to one side to reveal Mandy Lang-Jones now seated at the table with Kenneth Manning and Eleanor Cavendish. "Tomorrow we'll take you to the night streets of Hollywood for a look at male prostitution, young bodies for sale to the highest bidder; high stakes for high money—. . ."

Orin consulted his pocket watch. He turned off the sound on the newscast. Again he seemed to hesitate before shifting the channels—as if withholding a moment he had to experience. Other times he seemed to be extending the anticipation. Lisa turned away from the screen.

Sister Woman's diaphanous sleeves glided before the imitated sky. Without sound, she seemed to be performing a seated dance with her hands. The telephone number appeared across the bottom of the screen.

Orin's hands reached for the telephone. He raised it to his ear, his mouth. He dialed once, twice— . . .

Dave Clinton: "Slave Auction"

"He's ready for combat! Ready to shoot! Tough, mean, and ready—and *just for you!* Ladies! The Combat Sniper!" The femmish older man in a tuxedo introduced the new act at Tiffany's, the city's most popular male-exotic-dancers nightclub for ladies only.

Bloused battle-camouflaged pants streaked brown, dark green, orange, army fatigue cap cocked over dark eyebrows, ammo belts criss-crossed on his chest, heavy-booted feet spread, imitation rifle at a diagonal before him, Dave Clinton thrust his hips out within the lighted sphere of the stage. More sexual than handsome, he had an uneven-featured virility, emphasized by a thick but trimmed moustache and a solid natural build. Under the cap, his dark hair was shortish, just beginning to thin.

"Wow!" screamed the middle-aged woman who sat nightly in one of the front tables of Tiffany's, just feet from the stage. "Wow!" echoed her daughter next to her. Others among the two hundred or more women filling the club to capacity added their approval—hollered, applauded, whistled from the darkness. They were all types—young, old, plain, pretty, fat, slender, even beautiful. They sat in tables closely arranged in ascending tiers about the round, just barely elevated platform.

"And you thought nothing could top— . . . Oops!" A naughty hand flew to the lips of the emcee. "And you thought nothing could *surpass* our Construction Worker in his hard, *hard* . . . hat!—and *he* used his drill *just for you!* . . . Now *shoot* at them, Sniper!" he said to Dave and he waltzed away.

Now a fattish woman with a coiled sculpture of bleached hair and a mask of makeup—"the hostess"—replaced the emcee; she was dressed in a long blue dress, cut in a wide *V* to expose heavy propped breasts. During each performance, she stalked throughout the audience, the wire of the microphone she held to her mouth trailing behind her as she rasped insults at the women, who greeted her with enthusiastic applause. "You're a bunch of savages!" she screamed at them now. "Horny savages! Shove it at them, Sniper! Assault 'em with your deadly weapon!"

From the glassed coop over the circular stage, slurred, taped words and music groaned:

Ya say ya got a body!

"I'll *say* you got a body!" a woman moaned. She ran up to Dave and clasped one of his scuffed boots. A bare-chested male attendant restrained her. She surrendered dramatically but easily. The hostess shouted at her, "Now don't you go and drown in all that wetness of yours, sweetie, cause the dancers might slip on it!" The women howled their appreciation.

I say if I can put a hole
right through ya— . . .!

"Through *me*, soldier boy!" screamed another woman. "Put it through *me*!" The hostess whipped at the electric wire, moving toward the screaming woman: "Honey, *your* case would require the Construction Worker's drill *and* an interior decorator!" The assaulted woman squealed with delight.

In the lighted globe within the staring darkness, Dave unbuttoned his shirt and froze into a sexy pose.

An' if I can shoot into your
heart— . . .

"You *got* it, honey! Shoot, Sniper! *Shoot!*" a voice exhorted. Echoed approval greeted her words.

The hostess yelled into the microphone, "What a roomful of disgusting tramps!"—arousing laughter.

In several gyrations, Dave tossed his body forward, back, forward—removing the fatigue shirt, slipping it off under the ammo belts, exposing his dark-furred chest.

"Whattaya want him to do, girls?" the stalking hostess yelled.
"Take! It! Off!" pled the women, on cue.

Then you ain't go no soul!

"You don't *need* one, Sniper!" growled a throaty voice.
"Show us what you *have* got!" another screamed.
"Like him to set up house *in* you?" the hostess aimed at the
woman, who nodded, "Yes, yes!"

Dave tossed his shirt to one side; grasping fingers rose out of
the darkness demanding it. Holding the imitation rifle in one
hand, he floated the other over his groin. As the women shrieked,
he closed his eyes, dredging private images, beginning a hard-on
to increase the mound under his pouch. It grew.

The roar increased.

To make sure he could strip without removing his boots, he
had slit the sides of the bloused pants. Even so, they tangled on
one of the boots. He had to hop awkwardly on one foot to
secure the stance. Laughter punctuated the lighted globe of the
stage. The laughter from the women was spontaneous, natural.
For these moments it seemed to render the early hoots of delight
forced.

"Clumsy damn fag!"

Defiantly, Dave stopped his movements.

From the darkness the same woman's voice said heatedly,
"This clumsy waiter! Spilled my drink on me! He was watching
the strip—and it's supposed to be for *ladies!* Fag!" she hurled
again at the waiter.

"Cunt!" the shirtless waiter, with bow tie and starched cuffs,
hurled back at her.

Shuffling sounds, protests, shouting voices muffled.

The hostess took quick action: "Whattaya want the Sniper to
do?" she incited the expected command.

"Take it off!" Screams of encouragement aimed at the stage
shoved away the incident. "Cummon, Sniper!" "Off!" *"Off!"*

Dave removed dark green briefs—he waved them over his
head as if they were a lasso. Stripped to brown-dyed jockstrap,
boots, fatigue cap, ammo belts, he thrust the rifle out, withdrew
it, thrust it again.

"Uh, uh, *uh!*" a woman's gasps punctuated each thrust as if she were coming.

"Rat-a-tat, rat-a-tat!" a woman gunned back with her bumping hips. Another ran to the edge of the lighted arc and grabbed Dave's legs before an attendant pulled her back. There was little resistance from the women—as if they counted on being stopped.

Dave held the rifle pointed out from his groin. He shoved his pelvis out and "fired." Hips jerking in spasms of simulated orgasm, he moved about the edge of the stage, then onto the main floor, gyrating his body along the tables, his crotch almost, almost brushing the shoulders of one woman; almost, almost connecting it to another's lips—as he reached for the bills of money they held out to him. The women's hands tantalized with the tips, luring him to them. A woman tucked a bill into the cleavage of her lush chest.

Dave's body bent, still dancing. His head inched toward the woman's breasts, the money peeking out between them. With his mouth, he fished out the bill. And he closed his eyes, releasing this image on the screen of his mind: *a beard-stubbled man in a low-dipped tank top, dark-flecked bare legs over lowered pants—* . . .

Other hands reached out, trying to stuff bills into Dave's jockstrap, the elastic band about his hips and buttocks. Gathering the bills, Dave removed the jockstrap, naked now except for an olive green pouch at his groin. With a flaunted tip, a woman "purchased" the jockstrap. Another raised her dress, held out her leg, and stuffed a bill into the top of her stocking. Dave squatted, legs spread. Arcing slowly toward the woman's thigh, he clenched the money between his lips and closed his eyes again, releasing another carefully gathered image: *a blond youngman in faded torn jeans, the crack of his taut ass showing—* . . .

A woman clasped a bill between her teeth. Dave's lips connected with hers. She released the money, pushing it with her tongue, as—eyes closed—he unleashed another memory: *a lanky, shirtless man leaning against a van, his cock exposed—* . . . Bills fell to the floor, at his feet; he reached for them and others with his hand. Kissing women at random now, he flushed out all the erotic male images of this afternoon's incursion into the cruising area of Griffith Park, images gathered to give him the hot charge he needed for his performance.

"Take it *all* off, let's see it *all!*" a woman growled, and there was real frenzy in her voice.

The hostess held out her microphone to the woman. "You'll have to settle for *this!*" The women applauded and laughed.

Dave danced back up the steps, back to the circular platform. The emcee floated out as Dave began to move beyond the cone of light.

"Too *much!* Wasn't the Sniper too *much*, girls?" the emcee camped. "Whew! . . . And now, for your further delectation, we present the ever-popular Lumberjack-off— . . . I mean, *jack*!"

The dressing room was full of lights, mirrors, sweaty male bodies when Dave entered it. The Muscleman had already gone on—but he was oiling his body again, obviously for the benefit of the Sailor. The Cowboy was testing different angles for his hat. The Construction Worker was practicing removing his pants without stumbling—always a problem. The Marine was preparing to go on.

"Get the girls hot enough for me?" the Marine drawled at Dave. Dave disliked him, and so did the Construction Worker and the Sailor—both open homosexuals. The Marine was always talking about how glad he was they didn't let "fags" in this place and about all the women he fucked for big money; the Muscleman would say, "Yeah," deepening his voice. It was true several of the women included their telephone numbers with the tips, and that some of the men hustled them. It was also true that not all the dancers—and *probably* not all the cute shirtless waiters—were homosexuals—but most were, or would be, or went—claimed to go—"both ways." Dave had made it with several of the performers and the waiters—and, yes, at times he suspected they were *all* "gay." He saw no contradiction to his "gay pride" in stripping for women; like most of the others, he played a role and played it convincingly.

"Man, if you can't turn them on yourself— . . ." Dave tossed at the Marine.

"Shee-it," the Marine said. "I got this Bel Air woman so hot after me—ask *her* if I'm a fag!"

"*Great* act, Dave." Jay, the owner, walked into the dressing room to congratulate him. "It's real *today*." This was Dave's first night as the Combat Sniper; before, he had been the Telephone Lineman. Gray-haired and squat, Jay resembled a wrestler past his prime. "I'm thinking of moving it up for the last act next week. *Terrific* response from the girls!"

The Marine glowered at Dave.

"The rifle's gonna become too obviously fake, though." Jay had provided it, and the ammo belts—his son's. He gave Dave the name of a place that specialized in "realistic" toy weapons. Then he told everyone: "Oh, and we're having a new act tomorrow, real daring, real *today*."

Jay liked to create suspense, even, at times, seemed to encourage fierce rivalry among the "macho" dancers—this resulted in even more sexual performances.

Soon all the dancers would gather on stage for the "finale." Now that the Marine had finished his act—winking relentlessly at the women as he stood almost naked for moments on the stage—the hostess was introducing some of the shirtless waiters.

"It would take *all* of these to satisfy *you*," she hurled at a conservatively dressed woman, "and there'd still be room to serve tea—and what do you think of *this* muscleman?" She touched the shirtless waiter's round pectorals. His waist was just slightly thickening, and, like some of the others, he did not appear nearly as young as he had in the subdued lights; careful erasing makeup almost concealed the creased edges of his mouth and eyes as he stood among the other shirtless men, all acting very masculine, not always succeeding. The hostess's fingers outlined the muscleman's abdominal muscles—but pulled away from the fleshier part. "You know who he is when he's not waiting on you hungry cannibals?" She licked the microphone. "He's a *star*, girls, a famous star of the cinema—that right, Oklahoma?" she asked the flexing man, who nodded. Then she brushed the waiters away. "I'm tired of all of you. Bring out the dancers!"

Now in abbreviations of their costumes, wearing just enough to suggest their earlier fantasy-identity—Dave and the other performers invaded the clearing. To the shrieks of women and the moans of loud music, the men stripped quickly to their pouches.

The hostess ended this night's performance: "All right, ladies, and now we wish you all pleasant—I mean, *wet*—dreams!"

Dave left quickly. In the parking lot, he got into his open jeep—the tough vehicle's ruggedness augmented his own. He loved the sense of "rough freedom" that driving it fast on the freeways gave him.

In his late, very late, thirties, Dave Clinton almost always appeared much younger. But there were those times—after a long, active weekend especially—when the disguised years ganged up, each day attacked. In the "gay world," few types survive the short erotic demarcations of cherished youth; Dave was the epitome of one of those: rugged, a "man's man," attractive to the young and the older. Earlier this year, in a contest that drew tough competition from the city's many cruising bars, he was chosen "Mr. Macho of the Year." He had no problem at all getting into the most desirable "private" bathhouses and orgy rooms in the city, even those that post signs—or have men guarding the door—to keep out "undesirables—fats, femmes, and over 35's."

Now Dave entered an area where sex occurs at night in the alleys of a dark two-block stretch of garages and parked trucks. His "combat" fatigues would blend well in any cruising area.

Often pointed out as an example of a "truly liberated gay man," Dave loved what he called his "real world." Not only was he desired in it, he was well liked—a rare combination in an arena where potential lovers are potential rivals for the same body. He was proud to call himself a "political activist" —organizing and participating in fundraisers for "worthy gay causes"—not the radical ones, though, which created the dreaded "negative images—the stereotypes we have to overcome," he would point out with conviction.

He had had several affairs, which ended after a few months, usually with mutual accusations of "infidelity." Now he was satisfied to live alone—in a tasteful, masculine apartment in an attractive building with a flower-spattered garden about a pool that shimmered like tinfoil.

Years ago he had aspired to be an actor; he had had a bit part in a movie by a famous closeted director. As a lifeguard in the film, he had warned a beach bully: "Careful with the ball." That was his only line. As "Clint Dave," he had posed nude for Stud Studios and appeared in *Partygirl* magazine.

Quite successful in real estate for a time—he charmed men and women with his easy, concerned manner—he was confronted by a shaky period in the business; and so two nights a week he bartended at the Modern Man, a homosexual "cruise" bar; and three other nights he stripped at Tiffany's. In college, which he hadn't completed, he had worked as a dance instructor in a studio.

Up to his later teens, Dave had been "into girls"—although he had been aware of a powerful energy when he wrestled on his high school team. Then early in college, he proudly announced his homosexuality, long before others tumbled out of the closets.

His best friend remained a very pretty heterosexual woman; Julie's male lovers were more jealous of Dave's special friendship with her than of each other. He told her "everything"—as she did him—and she understood him as well as anyone else—as he did her. She would not go see him dance at Tiffany's, though; and there had been a few strained minutes between them recently when, driving past a "leather bar" on Santa Monica Boulevard, they had seen two men, both in black leather. Around the neck of one was a studded collar; a leash was hooked to it and held by the other man. "Ugly—and silly; ugly," Julie had said. Dave had explained earnestly that everyone knew "gay S and M" was strictly charade among consenting adults, no real force involved; "and it might even be the new frontier of man-to-man sexuality," he said—and added that he himself was not "into it." That was true—although days earlier he had bought a pair of tailored black leather chaps, and a black biker's cap—both items still unworn.

Tonight many bodies cruised the sexhunting area, into the crevices of the alley. Dave parked on a side street, and walked into the strip of darkened buildings. Several men floated by. A handsome dark man stared at Dave and disappeared behind a parked car. In the garage, the two men were about to reach for each other's cocks when lights smashed the darkness. "Come out, *fags*!" a woman's harsh voice said.

In the bath of light from the car's spotlight, Dave saw a white male cop and a black female cop.

"You try to run, and I'll shoot your brains out!" the woman's deepened voice promised.

The handsome dark man with Dave was trembling. Dave was cool. There had been nothing they could have seen, although it was not rare for cops to make up heated lies. More often, their incursions into sealed known cruising areas were just harassment. When the cops asked them for identification, Dave understood why the other man was so terrified. "You from I-ran, huh? —came here to suck cock, huh?" the male cop said in a Southern redneck drawl to the frightened man.

"Cause where he's from the Aya-toll-ly executes queers," the black woman said.

Breathing in to force back his anger, Dave did not protest— they would turn on the vulnerable man, he knew.

The two cops asked them routine questions—names, addresses—writing on white cards; a tactic to pretend to have a record of all cruising homosexuals.

The woman's fingers slid up and down the holster. Both cops got into the car, waited, the light left glaring on the two men. Defiantly, Dave put his arm around the Iranian student; the other's shoulders still trembled. Hugging him the length of the alley, Dave walked him back to his car, assuring him the white cards had no validity.

Still early. Dave called Julie from a booth. Neither went to bed before two, often talking late at night. He hoped she'd be alone and ask him over. She was but didn't. Dave told her how successful his new "Sniper" act had been, and then he told her about the incident in the alley. "Ugly," she said, but he wasn't sure what of everything he'd told her she was referring to. She broke a date they had made, though tentatively, for early dinner tomorrow before his performance.

The next day Dave drove his jeep to Griffith Park, to gather fresh sexuality for tonight's performance. He always showered before going to the park, but not after—to preserve the sexual connections. It was a warm erotic afternoon.

Several miles up the paved winding road, he parked in one of many indentations of dirt, ground into filmy dust by countless cars. An attractive youngman looked back as he drove by—and made a quick U-turn. Dave proceeded down the nearest trail. Moments later, in a cove carved by branches, an enclosure not unlike a large nest on its side, the two men faced each other. Both were shirtless. Similar sculpted cutoffs on each exposed firm, tanned legs over heavy hiking boots and logger's sox.

Feet planted firmly, thumbs hooked toughly through beltless loops, the two men aimed narrowed looks at each other. The other man was younger, mid-twenties. The two squared off, waiting for the triggering move. Dave drew—pulled out his semihard cock. The other toyed with his so it would match Dave's. Ready, he released his "six shooter." Glancing slightly sideward, neither moved. The hardened cocks aimed at each other. Do or die, weapons were drawn. If the other resists the challenge and leaves at this point, within the mutual defeat of frustration he will be the victor—by rejecting—the other left toughly slouched, eyes a sexy squint, proud cock abandoned.

A draw! Both groped each other simultaneously. Now their cocks fenced. Pants sliding to hiking boots, the two men kissed deeply. Their fingers probed hair-brushed buttocks just as deeply. Dave coaxed the other's head down; the younger man swallowed Dave's cock expertly. Now Dave raised the man, lowered his own head, and sucked the other in sure strokes. Then he leaned against a low branch, cocked one hairy leg, and let the other man suck him for a long time. He pushed the bobbing head against his hips, miming force. It was important that he didn't come, and so Dave removed pressure from the man's head. The man jerked off into his own hand while Dave's cock was buried in his throat. Seeing the thick cum jetting, dots of it spurting hotly on his bare legs, Dave felt the rushing hot charge he needed for tonight.

As he moved back alone to his jeep, he looked down the hill, far away. Yesterday he had seen a figure rushing into dense thicket and carrying something pointed. Hunting was, of course, outlawed in the park. Probably just a kid with a toy rifle—but it was that which had given Dave the idea for the Sniper costume—which, on the telephone later, Jay had immediately approved as "timely."

Collecting other erotic images for tonight from among the army of exposed cruising bodies, Dave drove out of the park.

At the store Jay had recommended for the "more realistic" rifle, the clerk said, "This is an almost exact replica of the M-16 weapon that our boys used in Vietnam; the real one could kill a *squad* in seconds. It's so light they could just hold it behind their heads and spray a whole area without looking back." There were realistic war toys all around. "Is your son having a birthday?"

My *son!* "No," Dave said curtly.

At Tiffany's that night, Dave's Combat Sniper was an even greater success. Next week Jay would definitely use it as the last number, he told him; tonight he wanted to end with a new, "daring" act.

When Dave had completed his performance that night and as he moved out of the stage, he heard a shrill whistle blasting out of the back of the auditorium. In the gray shadows, he watched a motorcycle policeman with knee-length boots strut down the aisles past surprised women. "All right, everyone freeze!" he shouted. "This is a raid!" The emcee and the hostess dashed away as if to hide. Now the policeman stood on the dance clearing. Legs spread and planted, looking down at the women through dark, dark glasses, he growled, "You women know the rules, right?"

Joining in the charade, the women answered, "Right, officer, right!"

"Well, you've broken them!" barked the dark presence. "And so I'm here to *bust* you!"

Applause—led by the advancing hostess, in pink tonight, with sequins in a vortex of hair.

"If you don't spread when I say spread, I can get rough!"

"I *bet* you can, officer," the hostess growled. "Stripsearch them all, all!" she told him.

Applause erupted.

"And if you don't submit," he said, "I got *these*." He dangled handcuffs.

Dave watched the scene intently.

Now the music began, and the "policeman" started his performance, subtly altering the motorcycle garb so that it became an adaptation of it—semi-cop, semi-outlaw biker in black. With a black-gloved fist, he held between his legs the butt of a coiled whip.

"A new presence!" the emcee shivered. "The man in black leather and a whip— . . . Ladies, the Leatherman! Grrrr!"

The hostess hissed at the women, "And you love him, don't you?"

Loud cheers answered. *"Yes!"*

The Leatherman uncoiled his whip.

Dave studied the dark presence in black leather. That was a costume hundreds of men in hundreds of homosexual leather bars throughout the country wore nightly. Almost all the "costumes" of the male dancers had appeared years ago in cruising bars. Now here they were before women. *Fantasies in common!* Dave heard the crack of the Leatherman's whip.

A woman screamed, "Ouch! That hurt so good!"

Another whimpered, "Oh, *dad-dee!*"

Dave felt a powerful, vague disturbance. Tonight he deliberately left Tiffany's through the ballroom.

This was one of the evenings when "gentlemen clients" are allowed early, because the second phase of the entertainment is provided by sexy youngwomen wrestling in mud pens.

Dave watched the beautiful women in tiny brown bikinis squirming and writhing in the gray brown liquid muck. It oozed down their lustrous flesh.

"Wallow in it, baby!" a red-faced man goaded them on.

"Deeper!" another man prodded. "Dig *deep!*"

"Dig *in,* hon!" a youngman who looked like a college student demanded, while others in his young group hollered, hooted, whistled at the girls covered with mud.

Some of the women with the men called out, too; most just laughed.

Dave went home, changed his clothes, and drove to Bolts, a bar he had never been in. It was known as "the heaviest leather bar" in the city; and it was located in a seedy section of East Hollywood, among crumbling assaulted buildings, their windows replaced by boards. Dimmed yellow streetlights hardly created shadows, merely pools of grayish night.

The bar's exterior was painted black. A reddish electric glow floated over its entrance.

A row of large, expensive motorcycles was parked on the curb before it.

Dave walked in. For the first time, he was wearing the tailored black chaps.

Others in the red smokiness of the sleazy bar—studiedly unkempt to evoke the aura of decay, with broken beer crates, gutted stools, patched walls—looked like the Leatherman at Tiffany's. They congregated here, some in heavy black jackets, cop uniforms; others wore leather vests or crossed studded belts or chains on their torsos. Some wore black leather gloves, sunglasses. A few dangled handcuffs. The smell—and the sound!—of leather soaked the rancid air.

Dave almost left. But a choking, not totally pleasurable excitement kept him there. He moved away from the more extremely leathered men who approached him—and from a man he was at first attracted to, until he noticed a ring piercing the right nipple of his bare torso. The excitement choked tighter. A man in worn jeans and denim vest—wearing a twisted red bandanna around his head—asked Dave, "Looking for a heavy scene, top man?" "Top man" is the master, the dominant one over the "low man" in "heavy sex." Dave stalled, drinking slowly from his beer, waiting for his own answer. The bandannaed man coaxed. "You can tie me up, do whatever you want." Dave left alone.

He returned the next night. And left alone.

On the third night he wore jeans, the chaps, a black belt, and the leather cap. When he walked in, a voice out of the smoky darkness said, "Wow!" Dave moved into a small back room off the main bar; more thickly darkened. Bodies were swallowed by eager shadows. When his eyes adjusted, he saw the bandannaed man kneeling, licking the boots of a man in full leather who twisted the other's nipples like screws.

Back in the less shaded part of the bar, Dave had a beer, to cool the fever that had increased amid the odor of leather in the heated shadows.

Outside, there was the snarl of motorcycles, loud, agitated. The machines idled, a menacing, even roar. Then one or more revved out a mechanical growl, tires screeched in short sorties.

Over the increasing angry murmur of the motorcycles, there were shouts now, sounds of a scuffle. A bottle smashed on concrete; there was the harsh sound of metal jangling. A man who had left moments earlier backed into the bar through the open door. Blood stained his face.

Through the pulled leather drapes at the door, Dave saw about ten motorcyclists lined facing the parked bikes of the men in the bar. The angrily purring machines were mounted by youngish, skinny, long-haired men wearing dirty jackets and insignias. Several were Mexicans and Negroes. They were brandishing lead pipes and bottles. Ugly scrunched faces twisted out words:

"Faggots!" "Cocksuckers!" "Fuckin' queers!"

A bottle burst into the open door. Other bottles and lead smashed on concrete, against windows.

"Next time we'll bring knives and guns, cocksuckers!" one of the mounted men screamed. Others echoed his threat. Motorcycle tires screamed away. It had all happened in perhaps one astonished minute.

Dave walked outside. Near the entrance lay a bloodied lead pipe. He picked it and flung it in the direction of the fleeing invaders. *"Cocksuck—* . . .!" He blocked the word. "Dirty fuckin' coward punks!" he shouted. On the street, other men, bleeding, reeled from the unexpected assault; the invaders relied on surprise.

Men tended the bloodied men. Someone called the cops. Dave waited to see whether they'd come. They didn't.

Next morning flotsam from a dream floated onto the brightness into which he woke: a bottle crashing without sound, a soft, subdued, almost saddened voice of a man—or a woman—or both—sighing, "Dad-dee— . . ." No. The voice said, "Wow, Dad-dee." The cracking sound of a belt. No, a whip.

In the mirror, Dave looked tired. He freshened his face with cold water, brushed his hair, running his fingers through the brush to remove whatever hairs were there without having to look at them.

Oh, Christ, it was later than one in the afternoon—he'd missed an appointment to show a house. Had Martin called him earlier? Or was that part of the dream? Martin saying something about a slave auction. A slave auction.

He dialed Martin, the owner of Stud Studios, the man who had taken the *Partygirl* magazine photographs that assured his job at Tiffany's.

"Honey, I thought you were dead when I called. Either that or you had five cocks—*large* ones—in your mouth; you couldn't utter a coherent *word*— . . ."

It irritated Dave that Martin was always doing nineteen-Fifties' camp, although he constantly told everyone he "just *loathed* queens, femmes, and sissies."

Martin affirmed with delight: "Yes, I called you about a mock slave auction to raise money for several gay causes—isn't that delicious? I'm providing the slaves from my—uh—famous stable of gorgeous models, all hunks, all types. We're selling invitations only to the hottest men. We'll auction the willing slaves—did I say 'willing'?— honey, it's more like *eager*! —we'll auction them to the highest bidder for a night of 'service.' Isn't that utter ecstasy?"

Dave's cock hardened; his body felt cold.

"We need three *divine* slavemaster auctioneers: the *very* best," Martin gushed on. "I'm asking Oklahoma and all his muscles, and Tim Pierce and *his* muscle—I could faint to utter the name. And *you*, Mr. Macho!"

Dave's throat tightened. "Will it raise a lot of money for a good cause?" he managed to say.

"Oh, yes, a *very* worthy cause," Martin assured him. "You know I wouldn't do anything to support one of those tacky fringe groups that give us a bad name. Anyway! We'll give the girls in their Adidas shirts at their tea-dances a shock, won't we?—when *we* simply overwhelm *their* donations! There'll be an elegant scaffold, and cells, and a— . . . Oh, wait—I'm being buzzed on another line!"

Sudden heat overwhelmed Dave's bedroom.

Martin returned to the phone. "Can you believe that *bitch*? Oklahoma *declined*, says it's not good for her image with *women*! The last time he was with a woman was when his mother *nursed* him, and even then I bet he— . . . What next! But I know I can get Buzz Saw—he's here from the East—and he'll be even better. To *die* for, darling! Simply to *die* for. And we want *real*—not *closet*—masters!"

Martin's words stirred the mysterious disturbance Dave had become aware of the other night. At Tiffany's? Then again at—
. . ." I'll do it," his voice said.

"I *knew* you would, you delicious hunk!" Martin's voice purred on.

The tone bothered Dave, the certainty. Martin was telling him that he and his partner had opened a new afterhours club—a euphemism for an orgy room. "*Very* exclusive, just beauties," said Martin, who was almost sixty and at best plain. "I'll send you a membership card; but if you just can't wait, simply go there; the attendant will recognize you from your pictures—he's *wild* about you. *And*— . . ." He stretched out the emphasis. ". . . —one room on the premises is *très* heavy, darling, *très* rough. Terribly *au courant*: leather slings for you-know-what, shackles, a tub for—*que sais-je?*"

Apprehension and sexual longing mixed, separated, tangled into one knot as Dave drove his jeep later that day to the park.

A Santa Ana condition was increasing, and the upper portions of the park were closed to automobile traffic because of "fire hazard." Cars park at the foot of the cruising areas at those times, and the men trek up the hills.

In his logger's outfit, Dave did that. But he didn't feel "on top of it" today. Weariness wound through the unfocused sexual desire, the hot disturbance, which turned cold. He felt very angered by Martin—his campiness; his constantly using, probably *mis*using, French when he was sure whoever he was speaking to didn't know the language; his— . . .

Dave started to make it cursorily with someone in the bushes. When a third man attempted to join them, Dave just walked away. Other times he might have welcomed the added sexuality.

He started walking down the hill, back to his jeep. Sitting on the trunk of a thick, fallen tree was a beautiful, slim, curly-haired blond youngman with dark eyelashes and azure eyes—one of the various types Dave's versatility was attracted to. The youngman looked eighteen. "Hi, Mr. Macho," he said.

Dave astonished himself. When the kid slipped invitingly into a cove off the road, he did not follow. He felt aroused by the kid, oh yes; but his sexual needs were in limbo during these moments, and the youngman's youth confused them further.

Dave drove to Santa Monica Boulevard, parked, got out, began to cruise the street. Growing weariness matched the burgeoning sexuality. *Martin's knowing tone* . . . In a usually favorite afternoon bar, Dave had a beer, talked to one or two people, friends; got cruised—and left.

He went home, lay down, got up, took a bath and a shower and fixed himself a large steak, blood-rare, the way he liked it. Today, when he cut into it and it burst into blood, he dropped the knife.

He decided to stay home tonight, watch TV until he fell asleep. Or maybe call one of his close friends, drop by, just talk? He looked in the mirror. Yes, tired. He dialed Julie's number. She was dashing out, she said. He began to dress. Western garb. Fifteen minutes later, he dialed Julie's number again; she was still there. He hung up. He lay back in bed and turned the television on with the remote control.

The late news: ". . . —gratitude to Mandy Lang-Jones," Kenneth Manning was saying, "for her continuing exploration into 'The Lower Depths.' Thank you, Mandy; those are cruel worlds you expose yourself to for our viewers." The man was somber for a few moments. Eleanor Cavendish said, "French diplomats— . . ."

Dave flipped channels.

That spooky Sister Woman. Dave shot her off the screen. Occasionally he'd watch her with some of his friends, marveling at her grand, spellbinding acts. One of his friends did a hilarious imitation of her, draping himself in chiffon. Tonight Dave wasn't up for her.

He'd go to Martin's new club.

Again the mirror confirmed his weariness. Was his hair thinner? He brushed it carefully. He almost pulled back on his decision to go out. Desire tugged. He put on a plaid lumberman shirt to go with the jeans and the cowboy boots.

The Santa Ana wind swept heat into the city and into his exposed jeep. West Hollywood swarmed with semi-exposed bodies. In the lot Martin had described, there were many parked cars. That meant many bodies to choose from inside. Like that of all other such "private" clubs, the entrance to Martin's was almost hidden, no sign, no name. These places burrow between buildings, then spill out into rooms and even other floors beyond the tight entrance. Dave parked his car and waited. He got out. The wind scratched with dusty fingers at his hair. Dave arranged it carefully, but the wind kept disheveling it. He walked under a single yellow light and up squeezed steps. Behind a half-door to one side of the landing sat a skinny youngman in a sleeveless black t-shirt. His fan?—Dave hoped so; the youngman was sexy, in a punky way.

"Hi." Dave waited for the adulation Martin had promised him.

The youngman eyed him. "You a member?"

"No, but— . . ."

"Can't come in. Private club."

"I know, but— . . ."

"Rules, okay?" the surly youngman said. "You gotta have two local I.D.'s, and— . . ."

"I do." Dave reached for his wallet. He stopped. He said firmly, "I'm Clint Dave"—he used his "model's" name—"and Martin of Stud Studios said— . . ."

"Hey, man," the youngman said. "I just got hired today, okay? and I don't know who Stud Martin is, right? Hey, all I know is they got rules, and you gotta be under thirty-five to get in. See?" He pointed to a sign:

NO FATTIES, FEMMES, ALMOST 40S

What had he felt at that moment? Outside in the parking lot, Dave didn't know. He let the wind howl at him. Had it really happened? To *him*? He wanted to rush back up the stairs, tell that fucking punk that he was Mr. Macho, *and* the Combat Sniper, *and* one of three slavemasters at the fundraiser, and that he was *not* almost— . . . But he was—he was almost forty.

He leaned beside his car, not able to muster the energy to drive away from the terrible place and the dusty entrapping night. It didn't help even when two good-looking men walking the steps into the club recognized him. "Stud model," said one. "Mr. Macho," the other said. They looked back at him longingly. Longingly? Or in amazement that he looked so . . . tired?

He drove home, desire squashed.

He called Julie. "Am I just imagining you're avoiding me?" He was blunt. They'd spoken a couple of times recently; each time she had "been on her way out."

"No," she said. "Dammit, Dave, you're changing and I'm not sure how. I mean, how do you really feel about all the stuff you've been telling me?—about those women shouting at you at Tiffany's, and the men shouting at the women wallowing in mud."

"I don't know," he said. Then he told her goodnight and hung up.

Weariness crushed him. The phone rang immediately again. But he didn't answer. He fell into roiling sleep, which became smoother, smooth, calmed. Twelve hours later he woke. When he went to the bathroom, the scratches of last night's weariness were gone.

The day of the slave auction, he looked great and felt terrific. Ten years younger, tanned; his body flushed from an earlier workout. He wore a black jockstrap under the hugging chaps, black boots.

In the enormous patio, he stood apart and watched the erotic parade. The auction was being held in the enclosed grounds of a secluded, unkempt mansion in a now-shabby part of the city. It belonged to an eccentric friend of Martin's who was in Europe, and it provided the perfect setting. The desert-seared wind dipped occasionally, but tall trees rising on one side into an uncultivated hill resisted its invasion. Almost two hundred invited leathered men sauntered about the grounds. Beer and sweat flowed.

More men had wanted—longed—to attend than could get in. Martin had insisted the invitations be sold only to attractive, masculine men in the bars. Leathered men roamed about; there were the ubiquitous chaps, leather pouches, vests, studded contraptions like harnesses formed by intertwined studded belts; leathered nudity on display throughout. The poses were tough, laughter coarsened. Waves of butyl and amyl nitrite saturated the air with sexual fumes, men constantly inhaling from small brown bottles or snapped ampules.

From where Dave stood on the secluded trail that pushed the courtyard into the slope covered with trees, it all looked like a sexual fair: flesh and leather rubbing against each other, rough men collecting in intimate groups—and everywhere the hints of "heavy sex."

The "auction block" was designed in a *T* flanked by steps. A row of six improvised "cells"—barred cubicles Martin sometimes used as props for his photographs—lined one side of the courtyard. Inside each cell were three or four or more men; some lay pretending to be shackled to bare army cots, or on the yellowing grass. There were more than twenty "slaves," good-looking, muscular men, others slender—all types, all sexual, all naked except for black leather pouches and studded black straps on their wrists and collars; delicate chains would be hooked easily to these. As the invited men studied them, the "slaves" performed exhibitionistically as instructed; they writhed and twisted in invisible restraint. Occasionally one or another of the milling men would recognize one of the slaves as a friend, and a spirited chat would develop.

A large wooden enclosure was filled with thick mud. For a further contribution, men could strip down—or not—and wrestle in the popular "Pig Pen." Muddied flesh writhed in the thick dripping brown ooze.

"Gentlemen!"

In leather chaps, vest, boots, his sweating body spilling in ugly folds that would have barred him from his own club, Martin was calling for attention from the mob of men wandering the sexual area. "Gentlemen! The goal of the fundraiser has already been surpassed!" he announced.

The men cheered.

Martin went on to explain what they all knew—the slaves had volunteered to be "sold" to the highest bidder for an evening of "service" to be determined by the master—*"and the slave,"* he emphasized. If the slave didn't like the person who bid for him, he could protest and be "freed" by someone else's new bid—even if it was less.

The men applauded the democratic consideration.

"It all goes to the fund, of course; and remember," he emphasized again, "it is all make-believe, charade. Take your fantasy only as far as *consent* allows."

Shouts of agreement, a few dissents.

"And now it gives me great pleasure—and a hard-on!—to introduce—although they need no introduction in the gay community—our slavemaster-auctioneers! . . . Buzz Saw!" A huge muscleman walked onto the scaffold wearing only a leather pouch, boots, and heavy oil. Shouts, whistles. "Tim Pierce!" He was tall, sinewy, menacingly sexual, wearing boots, a tangle of gleaming chains on his torso, and tight leather pants that revealed an enormous bulge between his legs. "Eat your heart out, Jimmy Steed!" Martin ad-libbed. More shouts, more whistles. "And Mr. Macho himself—Clint Dave!" Still more shouts, still more whistles. Sustained applause for the three imposing men. "Just gaze upon all these daddy-hunks!" Martin drooled.

Dave's excitement was lanced—sharply.

"Take it off!" screamed one of the men.

"Off! Off!" a chorus chanted.

Martin went on: "Because everyone is contributing his talents to this worthy cause of— . . . of— . . . unity . . . this very worthy cause! Uh, because of that— . . . Our slavemasters will be rewarded by their choice of any of the gorgeous slaves. Whoever has bid for the one they choose will have the option of getting his money back; donating it anyway— . . ."

Boo! Boo! Boo!

". . . —and getting a special *surprise* gift!"

Acquiescing cheers.

"And *I'll* double the original bid prize," Martin got swept away.

"But first! Let's dance! There'll be a prize for the best couple."

On the platform with the others, Dave couldn't believe this shattering of mood would be allowed.

But as soon as the loud music poured from the speakers, the heads of the leathermen begin to dip back and forth in rhythm; now the men danced, churned enthusiastically. Although the small hardcore of "heavy leathermen" takes its rituals very seriously, the larger contingent on its wider periphery can slide in and out of the charade and into campiness, especially when the split is lubricated by liquor. Several of the slaves came out of their cells to join the dance, two with each other. Three judges chosen at random by Martin selected the winning couple.

Summoned to the platform, the two, one in a harness, the other in leather pants, were given $100 gift certificates "donated by several committed gay businesses." In appreciation, the two dancers executed a few winning steps.

"Fred Astaire and Ginger Rogers!" a husky voice shot out.

Hoots fought with concurring sounds.

"We just met on the dance floor," the man in the harness said.

"Whoevuh you are, Ah have always depended on thuh kindness of stranguhs," a voice drawled as Blanche Dubois.

Laughter attacked the boos!

"After all, tomorrow *is* another day!"

The boos surrendered.

A deliberately coarsened voice did Bette doing Tallulah: "Fasten your seatbelts, it's gonna be a bumpy night!"

Laughter and applause won.

The camping stopped when the first two slaves were led up the steps by Buzz Saw. The serious performance had begun. About the courtyard, men slumped into studied poses of contemptuous machismo. Slowly, dramatically, the first two slaves trudged up the steps, pretending to fall, being pulled by thin chains snapped onto their collars, which, like the "wrist shackles," were so loose the men could easily squeeze out of them. On the platform before Tim Pierce, the slaves mimed great agony.

Waiting to one side of the platform—the three auctioneers would take turns—Dave felt a terrific rush at the display of dominant and dominating male flesh! He increased the rush with a deep breath from a brown bottle of amyl. The fantasy was overflowing now, conquering reality. Dave was aware of a heated gathering current, and he was riding it.

"What am I bid for this— . . .?" Tim Pierce slurred. The eager slave groped the slavemaster's engorged groin; the slavemaster thrust him back and spat on him.

"Whip him with your cock!" an aroused voice cried. The bids rose.

The heated current flowed *against* Dave, and then, swelling, it rolled again, flooding the scene and him.

There was an altercation at one of the guarded entrances,

behind the scaffold. Each of the gates was being overseen by
two or three beard-stubbled men. A slightly drunk middle-aged
man in frayed leather was trying to come in. Martin shook his
head emphatically—*No!* Dave went over and said softly, "Oh,
lettim in." The men did. The man staggered into the courtyard.
Martin shot an annoyed look at Dave.

A muted, unwanted echo— . . . It pushed against the resur-
gent current sweeping Dave.

"This slave's got a good fuckin' asshole on him." Buzz Saw
was going through his auctioneering. He slapped the exposed
buttocks. The slave looked at him in flashing anger, the slap red
on his flesh. He slapped back, hard, at Buzz Saw's bare round
buttocks and stalked off the platform. Another body replaced
his. "What am I bid for this hunk of meat?" Buzz Saw was
unperturbed. "This unworthy fucker. Kneel, fuckin'slave!" The
slave bowed his head.

Despite the increasing clutch of the fantasy, the tension snapped
occasionally into laughter. Two slaves didn't like the men who
bought them and chose a lower bidder. Shattering the tension
further, one slave bid for another—"I'm versatile," the husky
voice said, and the sale was made. A "master" among the
guests decided to be a spontaneous "slave" and jumped on the
scaffold to be sold. The slaves were going for about $30,
slightly more; one or two for less.

"Who wants this dirty pig?" the muscular man pulled at a
slave dripping with mud from the pen. The charade grew darker.

Now it was Dave's turn on the platform. He felt pulled by
welcome fire. Immediately he was the best of the auctioneers.
He vaunted "prime stock." He prodded a higher bid by probing
a "slave's" buttocks, arousing the bidders, raising bids. He
"weighed" the balls of one slave in his hand. "Bid by the
pound for this one!" he tantalized. Inspired, the slaves groaned,
cringed, pled. The black pouch of the next slave reached low on
his thigh. Dave pulled the tantalizing pouch off, to auction him
"by the inch." But the pouch had been stuffed. So Dave
whirled the man around, exhibiting his firm ass, forcing him to
bend down "and show your wares." The bent man licked
Dave's boots hungrily. Sexual fire imploded in a series of jolts

inside Dave. Now he whirled in a vortex of new desire, found at last. He pushed the head of the cringing slave against his boots.

The men in the audience swam in those boiling waters. Throughout the courtyard, orders echoed those coming from the block, as spontaneous masters and slaves extended the boundaries of the auctioneering arena.

The next slave was the blond youngman who had called out to Dave in the park, whom he had not followed into the bushes. Not inexperienced at all, then, and at least twenty-one—they all had to be. The youngman dropped to his knees. Then he looked up and whispered. "My name's Chip. Choose me as your slave, Mr. Macho."

The audience applauded the groveling slave. More heads disappeared between planted boots about the patio.

"Thirty-five dollars!" Dave spat in disgust at the bid. "Just *look*." He squeezed Chip's pouch, no stuffing. "Forty dollars? Only forty dollars for *this*?" He lowered the pouch for just an instant. Now he cupped the mounds of ass. The bids rose. *"Sixty* dollars Just *this* is worth that!" He pinched the youngman's nipples. "Seventy measly dollars! Show 'em what you can do!" he commanded. The youngman's tongue traveled up and down Dave's boots, crotch. "Lick!" Dave ordered. He was in it, really in the world that beckoned; he was learning to swim in the most turbulent ocean—and to do so expertly. The bunching disturbance of the past few days untangled. He held the licking head down. The bids soared. Eighty dollars, eighty-five, ninety, ninety-five.

"One hundred dollars!"

"Sold!" Martin stopped the bidding, which he would have to double if one of the auctioneers chose this slave—and it was very likely!

The man who bought Chip was dark, brooding, good-looking, young, masculine. Dave felt apprehensive about that.

The auction was over. A huge success!

The slavemasters would now choose their slaves. The muscular auctioneer chose a muscular slave, and they kissed; the sinister auctioneer chose a sinister slave. Dave chose Chip.

Chip rushed over and knelt at his feet.

But the original bidding "master" disagreed; he began pulling at Chip's loose-chained collar. Chip shoved the hand away. Martin said firmly to the dark young master, "Now don't be a *sore loser*." The dark youngman said, "Fuck you!" He and Dave faced each other.

Martin said firmly to the dark youngman, "I will *not* have roughhousing, this is a *peaceful* party, you want your money back?" The handsome man said yes, got it, and without waiting for his "special surprise" stamped out.

The patio turned into a mass of bodies.

"You had enough of this shit?" Chip asked Dave. "Of course, you're the master, but, me, I'm ready to have a private party; why don't we go to my place?"

Chip's apartment was two pretty rooms in the Hollywood Hills. The walls were plastered with posters from *A Chorus Line, Evita,* and *The Pirates of Penzance*.

"I'm going to be a dancer," Chip said. "I've already done a TV special—in the chorus, but featured." Naked, he spun about and landed at Dave's feet. He stood up. "Wanna drink?"

"Yeah," Dave said.

Chip brought the drink. Wine and Seven-Up. "I know it's crazy, but I like it. Want me to worship you?"

"For a start," Dave lowered his voice. He began pulling at his own cock.

Chip pushed his hands away. "I'll take care of that, master. Order me!"

Dave spread his legs assertively.

"Want some *real* amyl poppers? That shit at the auction—ugh!"

"Yeah," Dave welcomed.

Chip popped the amyl ampule, held it to Dave to snort, snorted it himself, and put it carefully into a silver container like a bullet; he placed several other of the small yellow ampules, like ready bullets, nearby. The pulsing chemical fumes enclosed everything in sex. Dave reached for the mounds of Chip's ass.

"Slap it, master," Chip said.

Dave slapped it—cautiously. On display on the platform, his actions had come easy, as if rehearsed for long. Now it was like starting out again, although the same excitement clenched.

"Harder!" Chip said. "Like this." He slapped himself fiercely. "And talk real tough and dirty, okay? Wanna start?"

"Suck my cock!"

"It's too soon for that," Chip said. "Gotta work up to it."
He threw himself on the floor and lapped at Dave's boots with
his tongue. "Tell me to lick your boots and do-it-good-slave."

"Do it *real* good!" Here Dave couldn't bring himself to call
this youngman "slave."

"Tell me what I'm doing, huh? I wanna hear it real dirty."

"You're licking my boots."

"Yeah—lickin' your fuckin' dirty boots!" The tongue pulled
in and out.

Dave lowered his chaps. Under the jockstrap, his cock was
anxious.

"Now tell me to lick your filthy jockstrap," Chip said. But
he didn't wait. He licked until the jockstrap was moist under
Dave's balls. Each time Dave reached to bring his cock out,
Chip would push it back in, pulling with his mouth at the strap.
Then he slid between Dave's legs.

Dave felt the dabbing tongue.

"Talk tough! Mean!" Chip swallowed Dave's cock. Dave
leaned back, groaning. Chip leaned away, too. He popped
another ampule, didn't bother with the silver container. He
breathed deeply from it—giving it to Dave to do the same.

"What all do you like?" he asked Dave.

"What?" Dave said. The amyl pulsed into his groin. He
removed the chaps.

Chip looked at him wistfully. "I mean, you wanna tie me up
and whip me?" he asked. "I got some whips. Or use your belt,
huh?"

Dave thought, Yes! But— . . .

Chip shrugged at the indecision, knelt again. "Say, 'Spit-
shine my boots, slave!' "

"Spit-shine— . . ." Dave's voice seemed to come from beyond
him.

"Say it *real* tough, cummon, like this— . . ." Chip dropped
his voice: "Lick my boots, fuckin' filthy slave!"

"Lick my boots, fuckin'— . . ." Dave bent over the arched
body, his hand fingering the blond knotted ass. He lowered
himself to the floor, lowering Chip with him, shifting his own
body to suck the youngman while he sucked him. Chip squirmed

away; Dave pressed his body against his, hugging him, rubbing his cock with his, his mouth about to kiss— . . .

Before Dave's lips could touch Chip's, Chip squeezed away. He reached for the drink of wine and Seven-Up, sipped it, popped another ampule, held it longer to his nose, gave it to Dave, who placed it on the table without breathing from it this time.

"I want to suck you, too," Dave said, "and then fuck you."

"I was in this orgy the other day," Chip said. "Two guys fucked me at the same time, but one had a small dick, so it wasn't such a thrill. I got lots of dildos, you wanna fistfuck me? I can take it to the wrist." He moved away, came back with a can of Crisco and three dildos—different sizes, all big, one huge. "Why don't you put your chaps back on and tie me up and stuff a dildo in my ass and wrap your jockstrap over another dildo and stuff it in my mouth and slap me with the other, and then you can fistfuck me."

"I want my *cock* up your ass," Dave said. He heard his own voice again. He looked at Chip's angel face. Blue, long-lashed eyes.

Chip said, "Ah, cummon, man, tell me to drink your piss." He began to slide from Dave's embrace. "And call me a dirty quee— . . ."

Dave choked the word by pulling the blond body up and pushing his mouth against the youngman's lips, kissing the unresponsive mouth. Chip wrenched away.

He bent over, offering his ass. "Go ahead and fuck me, then," he said.

In frustration and confused anger, Dave pushed his cock into the waiting hole.

Chip's voice moaned. "Fistfuck me, master, cummon, master, push your fist up my ass, Mr. Macho, shove it all the way to your elbow, fuck me with a dildo, Macho Man, then shove your fist in!" He ground his ass.

Dave reached under for Chip's cock. It was soft. But Chip's growling continued. "Yeah, yeah, cummon, master, be mean, push your . . . !"

Dave pulled out his cock, softening, not coming. Soft.

Chip turned and looked at Dave's cock as if it were a wasted offering.

"Can't come, huh?" Chip said. He popped another ampule of amyl. "I guess I'll come."

"How do you want to— . . .?" Dave started, trying to order the rebelling emotions, contain them until he could understand, try to understand them.

Chip knelt on all fours, reached for the largest dildo, closed his eyes, and shoved the dildo into his ass. He said to no one, "Yeah! Punish me hard for being dirty and licking your filthy boots and eating you out; punish me hard, use that fucking belt on my ass, shove your fuckin' fist in, cummon, be mean!" He tried to push the dildo more deeply inside himself, but it was buried to its fullest length. Coming, he yelled, *"Punish me for being a fucking queer, Daddy!"*

Please don't punish me, Daddy! Dave thought he heard a buried voice scream that out of his own drowned past—or was it just the echo of Chip's? Dave sat on the couch.

Chip removed the dildo, sipped the "crazy" drink. "You know," he said, "us kids are really lucky. I mean, when you were my age—I just turned, twenty-one, ugh, but I look younger, don't I? I *know* I do—you think I look eighteen?—I *know* I do—when you were my age, I bet you wouldn't do the things I did. I mean, liberated things and stuff."

He sat down, legs tucked under him. "Being a slave at the auction—that was a rush. You played the auctioneer real good, too—just an act, huh? You couldn't really get into it for real, could you? Actually, you don't *act* like your photographs." He shook the glass in his hand, dissolving the ice. "I guess all you guys did was fuck and suck. And kiss, huh? You still like to kiss, don't you? Yeah, I noticed." He sucked a piece of ice into his mouth. Then he spat it out. "Cold," he said. "The ice is sure cold."

Dave felt a deepening confusion, a growing fatigue, a sense of betrayal—cheated by a world he had helped to create and which he was not sure he understood anymore, knew only that it was now preparing—indifferently—to shut him out, discard him.

Lost Angels: 5

"What are you going to tell her?" Jesse dared boldly.

"I'll just tell her— . . . I'll tell her: I am here."

Orin's words pulled at Lisa. They were the same words he had reacted to the other day when she had spoken them. She stopped stroking Pearl. Had he spoken them just now in threat aimed at Sister Woman? No, Lisa was sure, when he went on easily, "I'll just tell her that I'm here. She already knows the old woman is dead."

His words evoked the figure banished since that early day of Jesse's clumsy question about the Cadillac. An old, old woman, dead. And Sister Woman. Lisa felt touched by two invisible presences.

"And now it's all up to Sister Woman," Orin answered Jesse James's question. He spoke in that soft, calm voice of his—as if all this should have been obvious. But he removed his hand from the telephone.

The sound was still off on the television screen. Sister Woman's gliding, slashing hands spoke their own language. Then they were dormant on her lap, and she bowed her head. The blue chiffon expired, released by her breeze like an exorcised spirit.

Lisa stood—leaving Pearl open-eyed against the pillow—and faced the screen. Until now, she had tried to ignore the woman behind the glassy unreality of the television.

Now on the screen appeared the unfurled flag of the country, waving in a strong wind, as if the gentle breeze that stroked Sister Woman and her veily robes throughout her sermons lost its control without her. Burning in white light, the luminous cross appeared.

Jesse longed to question Orin further. The old woman— . . .?

But he had shot out his question about what Orin intended to tell Sister Woman and Orin had answered, and now Jesse felt only relief that his words had not unleashed Orin's fury, angered probing of him. And it was clear from Orin's set lips that he would say nothing further now.

Orin turned off the television and went into the bathroom.

Lisa returned to Pearl. "Don't grow up," she told the doll, "stay pretty so I can!" She felt Jesse looking at her; she laughed softly, erasing the strange words. Jesse's look continued on her. She met it. Both looked at the closed door of the bathroom.

When Jesse heard the shower running, he stood over Lisa, looking down into her breasts over the loose opening of her nightclothes. He saw the nipples—no, just the pink outline of the nipples. He assured himself the shower was still running. He sat next to Lisa. With one long finger he touched one nipple. It hardened. Lisa closed her eyes. Jesse cupped her breast. The spraying of the shower stopped.

Jesse withdrew his hand and stood up. Sliding under the sheets, Lisa grabbed Pearl. When Orin came out of the shower, Jesse marched past him, feeling rage as he closed the door of the bathroom behind him. Orin stared at the locked door, and then his gaze grabbed at Lisa. Her eyes were closed; her breasts rose up and down, up and down under the light cover of the sheet as she breathed nervously.

In the morning, again Orin was gone when Jesse woke. But this time he felt no apprehension, just a surrendered relief— Orin had gone to pay for that day's full rent. Lisa was still asleep. Jesse took his turn in the bathroom. When he came out, Orin was back; his sly smile confirmed what Jesse had conjectured about the rent. It was now difficult to know when he expected them to pay their share, or a portion; he would indicate that simply by placing his money on a counter, a table, wherever—and pull back, waiting for them to respond. They did.

"Guess where we're going today, Jesse?" Orin asked.

Lisa looked down at Pearl Chavez. Bring her along today or let her stay?

An hour later—after breakfast, which they split equally—they stood on the white terrace outlining the Griffith Park Observatory and looked down into the acres and acres of trees, coves, brush, craggy rocks jutting up intermittently—a piny forest and a palm-treed jungle; caves, cliffs, escarpments.

Indeed the park is so vast that, years ago, a hermit was discovered to have been living there for what was variously claimed to be several months, a year, more—unseen by anyone. He lived in one of the hundreds of coves created by intertwined branches overhanging sudden hollows and covered over with fresh leaves each new season. He kept his few belongings there. At night, when certain sections of the park close—the upper levels at sundown, the lower ones when night blackens—he would scavenge for food left by picnickers. He knew where water was to be had, from which of the network of pipes that water the park he could drink; he learned which berries to eat. When he was finally "captured," a newspaper photographer caught a messianic-looking man staring in shock at the camera. Behind him, on a small elevation of green, stood a terrified deer. The man was committed to a mental institution.

The size of a small city, the park rises in many hills, cut into by countless trails that connect, split up, crawl through cluttered brush, emerge out of overhanging trees, which at twilight turn ashen green.

During the season of heat and wind, the park is vulnerable to fire. Old scars are covered over by indomitable new growth, new wild grass, wildflowers; recent scars are blackened with ashes and the broken dead limbs of charred trees, creating a surreal cemetery. Especially during the Santa Ana winds, the upper portions of the park are blocked, but only to vehicles, not to the intrepid hikers and sexhunters.

On the crest of a hill is the Griffith Park Observatory. Surrounding an obelisk like a tall needle are life-size statues of six scientists who studied planets and stars. Their hands are held in the attitude of hopeful prayer. Flanked by rows of ever-present oleander and paths that burrow into green depths is a carefully pampered lawn of grass bordered by walks leading up white steps toward the wide-stretching facade of what looks like an Egyptian temple topped with a green dome. Inside, the dome becomes a seemingly depthless sphere on which the sky, stars, planets—even stars in collision—are reproduced several times daily by intricate lenses, prisms, lights contained in a huge dark metallic globe that rotates on the floor in the midst of rows and rows of comfortable seats for the spectators to witness the heavenly configurations.

Beyond acres of descending green, and beyond the scattered orangey roofs of houses, from the back of the Observatory, Los Angeles looks like a scrambled jigsaw puzzle out of which distant buildings emerge—and the city fans out for miles and miles and miles until it connects with the ocean.

The day was hot. A pacifying stillness had replaced the sporadic thrusts of wind; a stillness that might as easily announce the death of this Santa Ana season as a mere stasis before greater fury. A "Santa Ana" is a wind that gathers heat as it blows across the sun-soaked deserts, a wind like no other. It can just stop, instantly; severed from its invisible source, it dies, a corpse of heat. Or dredging up its own violence, it can push again, seemingly out of nowhere.

Orin had led them expertly across the lawn of the Observatory, up its outside steps, and to the back terrace of the domed building. Telescopes, set into operation by a few coins, line the rounded wall. Orin dropped coins into one of the telescopes. He swiveled it in a full arc of the park, then pointed it at a mass of gathered green, far away, in the park's deepness. He adjusted the telescope, held it, held it.

What is he always looking at?—*for*? Jesse wondered.

Abruptly abandoning the telescope, Orin faced Jesse's stare.

Jesse looked down at his boots and marched a few steps. "I bet this is the exact spot where ole James Dean got killed in that movie." Jesse lowered his booted foot assertively on one exact spot. "Here!"

Tourists looked down earnestly at the designated place.

"I don't think it was James Dean who got killed," Lisa tried to remember; that movie wasn't one of her "all-times," although it had been shown with one that definitely was—*The Grapes of Wrath*: Ma Joad so loyal, so strong—and nobody seemed to know that *she* was the strongest one. "I think it was the other boy." She leaned over the concrete ledge. Below was another semicircular tier—and skinny yellow flowers fluttering next to pale blue ones like tiny stars! And a willow tree! A real willow tree—just next to all those oleanders! She looked over toward Orin and Jesse and said, "You know, they're poisonous, oleanders; that's how they all got killed in *Dragonwyck*. Gene Tierney." The thought of the exotic beauty made Lisa suck her cheeks in imitation of the doomed star. *Leave Her to Heaven*, the— . . . She didn't let herself think about what she did in that one. Lisa had loved the movie about the jealous woman who loved intensely, but it bewildered her.

Tourists wandered all about, leaning over, peering down, poking each other, putting coins in the telescopes which destroy distance, clicking cameras, "ahhing" at everything.

Bang! Bang!

"Sniper!"

"Oh, my God!"

People screamed, scrambled, some threw themselves on the concrete ledges.

Lisa crouched. Jesse began to; but when he saw that Orin did not budge, he straightened up, and felt a seizing excitement. Orin stared away into the park, toward where he had pointed the telescope.

Bang!

A figure jumped off a lower ledge.

BANG! Bang! Bang! Close, then more distant reports.

Someone laughed, then someone else did, too.

"Just popping firecrackers!" The teenage boy who had screamed *"Sniper!"* roared with laughter at his friend thrust out another popping firecracker into the distance and then, smirking, ran around the base of the Observatory, back up the path to the walk. Almost everybody laughed in relief. One old man cursed the pranksters: "Nasty bastids!" The teenagers ran off, shoving upraised middle fingers behind them.

Just like Orin to remain so cool, Jesse admired. Look at him still staring ahead as if in those moments of simulated shots and real pandemonium, the greenness would reveal something to him—*only* to him. Jesse's eyes followed the direction of Orin's gaze—down, beyond, toward a mass of trees behind large craggy rocks. It looked like a jungle down there.

An exuberant, hefty woman nearby said, "Well, that's what *I* call a good scare!"

"*Are* we going to see the stars in the Planetarium?" Lisa asked Orin impatiently. She hadn't enjoyed the incident.

"Not today," Orin said. "See more of the park."

"Okay—if you promise me the moon," Lisa said, evoking Bette Davis in *Now, Voyager*; she had wanted the stars *and* the moon, and that man who claimed to love her told her that was too much to ask for!

When they reached the moody car, Lisa was surprised to realize she hadn't left Pearl there, as she had thought; she'd left her in the motel. She felt guilty.

Three teenagers hovered admiringly about the Cadillac. Jesse strutted to the driver's side; he was glad Orin waited till the kids walked away before *he* got in the driver's seat.

Before they felt it brushing against them, they heard the urgent murmur of the rising wind swirling through dark trees. At first only a few trees shook, their branches attempting to thrust the wind away. Then it pounced more angrily—and on others. Soon every green thing was set into urgent motion.

They left the top of the car up as they drove through a tunnel. It enclosed them in a startling darkness after the yellow heat of the park; and then they drove up, past pools of wild orange and blue flowers and hills deserted at times by any verdure, at times forested. Orin braked the car by a patch of gray decay, leafless dead twigs and branches, dead vines like disintegrating brown lace; dying trees. Against this, the wind had shoved brown leaves, tinged desperate purple. Orin fixed his gaze on the dead area.

"It's ugly!" Lisa's words jolted.

Orin drove on, leaving behind the patch where decay had gnawed outward.

Off a sandy indention, he parked. A gathering of rocks rose beyond the shrubby trees. They got out of the car, into swirling hot air. Orin found a slender path, and Jesse and Lisa followed. This was not the spot Orin had pointed to earlier; they were now on the opposite side of the park. They had to stoop low to make their way past greedy branches. Orin would hold one up for Lisa to squirm past. Jess had to bend very low. They walked into an enclosed cove. They were like exploring children discovering secret places. The sun stabbed through in golden shafts here, creating a magical enclosure. The piny odor was thick, sweet. Twigs had formed a shelter like a dome, the green at their feet was soft. They stood within the high leafy hollow. Tiny red berries spattered red dots on the branches of a vine.

"I hope there're no snakes," Lisa said in a child's voice.

"Too shady," Jesse tried to sound knowledgable. "Snakes lay in the sun."

"Snakes thrive in the white darkness or in the dark sun," Orin said. Then he laughed.

Because of that, "Where'd you learn to talk so crazy, Orin?" Jesse ventured, but lightly, making sure he could retrench during what seemed an allowed moment.

Orin chose to answer, in that easy way. "Used to read to her, tell her stories—when she was almost blind. But she heard things, 'saw' things—in her way."

The woman who had willed him the beautiful car—and what else? Jesse waited for Orin to go on, but he didn't.

Lisa was glad to pull away from the disturbing words. She bent to gather some long stems with soft buds on them. This might be heather, she thought, like on the moors in *Wuthering Heights*. She looked through an aperture of branches and saw the craggy rocks. "You think Heathcliff and Cathy finally found peace in heaven?"

"Hell's easier to get into," Jesse laughed.

A twig severed a blade of sun and cast a shadow like a brutal scar across Orin's face. A swirl of wind entered the cove and rushed out, leaving silence. The shadow shifted with the scurrying wind. Now it slashed darkly across Orin's deepening eyes. He looked angry, or sad. The shadow moved again, clearing his face of all expression. Then a glance of light from the slanting sun heightened the gold in his hair, and he looked luminous.

This place, so beautiful, so intimate, gathering them tightly—it evoked that naked night in the motel—and this morning's sexual moment for Jesse. What if he just went over now to Lisa and kissed her, drew her to him and kissed her? he wondered defiantly. She looked beautiful leaning against the branch, the blouse lower on one shoulder than the other, holding those stems with the furry buds. If he did go to her that way and Orin protested, whom would she choose?—*if I just went over to her, put my arms around her, and kissed—* . . .

"Then why don't you do just that, Jesse," Orin said—and he left the cove in the direction of the naked rocks.

Jesse's head bolted back. He felt a chill in the heat. Orin had read his thoughts! Fear jabbed. *How?* And then, with flooding relief, he remembered that only seconds earlier he had said hell was easier to get into, and *that's* what Orin meant—a joke; why don't you do just that? Of course. Jesse laughed aloud, shedding the chilly fear.

Lisa walked to Orin, who stood beyond the cove and on the craggy rocks; she held her bouquet of "heather." Then Jesse was there with them. The wind whipped about them, capturing them together.

After moments, they made their way back to the car along a different trail.

Lisa had seen the way Jesse was looking at her, had felt the powerful sexuality; and for moments—until he walked off—she thought it came just as powerfully from Orin.

They drove out of the park, into Franklin Avenue. Palm trees leaned away from the wind. They drove up the residential end of Hollywood Boulevard, up into Laurel Canyon.

"Orin, Jesse—look!" said Lisa. "Oh, too late!" Because other cars were driving so close, neither Orin nor Jesse had been able to see what had excited her.

"I bet she saw one of those movie-star-homes maps for sale," Jesse said; he'd been tempted to buy one himself. Little boys stand along Sunset with placards advertising the maps. Lisa had never commented on that, actually looked away in disdain.

"I wouldn't want one," she said. "Everyone knows you don't see anything but trees . . . Oh, Orin, please, please let's go back," she said dramatically. "It looked like an old *real-*movie-star mansion."

"Yeah, let's," Jesse took easy sides.

Orin turned off the road, to the right. He waited for the flow of traffic on Laurel Canyon Drive to break. Then he made a swift U-turn back to the house Lisa had pointed out. "Drive as slow as you can, it disappears right away," she instructed.

It crowned a hill. Orin made a quick turn into a fan of dirt. They got out and looked up in awe at the exposed portions of the old mansion.

Steps worn away from countless pressing footsteps led to the magnificent house—now the near-corpse of a gray mansion. A white—dirty white—balustrade separated it from a sharp decline, carved by greedy torrents of water rushing down from the upper levels of the canyon, seasonally razed by fire. To the side of the house was a rotunda, overgrown with wild flowers. Intermingling through them, indomitable, were weeds. Only a portion of two more storeys, each retreating farther against the green escarpment, was visible now. At irregular intervals, round balusters had fallen out like gouged teeth.

"What you lookin fer?" a skinny blond boy emerged from a side of the dirt road.

"That house," Orin said.

A thirtyish man, perhaps the boy's father—he had the same dirty blond features—appeared. "You lookin' for an apartment?"

"Might just be," Orin said.

"Might," Jesse concurred.

Lisa knew this was Orin's way of allowing her to see the house; she felt elated—but saddened by the abandoned state it was in. Still, she would get to see it, imagine it as it had been.

"Half of the place is rented units." The man pointed up. "We're movin out. Places hard to find in Los Angeles now; we'd let our apartment go at the same rent—nobody knows the difference—for a consideration."

"What about the rest of the house?" Orin asked.

"Belongs to the old ladies," he man said.

"Twins," the boy said.

"Triplets," the older man corrected.

"Can we see it?" Orin asked.

The man led them up side steps shaded by shaggy trees. At the top, a long semicircular veranda was chopped off by a wall—by what looked like a makeshift barricade: bare bricks piled one on top of the other in odd rows, cement hardly holding them together, paint smeared, white, gray—as if it had been flung against the bricks, paint melting in long fingers.

"Part of this was a guest house, part of it was servants' quarters," the man explained. "The old ladies had to rent cause they run out of money. There's four, maybe five apartments in all; can't tell cause some of 'em's broke into rooms—could be more."

Smoking, a surly girl in Levi cutoffs sat on one of the white marble-vined railings. A shirtless youngman with glasses lolled with her. "You movin' in?" the girl asked.

"Maybe," Jesse went along with Orin.

This was certainly not the part of the house Lisa wanted to see. She looked beyond the makeshift wall; the rest of the mansion was draped in seclusion.

Following her look, the man laughed. "The old ladies made that wall themselves so nobody'd go over."

"Who wantsa?" the little boy said, becoming nastier. "Them's mean bitches."

"Don't worry," the man said to the three, realizing he might talk them out of the deal he would be proposing. "We never see them, don't even pay rent to them—a man collects it."

"You oughtta see 'em," said the boy. "Seen 'em once." He tried to imitate the careful, erect movements of the sisters. Then he broke up laughing.

"Know who owned the house first?" the man tossed. "That king or prince—whatever he was—who married that American woman. Lots of movie stars—old ones from a long time back—lived there or visited a lot."

Lisa held her breath. She just knew it. Just driving by the house, she had sensed its magic spirit.

"The old bitches're twins," the hideous boy said.

"Triplets!" The man reached out to smack him. "I've told you: Two is twins, *three* is triplets—and there's three of 'em!"

Even on this surrendered side of the mansion, there lurked the ghost of grandeur. Crumbling entryways revealed portions of carved figures, eroding. The dark corridors were arced with wooden beams. Fleurs-de-lis were buried under careless coats of thin, chipped paint.

"Here's where we live," the man said. A youngish woman

was cooking on a small electric stove. Along the halls, other desultory forms roamed into the "apartments." They were like gypsies who had invaded a mansion. "We rent these two rooms." Gold filigree—tattered, greased-over—ribboned tall, tall windows. Once they had contained designs formed by myriad panes of colored glass. Now many pieces were broken or missing, some replaced by plastic blocks turning darkish yellow in the sun. Other panes more recently shattered were covered with cardboard among the remaining delicately tinted glass. None of those living within the crumbled elegance of this portion of the house seemed aware of its buried beauty.

"You wanna have it?" said the woman. "Places are hard to find in Lesangeleez. We're going back. Lesangeleez's had it for us. You pay us three months' rent, it's yours."

"No," Orin said shortly. He walked out along the darkened corridors and into the round veranda blocked ahead by the carefully glued bricks. Following, Jesse and Lisa saw him jump the barricade easily, limber as an acrobat.

"Hey, don't, bastard!" the boy shouted.

As Jesse helped Lisa over it and then jumped the wall himself, they heard protests behind them. Then the boy's father said, "Aw, let 'em."

Orin stood on the terrace of the main part of the old mansion. Trees shabby with age and lack of attention crowded about the walls, trees so thick the wind didn't threaten them. No matter what the time of day, they would shelter the house from sunlight, and so there was the atmosphere of stopped twilight. Within it, a murmuring silence collided with the anarchic sounds of cars on the drive below. Extending from white striated paths guarded at intervals by stone lions were circular enclosures, where careful gardens had once been pampered. Now weeds conquered an occasional flower—a brave rose beginning to die before it bloomed fully.

Orin walked along the terrace. A series of three double doors led into the house. One was open. Orin, Lisa, and Jesse James looked into the enormous room. It seemed to have been preserved in mothy dust. The ghosts of drapes, gray through years of neglect, hung mournfully in uneven folds. The once luxuriant furniture was punctured in places, chunks of graying cotton clotting. Crooked chandeliers—protruding wires indicating they no longer worked, pieces of glass missing—did not gleam. A fireplace over which there had been a peacock shaped by blue, green, purple tiles was full of ashes. Twigs that had once been the stems of flowers crumbled at the base of chipped vases. The veil of dust, and the static twilight, turned everything in the room gauzy gray.

Orin walked into this house built by a king or a prince. Lisa and Jesse entered more cautiously.

There was a grand piano. Over it was draped a frayed Spanish mantilla. Many photographs rested on it—the only objects not covered with dust. Their glass panes were shiny, freshly polished. There was a photograph of a man and a woman on separate horses.

"Tyrone Power!" Lisa gasped at the photograph of the dashing movie star. Then she gave it the slightest shove when she remembered what he did to Linda Darnell in *Blood and Sand*. But then she couldn't help run her finger over his thick beautiful eyebrows. She sighed at each photograph. "Garbo! Dietrich!"

Orin stared at the largest of the many photographs. In it, three pretty young girls, identical, smiled at the camera. They wore white lace dresses to their ankles, wide-brimmed lace hats like halos; white fringed sashes gathered the dresses loosely about their waists. Arms about each other, the three were framed against the veranda of the house—gleaming white and surrounded by thriving blossoms, vines, trees. In script that might have been made by the same hand, were inked three names, one under each figure, each name preceded by the flowing word *Love!* "Love!—to Daddy—Rowena." "Love!—to Daddy—Emma. "Love!—to Daddy—Nora."

Jesse and Lisa peered at the picture. Carefully Orin relocated it more centrally on the mantled piano.

A staircase curved up to a balcony which led into deeper shadows, blackness. They heard footsteps, soft, as if the shoes that created them were covered with dust. All three looked up. Halfway down the steps stood an old woman in a white impeccably clean lace dress. A white lace hat framed her silver gray hair. A fringed sash embraced her middle loosely. She looked at the three invaders. Expressionless because it was heavily powdered in layers of whiteness, the face was like a thickened mask.

"Who are you?" It was not the woman on the staircase who had asked that; it was another, higher up, on the darkened balcony. She moved into a lighter shadow. She too was dressed in white lace dress and hat, fringed sash. Her face, too, was chalked.

"Good evening, ma'am," Orin said.

"Who are you?" said the woman on the stairs.

Lisa and Jesse James began to back away.

The woman on the balcony called down, "Did you know that Emma died? There's only Rowena and I now. Did you know that?"

"Yes, ma'am," Orin said gravely, "and we came to pay our deep respects to Miss Emma, and regrets to you both for your great loss."

"Oh. . . . ." The woman on the stairs sighed.

Then the voice of the woman on the balcony came wearily, "Thank you for your concern and courtesy. Yes, she— . . . But she's with *Daddy* now, and— . . ."

"She is," Orin said.

Abruptly, the woman on the balcony took a step forward; she rasped, "Leave us alone. We're not selling this house, not ever—leave us alone."

Orin moved back, joining Lisa and Jesse on the dusty veranda. Ancient leaves scattered as they walked across it. They jumped back over the glued barricade. The dirty-blond boy stood there.

"I tole you—them bitches is *mean*," he said.

"No," Orin said.

They walked down the stairs. In the car Lisa didn't know what she felt. She was thrilled, yes, by the haunting presences of the great stars; but the house had given her the feeling that she had attended a belated funeral.

In the car Orin looked at Jesse and Lisa. "What happens to people—why?"

They drove back to Hollywood, and they ate at a Sizzler Steak House. Each paid for his own. Jesse had gambled and lost; he should have had the hamburger plate instead of the expensive steak.

They drove aimlessly about the city—along blighted streets, nighthunters beginning to prowl, men and women; along dark, sleazy streets with arcades and porno book stores; downtown— where tramps wandered among the towering, new glass buildings. Occasionally Orin would look at his pocket watch. He turned on the radio. The news. Checking Orin's expression, Jesse reached out for the dial; Orin did not disapprove. Jesse found the Western and country station: crushed dreams restored, hearts mended by the power of new loves. Again, Orin checked his watch—and they drove back. The prostitutes on Western Avenue were thick in the hot, black night.

Orin had left the television on in the motel room. The radiating blue light told Jesse what station it was on.

"God's heart breaks, the angels weep," Sister Woman was saying. Her hands opened slowly, releasing nothing. "I had a vision— . . ."

Brother Man said, "You saw the messenger?"

Lisa looked away from Pearl, propped on the bed, and at the woman on the screen. Lisa *really* looked at her for the first time, allowed herself to.

Jesse, too, watched the now-familiar woman. He and Lisa flanked Orin before the screen.

Sister Woman said, "An important messenger has arrived. To burn in the blazing caverns of hell? Or to bathe in the glorious blood of Christ?" She withdrew some of the rage, only some. "Pray for the right choice! Which shall it be?" She cleared an invisible space with the phantasmal gestures. *"Which!"*

Lisa saw Orin's lips move, slowly, forming soft words, words familiar to her now—she could read them on his lips:

I . . . am . . . here.

Threatening Sister Woman? Had she done something to the dead old woman? What was she to— . . .? Lisa blocked her questions.

The grasping hands of the studio congregation reached toward the conspiring forces Sister Woman invoked.

Mrs. Stephen Stephens III: "The Family Unit"

Through a narrow partition in the swinging door that led from the white kitchen through the ecru breakfast room and into the pale gold dining room, Hilde saw Mrs. Stephens touch her temples, the edge of her auburn hair. More nervous than usual, not from the stitches, certainly not—they had come out weeks ago; that wasn't the cause. It was Tessa, her first Sunday dinner since she had "returned."

By moving slightly, Hilde located the dark-haired older daughter. She sat to Mrs. Stephens's right. Mrs. Stephens had instructed Hilde to tell all the help to let the youngwoman know how *fine* she looked, and Hilde had done just that, although nobody could fail to see that Tessa looked like a semiresurrected corpse.

From her limited vantage, Hilde could not see Mark, but he would be sitting next to Tessa and wearing his glasses. Was he? Yes! Hilde saw, when she edged closer to the partition, and farther to the other side. There he was, restless as usual, battling the light salad, and, yes, wearing those thick black-framed glasses which he used only now and then, with no pattern except one: always during Sunday dinner.

Hilde pushed the door just a breath, to locate Linda, next to her father. If she got any darker, she'd be the color of that awful day-maid, Hester! Hilde would have fired her in a minute, but Mrs. Stephens felt guilty about those people—even to the point of driving to God-knows-where-she-lived to pick the black woman up when they required extra help on a Sunday. . . . Linda was wearing a powder blue dress. Good! It was the judge's favorite color and would soothe him.

Barely touching the door, Hilde allowed herself a farther

fraction of vision for a full view of the judge's imposing back. Noticing, as she always did, how erectly he sat, she was inspired to straighten her own back even further. He was savoring—she knew—each crisp bite of chilled lettuce, flavored just exactly right with her own dressing. It was an indulgence that she—and, she felt certain, the judge—lived with, Mrs. Stephens's insistence that the salad be served *first*. Her family was, after all, new, *acquired* wealth, whereas the judge was old, *inherited* wealth.

Already, the judge had had his two before-dinner Dubonnets, Hilde knew, with the pleasurable sense of ritual having been restored. She had often made a point of being near the room, preferably *in* the room, when the judge would point out to new visitors that two Dubonnets had been *his* custom long before "that Rockefeller feller"—that brought appreciative laughter and, always, a smile from Hilde—had learned it, from *him*. Mrs. Stephens drank bourbon, like her Texas father, after whom she had been named—a loud, vulgar man with a flushed face; Hilde had overheard him refer to her as an "imported servant." And he called cornichons "sour pickles"!

Hilde moved to the right of the partition and saw Linda lean slightly—sway—toward the judge. She had a way of doing that throughout dinner. Then the judge's posture would yield, for a second, just a second, in fond acknowledgment of his younger daughter.

Through as wide an opening as she ever allowed herself, Hilde saw the judge place his salad fork, tongs down, on his plate. He did that soundlessly, and he leaned back. Across from him, Mrs. Stephens did the same, except that *her* fork created a slightly unpleasant tinkle. Without having to see him do it, Hilde knew the judge blinked at the unwelcome sound.

Hilde whirled around to the white maid sitting on a chair at a small table and waiting to be summoned. Hilde made a signaling sound, like a hiss, and the maid rose, smoothed her uniform, and marched invisibly as she had been instructed to do from the white kitchen, through the ecru breakfast room, and into the grand dining room to gather the salad plates.

When the door swung widely, Hilde stood there for a full view of the Stephen Stephens III family seated in the magnificent pale gold dining room and about to enjoy her superb Sunday dinner. Mrs. Stephens, Tessa, and Mark on one side, the judge and Linda on the other. A bottle of Pinot Chardonnay commanded the table, for now. *Everything was in order!* The serving maid entered.

At the sight of the maid's subdued presence, Mrs. Stephens touched her face, Tessa gathered her hands on her lap and looked at them, Mark pushed his glasses closer to his eyes, Linda leaned away from the judge, and the judge sat upright as if in the presence of an undeclared enemy.

Now! Hilde moved her large, solid body into the white kitchen and faced the prepared ingredients for this Sunday's special dinner. Prepare all of Tessa's favorite foods, Mrs. Stephens had instructed her at least five times; and the judge had nodded, once, in assent.

Stroganoff! Superb! In the grand tradition! And *not* served on rice—as Mrs. Stephens might have wanted but never said so— but on golden noodles.

Before her, already flavored with exact measures of paprika, ground pepper, and salt, the julienne strips of prime filet mignon awaited transformation. A creamy cloud of sour cream was ready. The one deference Hilde made to the ordinary—to Mrs. Stephens, of course—was the addition of . . . mushrooms! That would have been barbaric had it not been that she used only two and diced them almost out of existence before she sautéed them in butter with the chopped onions, *their* flavor further asserted by the dry white wine. On another plate, aloofly alone, the skinny slivers of cornichons, those little imported delicacies that brought a delectable shock to the creaminess, were ready.

When the butter in the pan released just the hint of a hot sigh, Hilde fed it the red pieces of meat. They sizzled, turned lightly brown, just a degree darker. With an expert movement of her hefty wrist, she bounced the heavy skillet, and the strips of meat responded to her unspoken command and turned over on their uncooked side to assume the same shade of brown all over. With a silver slotted spoon, Hilde fished out the pieces and allowed them to rest, briefly, on a separate, warmed plate. Now the onions, wilted quickly—and the detested mushrooms for

Mrs. Stephens! In the skillet the white wine released an unmistakable aroma, altered into another just as delectable by the addition of the sour cream, which mustn't curdle, just be heated enough to rewarm the strips of the filet, returned to the skillet.

Now the cornichons! Hilde slid the green moist slivers into the tanned creaminess. They floated proudly in the sauce. The aroma would filter into the dining room like an announcement of perfection. The judge's nostrils would sniff just barely to accept her culinary bouquet sent from the sheet-white kitchen, through the ecru breakfast room, and into the faded-gold dining room crowned with a chandelier of cut crystal.

The judge received the bouquet, and leaned back just a tilt, savoring it deliciously. Not even Perino's Restaurant, where *he* had lunch, could boast the excellence of Hilde's stroganoff. She was a superior woman, his housekeeper, brought here from Europe by his father while on a tour. Hilde was one of the few people the judge respected, and trusted. Of course, they hardly ever spoke, but their silence contained total understanding. Iron-gray hair trimmed weekly, dressed in a subdued-toned suit that rejected wrinkles, his tie centered exactly, the judge faced his family. Intact!

Oh, would Hilde remember the mushrooms? Alana Stephens wondered. She was trying, unsuccessfully, to keep her hands from her temples. The incisions had healed more easily this time. But did she look better than, or even as good as, after her first face-lift? She had been horrified to see Margaret Manfred at Chez Toi; *her* face looked as if her features had been erased and painted on.

Stroganoff, Tessa knew. She had not eaten meat in weeks. Stroganoff. Her favorite, everyone kept saying. *Was* it her favorite? Or had she just once claimed it was, to please her father? If it had ever been her favorite, was it, still? A twist of nausea alerted her to the possibility of change.

The fucking sour pickles, Mark thought.

Linda smelled the stroganoff and wished, just for once, it would be served on rice. Later tonight she would have a hamburger on her way to the West-Sky. Would they let her in after what happened the other night?

Accidentally, Alana's foot touched her older daughter's. Tessa winced. In panic—knowing this would annoy the judge but having to do it—Alana pretended to drop her napkin. She bent for it—saw Tessa's hands knotted into hard fists—but saw also what she dreaded: Tessa was barefoot. Rising, Alana faced her trim husband and smiled. She felt the skin pull inordinately. Were the smile lines gone? Please no!

The maid appeared with the noodles, and they served themselves, the judge with a flourish. After all, this was all, all his, his creation—everything was an extension of him, yes.

Now the maid was coming around with the asparagus tips. The judge could not believe it: The sauce was thick! No. The light swimming in from the distant pool had created the illusion of thickness. He smiled inwardly at his momentary accusation of Hilde; he felt—somehow—she would be sharing this moment of doubt—doubt turned into triumph—with him.

As long as it clearly established another well founded tradition, the judge could—might—accept the breaking of one. There were, of course, several contingencies, the main one being that it be broken in an orderly way, and to bring about tighter order. Hilde had done that by asserting that it be she who would serve the main course when it was a specialty. Her heavy but solid and firm body would appear, affirming her silent presence loudly. She would hold a platter, a dish, firmly, as if it were a gift to be released only to its qualified recipient. When she served, she did not bow; she just leaned—like Linda. The judge would nod in acknowledgment when she stood at his side.

Mrs. Stephens was served first. Hilde knew she would look for the mushrooms, perhaps even shoot her a subtle reprimand; so Hilde stared straight ahead. Then she moved to Tessa's side. Glancing down, she saw the girl trying to avoid the meat. Hilde thrust a warning look at the judge; the judge intercepted it and its meaning and fixed his eyes on Tessa. Feeling the onslaught of the collected stare, Tessa lumped pieces of meat on her plate.

Now Linda. Hardly any noodles on her plate! Hilde dismissed any possible implication of insult: The girl was always watching her figure. And now Mark—certainly he hadn't deliberately spattered the sauce when he placed the serving utensil back; she actually had had to retreat slightly. And *now* the judge! Hilde gave the plate a slight shake, to expose the cornichons prominently. The judge served himself, asserting the abundant presence of the green slivers. Satisfied, he made his usual slight nod toward Hilde. She returned it just as slightly.

Hilde marched out, having left her profligate gifts.

The judge felt a hearty appetite grow at the spectacle on his plate—golden noodles, tanned stroganoff, bright asparagus tips. He looked at Tessa, demanding to read appreciation on her face. Tessa's lips pulled at the edges as if she were practicing to shape a smile. To the judge, it seemed that she was leering. He looked away, glancing at Linda, wearing blue, light blue. Soon conversation would begin.

Instead, the telephone rang. Alana Stephens's heart skipped. Not possible. He was brazen, and she loved his daring, but he couldn't be *that* daring. Somewhere in the house, the phone was answered. The judge had instructed that only calls that came to him on a special line were to be conveyed at Sunday dinner. All other calls were written and then given later to the recipient. Otherwise, Sunday dinner was never to be interrupted.

The judge felt particularly satisfied today. On so many levels he had done *right*. With his daughter, and in court. Yes, the man deserved to die. The judge had cast the deciding vote, had written the majority opinion: "Motive was not ameliorative. Crime defined itself. Crime *is* cruel and unusual, not its punishment; punishment is an assertion of order against anarchy." In that opinion, and often in others, the judge quoted his grandfather; that great-man's opinions filtered down, intact, through Judge Stephens, to soothe our troubled times. From his symbolic perch on the highest court of the state, Judge Stephens had read his opinion. One more step and he would be appointed—
. . . Yes, one more step and he would have what he wanted more than anything else in his life except perhaps— . . .

That damned art piece of Alana's! His eyes had drifted involuntarily, as they often did, toward it in the room beyond. Framed in silver, the white canvas surrounded a plastic half-sphere filled with floating mercury. Within the enclosure, the mercury would form different dripping patterns. When a certain concentration occurred, the circle turned, to create new twisted shapes. It was like a Rorschach print, a silver Rorschach, melting—and its disordered unpredictability set the judge on edge.

Enough! He savored the first bite of stroganoff. Ah, the exquisite texture of the sauce, the inspired touch of the cornichons! He glanced at Alana, to keep his eyes from moving toward the mercury "art"-piece. Was she still sulking about his ruling? He didn't mind. She was harmless in her flagrant liberalism. He even encouraged her charity events, and her lunches at that vulgar Chez Toi. Harmless. His friends on the bench treated all that with proper deference—they had wives, too! Harmless. Her attitudes, breathlessly expressed, had lent a welcome touch to a good story about him in *Los Angeles* magazine. The article said he allowed her "activism," listing her various causes and charities—and the classes she attended; she was always taking classes at the university. Harmless. That had all made him seem wiser, tolerant of human foibles.

Next time, she would insist—demand—that Hilde put more mushrooms and fewer cornichons in the stroganoff, Alana Stephens promised herself. The dish had a harsh taste. And the wine was too dry; she liked it fruitier. That, of course, was the judge's choice. And look at him—so proud because he had had his way, always, always.

Tessa licked around the piece of filet. She had *always* despised stroganoff, she knew now. A piece of the meat punctured by the fork, she lowered it to her plate. It made a sound much louder than she intended, because she felt all eyes on her—but mainly her father's. She looked at him, and his stare was forcing her to eat the meat. She raised the fork again. Before it reached her mouth, she saw it—stripped, tanned, dark-tanned. Like Linda. She gobbled the piece of meat and swallowed it.

Leaning toward the judge, Linda looked at her sister. Why did she have to come back? She poked at the stroganoff, searching for mushrooms, separating the noodles. Tessa's favorite dish, ugh.

Mark pushed down his anger with the creamy sauce and filet. Tessa's fork rested on her plate again. He studied his sister. He felt guilty. But what could he have done? What he did: stand by, watch, not protest.

The long windows in the dining room had been left bare to allow the perfect garden to "enter," and it did, with enormous roses in a harmony of colors, including a rare bud Alana cultivated, caring for it herself. It was a pale, pale lavender rose that defined its color only at the edges of the extravagant leaves. It was a work of beauty, and she felt she had created it.

Alana could have good taste, the judge would allow, but not always. Some of the modern art works she acquired—like the despised mercury piece and other swirling, coiled things—were monstrous. He had, however, adjusted to the pool. It still ruined the elegant old house from a certain angle, he constantly noticed, although it had been added years ago; it clashed with the classic architecture of the house. But there was one compensation: Linda loved it. During a particularly difficult review of a case, he would even walk to the window, knowing she was lying there enjoying the sun, tanning more deeply, her hair streaking blonder. He would wait at the window until she would "feel" his eyes—though sometimes he encouraged that awareness by making an accidental noise—and then she would look up, slide her sunglasses off her eyes, and stretch her long arm toward him in greeting. She was the only one of his "children" who had never distressed him. He had always known she would be like him.

Linda leaned one golden shoulder toward her father. The tip of a smile touched one side of his lips. He was aware of Tessa's dark eyes. He had pulled them to him. He had won.

Mark saw the knotted stare between the judge and his sister. She looked like a depleted Cassandra, all visions of doom erased, or just blurred. He touched her on the arm, to break the powerful stare.

"Tessa! How do you like the stroganoff?" the judge asked the girl. "It's your favorite."

She swallowed another piece of meat. She almost choked on it, coughed. Alana held a glass of water to her. Mark was about to get up, to help her, when the coughing stopped. "My favorite," she said. "Thank you, father." She forced another piece of tanned meat into her mouth so he could see her.

"It's our way of welcoming you back into the family unit," the judge pronounced.

"Yes, yes," Alana Stephens said eagerly. "We should have a toast." She reached for her glass, began to raise it, but nobody followed. She sipped from the glass. At the end of the meal would there be a telephone message for her—and, if so, and it was from Rob, how would he phrase it?''

Mark let his knife fall heavily on the plate, knowing his father reacted to sounds as if to an attack. The judge stared directly at his son for the first time since they had sat down to dinner.

Wearing those glasses he doesn't need! How dare he make that noise at the dinner table? Strange boy—not in the family tradition. No, not *yet*. But he was young—eighteen?

"And your car?" the judge asked Tessa. "How do you like your new car?''

"Her new *red* car," Alana Stephens encouraged.

The car was parked where they had shown it to her the day she came back. Tessa reached into a pocket of her skirt and brought out two keys, a metallic keyholder. She held them out, acknowledging the gift. "Thank you, father, mother." She remained holding the keys suspended over her plate. "I intend to drive it— . . .''

"That's what it's for," the judge barked.

". . . —very soon," Tessa finished.

"Well, it's a beautiful day for a drive," Linda encouraged her sister to leave.

"Did you enjoy the day?" the judge asked his younger daughter. "You can't get any more tanned, my goodness.''

"Give me sun every day any time, Dad," Linda said.

"Yes," the judge said.

"Mark went to a fascinating lecture yesterday at school—the day before?" Alana introduced conversation. "Didn't you, Mark?''

"What was it on?" the judge asked dourly, knowing he would disapprove.

"It was postponed.''

"What's the lecture *on*?" the judge demanded.

"On nothing," Mark said.

The judge controlled a wince.

"How fascinating," said Alana. If there was a call, how could she get away tonight? It was Sunday—and evening—so she couldn't be at the psychiatrist's, or at a charity, not at luncheon at Chez Toi— . . . Chez Toi! Jimmy Steed at Chez

Toi. Such a vulgar man, and he had stared at her so openly. Still, she felt a wave of warmth at the incongruous memory. . . . Her eyes floated in an arc, from Tessa, to Mark, Linda. She felt a plunging desolation. She turned around, searching out her lavender-tinged roses, but she couldn't see them from here. She faced the table. She brought her napkin lightly to her eyes, feeling the origin of tears. But there were none. Why? Why should there be tears? But why were there none?

"Tessa, eat!" the judge ordered. "You're so thin, thinner than ever, look at Linda."

"I am eating," Tessa said. She dropped the car keys, and picked them up, held them up, put them on the table beside her plate. She realized she wasn't wearing shoes. She froze. She would have to remain at the table until everyone left, except Mark; she had to whisper to Mark to bring her her shoes, which she had left— . . . Where?

So spooky, Linda thought. The other day she'd actually felt a chill when she had removed her sunglasses and turned to see her standing there staring at her, just standing there barefoot. True, she was already a little nervous from the night before. She'd taken off her top, and the fucking redneck bouncer or guard or whatever he was who had wanted to ball her, dragged her out and— . . .

The world has to be put back in order, the judge thought, looking at his older daughter. And that was what he had done, for her own good, and for his world. *The* world. Soon she would be as she had always been—highly intelligent, perhaps too sensitive and— . . . yes, moody; she had always been moody, but she would not be— . . . not be— . . . He was looking at the dripping silver mercury! He would have Alana move it into her bedroom. But, he realized quickly, her bedroom adjoined his, and then he would have to be aware, when he woke at night, that it was in the next room—dripping, dripping, changing from ugly shape to uglier shape. He looked at Tessa again. He had won over *them!*

"Is he going to die?" Mark's words severed the judge's relentless stare on Tessa.

"Oh!" Alana's hands shot to her temples.

"The black man," Mark said softly.

"Yes!" The judge pronounced sentence again.

"There's going to be a protest," Mark said. "And I'm going."

"If you— . . .! He deserves to die," the judge said.

"We all deserve to die," Mark said.

"Die," Tessa whispered. As if a shock of electricity had charged through her body, she stood up, rigid, the car keys clutched in her hand. Her eyes closed. *"Die?"* she screamed the question. Then her words poured out in a torrent of gasps: "I want to thank you, father, for saving me from that evil sect I was foolish enough to be seduced by, and I want to thank you from the bottom of my heart for hiring Dr. Phillips to find me and turn me over to Dr. Emery to depro— . . . deprog— . . . save me, and for letting me stay with him and Mrs. Emery and their other wards until my mind healed and cleared, and I want to thank you for allowing me to come back, and for the stroganoff, my favorite dish, and for giving me everything anyone would be grateful for and teaching me so that I can now recognize that I did wrong to run away to those miserable misfits, and I want to apologize for all the heartbreak I caused you and mother and for not eating this delicious meat and for shouting, *Fascists, fascists!* at the police who were doing their duty, and you were right, father, always right, just and merciful, and you know what is right for the family unit, and I want to say how deeply and profoundly grateful I am to— . . ."

The judge was looking at her with outrage.

Alana felt depression weigh more heavily, crush her. She felt again the beginning of tears, but there was still no moisture. Was it because her skin had been pulled too tight? she thought crazily. While she was having her face purged of loose skin, Tessa had been having her brain purged of all that— . . . that— . . . *What?* What had it been?

"And I want to say that I was wrong, was wrong, was wrong, was— . . ." Tessa's words garbled into sounds, her eyes remained shut.

The judge had listened to his older daughter's words as if they were those of a defendant he would grant no mercy to. "Only order allows us to endure," he said.

"I know that!" Tessa shouted. "Certain things cannot be allowed!" Her hands covered her closed eyes.

Mark stood up, next to his sister; she had backed away from the table, as if in horror of it. He held her by the shoulders, shaking her gently.

"No, Mark!" she yelled. "Let me finish!"

He kept shaking her, pulling her hands from her eyes.

The telephone rang. Alana Stephens grasped her napkin tightly, wringing it, choking it.

Tessa screamed, "*Father!* You have saved me! from becoming one of those people! who upset the order of everything good!—and I want you to know that I know that and that I will never run away again, and that I— . . . that I— . . ." She squeezed her eyes shut, words pushed out of her clenched lips. "I you thank doctor sect perfect order run right right did what thought come back come back back— . . ."

Mark shook her strongly now. "Stop, Tessa, stop!"

Tessa opened her eyes and looked at her brother in sudden recognition, recovering. She located the car keys, which had fallen to the floor. She touched Mark's arm, briefly, as if afraid to contaminate him. "I—want—to—go—for—a—drive—in—my—new—car." She controlled each word.

"No," Mark said.

"Let her go," the judge ordered. "She needs to be in control of herself."

Mark took the keys from Tessa. She looked at her hands as she walked outside to the pool. The water reflected the angled sun. Silver rivulets lit up the beautiful dining room. A shaft of light shot into the melting-mercury piece.

Mark faced his father. "How the hell does it feel to know that in one fucking month you affirmed the death of a man and had your own daughter brainwashed just so that she couldn't think the thoughts that threaten you and your fucking family unit?"

Linda placed her hand lightly on her father's knee. It was that, that warmth, which kept him from getting up.

Alana Stephens looked at her son, and she felt a new sensation, a new feeling sparked by Mark's rage. No, it wasn't new, it only *felt* new, each time. Pride at his rage. The telephone was ringing again. Why didn't somebody answer!

Linda withdrew her hand, to reach for her wineglass.

Feeling the absence of the warm hand, the judge's body bolted up. He stood rigidly facing his son. "Sit down!" he commanded.

Mark did not. He looked out the window. Tessa still stood there desolately. The shimmering reflection of the pool seemed to envelop her in an aura of unreality, as if it were pulling her into a silvery hazy limbo, sucking her in, making her disappear.

"Sit down, Mark!"

Mark still did not.

Alana looked at her husband. "I want to tell you, Stephen, that two weeks ago, on the high recommendation of one of the women we regularly have dinner with, I hired Jimmy Steed, and I may have an affair with a youngman half my age—a male stripper I met at one of those clubs for women only, on one of the nights you thought I was at one of my silly classes. He may turn out to be gay, but I don't care. Stephen, you are a tyrant, a bully—a cruel, cruel man. You've destroyed me, destroyed your daughters—yes, both of them. I kept it from you that Linda was pulled out of a club they call the West-Sky, and— . . . Oh, yes, and you're trying to destroy our son. And I'm proud of him, proud he stood up to you, Stephen—and that he looks like *me*! . . . You've kept me a child, Stephen, a silly child at times. Stephen, *you're* the criminal. I know I've come to seem ridiculous to you, and even to others, and so it will amaze you to know that I really care, I really *do* care about injustice. But— . . . But I've never been taught—I've never been allowed to learn!—what really to do about it!" She looked at her son's face, she looked at Linda, she saw the judge still standing. But they were not looking at *her*. Hadn't they heard her words? No—because again she had not spoken them, had screamed them, again, only in her mind.

Hilde lunged in, carrying the silver dish of stroganoff. She had heard the angered voices. But this, her impeccable creation for Sunday dinner, would restore order—that, and her reassuring presence next to the judge.

Unaware of her, the judge's hand jerked out in anger at

Mark's refusal to sit down. His hand hit the silver serving spoon. Hilde clung to it in soundless horror, but it was too late. The creamy sauce splashed hideously on the judge, smears of it dripping, extending. Her own uniform was spattered.

Instantly Linda was dabbing with a wet napkin at her father's tie, shirt, jacket. The judge sank into his chair.

Alana looked out in the direction of her lavender roses. Instead, she saw her first-born daughter staring into the shimmering pool. Mark was still standing. She glanced at the judge; he seemed surrounded by the hands of his daughter and that despised woman.

The judge looked down and saw a tiny sliver of green cornichon clinging to his white shirt. In horror he thrust it away. His eyes were pulled to the dripping mercury piece. Like excrement, he thought, like silver excrement.

Delicately, Alana Stephens brought her wineglass to her lips. She sipped from it as calmly as she could. And, Stephen—she added to the litany of loss she would never speak aloud—you aren't even capable of seeing the beauty—the rare, rare, exquisite beauty—of the lavender roses I've created.

Lost Angels: 6

Once it was Grauman's Chinese Theater—a Chino-Deco palace with gold-gilded curled edges like pagodas, Oriental-suited ushers, fountains gushing painted water, tiles shaping exotic birds. Premieres of annihilating tawdriness were held here. Search-lights carved a white cone into the astonished night. Within its circumference, dazzling film stars waved at the bleachers filled with shaggy, dreamless faces. Once, during the premiere of a film starring the great Norma Desmond—herself later pushed by scandal into madness—a child named Adore was trampled to death while fans surged, not in adulation at the stars but in empty rage against each other's drabness.

Now a vast corporation has converted the famous theater into a triplex, its once proudly gaudy facade violated by harsh jutting extensions to accommodate two more theaters. Lines of people tangle confusedly along with constant bands of tourists identifying hand- and footprints, with carved signatures, in the cement blocks of its outdoor foyer, a courtyard boasting the imprint of more than 160 stars—a tradition begun, it is said, when Norma Talmadge stepped accidentally into a rectangle of fresh cement.

"Gene Tierney!" Lisa gasped. She bent reverently to touch the outline of the star's hands. "Can you believe *Gene Tierney* actually bent down here and did this?" She placed her hands, exactly, on the grainy indentations. She hummed the tune from *Laura.* But the memory of what she'd driven away yesterday— what the star, or the character she had played, had done in *Leave Her to Heaven*—had been pursuing her since she had begun to mention it in the park, reminded of the star by the poisonous oleanders in another film. "She threw herself down the stairs and killed her unborn baby?'' She tried to obliterate the nagging memory by thrusting it out.

Orin who was reading a newspaper he had just bought from one of the metallic and plastic racks lining the streets of Hollywood, raised his eyes. He touched Lisa, just barely, on the hand.

"You're always talking about dead babies,'' Jesse James said. He was trying to contain his burgeoning excitement at the prints. He was looking for James Cagney's. Had to be here. Maybe his block of cement would be dated the year he was in *White Heat*—but what year was it?

Lisa thought of Pearl Chavez, left in the closed heat of the indigo Cadillac. She tried to remember the name of the character Gene Tierney played in the film, but she couldn't now—overwhelmed by so many sensations; so she called her by its title. "Leave-her-to-heaven also scattered her beloved father's ashes to the four winds while she rode on a horse.'' She tried to offer that in defense of her. The unsettling memory of Ellen Berent—Ellen Berent, that was her name!—making herself up carefully in order to look beautiful when they found her, and then throwing herself down the steps to kill the child inside her, was not assuaged by her narration of the ash-scattering scene. And then she realized why—really *why*—Leave-her-to-heaven had killed her baby. She loved her husband so much, so much—remember?—and he was the same actor who left Forever-Amber and took away *her* child—and no matter what he said, he *couldn't* have loved Leave-her-to-heaven—the way he took up with her sister, that mealymouth! "Ellen loved him so much,'' she said aloud, satisfied with her discovery of Ellen's justifying wound, "and it was *him* who was so mean! . . . Lana Turner!'' she sighed. "*She* sacrificed so much for her daughter, like Joan Crawford.'' She caught herself addressing the milling tourists, who listened to her attentively. She walked away, joining Jesse.

"I found Bogart, Robinson—but I can't find Cagney!'' He was becoming anxious.

"Well, you certainly know a lot about the old stars, for such young people,'' a fat happy woman said to Lisa and Jesse. The woman was with her husband. When she spoke, her flesh jiggled in a jolly way; and she had a way of breathing twice, a normal breath then a short one.

Lisa explained: "Oh, I saw all the great stars—in a theater which was going broke until the owner decided to show only the all-time greats; two each night; sometimes three, on weekends," she collected the cherished memories.

Orin leafed anxiously through the pages of the newspaper, his eyes raking the columns of each page.

The elated woman said, "Well, it is certainly very nice to see young people interested in real culture."

"Those were the happiest times in my life," Lisa said. "Until now." She touched Orin, lightly the way he had touched her, and then Jesse. "I saw Joan Crawford, Bette Davis, Jennifer Jones, beautiful, *beautiful* Hedy Lamarr, Lana Turner, Rita Hayworth, Vivian Leigh—you know, that *is* how you pronounce her name—Gene Tierney— . . ." She paused. "And Marilyn Monroe. When she died, they *all* died; that's when the all-times ended."

"*James Cagney!*" Jesse placed his booted feet to the side of the star's prints, straddling them, his stance wider than Cagney's. "Come and get me, coppers!" he mimed. It still didn't sound like Cody's last line.

"Well, aren't they remarkable, for such young people?—so much respect for the past," the woman said to her husband.

The man agreed; he was staring at Lisa's body.

Orin threw away the first section of the newspaper. Its leaves opened and sailed into the wind.

"I would have been a movie star for sure if it would have stayed the way it used to be. But it's all changed." The two strange movies they had seen the night Orin chose them haunted her—but not like the "all-times," she told herself, not at all like that.

"Well, you certainly should be congratulated for seeing that," the woman said joyfully. She was about to move away with her husband, and then she turned back. "Well, now, haven't I seen you three before somewhere?" She pondered for a moment: "Well, I'm sure it was at one of the other many beautiful sights in this city!" she enthused. "Well, good-bye, Lord love you!" They moved away, along the petrified prints of dead stars.

As Lisa, Jesse, and Orin walked farther along Hollywood Boulevard, they passed the inheritors of the street, the scraggly bands of dispossessed drifters and exiles, the banished young and old, but mostly young—like the tattered lurking souls of the faded stars, whose names—contained in the tarnished copper stars in the sidewalks—they walked on, dishonored tribute to buried glory.

They sat on Sunset Boulevard in a real railroad car converted into a hamburger restaurant. Across from it, rose a beautiful Art Deco building with stone maidens mounted on layered pedestals; but it was all peeling; renovating machines surrounded it, giant tubes, hoses, wires buried into it like implements for critical transfusions.

Orin shoved the newspaper away. He'd been moody since this morning, although once again he had paid the day's rent by himself. It did not alarm them—too much—this time when they woke to find him gone. "What you looking for in the paper?" Jesse tried to sound casual.

As if in answer, Orin said, "We'll go to the park this afternoon!" Instantly his spirits seemed to rise.

Jesse's thoughts bunched; he sorted them out. Did Orin see something—someone—in the park yesterday, when those kids scared everyone with their firecrackers? He remembered the area Orin had stared at, first through the telescope, later while everybody scurried. It had looked like a jungle—a forest and a jungle. When they heard the shots, everyone had thought it was that escaped veteran who— . . . The veteran! The veteran the news kept talking about, reporting sightings everywhere. Was it possible he was there? And Orin saw— . . .? Jesse's thoughts jumped: Would there be a reward? Would they be heroes? His smirched past—would it matter then? *But whose side would Cody Jerrett be on!* "That escaped veteran." That's all Jesse said, and he said it aloud.

"Oh, you!" Lisa teased Jesse. "You and those movies!"

"*You* should talk," Jesse threw at her. She had made his suspicions and deductions seem stupid to himself; she had also kept him from seeing Orin's reaction. But what was there to see when— . . .?

"He's in the park; I saw him," Orin said.

"*Saw* him!" Jesse blurted out.

"I even— . . ." Orin stopped. He seemed to study them.

"Jesse!" Lisa reprimanded. "You actually believe *everything* Orin says; he's teasing you, can't you see that little-boy smile just about to burst on his face?" There was a beautiful aimlessness in their life—a loose continuity disturbed only by the possible ghost of an old woman, and the distant presence of Sister Woman's glassy image. Orin's and Jesse's words had hinted of pulling in another invisible presence.

Jesse did not see Orin's face break into the little-boy smile, but Lisa's words accusing him of gullibility stung, badly. "Shit," he said—a word Orin didn't like. "It's not so, that I believe everything." Cody didn't. Cody distrusted people, learned to— the hard way. "If I— . . ."

"Awright, kid." Orin actually did an imitation of Jesse imitating Cagney!

All three laughed uncontrollably.

Orin paid for their food.

Outside, the wind pushed.

The song on the country and Western station proclaimed the power of devotion; they drove down Franklin Boulevard in the commanding Cadillac. Everywhere, someone looked at it, pointed, admired.

This spell of unseasonal heat was breaking records, the news interlude on the station announced as Lisa looked out at the lush vegetation.

Confused, flowers that grow only in deepest summer were pushing out in despair in this time of heat, blooming lushly before the usual cool weather of this month returned to kill them.

Lisa sat in back with Pearl. The proximity to Jesse—and Orin—when she sat in front, became, at times, more frustrating than pleasurable, because it stopped there. So there were recurrent times when she moved away from the sexual currents; other times she wanted to swim in them.

Western Avenue cuts Hollywood in half. At that corner derelicts not yet ready for skid row gather as if in preparation, harsh initiation. Ubiquitous avengers, the police prowl in slow cars. At that point of Western, the raunch gathers. In a stuttering fit of attempted "class," a shop at the corner displays a clutter of "art works" in its windows; its most prominent piece is a harsh reproduction of a hugely hung David painted gold.

Then that street slides away into Los Feliz Boulevard, the haughty street along which—and in the lofty hills—grand homes stretch in settled wealth, lawns perennially sprinkled in water-spurting stars. The dark Cadillac moved past the several entrances to Griffith Park. Lisa was relieved they didn't drive in. She wanted to see the Planetarium, yes—but not if it was going to create more of that disturbing talk, and Jesse's fired imagination. She fluffed out Pearl Chavez's dress. She had eyes like hers but the doll's were dimming.

Chopping off a whiny song, Orin set the radio on to the news station.

". . . —of an investigation into the shooting death of an unarmed black woman by Officer Norris Weston several months ago. The Internal Affairs Division of the police department has recommended that no further action be taken, asserting that Officer Weston acted responsibly in defense of his threatened fellow officer. In the city for a fundraiser for various liberal-identified causes, Senator Hutchens called the finding 'a blatant miscarriage of justice.' The white senator's remarks were denounced as 'inflammatory' by Cardinal Unger, in the city for a meeting of church hierarchical figures. . . . A sweep of male and female prostitutes netted— . . ."

To assert his independence further, Lisa's remark still smarting, Jesse turned off the voice on the radio—but did not switch back to the country and Western station—and asked Orin, in a small voice, "Awright, kid?"

"All right," Orin said.

That was what was so damn confounding to Jesse. Orin's unpredictability. The same thing that angered him one moment, he accepted easily the next. Sometimes Jesse thought in terms of a "struggle" between them; but when he tried to define it, it would all evaporate. And there were all the unallowed questions about the dead old woman—who probably made these idle days possible—and that weird Sister Woman; she seemed to have been talking about Orin last night. And how were he and Lisa involved—if they were? Part of the "evidence" Orin seemed at times to be collecting?—the way he studied the shape of things, investigating; actually sniffing at things as if to detect what might be hidden in them. Yes, something to do with Sister Woman? For her? Or something to do *to* her? He didn't dare ask any of those questions, though: He felt secure in the indolence— now—of this time. And he liked to hear Orin talk. He liked that increasingly, would often make comments to elicit Orin's strangely clear declarations. Like now.

"That senator and that cardinal— . . ." That's all Jesse needed to say.

"You can't tell what *side* people are on until the exact moment comes when they *do,*" Orin said. "You just can't tell until people *do.*"

Jesse leaned back to listen.

Aware of a certain rhythm his words assumed, like an incantation—a rhythm she had noticed as far back as the long trip across forests and deserts and into Los Angeles with him— Lisa listened. It was like the rhythm that the wind can create on the ocean, private murmurings which become yours.

"See, God created order out of chaos," Orin said. "Now *that* was good, no question about that, a-*tall*. But what he created, and what *it* created, is *it* good? The act, see, is different from what comes out of it—can be. If God hadn't thrown out the lost angels, he would have had to surrender heaven—but if they hadn't rebelled, there wouldn't have been Jesus. So the angels deserved to go to hell, but their *rebellion*, see—was their rebellion good? And if so, don't they deserve to be led out of hell?"

Jesse felt the intense words. Even when Orin asked a question at those times, the sound carried certainty, as if *he* knew.

"Can God be wrong, Orin?" Lisa asked. With her fingers, she pulled up her hair, to get a breeze on her moist neck. The wind whipped her hair about recklessly. She saw Orin's eyes framed on her in the mirror. She kept her hands behind her neck. She wasn't even sure whether she believed in God—but she wanted to hear Orin.

"Depends," he said with finality.

He made a dangerous U-turn into nervous traffic, and Jesse knew: We are going into the park.

The lots about the Observatory were full. They had to park on a slope of a hill and walk up. Hundreds of early-summer tourists littered the grounds; with cameras and hot dogs and in shorts and pulled-out shirts and blouses, they roamed like immigrants from 1955.

"The planet show goes on in fifteen minutes!" Lisa read the schedule outside the entrance. She wanted to see stars and planets.

"We got time," Orin said; he walked around the back of the green dome, where they had stood yesterday. Lisa moved along resignedly with Jesse. This time she had brought the doll with her.

On the highest tier, Orin stared at the acres of wilderness. Jesse followed his gaze—far along wild growth, farther to a jutting fortress of exposed rocks in distorted shapes, beyond, to a short leprous patch of burned ground after a decline, and then, rising onto a green hill, to a bolted enclosure of trees. *He does think there's someone there; maybe he knows it!* Jesse's excitement resurged.

"Time for the planets," Lisa said emphatically.

They walked past the white portals and into the wide foyer of the Observatory. Inside, there are displays of extraterrestial stones and photographs, harsh craters like modern paintings.

Under a spherical ceiling on which are painted nude figures in ambiguous struggle, a gold ball connected by wire swings—a pendulum threatening to overturn each of a series of colored pins arranged at the base of a deep round stone pit. A placard identifies this as "The Foucalt Pendulum" and explains that the pendulum revolves in rhythm with the earth's rotation, knocking down one pin every eight minutes.

Now it swung, missing a pin—several already lay slaughtered at the base of the deep cylinder. It missed again, came closer, swung, missed again, closer, missing again. Over the edges, looking down as if into a well, crowds of people waited eagerly for the ineluctable gold ball to topple still another pin. It did. The pin folded over. There was a collective sigh, then applause, then cheers.

Flowing in with a current of bodies, Orin, Jesse, and Lisa went inside the largest domed structure, a huge auditorium, seats arranged in concentric circles. A giant, round machine waits to duplicate the universe. An awed hush gripped the full hall, which deepened into black; then the dome lit up: dusk; then a rim of night filled with vagrant eager stars; then: night— deep, dark—and stars, stars, stars! A voice announced the names of the planets as a white arrow projected on the reproduction of sky located them. The signs of the zodiac, imposed on the constellations, drew "Ah's!"

When it was over and they were outside, Lisa said, "It was just like the sky used to be, remember?—full of *real* stars. Couldn't you just sit in that planetarium and pretend you were floating away from this old world?"

"You sure could." Jesse had been impressed.

"Can't, though," Orin said.

They drove out of the park, each awed by the universe.

The elegant Cadillac had entered the old Pasadena Freeway, the oldest, grandest, and most inadequate, of the city's 600 miles of freeways. It is narrow, with quaint lamps out of another era, the Los Angeles of the Forties. Grass borders usher cars into unexpected bricked exits.

The Cadillac glided out of the freeway. It moved into the elegant old city of Pasadena. It was as if the trees were bleeding gelid red blossoms. There were solid fields of flowers of all shapes and colors. From the distance, they looked like exotic rugs draping green lawns. Houses of old grandeur, even steepled Victorian creations, magnificent rococo buildings, challenge the encroaching landscape of plastic and squares.

Jesse's guide said this city had more roses than— . . .

"What did you do back in Indiana so you had to run away, Jesse?" Orin asked.

Both Jesse and Lisa looked at him in shock. He had broken his asserted demand not to invade the past.

"What!" Jesse grasped for time to frame an exact answer. He felt the same coldness he had experienced the day in the shadowed cove of the park when Orin had seemed to read his thoughts about Lisa. "Tell us about the old woman in Salem, Orin," Jesse actually asked that—doing back what Orin had done to him that other afternoon, countering his probing.

"Toldya," Orin said easily. "She died. Almost two weeks

ago now. What did you leave back there, Lisa?'' Orin extended the sudden, threatening invasion.

"Nothing!'' Lisa said in a firm voice. "Nothing—because that was all there was—nothing!'' Why! Why was Orin doing this?

"Just joking?'' Jesse offered weakly.

"Just joking,'' Orin pronounced.

They stopped to eat in a red and black restaurant: red curtains, black vinyl booths. Orin broke the profound silence—he announced the treat was his, "and the sky's the limit.''

He's making us trust him, Lisa felt she understood now, that's why he asked those questions, and why he pays our expenses only sometimes but more and more. He wants us to *trust* him. She felt better now, sure that the violating incursion into past shadows would not recur.

Evening. The heat settled into the night. Orin drove about the city. He turned the radio to the news: ". . . on tonight's television news in response to Mandy Lang-Jones's report on prostitution in her series on 'The Lower Depths.' And she interviews Councilwoman Patty Peterson, whose office has been deluged with calls demanding a cleanup of the sordid streets. Councilwoman Peterson asserts her belief that more arrests and harsher penalties are the answer— . . .''

"Our bodies! belong! to us!'' Lisa chanted from another newscast.

" . . . —in the canyons is causing anxiety among firefighters. Police suspect arson— . . .''

This time it was Orin who found the country and Western station—and Jesse James quickly told them of a place he'd read about in the entertainment section of the paper. They went there.

It was a beer bar for "cowboys'' from the Valley, a portion of the San Fernando Valley just minutes from the city. Almost everyone was in Western garb—the grandchildren of the men and women who had fled the smothering dust and wilting heat of the West in the Thirties; grandchildren who now fled to the Valley, away from "niggers.''

The best country bands and singers perform here, a place pulsing with redneck energy. Bowing to request a dance, Jesse

swept Lisa into the dance floor. She liked his strong hands
around her tiny waist, like Rhett's about Scarlett's when they
scandalized Atlanta society by dancing at the fundraiser while
she was still in mourning, she told Jesse, who was delighted and
whirled her around even more. Orin enjoyed himself, too; that
was so obvious that Jesse and Lisa coaxed him into the dance
area. To their astonishment, Orin swirled expertly with Lisa.
They became stars, getting special attention on the cleared
floor! Orin's lengthening reddish hair sparkled in the colored
lights. Jesse was chagrined by the sensational performance,
which got applause.

In the motel now filled with good humor, which had grown
during the ride back—yes, Orin wanted them to *trust* him—Lisa
stood in front of the mirror, having finished her shower. She
studied her naked form as far as that mirror allowed. She
touched each breast simultaneously with a finger, rubbing it
until it tingled and felt erect. She moistened two fingers with
her tongue. She touched the nipples again. She had enjoyed—a
lot—the attention she'd gotten at that dance place earlier, and it
was obvious that both Jesse and Orin were proud to be her
partners. During those minutes, she had been certain that, yes,
she loved Orin and Jesse. *Could* love them, she inserted an
unspecified contingency—for later, if necessary.

Now she put on her nightgown, arranging it so that the
parting in the middle of her chest showed prominently. She
allowed one shoulder of the flimsy material to fall loosely so
that the effect would be one of pure accident. Quickly, she
raised the nightgown. Again, she lowered it, even more boldly.
After all, Orin had held her closely when they danced. *Very*
closely. Radiant with sexuality, her hair wet and wavy from the
shampoo, she walked into the bedroom.

Jesse had been sitting down. Seeing her, he stood up, took a
step toward her. "Knock your eyes out!" he blurted Cagney's
line when he saw his girlfriend Verna in a black negligée, or did
she say it?

Lisa looked flirtatiously at Orin. She had glanced at him a
second earlier and seen clear desire. It turned into fury!

He lowered his head so that he gazed up at her.

Lisa felt cold-heated terror, felt exposed, naked, trapped. She raised her nightgown over her breasts. She rushed to Pearl. She covered herself with the bed sheet. When she looked back at Orin, the anger was gone. Had she imagined it?—it had all occurred in one second.

Orin turned the television on. ". . . —the adversary, like a roaring lion, goeth about seeking the ruin of souls," Sister Woman was whispering.

Jesse looked wistfully at Lisa. Why had she acted so strangely? What had Orin's reaction been?—he hadn't seen it.

Hearing the woman's voice, Lisa sat up in bed. She saw the telephone number across the television screen. And Orin was dialing on the telephone! Sister Woman's eyes, dark outlines containing almost no color now, stared from the screen; eyes whose paleness reflected only black.

"I want to speak to her! . . . Yes, you can! . . . No, to *her*! I said, to *her*!" Orin demanded into the telephone.

Did he really dial that number? Jesse looked at the red gash of the woman's mouth, issuing words he did not hear now. He heard only Orin's.

"He isn't talking to her!" Lisa saw Jesse's confusion, and she pointed to the screen.

"They've got lots of operators," Jesse said. "*They* answer."

Brother Man bowed his head. Sister Woman grasped the arms of her throne. The breeze brushed her hair. "Deliver us, O Lord. Purify us in the blood. Slay us in your spirit. And you, out there, soldiers of God, challenge the evil prince!" Her strange eyes gazed down as if at a presence pulling violently at her. "I bind you, Satan, in the name of Jesus! I plead in the blood of the Lamb! The Lord rebukes you!"

Wails rose from the studio audience.

"I want to speak to her," Orin repeated each word into the telephone. "All right, then, this is the message: Tell her *Orin* called. Tell her: that I am here! Exactly that." Anger smirched his face. "The old woman is dead—like I wrote her—and I am here. Tell her I want the proof now!" He hung up ferociously. Depression was carved into his face. Rage and pain seemed to pull at his features.

Again! *I am here.* If not a threat, a secret message? And proof— . . . Lisa looked away from the menacing screen.

The televison camera shifted to Brother Man, only him. He mumbled prayers. Alone on the screen, he looked real, flesh and blood; in her presence he faded. The camera reached back to reembrace Sister Woman. Her hands were clutched.

She said, "All grief will be lifted. Jesus promises it, and through him I promise it too by the living God." Her crystalline eyes stared into the camera; her hands were clenched on her lap. The sigh of her originless breeze touched her hair, once, in awe: "Proof . . . of the wondrous . . . fireworks of God!" her mouth shot out the words.

Jesse and Lisa heard Orin inhale, long, as if pulling the woman's words into himself. His eyes closed as if to contain them there.

"Neither shall there be any more pain. *That* is the promise; it will be kept. Call!" One hand sprang to violent life, the other remained clasped in her lap. She flung out that one word, forcefully, and then paused, paused, paused. Now the purling voice resumed: "*Call!* . . . on the Lord."

The wrenched emotions seemed wiped away from Orin's face, suddenly beautiful.

Over the image of Sister Woman kneeling in prayer, the announcer's voice exhorted viewers to send in their petitions and their gifts of love, especially now for the "marathon spiritual meeting—the largest revolution of saved souls ever"—which would occur, he reminded, this weekend, Sunday, "in the Silver Chapel on the Hill."

The camera pulled farther back on the phantasmal kneeling figure of the chiffon-draped woman—and on the hands quivering toward her in the studio.

Jesse waited for Orin to pick up the telephone and dial again. But he didn't.

The Lecturer: "On Nothing"

James Huston, the guest lecturer, looked out the window of the room in which he would soon speak. The campus was flooded with green grass and white sun. Shadows cast by the Rodin statues in the sculpture garden he had just passed were almost as beautiful as the carved bodies themselves.

It always astounded him anew, this city of bodies and souls. He did not consider it the flippant land of the inherited clichés. To him it was the most spiritual and physical of cities, a profound city which drew to it the various bright and dark energies of the country. All its strains, of decay and rebirth, repression and profligacy, gathered here in exaggeration—as exaggerated as actors in Greek tragedies. Its desperate narcissism—which acknowledged death in extended summers under seasonless skies—and its vagrant spirituality—which burgeoned into excess—were manifestations of a fury to live, to feel, to *be*, here on the last frontier before the drowning land—the snuffed sun, the darkened shoreline.

Now the sun was so white it glazed shadows silver. Momentarily mesmerized by the dazzling brilliance of this day, the lecturer forced his eyes away from the open window and faced his audience. He would not speak in a large auditorium—he needed to watch his listeners. More than a dozen rows of at least as many seats ascended in a widening arc about the lectern where he stood. Unprepared for the heat, the air-conditioner created a sweaty breeze.

Angular, moody dark good-looks and a slender survivor's body made James Huston appear younger than his fifty years. He was wearing a casual tan jacket, a loosened brown tie over an unbuttoned blue shirt.

This afternoon's was a typical audience. There were the students, at least a few assigned to attend by professors who would themselves not be present, their statement on the lecturer's controversial life and views. Many were here simply because he was famous, some said notorious, the author of several books that described his turbulent life—"raging equally in sexual and intellectual promiscuity," this morning's newspaper had said. Here, too, were those he called "the grand inquisitors," faculty members who came only to denounce his lectures in articles in their "intellectual house organs," full of that-year's positive answers and arcane language. Among both students and teachers, of course, he had as many supporters as detractors. His invitations to speak came as often from those who derided him as those who admired him, who found in the seeming anarchy of his words and works an artful form, a saddened intelligence, and a respect—perhaps anachronistic—for what might be called the "soul."

A dark, intense good-looking youngman marched to the front row and remained standing until he was certain the lecturer had noticed him. Then from his pocket he took out a pair of dark-rimmed glasses—*daring me to tell him anything he might learn from*—and put them on carefully before he sat down. *I've seen you before*. At the other end of the same row, a tanned brown-haired girl in sleeveless dress uncrossed her brown legs— *you will listen only when I speak about sex or bodies*—and leaned back as if exposing her limbs to an admiring sun.

Them, James chose the two. At his lectures, he would select a few in the audience to use in gauging his effect. Varying factors elicited his choices—indications of intent attention, intelligence; cynical defiance; hostility; and, yes, beauty. He would give them names, assigning variegated lives and reactions to them. That made his remarks more intimate. He would name the good-looking youngman— . . . Mark. The girl would be Adorée.

Scanning the filled hall, James Huston chose others: a male professor—Dr. Admas—already mentally writing his scathing, remorselessly obscure "post post-structuralist" critique of this lecture; a pretty woman, an untenured professor, with him— Ellen, perhaps an agnostic critic; an older, carefully arranged lady—Mrs. Loomis—who subscribed to every lecture series and knew nothing at all about him; a fiercely intelligent plain youngwoman with a thick notebook waiting to be filled—oh, yes, Joan; a well-built athlete—Joe, who else?—who at the moment James's eyes glided toward him stretched his young body in blatant competition—*youth is not acquired, Joe!*; two pretty young girls, determinedly insouciant, hugging and holding hands—Sally and Lorry; a black, very black, youngman with rage ready to scorch—*what name?*; a Mexican girl—Gloria—her face defiantly brown without "Anglo makeup"; and a surprising presence, a rigid, crewcut older man, either a director of continuing education or an undercover officer making sure the lecturer was not subversive—Mr. Hartzell! He might choose others as he spoke. . . . Hilton—he gave the black youngman an uncommon name.

"Flawed perfection or perfect flaws, accident or fate, salvation or betrayal," James Huston began his lecture, softly; always without being introduced.

Faces looked up startled.

"We will perhaps discuss perfection and what we accept as such, and the expectations arising from it. Completeness—no possible substitution—might be a component of the perfect. Salvation—I speak in the conventional sense—is therefore perfect; there is no substitute for salvation." The last three words formed a phrase he used in every lecture he gave, every book he wrote. "From attempts to substitute it, all neuroses stem, and from thwarted expectations, broken promises—neuroses being realistic disappointments carried to an extreme."

He deliberately provoked laughter early in his lectures. The expectation of the outrageous conclusions he was known for added interest, and prepared attention for the seriousness of his discourse. Even in his humor were careful clues of his personal intention, the steady dismantling of what he had once believed in: "meaning" and "reasons"—sought in religion, philosophy, psychology, art, finally life; unfound. His lectures were laments for, and rages against—at times subdued, at times overt—deceiving mythologies, betrayals. Each lecture brought him closer to the death of hope.

"Black is the total absence of color. So is white—the opposite of black. Black and white are perfect. Yet black results from the total absorption of light rays, contains all colors; and white reflects—rejects?—them all. A contradiction? An imperfection? A mystery! The recurrent subject . . . along with sex.''

Joan skipped a page for retrospective illumination. *You have pretty hair, Joan. . . . Hilton!—certainly you did not find bigotry in that? Or do you see it—correctly—in every white face, hear it out of every white mouth?* The doggedly skeptical Dr. Admas was making a note on a paper: *"The structuring absence of his lecture is the modernist discourse that he ignores."* Something *that* pertinent! And Mark— . . . *It was here, in this city—* . . .

''What would a contemporary lecture be, without a reference to sex—or dreams?'' he clarified for Joan, who nodded. Adorée of the brown satin legs smiled appreciatively. But Mark frowned at the supposed flippancy; so James explained further: ''I used sex only to hold lack of attention in abeyance—soon, I will, I promise, use the word 'fuck.' '' There was receptive laughter— but Mark secured the barrier of his glasses by placing his hands on his temples.

''Gray, not so coincidentally, is an imperfect absorption of those rays—the flawed middle, gray age.''

Mrs. Loomis touched her dyed temples and felt surrounded by so much youth!

I didn't mean you, you have been so wounded by Mr. Loomis! ''In the beginning was the word, St. John tells us, and whatever else *Genesis* may be, one might see in it a metaphor for literary creativity, the *word* ordering *chaos*, bringing—one hopes!—light! Much of the rest of the Book is bad revision,'' he continued still lightly to court their intelligent attention. '' 'In the beginning the earth was without form, and void; and darkness was upon the face of the deep.' Science and *Genesis* agree. 'And God said'—and here begins the controversy—'Let there be light; and there was light. And God saw the light, that it was good.' But what did that good light reveal to a myopic God? In our time—in my time only—Dachau! Bangladesh! Viet Nam! . . .'' He thrust the scorched images at them.

The audience reacted in bewilderment to his sudden ferocity. This was his first clashing indication of what they might expect.

Now he drew back to abstractions: "And plagues, fires, the unholy wars, inquisitions and burnings at the stake and by napalm and gas. Now the darkness becomes benign. It snuffs out the cruelty of that 'good' light."

Mark seemed about to remove his glasses, paused. Mrs. Loomis looked about the room, to watch the reactions of the susceptible young—and report to Mr. Loomis, who would not listen. Dr. Admas loosened his antagonism—but only because Ellen was clearly interested.

Outside—where he looked—shadows clasped, commanded by the sun.

"Questions. Important questions. Before one can find answers, one has to find questions; meaningful questions require meaningful answers." He reached in his pocket for a slip of paper. He read, " 'What are the forces that deconstruct a text?' " Oh, that gave Dr. Admas an unexpected thrill. Perhaps he will even write, *"There are times when he is almost capable of an intelligent—. . ."*

Joan frowned. Instead of removing them, Mark adjusted his glasses.

Please, Joan, Mark wait! James Huston continued to read from the paper: " 'Is the contemporary novel dominated by metonomy or metaphor?' " *Please!* " 'What are the major differences among modernism, post-modernism, and post-post-modernism?' . . . Important questions—they were discussed heatedly at a recent conference on criticism. . . . *Babble!*" Joan and Mark relaxed. Dr. Admas slashed with his pencil at what he had spiritedly begun to write. "Ask *important* questions! Did God weep when he flung the lost angels out of heaven? Did the *angels* weep? When they fell from cloudy grace, did their tears precede them as if to quench the fiery red damnation? *Who* wept? *That* is important. Were the rebellious angels the first radicals against the lineage of totalitarian tyrants that begins with God?" *Hilton is thinking of white devils shedding black blood*. "And were any of the angels black?" he addressed him.

Hilton nodded.

"Imagine the rage of betrayed angels! . . . And imagine what a dreadful childhood Satan must have had.'' He moved deliberately from the somber to the seemingly flippant, but even then his tone was bruised by bitterness. Mark did not laugh. *You want*— . . . James Huston turned away from his gaze. He looked outside—at the scattering geometry of shadows and light. '' 'Be wary, be watchful, for your adversary the devil, as a roaring lion, goeth about seeking the ruin of souls,' so says that often overrated work, the Bible.''

A gasp, controlled—after all, they were sophisticated. Mr. Hartzell glared. Mrs. Loomis pulled in her lips in indignation—no, she was applying lipstick! What was the relentless Dr. Admas writing now?—*"He does not address the serious questions he sometimes manages to stumble upon, like the matter of intertextuality and decentering the subject."* ''Again, that has nothing to do with my lecture. I simply quoted one of the favorite sayings of the greatest television performer of our time—Sister Woman, in her nightly series on salvation!'' They laughed; she was famous, all knew who she was. When he could bear it, James Huston watched her, at times laughing in outrage, always appalled by her terrifying, hypnotizing power. ''Again, I am merely making sure you're listening—you might miss what you've come to hear—sex! blasphemy! . . .'' He stopped. He said softly, ''You must understand by now that I inherited the sanity of mad parents.''

Startled, Mark met his look.

A connection, Mark? From where, before? ''A beloved mother, a despised father—but it was the same, wasn't it?—because it was all *passion*.'' He felt Gloria's accusing brown gaze. *Of course, you have a despised mother!* He sought Adorée, who cocked her head and blew softly on the sunburned portion of her breasts. Was it the lingering sadness Gloria had evoked that fanned even over Adorée?—*Adorée, will you come to hate your beauty?*

''What shall we substitute for salvation?'' he asked. ''Meditation, Quaaludes, neostructuralism? The arrogant perfections of the sciences? Mathematics! Yes, and then the perfection of love. Love,'' he pulled easily at their attention. ''We will of course accept, all of us, that love is perfect,'' he promised. ''There, we start with a clear given.''

Sally and Lorry kissed each other like two birds. Many other bright faces relaxed. Yes, they accepted that love was beyond assault—and good, always, to hear about. Dr. Admas sighed audibly, thinking, *Inverse romantic anachronism!*—and he will write in his pad: *"But then, his works have always shown a complete lack of consciousness about the implied reader and the narratee— . . ." Mark! On a white beach! And now you've come to claim something from me. Can I give it?*

"Mathematics is perfect if it solves the meaning of the unknown factor. An important phrase!—and not accidental: the unknown factor. Its solution is assumed by only one other institution—religion, which relies not on hard axioms but on flaccid faith."

Joe laughed heartily.

"We can even draw a picture of ineffable perfection and meaning simply by plotting an algebraic equation on a graph."

Joan flipped over a page with a sound that trumpeted ready understanding.

"Swedenborg tried to find God in arithmetic, too—but then Blake tried to draw the soul! Shall we substitute for salvation the graphed algebraic equation that shows us the exact location of the unknown factor? The unknown quantity—another important phrase! Retain it for later. The unknown quantity of X will be revealed in intersecting lines! Approach with awe!"

He drew on the blackboard one horizontal line and a vertical one, intersecting. A giant cross. And then he plotted loosely an algebraic equation. "Here is the outline of perfection—not only the solution, but a picture of X, solved! And it has poetry—shadowy reflections, mirror images." He pointed to the portion of the graph above the horizontal line, then below it, symmetrical forms. "The conscious and the unconscious, reality and dream. And the solution of X?" He turned around. "We have been deceived. There is not one constant. X. X is not the immutable; it changes from graph to graph, now plunging below the horizon into minus, now soaring over it as plus! . . . And there is the problem of prime numbers, a mystery pondered for three thousand years—the utter perfection of being able to find every number divisible only by one and by itself—such extravagant poetry in mathematics!—the mystery deepening the higher the number mounts. Supposedly finally solved—like the origin of time. . . . And zero! Invented to make mathematics work. Without it pyramids and buildings fall. Without that nonexistent zero. Even its shape is flawed, a squeezed circle. . . . More betrayals! The infinity of a geometric progression, which multiples itself but never tallies! The backward infinity of a square root, which divides itself endlessly, never reaching its origin. Both acknowledge in imperfect poetry that demarcation which does not exist—zero. Something so elaborate from nothing? Like the universe, created by a series of accidents in perfect collusion—collision—uniting into inevitability? . . . But keep that in abeyance, a hint of coming attractions, in the tradition of the great movie serials, to which I owe so much of my episodic and suspenseful mode of presentation!''

Spreading its powerful rays, the sun spattered shadows of trees outside—white splotches on the grass.

With his hand—wet with sweat—James Huston wiped away a portion of the graph he had drawn earlier, creating a blurred void where the spurious ''solution'' had been found. He felt an enveloping sorrow as he slashed a cruel X within the smudged void. ''Had mathematics not betrayed us, there— . . .'' He pointed to the intersection of the X. ''. . . —*there* would be God. But not impaled in masochistic splendor.''

Assertively, Joan drew an X on a single page. And Mark removed his glasses for a moment, pretending to clean them, then replaced them. Gloria pressed her lips together, as if assuming an attitude of prayer. Clumsily, Joe touched his round shoulder, attracting, attracted. *What will become of you, Joe? —when answers are no longer given to you and you must ask questions?* Dr. Admas underlined what he had just written with dramatic flourish: *''Aha! The imaginary signifier!''* He whispered something to Ellen, who brushed his hand away.

''As long as death exists, free will does not. Except perhaps in suicide. Have we arrived at a possible act of perfection—the one action in which fate embraces choice?'' The question had slid into his lecture, the soft words asked to himself. But having spoken them aloud, he forced Mark to look at him. A clue! Mark did not nod in assent. James Huston drew back his private question, from them. Then: ''God is love is perfect is omnipotent.

Then why do we ask so little of him? Tiny petitions for tiny improvements of our not so tiny lot. Why not ask that grain grow in a rage across the barren soil of starved countries? Why not ask for justice for the poor," *Gloria,* "and for the violated," *Hilton,* "the walking dead," *Mrs. Loomis?* "Why not ask that we grow wings and soar like angels," *Joan?*—"although, as we have seen, our angelic ancestors did not fare to well with *theirs."* This time he rushed on, obliterating laughter, "Why not ask for the moon *and* the stars," *Ellen?* Why not ask that we . . . never grow old, " *Joe?* "or die," *Adorée?* Or for sustaining hope? he asked himself but looked at Mark. "It is true that we are created in the image of a small, mean God— whose contemporary high priests— *psychiatrists!*"—he spat out the word— ". . . —are deep betrayers, providing answers even where there are no questions. Puncturing dreams. . . . Like the lords who bought indulgences for their evil by giving money to the holy church, the rich pay their analysts to absolve them of deserved guilt. Atonement by psychoanalysis! Oh, yes, there are times when guilt is justified, should be exposed—and then allowed to roil and burn in expiation!" *Mark, your eyes—are they brown?—like mine?* "Perverted psychiatry provides the perfect climate for capitalism—and terrific alliteration."

Mr. Hartzell's pen had gone crashing to his pad! Adorée was glancing out the window. James yanked at her attention: "The legs part, and the cunt receives the cock— . . ." She looked up with full interest. "The legs part, the moist cunt receives the panting cock; the legs part and the ass receives the cock. An orifice is penetrated, orgasm occurs, time stops, a stasis in infinity and boredom. Perfection perceived only in the memory of a fleeting moment. Gone. It is always, That *was* a good fuck; never, This *is* a good fuck. I keep my promises, you see; I have used that word! So much for the betrayal of sex!"

Now he pushed anxious words into their laughter. "The body withers, the appetite has gone, the face is gaunt, bodily functions rebel. Lassitude, nausea, constant apprehension, the pulse races, there are moments of fever accompanied by chills. The desire to sleep is overcome only by the inability to do so. In the extreme one dies—but more often kills another, or both. What malady have I described? . . . Love."

There was laughter mixed with nervousness, a contingently welcome release. Dr. Admas wrote: *"And! More important! —Love is a historical construct!"*

"Obviously I wasn't serious. Love is perfect." He looked at Sandy and Lorry, so pretty, sitting so close. *Don't listen now!* "We know, all of us, that without love life is meaningless. We accept love as perfection. The only completion of the incomplete. The *sine qua non* of life. *Sine. Qua. Non.* Not *Synanon.*" He bent over a nervous youngman on the front row—the youngman frowned, flustered. "Although, come to think of it," James Huston said with kindness, "the Synanon of life isn't bad, it's better—leave it! The Synanon of Life!" The youngman beamed. "Without love, disorder reigns, life is meaningless."

There was a sense of relief in many in the audience. A few leaned forward, not convinced where he was leading them. Mrs. Loomis looked proudly about, as if *she* had created an atmosphere of love for this generation.

If only Mr. Loomis had helped to do it for yours! James looked out—drawn steadily by the wavy whiteness of the day and its dark shadows, and he remembered Meursault, in Camus's *The Stranger*, the apathetic man rushing at fate, facing the Arab he would soon kill only because the sun was attacking his eyes—the Arab he will soon be "killed" by, *his* death thrown back at him by the hypnotizing sun. Quickly James looked at Mark. The youngman's eyes . . . *demanded!*

"To say love is to utter the ineffable. Who dares question the perfection—the utter need, the hunger—for love? Love makes the world go round, the earth move."

Even Gloria and Hilton nodded, lightly.

"The tyranny of love," James Huston said with disgust. "The deadliest myth! The cruelest. Perhaps."

Some of the listeners erased a portion of their notes, others drew a line, lines.

"Heloise and Abelard bound—paradoxically!—by castration, Romeo and Juliet bound by poison, Lancelot and Guinevere and Arthur by bad sorcery, Catherine and Heathcliff by damnation, Othello and Desdemona by love as flimsy as a handkerchief or a flickering candle! Hamlet and his mother bound by a dead father in purgatory and a live one in hell. And consider Oedipus and his *father,* Electra and her *mother*—oh, there was disguised doom in the house of Agamemnon! And the endless frustration of 'Terry and the Pirates'!'' Fiercely his voice swept away the laughter. "Tragedy weaves, winds, wends through romance, is shot through—injected, infected—with pain. Masochism, if not its synonym, is its twin. Listen: 'I killed her because I loved her so much.' 'I love him so much I'll kill him before I let him go.' And this one—have you heard this one?—'God so loved man that he killed his only begotten son— . . .' '' He inhaled, felt sweat, anger, pain. His eyes moved from row to row. "The tyranny of love,'' he echoed himself. "Demanding patriotic *love* to support injustice, beatific *love* to entrench repression—an excuse for all the horrors of history! Oh, the Bible reeks with God's love!'' He stopped. "But we were talking of *romantic* love, *faithful* love—demanding selfish 'fidelity'—more ruinous to sex than impotence. It is only the *totalitarians* who demand monogamy!''

Sandy and Lorry left. He blessed them silently. *You can walk out in protest, yes—because 'love' has been allowed you only too recently. But wait.*

Mark pushed firmly at his glasses. That puzzled and disturbed James. What was the youngman reacting against? *Do your parents have lovers? Oh, let them! That is perhaps all he—she— has!* Feeling betrayed, he said, "Hatred is more honest—one expects the plunging, slashing knife. Love is dishonest—it kills with breaths and sighs—and withheld attention.''

An eager youngman joined Dr. Admas; clearly a disciple— Julian. Ex-psychology major, lapsed structuralist, born-again Freudian, majoring in film criticism, with Levi-Straus, Michel Foucault, and Jacques Lacan at his very fingertips.

"The madness of art—which is also its greatness but I won't emphasize that now—is that it attempts to contain chaos. The artist plays the great old madman, God, whose awkward creation—it *is* awkward—is nothing to emulate, although modern painters have tried.''

Beyond the window, sudden wind attacked tall trees. Sunlight cut across the lawn in slender blades.

"If only art did not posture as truth. If only it did not pretend, as Shakespeare said through Hamlet, 'to hold as 'twere, the mirror up to nature.' The mirror is, of course, total reversal. If only art would settle for . . . magic! . . . like Blanche Dubois for Chinese lanterns. But, no, it seeks to contain chaos. discover truth, and enclose all neatly within the covers of a book, the frame of a painting, the latitudes of a screen. It imposes meanings where there are none. It violates experience itself. The greater the artist, the greater the lie. Contain anarchy? Semantic contradiction, actual impossibility! Proust denied the power of the past by making his memories—forever—a part of our present. Joyce erased the unconscious by deleting the period and the comma—consciously. Freud disproved the unconscious by attempting to interpret it through clever consciousness. Wolfe belied his premise by contending that you can't go home again. Bergman converts faces into landscapes to reveal a 'truth' possible only through artificial exaggerations by the camera. Kubrick's monolith is a miniature enlarged. And Moby Dick, is, finally, a whale.''

He waited for Julian's gasp. Julian waited for Dr. Admas's. It came, with a look of indignation, and was quickly drowned by Ellen's appreciative laughter. And Mark smiled. And Joan. *Joan, if you let your hair loose, you will be transformed, like the heroines in the romantic movies you will never see; I am increasingly fond of you. Adorée has only a flashy beauty. But you! You, Joan—you have— . . . pain.*

"Thank God for Margaret Mitchell—no betrayer, she!—we will forever wonder whether Scarlett got Rhett back." He was sorry Joan didn't write that in her notebook.

"Milton set out to justify the ways of God to man and justified the ways of man to God. And what kind of heaven was it in which *angels* were not happy?" He looked down at Mark. *The edge of the shore, it was summer, you stood—* . . . "In *Death in Venice*, Mann would have us believe that the ineffable Tadzio destroys the professor, whereas it is the professor who 'kills' the youth—by dying. Tadzio's beauty is sealed forever behind a pair of closed, no longer obsessed, no longer adoring eyes—the eyes which created the beauty." *Could he have released him from that imprisoning gaze—freed him—allowed him to live after his own death?* . . . "Antonioni tilted *Blow-Up* into ruinous interpretation, belying his own premise, by nudging us to believe that a crime *did* occur in the park, where the mystery should have been left, in the heart of the breathing trees. Welles destroyed an essential secret by revealing to us what 'Rosebud' is to Kane alone.'' *Meursault knew he shot the sun.*

"Now explore the process of canonization. We are, after all, speaking about perfection, and what could be more pure— perfect—than the purity of a saint?—shaped by good works, four miracles. And martyrdom. Appointed angels and warring demons, priests assigned their arbitrary roles, are set out to rake the life of the proposed saint. The advocates of the angels dredge up good, the advocates of the demon dredge up evil. The same life will provide opposite meanings. And the actual life lived? Erased. Now will the angels welcome a new saint, singing his praises into heaven? Or will the sleazy sleeping corpse, retired from a weary life, be resurrected in despair for still one more goddam rejection! . . . Which brings us easily to what is fondly called a senseless act of violence perpetrated, always, by a 'misfit,' the misfit being the one who fits most perfectly into the perfect flowing harmony of coincidence that creates the moment of explosive intersection we call fate! All one has to know about a killer is that he/she killed, and a process similar to that of canonization will occur. A whole life will now be seen as having moved toward one act. The dull, gray incidents of that existence will be colored with the garish colors of inevitability. All redefined, all in retrospect. Where would Christ be without his goddam crucifixion?''

He had delivered his last words with such intensity that the audience withheld reaction. Gloria touched her neck, as if she wore an invisible rosary.

You do! Anger poured out: "Yet why are wars, starvation, exploitation never called meaningless acts?—their perpetrators never misfits? No, those are noble causes determined by wise kings and corporate presidents!'' Sweat streaked his face, wet his chest; a wet coldness.

Outside, the sun knotted the shadows of trees on darkening greenness.

Now the lecturer assumed a growing cadence: "Rolling clouds of steam and mist, within which planets swirled, crashed, and collided—the fission of the universe—a centrifugal force flinging out chips of rock, and one splinter became the earth, and in a million years or seven days, trees grew under a mesmerizing sun, and in the sea fish and oysters and caviar for the rich thrived, and the ape found his spine and became upright man—and some among the hairy new breed were eaten by dinosaurs, some escaped when a pursuing tiger sank into a pit of tar while a weeping mastodon watched and others of the upright creatures were saved by wolves, and caves were carved and collapsed in earthquakes, or fell under lava and ice, and years passed, Babylon fell, Rome followed, and Lot's wife looked back leaving a wake of unending anger, Ezekiel saw the river of blood and fire to come, and the unknown factor loomed over Calvary, and there was war in heaven as apocalyptic horsemen pillaged the plains with war, strife, famine—and death was the pale rider—and fire, hail, and blood, plagues, woes, pestilence, seven vials containing the wrath of God as heaven and hell collided and the earth darkened, the sun was blinded, stars burned, the air darkened, and the poisoned sea gave up its dead—but only some—and the four winds of the burnt earth blew sand trying to wipe away the tears and the scattered sorrow, pain, and death, as promised, and years passed, the great wall of China stretched beyond the pyramids made by a thousand Sisyphuses, Buddha sank into eternal bliss, Allah was praised, God made hefty sacrifices, and time flew because we were having fun as captive kings and princes became slaves, and heads fell to the guillotine and tea bred revolution as new oppressors thrived in place of incestuous kings, who made a comeback to kill more poor, and Salem witches burned in innocence but their ashes burrowed in vengeance into the dark soil, and—here comes another giant leap—years passed, dust swept crops away and the rich took their lives because their money was gone, temporarily, and depression came with Freud and Hoover, followed inevitably by films and premieres during which the dreamless were trampled under tangled cones of searchlights like confused unknown factors—I forgot radio and the World War— . . ." *and a father raged in wounded anger and a mother loved and was loved too much and a dog died in the wind in Texas and was not buried deeply enough, and decayed in the summer sun and was not resurrected but dug up again to be reburied more deeply, and I saw the rotting face of God on my dog, and the first myth died, and then all the others followed easily and that is all you need to know about me* ". . . —and freight trains carried men and women fleeing poverty and dust, and Tangueley's art machine refused to destroy itself in the desert, and out of all that and eons of time—recessive genes devoured by aggressive ones—out of the sand gathering to create man and woman, the pink and blue and cubist periods, the spinning sun, the generation of vipers flourishing, out of all, all that, two individuals emerged separately and miles apart on a lazy afternoon to drive their cars on the same street and *crashed*! It was all, you see, an accident.''

Shocked laughter, uncertain scattered applause. Mark laughed aloud. *But I've given you nothing, Mark.* Adorée relented in her sensuality, and James realized how young she was.

The lecturer studied his audience again. They were appreciating him, yes, but most did not understand how much horror he had poured in constructing his inevitable absurdity. And so he laughed with them as their laughter continued to grow and he said, "The road taken is an important as the road not taken. If Dorothy had followed the *green* brick road, she might have ended in heaven with God, instead of back in Kansas with her aunt. Such are the risks, or treacheries, of free will."

Joan didn't laugh now. Mark stopped. James Huston tried to make the others understand. "The horror, the horror of it all in that journey to the heart of darkness, which is the darkness of the soul—and, in between, a long good-bye." *What can I give you, Mark, Joan? What should I give you, Mark? Joan, will your unappreciated intelligence force you into lucid madness and send you searching through the precious trash bins of your mind? Gloria, you have your inheritance already—a Catholic Christ as indelible as a tattoo carved on your heart. And you, Joe . . . Joe, learn the example of Sisyphus! Hilton!—my white face will distance us forever! It is too late, Mrs. Loomis, it is too late.*

He broke his own trance. His voice was firm. "As easy as ordering the universe, to find meaning within life, whether in art, prayer, or sex. Only God could attempt order out of chaos, or so his reporters claimed, but he botched it—just look around for ample evidence that either God is evil or destiny is chance!'' Dots of perspiration quivered on his eyelids. The faces before him blurred as if he were viewing them unclearly through water or clearly through tears.

Beyond the room, shadows spread under the blazing brightness of the afternoon.

''The only liar greater than the artist—greater only in the sense of degree—is the critic, who interprets the artist's lies.'' He did not bother to aim that at Dr. Admas and Julian. ''And too often by imposing ugly lies on, oh yes, very *beautiful* lies! Critical interpretation is the greatest lie.'' He smiled when he saw how many in the audience—including Dr. Admas, and then Julian—wrote that down. ''Critics, like the blessed apostles, pump meaning into coincidence.''

James Huston sighed. And then as if he were rerunning a film—already shown, a film of his ideas, spliced but run now in fast motion—he said, ''Fate finds its accident, art interprets life, life interprets art, both fail to contain anarchy, anarchy is perfect disorder, death shapes life, in the beginning is the end, the end redefines the beginning and all in between, all possibilities become only one, inevitability exists only in retrospect and random interpretation, accident is inevitable coincidence! To have meaning, life should start with death!'' He stopped abruptly. In startled revelation, as if to himself, he said slowly, ''Perhaps all life *is* flashback, feeble interpretation of that first—and only—meaningful act, the burst of fire that created life, the first and only mystery.'' Outside, as the whitening sun intensified the darkness of shadows, James Huston said softly: ''If one could end life as perfectly as in the carefully constructed ending of a story, brought to the moment of one's great triumph, greatest loss, a mixture of both in a moment of epiphany. Alive, forever, remembered always that way, and not in . . . *creeping* anti-climax!'' He sighed deeply, a muted gasp of pain. ''I see life as a dance before the void. One should perform that dance as beautifully as one can, in as perfect a choreography as allowed—defying while acknowledging the darkness which will end . . . our long life sentences. A *defiant* dance before the triumphant void.''

He allowed a long silence, and he thought he heard within it a sound like that of flapping approaching wings, invisible wings. The rustled leaves of trees, of course; just that.

"Questions! Find questions! Obsessed with finding solutions, we ignore the importance of mystery. Let mysteries remain unsolved—like the mountain climbed because it is, simply, there. Solved, interpreted in 'answer,' a mystery is no longer that, was *never* that! Move *beyond* interpretation, into mystery! Between the mysteries of life and death, there is no proof, no answer, no solution, merely evidence: *I am here!* . . . Finally only mystery is to be 'found.' The Rorschach patterns are silhouettes of each man's mystery. To each his own 'Rosebud' destroyed in the private fires of locked memory. . . . We have arrived at the subject of it all. The mystery of mystery." He felt despair flood, drowning the shreds of hope, sweeping it away into nothingness, this white, hot afternoon. He searched for words to announce that death—and to finish his lecture. "Nothing I have said can stand scrutiny. By speaking, I have contradicted everything I've claimed. It is all incorrect. All contradiction. And what may not have been that, became so when it was uttered, betraying the living it presumed to speak of, and from. I was speaking all along about . . . nothing," he ended.

Mark stood up angrily. He dropped his glasses. He took a step forward. There was the sound of crushed glass.

James Huston looked at him—knowing he was demanding more. *I remember you, Mark. I may have seen you on the beach, a shoreline, perhaps you waved—but I saw you long before that, in my mirror, myself your age, years ago, my youth reflected in you.* James resumed, as if he had not ended his lecture. "Yes, I was speaking about nothing—but with one important exception: In the defiant movements of that dance which acknowledges the triumphant void— . . ." He stopped. *Do I believe this? Do I still believe this? Am I speaking to this youngman—whoever he really is, whatever he really wants—or only to myself?* ". . . —in those defiant movements there should be— . . . might be— . . . will be . . . a kind of meaning . . . which may— . . ." *perhaps!* ". . . —allow hope."

Mark nodded.

Accepting that reprieve?

There was buzzing tension. Then silence. Then tension and silence were swept back by applause.

Applause! The irony, James Huston thought angrily, the irony of that applause! He turned away from it and from the shared imaginary lives, which had ended, and he looked out the window, where shadows on the lawn had grown into black blossoms.

Lost Angels: 7

The Santa Ana wind moaned into the dark park. Gathering heat from the distant desert, enraged it invades the city, creating the season of heat and fire.

Orin, Lisa, and Jesse James moved against the harsh vista of twisted trees and craggy rocks stenciled on the orange luminescence of fire miles away in the outlying canyons of the city.

Orin had parked the Cadillac on a street where houses bunch at the base of Griffith Park. Then they walked past the chained rails that bar vehicles from entering the vast park after ten-thirty at night.

This morning Orin had said; "Trust me . . . please?" Those words, pronounced softly, slowly, like a powerful incantation—those words and his saddened, pleading, deepening blue eyes underscoring them gave the aimless day its only order. *Trust me.* As they rode in the dark Cadillac off and on the maze of freeways, to the beach, stopping to eat, to Hollywood—Orin paying for everything, everything, hesitating only after the expensive dinner as if to reinforce their promise of trust—his words wafted Lisa and Jesse throughout the day. Trust me. The silence of the day—enforced by Orin by asserting his own—itself became hypnotic, containing only that exhortation, *Trust me.* And leaving in abeyance the rushing questions about last night's unfinished call to Sister Woman, it promised contingent clarification—and perhaps more, based on tonight's loyalty. They wandered about the city, rested in a statued garden. Toward evening, the sun had turned ferociously orange, a conflagration of the days of heat, which was burrowing into the very soil of the city.

Now black heat poured into Griffith Park—their destination

implicit this whole mesmeric day; they had known it, or so it had seemed to Lisa and Jesse, when the car approached the night-shrouded park. *Trust me*, the haunted eyes had exhorted.

In the hypnotic wailing dark heat, Jesse and Lisa walked with Orin past the black ruins of charred areas, past secret coves and hiding paths. Ravaged trees twisted into violent shapes under the mottled gray of a spectral moon. As they advanced up the deserted roads, they heard the harsh exhalations of the pillaging wind.

Far beyond, at the top, the Observatory swam in a pool of electric light radiating from its base; surrounded by darkness.

At the end of this night's journey, Jesse James felt certain that, like all the heroes he admired, he would have a destiny. Orin promised it. *Trust me*. Jesse raised his chin. They made their way up the concrete road.

At first the park's contorted darkness had frightened Lisa. But as she moved along with Orin and Jesse, her fears faded. *Trust me*. And she had—from as far back as the desert, perhaps before that, days ago, but certainly from the moment of saddened silence when he had dug a grave for the slaughtered bird under the only shade he could find in the desert. She had not told him this, but on that day she had become eighteen. *Trust me*.

Even Orin was drenched in sweat when they reached the edge of the lawn that leads to the Observatory. The invading desert heat increased in layers. They moved into the path that veers down to the left of the three-domed building. Away from the dying yellow lights of the park's scattered lamps, they hiked into the branchy depths of the park, farther, deeper, under clawing limbs, tunnels carved by bent trees, past oxidized pipes like orange decayed veins, which feed the Observatory its power. Farther. A collapsed tree blocked their way. Orin led the way over it. It was now as if they had entered a tunnel of the night itself, the park's true wilderness. Huge powerful trees interlocked.

They reached a broken crag, a small cliff, which dropped into a path of fire-scarred land. Moonlight swept the burnt skeletons of trees clinging to the dead earth on a plain as desolate as a plundered graveyard.

Ahead, on another small hill, a mass of trees formed the heart of the park's darkness.

They stood on the edge of one hill and faced the other across the burnt waste. Here, rocks jutted from the earth in distorted protrusions. Orin climbed onto the blackened stones. Lisa raised herself and stood beside him. Now Jesse was with them. On that jagged crest, they stared across the escarpment separated by a decline and the desolate stretch.

Then Orin bent and forced a heavy rock over the stone rim. The crashing noise pushed against the howl of wind.

Out of the clotted darkness ahead, a lone form seemed to emerge. The wind shoved trees to one side, then the other, wiping away the outline within the shifted darkness of clasped branches. Now across the barren spread, there was nothing, only frantic trees.

Against the glow of distant fire, Orin, Lisa, and Jesse James stood on the crags and faced the dark.

PART TWO

Lost Angels: 8

"I didn't see *anything!*"

Inside the motel, the spell of the night shattered like black glass. For Lisa. For Jesse.

"*Nothing!*" Lisa emphasized her first denial. She wanted to erase what she had seen—thought she had seen, only for a moment—in the park—and, with that, to erase even her lack of fear then; it disturbed her now, now that they were in this room of past safety. To assert that safety, *its* reality, she went to the bed and held Pearl.

"I didn't see anything either," Jesse said. He resented the way Orin had prepared the day.

Orin sat at the table of the room, which had become their home since they had arrived in Los Angeles just days ago. He reached for some stationery in a drawer of the table. He found a pen. He sat there, pondering. Then he wrote numbers.

Jesse threw himself on the bed, weary from the long night journey. He didn't bother to remove his boots. He knew what had only festered before like a buried splinter: Orin controlled them, their reality. What if there had been someone out there and we— . . .

". . . —were in danger?" It was Lisa who had spoken the words Jesse longed to form. "Not that there *was* anyone," she thrust away. "It was just one of your weird tests. And you tricked us, just to scare us—acting strange the whole day. Trust me, trust me, trust me! you kept saying over and over. And you made all kinds of promises!" Her voice was firm—she pushed Pearl away.

Orin looked quizzically at her. "You weren't in danger; I had

223

already made sure of that—wouldn't put you in danger, you know that. Just wanted him to see you, and he did.''

Why? Lisa didn't allow herself to ask that question; he almost seemed to want them to.

Why? Jesse sat up, wishing he would ask that. Why did you want ''him'' to see us? . . . Look at him acting like he's been there before, even talked to whoever is there—if there's anybody!

''And I only asked you once to trust me, that's a fact,'' Orin said, ''and I didn't make any promises, a-*tall*.''

''How can you— . . . ?'' Lisa stopped. He was right.

He was right! Jesse knew, startled. But it had seemed otherwise.

Lisa frowned, withdrawing her further accusations for now. Why had it seemed, so powerfully, that he exhorted all day, and promised— . . .? Quickly, Lisa decided to remove Pearl's hat—it was badly frayed. Pearl Chavez—the real Pearl—hadn't worn a hat anyway. But neither had she worn this fluffy dress. Why had she called her Pearl in the first place? She didn't look the half-breed who had seen, in silhouette through a window, her father kill her Indian mother because he found her with another man—but really because the Indian woman hated her daughter. No—*this* Pearl looked like a little girl playing grown-up.

Still so cool, like nothing's been said. Jesse studied Orin. *Was* there a man in that park? When they stood on those rocks, he had been sure the outline was that of a man. He had felt a stalking excitement, as if he were in a movie with Cagney. Now, in this room, everything only ''seemed.'' ''You really serious you know someone's out there, Orin?'' He disguised his grave tone in casualness.

''You know as well as I do, Jesse,'' Orin said. He drew a line across the paper, adding some figures.

Jesse bit his anger. There it was again. Answering but not answering. ''Why did you want him to see us?'' He was instantly elated by his boldness; then an overlap of apprehension lessened his elation. There were certain questions whose answers he might not want to know—Orin seemed to count on that.

''He's got to trust us,'' Orin answered, as if the answer was obvious.

Why! Again Lisa drowned the persistent question. He wanted them to ask a reason because that meant they accepted a presence out there, and God knows what he'd come up with, in his mood. She saw Jesse about to ask more. "Stop asking him questions, Jesse! He'll make more things up!"

Jesse was glad to agree; he wasn't sure he *would* have asked any more.

She had walked into that frightening park at night! And yet she hadn't been afraid! *That* bothered Lisa, now. Again her strong voice accused. "I don't even believe you talked to that weird woman on television." She had to render it *all* unreal.

Oh, oh. Jesse winced at the powerful accusation. He, too, had wondered about that. . . . And just look at her! Jesse admired Lisa; one moment playing with her doll, and another moment confronting Orin like that—and Orin taking it. Or just allowing it. For now.

Orin drew another line across the paper before him. "What?" he asked her.

Pretending. "If there is anyone out there—and we captured him—would we be heroes?" Jesse remembered having asked that question, but he didn't remember an answer.

Orin laughed. He set aside the paper on which he had computed. "For finding someone who just walked away from a hospital?" he questioned back. " 'Cause he wanted to be free?" He looked into his wallet.

How many individual gatherings of paper-clipped money were left? Jesse wondered. There's got to be more! He and Lisa weren't contributing anything now. That was one of the ways Orin was able to run things so easily, buy their silence, which contained a hundred new questions each time one seemed to be answered. And! Nothing kept Orin from simply leaving them.

Lisa challenged, "And who cares if someone's out there—as long as he's not hurting anyone." She heard her last words and felt apprehension. "Would *you* turn him in—*if* he exists?" She deliberately did not address either one of them directly.

"Depends." Jesse startled himself. He had used Orin's ready answer, and it had come automatically, Orin's word.

Lisa glanced at Jesse. Was he *trying* to sound like Orin? "What if there was somebody out there and he *shot* at us!"

Damn right! Jesse got up, stood near her—an ally.

"He doesn't have a gun, no rifle; told you—I made sure of that. He just had to see there's three of us— . . ."

So he's been out there alone, those early mornings; talked to whoever— . . . if— . . . Now Jesse was sure he didn't want to hear any more, not tonight; now everything was confusing, and everything could turn threatening.

With an audible slam, Lisa closed the bathroom door behind her. She, too, was undecided how much clarity she wanted for now.

Jesse leaned over the table where Orin had been writing on a piece of paper; there were several numbers followed by many zeroes. Many, many zeroes.

Anger. Confusion. In the bathroom, Lisa startled herself in the mirror. Her face was smeared with dust from the park. She washed herself. She still looked different.

She removed her clothes. Her breasts looked fuller. She got under the shower, letting the water wash away the park's darkness. Orin scared her less. She turned off the water. Maybe she was just getting used to him. She dried herself, wrapped a furry towel about her wet hair. She touched her nipples, delicately, moistened her fingers with saliva, and then touched them again. Sexuality hugged her.

Last night when she had come out with her nightgown lowered, there had been that awful moment of Orin's anger. Now she needed to confront it.

She slipped on her nightgown, the sheerest one she had. No underclothes. She dabbed water over her breasts. She reached for the door knob, then stopped. This time she moistened the part of the material that veiled the upper portion of her thighs, so that it revealed her flesh there, and a hint of her pubic hair. She felt happily defiant, and emboldened by the fact that on that earlier night there had been clear desire when Orin saw her. She had retreated too quickly from his *possible* anger, anger she was almost sure now she had only imagined.

She walked out and stood very still in flimsy nudity.

"Hot as pistols!" another of Cody's lines shot out of Jesse when he saw her.

"*Lisa!*"

Lisa felt the lash of Orin's anger. It *had* been there before, and it was there now—fiercer!—in the way he flung her name. In the bathroom she had been one person, a new one; now quickly she was another, who belonged in this room. She breathed deeply, as if to retrieve the bold part of her. But that briefly born "her" did not return. So she grasped for words from her treasured "all-times," words which would save her. But *which*, now? All she could remember were lines of surrender and loss. The moisture of her breasts and thighs increased with perspiration. She felt paralyzed in a nightmare—Orin's.

Jesse inched toward her, toward her breasts pasted against the material as thin as tissue, the smudge of auburn between her legs—a beautiful, sexual woman, who wanted him, them.

Lisa grabbed Jesse's look of desire. She straightened her body, asserting its exposed sensuality, Jesse's look giving her assurance that she hadn't done anything bad.

"*Lisa!*"

She felt herself whirling in the vortex of Orin's fury. Why had she done this? Why!

' Jesse's hard-on was so demanding he clutched it—not caring what Orin would say. He put his hands about Lisa's waist, lowered them to her buttocks.

"Leave her alone." Orin's words were emphatic whispers.

Lisa rushed to Pearl on the bed. She covered herself with the bed sheet and pushed Pearl against her stomach.

"Hey, you listen— . . ." Jesse's challenge shot out at Orin. You controlled us all day, Orin! he didn't say aloud; you took us with you to that goddamn park to scare us, or test us, or whatever the fuck you're doing, and you're still doing it, and I know you want Lisa as much as I do! Jesse walked over to where Lisa lay in bed. He held the edge of the sheet as if to uncover her.

"Jesse." Orin's word warned—so softly.

And yet, Jesse saw, Orin's look was on Lisa, on her body. If he pulled the sheet at the moment of Orin's desire, then it would happen, but if at that moment anger raged— . . . He let go of the sheet.

Lisa reached for her robe, put it on, sat up fully covered. "I was just playing," she whispered.

"Just having some fun," Jesse mumbled.

"Nothing wrong with a little fun," Orin released them all.

Jesse laughed in eager relief. He sat on the bed with Lisa—not touching—to assure that everything was all right again.

"Shoot, you can even change your name if you want to, Lisa—haven't in a long time," Orin offered in his light tone. He sat with her and Jesse on the bed. "Medea," he said. "You can be Medea. Know who she was? She was a woman who let lust rule her, gave up everything for it, couldn't control it—so lustful she killed her children."

"No one should kill their children!" Lisa protested. She brought Pearl to her breasts.

"Sometimes people do—without *really* killing!" Pain deepened Orin's blue eyes. Then he said, "Didn't mean to scare you, Lisa—sorry if I did. What I was telling you—they're just stories, about Medea and everything—like your movies, see. The old woman, she had lots of books, liked to read—oh, she really loved to read! When she started losing her sight, she got the biggest damn magnifying glass you've *ever* seen!" He laughed briefly. "I read to her—stories, legends, myths. Lots from the Bible. She liked that better than almost anything else. Except sin," he breathed barely. "And she loved listening to Sister Woman preach."

Jesse's lips opened, formed silence. Lisa softened her breathing—nothing must stop these words of revelation.

Orin bent over and touched Pearl, as if to make her more comfortable for sleep. "Yeah—the blind old woman," he said. "She loved those old stories and listening to Sister Woman promise salvation—for *sure*!" He covered his face with his hands.

He moved away from Lisa and Jesse. He stood at the wide window. "For *sure!*" he repeated, the way he often said "a-*tall*." The drapes were drawn against the night. He parted them and peered out into the simmering darkness.

"That's why she left Sister Woman all that money—but *only* if she can prove to us that God is as powerful as she says—as she *promised*. Powerful enough to— . . ." He stopped, as if inspecting the glass-shielded night. "Every time she got me to write that Sister Woman, when she knew she was dying, toward the last, she'd insist, 'Tell that Sister Woman before she gets one penny, she's got to show us *proof*. Proof!—in the fireworks of God.' ''

Proof of *what*, Orin? *Proof of what!* But Lisa knew she wouldn't ask. Perhaps didn't even want to know—not now.

Mick Vale: "Mr. Universal"

When he saw Robert Newman commanding the entrance to Harry's Gym, Mick Vale immediately abandoned the Pec-Deck machine on which he had been blasting his chest muscles. Mick—Michelangelo Valenti before he emigrated from New Jersey to "the mecca of bodybuilders"—felt the striations of his pumped pectorals pull like the fingers of two tightly clasped hands. Strong hands. In the learned semi-swagger of a prize-winning bodybuilder, he sauntered to the area of the free weights, the barbells and dumbbells. All physique champions and serious contenders from around the world trained at Harry's.

Other hugely developed bodies that had been stretching, pulling, and pushing on the padded seats of the contraptions that resembled electric chairs, discarded the machines' cams and levers and insinuated themselves dutifully among the men who were heaving the iron weights, up, out, down, over; pulling and stretching cables; chinning on and dipping between bars.

The machines faced the racks of free weights across the room like weapons of the opposing armies they represented. Mirrored walls, surrounding, multiplied the warring equipment. More than twenty men, with muscles so big they seemed attached, worked out now, early afternoon. The meat-slabbed bodies were barely covered with ripped t-shirts, cutoff pants, tattered boxer-style trunks. Harry's outlawed bikinis and brief trunks and bare torsos, to assert its nonsexual buddy-to-buddy, man's-man to man's-man masculinity. Portions of defiant muscles peeking out of the cultivated tears emphasized the forbidden eroticism.

On an incline bench now, Mick prepared to do a set of presses; these work the upper pectorals so that they flare and sweep to the crown of the deltoids. Hands slightly wider than

230

shoulder-width, he held the weight, poised overhead, then lowered it—slowly—so that the full range of movement would
allow each muscle its own awesome moment. Seven repetitions.
Finished, he stood, feeling the ultimate rush of the bodybuilder,
the "pump"—muscles engorged by fresh assertive blood.

Mr. Venice Beach, Jr. Mr. America, Mr. America, Mr.
International, Mr. World—these were only some of Mick's
physique titles. He faced the mirror. Dark, good-looking, not
tall—he claimed to be 5'-9" but wasn't, not quite—he weighed
between 200 and 210 solid pounds. Through the pieces of his
chopped t-shirt, his muscles shocked each other in mutual,
admiring discovery, then, recovering, competed for attention.

In the bodybuilding magazines, there is a stock vocabulary
used only on crowned champions. In that language, Mick Vale
would be described like this: "His shocking triceps are carved
like horseshoes, his massive arms bunch into incredible baseball
biceps, his fantastic lats flare like bat wings, his mind-boggling
shoulders spread as wide as a barnyard door, his fabulous
abdominals knot like ropes, his unbelievable thighs are thick as
oaks, his fabulous vascularity resembles a road map, he is
massive but ripped to shreds."

"Looking good."

"Oh, hi, Bob!" Mick pretended to have just now seen the
man he had been performing for—Robert Newman. Only the
top champions were bestowed the right to call him "Bob."

As always, Newman was dressed in tailored clothes of casual
formality. Shortish, slender, a man in his middle fifties, with
graying hair, he had the sharp face of an eagle, dark eyes that
asserted they missed nothing except what they chose to ignore.
He was one of the most powerful men in the world of
bodybuilding; only his archrivals, Dan Lurie, Joe Weider, and
Bob Hoffman, came near or surpassed him, depending on which
loyalist was consulted in that bitterly factious world. Newman
was publisher of *Muscles* magazine, president of one of the
three federations that ruled over most of the leading physique
competitions, a man with the papal power to excommunicate
any bodybuilder from the small world of perfect bodies.

Newman moved about to study Mick's body from different
angles, as if Mick were a sculpture of flesh and Newman the

sculptor. Mick slipped off the torn shirt—that was allowed when Newman was here—clasped his right hand over his left forearm and, inhaling, raised his chest, almost parallel to the gym floor. Newman's eyes raked the sweating tensed body. Now Mick thrust his arms up in a U over his head, fists out, flaring legs slightly arched.

"You have a good chance to be Mr. Universal this year," Newman dropped the ineffable.

Mick felt blood pulse in ecstasy into every limb of his pumped body, every vein, every artery. He had already announced that he was entering the king of all contests, the one that proclaimed the most perfectly built man in the world, a contest open only to the superstars. The Mr. Universal!

"That's because I've been using all your principles!" Mick was finally able to gasp.

"Obviously," Newman acknowledged.

It was possible to lose the top title with Newman on your side, but it was impossible to win without his approval. He asserted his narrowed choices (the top six, then three, then— some said—one) by insinuating his contingent power over contest judges—gym owners, ex-champions, photographers, others in the field who stood to gain from his support.

No one out of grace ever placed in a top show. Those who fell—by nature of having entered a forbidden contest, endorsed a rival's products, whispered a word of criticism about Newman, or trespassed within a shifting code of "morality"—were further banished from the pages of *Muscles* magazine, which claimed, as the other three top bodybuilding magazines did, to have the widest circulation in its field, in the world.

A millionaire over and over, Newman owned an empire of health products, gym equipment, and hand-picked perfect bodies from whose ranks champions emerged. He did not own exercise machines. A rival entrepreneur had beaten him to them. Their use was too wide for even him to contain, and so *Muscles* magazine carried a monthly article denouncing the efficacy, safety, morality, and patriotism of the "unnatural machines." That is why Mick Vale led a small exodus away from them.

Until the last decade, bodybuilding had been a tacky, esoteric affair, contests held in drafty high-school gymnasiums or Y's, winners standing on quivering boxes covered with graying sheets. Now, choreographed displays of superb bodies posing against colored backdrops and to the gushes of music usually from movie-epic scores—were televised, sold-out, standing-room-only affairs held in major auditoriums before thousands of committed, demanding fans.

Even so, only the top men can make a living from body-building. Mick was one of those. He sold mail-order courses revealing his "secrets," conducted seminars in gyms all over the country, gave guest exhibitions as a draw in minor contests; and was paid a smart secret salary—augmented by a full supply of expensive health products—by Newman, in exchange for his name on ghost-written articles, endorsement of products, and photographs of him working out on Newman Equipment. That, added to constantly growing prize money, allowed Mick to live very well.

Mick heard a despised roar of vulgar laughter. The Gorilla had just entered the gym, he knew without looking. The Gorilla— Mick dubbed him that in secret—was Herbert Lichtenstein, Mick's main rival in the Mr. Universal, a man who seemed crushed by his own rampant muscles. He was last year's Mr. Universal. And there he was now, clowning his way into the gym, slapping ass, parodying other bodybuilders. Look at his waist, Mick thought triumphantly. Herbert claimed it was 30 inches, but Mick knew it was closer to 36. Photographers knew how to obscure that fact. Most bodybuilders lie about their arm size, waist girth, and age. Mick himself claimed his 32-inch waist—admittedly hard and ridged—was 29, exactly the way he reversed his age.

"Of course, you'll have to face Herbert— . . ." Newman waved at the Gorilla, who smiled broadly and waved back. ". . . —unless he retires this year; hasn't decided." Champions often did that—retired after winning the top title. Losing it was remembered more than having won it.

"You know which of your principles I found most beneficial, Bob?" Mick recited what he had to say. "The Newman Prime-Attention Principle." This was simply working more on the muscle you felt needed improvement. Obvious techniques known for years to bodybuilders were rebaptized by Newman into new "principles" bearing his name.

"And did you try the Newman Perfect-Imperfect Principle?" *I* introduced *that*! "All the time," Mick couldn't help but mumble.

"I saw you on the machines." Newman reacted to the tone by placing a bomb between them.

Mike defused it. "Just trying them out, Bob, so I can say in interviews why they don't work. Didn't even give me a pump."

"Sandra and I would like to have you to dinner," Newman bestowed. "Tonight?"

Mick gasped, "I'd love to have dinner with you and San— . . ."

He had seen her photographs in Bob's magazines: "Robert Newman's biggest fan, his beautiful wife, Sandra." ". . . —and Mrs. Newman," Mick retreated. He'd have to call his girlfriend, Josie, to tell her he couldn't make it tonight. She'd understand. Dinner with Bob and his wife! And at a time so close—*so very close!*—to the Mr. Universal Contest! God! Mick would have canceled attendance at the funeral of a beloved for this.

"I may be able to offer some pointers on your posing routine," Newman said. Those "tips"—sometimes granted in the gym—Mick himself had earned some—were valued not so much for their instructive quality as for indications of committed support. Newman was now offering private instruction along with dinner. "What do you pose to?—*Exodus? Dr. Zhivago?*" Every silver cloud has a dark lining, and Mick was slightly chagrined that Bob, who had seen his routine many times at shows, didn't remember. "*The Ten Commandments*," he said. He had tried it privately to the return-to-Tara theme in *Gone With the Wind*, but Josie made a strong case against evoking the image of Scarlett O'Hara with her fist clenched swearing to lie, steal, cheat, and kill and never be hungry again.

"*The Ten Commandments*! Excellent! Six-thirty, then. We eat early." He gave Mick a printed map to his home in Encino—a rich suburb in the outlying San Fernando Valley of Los Angeles. Mick was grateful for that; he doubted that he could have steadied his excitement long enough to write directions.

"That new bodybuilder shows promise," Newman moved

toward a youngman doing heavy squats. He was always scouting for potential champions; he would then claim to have built them, no matter how long they'd been training.

There is a forced euphoric camaraderie among bodybuilders in a championship gym—they *must* be regular guys, even when, as is often true, they despise each other. It is, after all, a world of constant, tense, internecine competition, further exacerbated by a religious seriousness and devotion to winning. This often produces raging bitchiness among the huge musclemen.

Mick was on his way to the showers when Herbert Lichtenstein—stripped to a cut t-shirt and trunks—sidled over. That waist wasn't a millimeter under 37 inches, Mick gauged with pleasure. The Gorilla was a notorious "joker," famous for crushing frail egos encased in huge musculature. He called out to Mick in his heavily accented voice, "Hoy, Mick, vhen ya gonna gain some veight so you can be really a competition? Ho, ho, ho!"

"When you get your gut smaller, Santa Claus," Mick said.

Blasphemy!

Weights clanged onto the floor. Nobody talked about the thick waistline of the acknowledged king.

"Vot?" Herbert's mouth shot open. "*Vot?*"

Newman stood between the two massive men.

What if he takes sides! Mick wanted to rush into the shower. Had he been too emboldened by Bob's invitation to dinner? Herbert was one of Newman's very top boys. A smile! A slight smile? The barest trace of a smile—at the edge of Newman's lips? Had Mick seen it or just hopefully put it there?

Newman left the gym. On his way out, he merely nodded at Joe Jones—"the Black Sultan"—a phenomenal bodybuilder with muscles like black marble who had defied Newman by having his hair woven into African tresses. Cold dark eyes barely acknowledged Newman's nod.

Engorged bodies resumed their stations about the machines and the free weights. Herbert Lichtenstein raised a loaded bar in a standing press, and then he flung it down with a quaking clang, as if it were Mick.

Newman didn't take sides! Mick exulted in the shower. He felt *damn* good. He had clobbered the Gorilla, and Newman had

not taken sides. If there *had* been a smile, that was added
victory. There were a few other bodies within the mushrooms of
steam—difficult to tell because the showers had small partitions.
Only by standing slightly forward were you able to see others
fully out of the hot mist. So often derided as "fags" because of
their devotion to the masculine body, bodybuilders are sensitive
to overtones of homosexuality. Although several of the top
champions are homosexuals, they keep their sexuality quiet.
Many contenders, who spend hours in the gym, make little or
nothing from their sport, and so find "sponsors" among homosexuals who glorify the muscular body. Some of them use
contests as showcases for that purpose. Several pose nude for
mail-order businesses and magazines directed at homosexuals.
Some—especially among the lower-ranked contenders—are
callboys, occasionally for women, but mostly, and by far, for
other men. None of that makes them "fags" or "queers" as
long as money or gain is involved; sexual identity is not defined
by same-gender activity. Unpaid choice defines that. Choosing
sex with other men in mutual, unpaid encounters makes a
bodybuilder "queer."

For these reasons, the ritual in the showers is a strained one,
where the strident enforced camaraderie in the gym bursts into
euphoric hysteria among the carefully developed bodies. Loud
laughter, anxious banter, passionate discussions of techniques—
thrust across the stalls by heads bobbing out of steam—anything
to dissipate the forbidden eroticism of perfect naked bodies
constantly comparing themselves, without looking.

Out of the steam, Mick Vale saw Bo Sanders, the quiet one,
a handsome blond youngman, an up-and-comer who had already won several of the lower-echelon, but necessary, contests.

"Been working on your delts, huh?" Mick was secure enough
to compliment Bo's when he felt his eyes on him. Bo said yes
and continued soaping his cock—disguising a hard-on? Mick
loved it when others got hard looking at him.

When he emerged from the showers, the Gorilla was gone.
Just like him to walk out sweaty, smelly. Mick was aware of a
buzzing excitement. Chuck Harris! Chuck Harris was in the
gym!—sitting on a bench and holding court. He was one of the
greats of the "old-timers"— one of the superstars of the Fifties,

the first to claim twenty-inch arms. One of the handsomest of the bodybuilders, he had made some *Son of Hercules* movies, in Italy—at a time when the short fad was passing. His last two pictures were unreleased, and he was stranded in Rome several weeks. Years ago he had left Los Angeles. A retired king, a legend. He owned a gym in the Midwest—or managed it.

The bodybuilders who, like Mick, had been inspired by Chuck Harris—his photographs—gathered about him now. Mick approached him. Though done carefully, the edges of his temples revealed they had been colored; still, he looked terrific for his age—over fifty! Or was it that the aura of his radiating myth still protected him? He was dressed in loose clothes, difficult to know what his body looked like; it seemed in very good shape.

Sure of his own fame—he was, after all, in the body magazines every month—Mick Vale worked his way through the sweaty delts, traps, and pecs gathered about Chuck Harris, and he introduced himself with a smile.

"Vale? Mick Vale! Yeah! Good to meet you, man!" Chuck Harris said.

"Great to meet *you*, Chuck." Mick meant it. It was so difficult to know what Harris really looked like—how old, how different—even this close up, because Mick's memory of him was so overwhelming that it stamped itself on the man surrounded by his fans, some of whom had not been born when he was winning contests. At age fourteen, Mick had pinned Chuck Harris's full-body photograph—for heroic inspiration—to the wall of the makeshift garage-gym where he had lifted his first weights.

"Good to get a look at my competition," Chuck Harris said. Wrinkles scratched his eyes as he smiled; the skin under his chin was beginning, just barely beginning, to loosen.

Competition! "You entering the Mr. Universal?" Mick asked casually.

"Yeah—Bob talked me into it. Said it was time we showed you new guys what we can do without drugs and machines."

It was true that many of the top champions were now well into their forties—maybe most of them—though they tended to linger at thirty-nine for six or seven years. Still, they had kept up with steroids, new techniques. Harris was older, belonged to a historical generation. Bodies had changed.

"Welcome back," Mick said. He felt an exhaustion that did not have to do with his heavy workout. That always felt great. He looked back at Chuck basking in the aura of a past which had *begun* over thirty years ago. Now, a comeback!

The image of the new Chuck, the middle-aged—old—Chuck, pursued Mick as he ran on the late afternoon beach from Venice to Santa Monica. How would he remember Chuck now? His bewildering concern was swept away by a loving breeze coupled with the awareness of what he courted on his almost-daily runs on the beach: the sight of his extraordinary body pulling eyes, eliciting whistles of admiration from women, and men, and some derision in falsetto male voices, mostly from skinny young punks. That did not faze Mick—not even the word "grotesque," which often flew at him—he accepted all that as envy, and it all acknowledged his proud specialness, a prized specialness that was worth the hours and hours of working out, worth the rigid diet, worth it all, a hundred times over and then some—worth it all, all, all—for this body, this uniqueness.

The ocean frothed blue and white. Hot clouds bunched on the horizon. What would Herbert Lichtenstein, the clumsy clown, say when he learned that Chuck was making a comeback? Mick did not like these feelings of protectiveness. After all, Chuck might turn out to be a formidable rival. He had said *Bob* had talked him into entering. Maybe he *is* in terrific shape! And if he was now taking, for the first time, some of the bodybuilding "aids," like steroids, whose effects were already being neutralized in the newer bodybuilders, then— . . . !

The sense of protectiveness evaporated like the sweat on Mick's cooling body as he lay on the sand on an isolated stretch of beach where the wind had formed clean rivulets. An early summer, technically still spring. He hoped this didn't mean that summer, precious summer, would be niggardly. Cool summers occur now and then in Southern California. Days on the beach, awaited for the eternity of a few months, are rationed. That then becomes a period of desolation for those who measure their lives by the length of summer. The beginning of summer always saddened Mick anyhow, because it ended the anticipation of it, and *another* summer would soon be over; that was the cruelty of spring.

Propping his head on his hands, Mick looked down at his body. It was beautiful. The Gorilla's remark. Maybe he *could* use a little more bulk, perhaps five, maybe ten more pounds—if he kept it defined. Tomorrow he was due for a shot of Decadurabolin, one of the many steroids—hormones—he and other bodybuilders use regularly for added bulk—although each must deny using them, attack them violently in Newman's magazine. He'd ask the doctor to increase the potency, and he'd double up on the oral steroids. Just before the Universal, he'd hit the zero-carbohydrate diet, and the day before, he might lock himself in a hot, hot room, dress himself in heavy sweatclothes, and take a diuretic—define the added bulk. Wait. Maybe the Gorilla, who was famous for his "psych-outs"—sabotaging the confidence of other bodybuilders before a contest—*wanted* him to bulk up, afraid of his striking definition.

He left the beach when the sun was reddening the clouds and the horizon glowered like distant fire—like a city on fire. There was a hint of gathering heat even in the moist air.

In his neat, two-room-and-small-kitchen apartment just a few blocks from the beach—with an awesome view of the sand and the ocean, so dark and dramatic at night—Mick called his girlfriend, Josie. As soon as they found a large enough place both liked, they would move in together. Of *course* she understood—*wow*—dinner with the Newmans didn't happen every day of the week. When he told her what he had said to the Gorilla, Josie was ecstatic. She was a pretty girl—and *not* one of those new women bodybuilders Mick disliked so much, making themselves look like parodies of *skinny* bodybuilders. Josie was on the curvaceous side. A great help to Mick, she kept track of his mail-order courses and gave him the needed support to sustain the rigorous training. She liked how people looked at him when they went out. And they had a good sexual relationship; she liked everything he liked, and told him so each time.

Mick dressed neatly—sport jacket, open shirt, slacks.

It was a bad time to be on the freeway—peak traffic—but he had to take it to get to Encino. Suddenly he and his perfectly kept 1965 Mustang—tan, in superb condition, like him—were in a traffic jam. One of the daily disasters that occur in Los Angeles—a stalled car—was paralyzing the freeway. Gawkers in opposing lanes created twin tie-ups as they slowed down to pay homage to *this* particular disaster. Mick felt moons of sweat under his arms, beads of moisture matting the curly hair at his forehead. It would be at least twenty minutes before this tangle unknotted.

Encino is a rich purgatory to which the not-quite-classy rich surrender, abdicating Bel Air and Beverly Hills. Even when large and resplendent, the houses are anxious in their shaky newness; determinedly *imitation* Spanish, *imitation* colonial, imitations of imitations.

Mick parked before a large two-storey house. It had a balcony from which carefully draped bougainvillea hung like purple-beaded necklaces. And arched stained-glass windows forming figures—muscular angels? The doorbell sounded the first four notes of Tchaikovsky's *Piano Concerto No. 5*.

"Hi, Mick, I'm Sandra."

Mick was astonished that Bob's wife had come to the door herself; he had expected a butler. They *must* have servants in this huge house. "*Really* glad to meet you," Mick emphasized.

Sandra was almost as good-looking as her pictures. She was wearing tight white slacks—and an equally tight, thick white turtle-neck, long-sleeved sweater. In this heat! She had dark brown hair, straight except for a swirl inward at her shoulders. Sensational shape!—the sweater was pushed out just right by her assertive breasts, held by a brassiere, to be that firm, Mick was sure. In her forties? She would have looked younger if it hadn't been for the deep-brown, creasing tan.

"Come in, Mick." Her swaying hips led him in. She looked like one of those not-quite-stars in the old, late-night movies.

Inside, Mick was assaulted simultaneously by cold air and a rage of colors. Hued light thrusting erratically through dyed window panes tangled and wrestled with the battling colors of the furniture—soft, velvety, whorehouse "Victorian" chairs, lamps, sofas, drapes; paintings—mostly of seascapes and landscapes, and muscular horses—contained in rococo gold-leafed frames. Josie would love this house, Mick thought approvingly.

One of the walls of the room was glass, which parted to connect with a portion of the garden. Mick felt a welcome breath of precious warmth coming from outside; he moved toward it. But Sandra pressed a button and the glass panels began to slide together to chop off the vagrant warmth.

Beyond the invisible wall was an enormous free-form pool. Something floated in it. A ball. Did they have children? No, it was a head. The head of Bob Newman wearing a yellow rubber cap. Before the glass panels joined, Sandra called out through the narrowing partition, "Mick Vale's here!" The head floated the length of the pool. Beyond view from behind the glass wall, it disappeared.

"Drink, honeybunch?" Sandra asked Mick.

"No!" Mick said in horror, both at the suggestion and the odd endearment, which might be overheard. Like many other bodybuilders, Mick had a drink now and again; had even gotten drunk after winning the Mr. America. He smoked a little grass, too. And that *one* time— . . . He pushed the thought away. It shoved back. *That* time he'd done cocaine. He looked around, as if Newman's powerful spirit would grasp his floating secret. His secret! Why did he have to think about *that*, now?—now, when he was here to do all he had to do to augment his chances at the Mr. Universal. His body could stand on its own. Other factors were now at play—like this invitation.

"Don't panic," Sandra said. "We have a drink now and then." She made herself one. A martini! She plunged three stuffed olives into the glass, and then added another, the liquid spilling. She licked the rim of the glass. "Pretending it's a Marrr-garrr-ita," she growled the *R*'s.

"You're late!" Newman's voice boomed. Bob was again impeccably dressed; he wore a scarf about his neck.

"Traffic snarl," Mick said. He would begin to shiver unless they lowered the air-conditioner.

"Just one of the prices we pay for living in Mecca," said Bob. He made himself a huge jingling martini with only one olive.

He'd better be on his toes, Mick reminded himself, noting that Bob had not offered him a drink.

Newman's extended hand directed Mick to sit in a certain chair. Soft, round, wine velvet, it swallowed his huge body. Mick tried to prop himself a little higher, feeling himself sinking to the floor, having to spread his thighs, curl his feet. Then the suction stopped. Still, he felt devoured by the carnivorous chair. Sandra kept looking at him. "Hungry?" She licked her lips.

"Very," Mick said, remembering Newman had said they ate early.

"Just a jiff." Sandra left the room.

To check on the servants, preparing dinner. Mick quickly pulled his eyes away from her swaying hips and faced Bob.

Newman sat on a chair that did not give at all. It elevated him at least one foot over Mick. Newman shook his head. "Drugs and machines—they're the curses of the modern world," he fired. "They will ruin God's natural creation. Remember—the bodybuilder is the artist of his body, and the body is the sanctuary— . . ."—he pondered the word he wanted—". . . of the soul."

"Oh, bodybuilding *is* an art," Mick certainly agreed.

"Drugs and machines! Deaths, destroyed livers, soaring blood pressure, baldness, shrunken testicles!" Newman raged.

Until he unleashed the last two horrors, Mick wasn't sure whether Bob was talking about steroids or machines. Mick didn't believe the frightening stories about steroids, injected or taken orally in dosages of up to more than fifty times the amounts used for conventional medical purposes—postoperative recuperation; they were given also to cattle, to produce more sellable meat. But what did doctors know about the *body*? Nothing. A *bodybuilder* knew about bodies.

"Sanctuary?" Newman still pondered the word that described the container of the soul. "Repository?"

Mick wished desperately he could think of the word. He felt constantly tested. And in a major way. How? Certainly Newman knew all the champions took steroids; he was the one who referred them—"for checkups"—to doctors who provided them.

Now Mick was grateful for the enveloping velvet of the hungry chair; his body was pulling some warmth from it.

"Show me a beautiful weight-constructed body fed with Newman food supplements, and I'll show you a beautiful soul; and if not, I'll destroy them both!"

Mick winced.

The unmistakable odor of hamburgers and onions wafted into the room.

Newman's cunning bird-of-prey eyes fixed on Mick. "You use steroids, Mick." The pause before the name turned his words as easily into an assertion as a question.

"Never!" Mick screamed. He cleared his throat. "They destroy the body."

"And?"

"Huh?" Mick was puzzled. Did Bob mean, So what if they do? "Unless it's— . . ." he floundered.

"What else! And what *else* do they destroy?" Newman pursued.

With enormous relief—which expunged some of the lingering apprehension over his having lied about the steroids—Mick understood. "The soul," he sighed.

"Right!" Newman approved. He leaned over as if to exchange a confidence. "But you'd be amazed, Mick, at how many bodybuilders take them, shoot them up in their arms, even in their buttocks!" He mimed the shooting up in the buttocks. "Now I'm a tolerant man," He leaned back, crossed his hands on his lap. "I know several top bodybuilders—most, perhaps—even my own—have experimented with steroids at one time or another. Even machines— . . ."

Oh, thank you, God!

"It is in the nature of the bodybuilder to try everything; he's a pioneer, pushing the frontiers of— . . . of— . . . pushing the frontiers. But if they continue— . . ." Newman leaned closer, more intimately. "That Joe Jones has been on steroids for years and years; several shots a day!"

So! The Black Sultan is out of favor, was Mick's first thought, in relief. No Negro had ever won the Mr. Universal. But the Black Sultan, as he was called, had a wide faithful following; several rival magazines were implying that the Mr. Universal

Contest was racist, and some of the others, too. "Word has been reaching me that he's off them now," Newman said. "Pure." He pondered his word. "The Mr. Universal is the greatest title bestowed on the perfect man."

"I know," Mick said quietly. Just the title—Mr. Universal! —made his heart pound.

"Did you know Chuck Harris is entering the Universal?"

"Yes—you encouraged him," Mick answered. He wished he could pull back that tinge of resentment: He tried. "He was one of my heroes." He couldn't help adding, "When I was a kid." Memories of the revered bodybuilder tangled.

"Do you know Ward Elder?" Newman proceeded.

One of the best bodies in the city—which meant the world. Sure, Mick knew him, cursorily—but, like everyone else, knew more *about* him. Right after he won Mr. America, he became notorious, hiring out as a callboy to men. Then Herbert Lichtenstein claimed to have seen someone shoving his cock into Ward's ass—in the shower of Harry's Gym! Late, when they thought everyone else was gone—but Herbert had remained for a few extra reps. The man with Ward was at first reputed to be Bo Sanders, but as the rumor twisted in that malicious world, several other names emerged, spreading selected indictment—and Bo's blurred. That was the year Herbert won the Mr. Universal.

"Ward's entering the Universal, too," Newman said.

Impossible!

"Oh, he's changed his ways," Newman said in a somber voice, "searched his soul. Deeply. Joined a Christian group. Born again! Introduced me to his girlfriend— . . ."

Ward Elder training secretly somewhere—and with all kinds of creeps praying for him—if that was true. Was it colder now, or was he just reacting to the chilling news? Newman was clearly announcing his narrowed choices. The Gorilla—Mick had assumed that; the Black Sultan, back in the fold because of outside pressure? Chuck Harris—*why?* Now Ward Elder! And himself. Who else? Bo looked awfully good today, delts round, arms— . . . But he wasn't ready. Still, Newman worked in mysterious ways. Mick felt increasingly on unspecified probation. He rubbed his hands for warmth.

"Cold?" Newman accused.

"Just cool," Mick said.

"Sandra and I heard this man on television, specialist on aging, famous scientist at UCLA," Newman explained; "said the way to increase the lifespan is to lower body temperature. He's done it with rats. So we keep the house cool and our temperatures low. . . . *Temple!*"

"What?" It was all coming too fast.

"The *temple* of the soul—that's what the body is! The body is the temple of the soul," Newman said. "Words and ideas, they just keep bouncing in my head like tennis balls." He leaned back, very satisfied with himself. Then he was deeply serious: "And *that's* what Ward Elder found out, the hard way—that the body is the sanctuary— . . ."

"The temple!" Mick said.

"The temple of the soul, yes." Newman paused. "Ward found it out the hard way."

The *hard* way, all right, Mick thought, letting everyone who had the money suck his three-incher—and everyone knows that's *all* he's got—when it's *hard*—and fuck his gluteus maximus—and all of it for free if it was another muscleman. Sure, hard! So now he's conned Newman—with all that bullshit about religion and getting married. Probably just wants to up his hustle price, and the Universal title would sure do it. Born again, right! Born-again hustler!

"Ward's a man of God now," Newman pronounced. He raised his hand in a mighty gesture of forgiveness. "I forgive him."

What about forgiving Cal Slauson—banished because he tried to organize a union of bodybuilders? Mick's anger surged. Cal— . . . Oh, wait, better not—better not forgive him. Oh God, the way that guy was—*is*—built! Funny the way people stopped existing, almost, when they were out of competition. . . . Cal's lat spread, and— . . . Fucking asshole, Mick wanted to shout at Newman. *We're* the champions, not you!

"Ward's past is sealed." Newman zipped his lips. Then he unzipped them. "Now you take Oklahoma and Jon Dodd!" he blurted. He closed his eyes, as if a great pain had struck him.

A great pain *did* strike Mick. "Who?" he said in a tiny voice. So that's why I'm here!

"The Fred Astaire and Ginger Rogers of the gay porno movies—*that's* what they call them!" Newman's pain deepened darkly. He soothed it with the last of the giant martini: the soaked olive. "Oklahoma was not his real name, of course—Morris Epstein, of the Jewish faith; and Jon Dodd was really Jonathan Manueles, before he dyed his hair that ugly yellow. They could have been Robert Newman champions! Instead they became prostitutes. Ho-mo-sex-u-al pros-ti-tutes!" he cursed each syllable. "Those parties they 'catered'!" His eyes fixed on Mick.

Mick prepared his confession: All Oklahoma said was it was a party, and we'd all be paid a couple of hundred bucks, even tips, just to hang around with body-cultists, maybe serve a few drinks, and they were not all men, there were just as many women, and I was inexperienced, Bob, new in the city, and neither Oklahoma nor Dodd told me we were— . . . He cleared his throat, revised his confession: I was real innocent, Bob, and— . . .

"And do you know they're *still* at it!—although Oklahoma is past forty and the other one at least that old—still blaspheming the palace of the soul— . . . Sanctuary?"

"Temple," Mike said wearily. And again reshaped his confession: I guess you could say I had lost my way along life's road, Bob; I was bewildered; I took the job without knowing. When they told me to take off my clothes— . . . When they told me to take off my clothes, I— . . . How would he get past the fact that he had? *Six naked bodybuilders serving drinks and people pretending to spill them accidentally on us and a voice kept saying, "Let's not waste a drop of this delicious— . . ."*

"After all I did for them. Oklahoma even bragged he didn't use my products."

Neither would I if you didn't give them to me! "Ingratitude, Bob," Mick said. "That's all it is." Oh, please, was that all about Oklahoma and Dodd? "You must run into that a lot—ingratitude—a man in your position and of your generous nature."

Newman sighed under the weight of it all. He nodded solemnly.

"Josie—she's my girlfriend, great girl, you'll have to meet

her, Bob, soon as we find a place we're moving in together—uh—
getting married—Josie was saying I'm one of the most grateful
people she's ever known—and she's known a lot, in her line of
work. I mean, she's a high-school teacher. Grateful to a fault,
that's what she said I am.''

"Din-din!" Sandra leaned sinuously against the doorway.
She was wearing a small silver apron, which formed a *V* at her
thighs, and she held a giant fork, up, in one hand. "Din-din's
ready," she purred.

She cooked? Mick followed them—and the odor of onions—
into the outdoor patio. The heat fondled him. He breathed
deeply, holding the warm delicious air, to thaw his insides.
Then the odor of the onions, intruded, made him cough.

Newman glared. "You coming down?"

"No," Mick managed to squeeze out.

The patio chairs were iron peacocks. Fiery coals glowed from
behind a cloud of smoke that almost concealed the barbecue pit
and almost dove into the pool. Slowly the smoke drifted away
and abandoned lumps of dead meat on a glowing grill. To one
side, a dish of blackened onions awaited the meat's cremation.

They sat at an aluminum table, from which a long slanted
pole emerged, holding an umbrella. Mick felt as if he had
moved out of the arctic and into the tropics. He opened his shirt
a button, not knowing how formal Bob wanted to remain at
dinner.

The table was clothless. Trays of relish, a plate of pineapple
slices, and a wooden bowl of salad that seemed to have waged
fierce battle with itself—tangled green, red, and something
yellow—squatted on the table. Unmatched silver lay heavily on
paper napkins next to plastic plates. Giant goblets awaited the
opening of a bottle of deep red wine.

"I love homemade hamburgers." Mick found he could speak.

"Sanda makes the best," said Robert Newman.

Mick realized they did not look at each other. Had they, since
he'd been here?

Sandra slapped a hamburger onto Newman's plastic plate. He
piled relish on it, topped that with the squirming black onions,
outlined it all with pineapple slices, and transferred resisting
chunks from the salad bowl into a smaller plate.

A giant hamburger landed on Mick's plate, and a smaller one on Sandra's. She sat down, duplicating Newman's embellishments on her plate. Newman opened the wine and poured it into the goblets.

Mick might have hesitated drinking it, if it weren't that Newman was proposing a toast. "To the Mr. Universal!"

Did he hold his glass out directly to me? "To Mr. Universal," Mick revised. The glass was so full the wine dripped onto his plate—like ketchup. Now he poked his fork into the meat. Not a drop of juice squirted out.

Sandra shoved her hamburger around the plate, gathering the assorted juices from the relish. Now she speared one of the yellow pieces from the salad. Looking at Mick, she popped it into her mouth, chewing it slowly. Mick turned to see whether Bob had seen that, but he was eating heartily.

"But *you* didn't take *your* clothes off."

Mick heard Newman's words, clearly, but he still couldn't believe their awful bluntness. So he *did* know about the party where he'd been a naked waiter. Mick began: "When they approached me, Bob, I didn't understand— . . ."

Newman almost looked at Sandra. "But he said no. He turned down that *Partygirl* magazine; they wanted him to pose nude."

Anywhere else, Mick would have lapsed back into his abandoned Catholicism, he would have flung himself on his knees and blessed God. Here, he could only sigh in relief, a sigh which came from every millimeter of his 55-inch chest. And so Newman was not talking about the party; he was talking about the magazine. He turned down being a centerfold because it would have destroyed his chance at the Mr. Universal.

"You wouldn't expose your sacred parts," Newman said.

Sandra said, "Yummy," and bit on her hamburger.

"Wouldn't even consider it," Mick said staunchly. "And they offered me a lot of money," he emphasized his moral fortitude.

"I've kept my eye on you, know all about you," Newman told Mick. "And you're clean as a whistle. Nothing to forgive you for."

Mick was so relieved he, too, topped the meat with brown

onions and relish, surrounded his plate with pineapple slices, and heaped salad onto his small plate.

"Nothing to forgive," Newman repeated almost ruefully. "Can you believe," his voice shot forth, "that Cal Slauson actually sent somebody to sound me out about his prospects for entering the Mr. Universal? Of course, I have nothing to do with his entering or not; that's up to the committee, the federation— . . ." he went on.

Please, please!—not Cal Slauson! Don't let him have forgiven Cal with his unbelievable lats and his— . . .

"I said, No, no, no!"

Bless you, God. Thank you!

"No, no, no, *no!*" Newman emphasized. "No unions! That's all he wants, to work behind my back, trying to organize bodybuilders. Well, unions have destroyed the initiative in this great country of ours. Bodybuilding has to resist, on behalf of the whole body politic. It's no accident that it's called the *body politic.*"

Accidentally, Mick chewed on one of the yellow chunks in the salad. It was cooked squash, still warm. Looking up, he caught Sandra's gaze traveling from one side of his wide shoulders clear across to the other. He pulled his eyes from the unbelievable thrust of her breasts against the sweater, the nipples a further outline; he wondered how long his eyes had been there.

Just like that, dinner was over. Sandra dumped the plastic dishes into a large can near the dead barbecue pit.

"I've offered to give Mick some pointers on his posing routine," Newman informed Sandra.

"Grrrreat," she growled.

"I think he has a *very* good chance of winning the Mr. Universal. *If!*" His eyes shot twice at Mick.

If— . . . Mick blinked twice.

"*If* he does everything right," Newman finished.

Mick felt as if all the muscles of his body were breathing in triumph; his lungs alone, formidable as they were, could not contain the excitement without gasping.

Newman pushed his chair back, rose, and disappeared into the frozen house.

Sandra sat next to Mick and said, "Wow, man, what a stud; you're gorgeous, sweetbums!"

Sweetbums! Josie was no liberated woman, but if he had called her that, she would have had a fit. He looked about in torment when Sandra propped her pretty face on her hands, elbows on the table, and studied him.

"Mr. Groovy, that's who you are," she said. "Turn profile." With a finger, she maneuvered his chin sideways.

"Wow! See mine?" She turned hers.

Mick wondered whether God or a surgeon had created her cute tilted nose. He didn't dare compliment her.

"It's cool, man." She understood his nervousness. "Bob's just fucking around inside for the posing. Lots of cats have great bodies—period—but you! You're really cute. Howrya hung?"

Jesus! Mick was sensitive about that. "Average," he said.

"Good," Sandra said. "That Ward Elder!" She defined a small distance between her thumb and her forefinger.

So Ward *had* been here! But how did she know that about him? For all the bullshit about his turning into a minister and having a girlfriend, Ward was gay; everyone knew that.

"Now you take Oklahoma!" Sandra said. This time she used both hands to measure a long invisible distance.

"You *know* Oklahoma?" If Bob didn't know about the party, did *she*?

The stirring music from *The Ten Commandments* thundered out of hidden speakers. *His* music! Mick felt thrilled.

Newman strutted in, taking giant paces in rhythm to the music. "Ta-ta, ta-*tum*!" he boomed. "Come," he said to Mick, moving back into the house.

Mick followed.

"Later," Sandra called out after them.

Newman led Mick through various rooms cluttered with gold-painted statues and mismatched soft furniture. The attacking cold air made Mick realize he'd be stripping to his posing trunks. Would he even be able to pose? The rousing music made him think, Yes, yes, anywhere!

As they moved down to another level of the house, Newman's walk became statelier, slower, more carefully paced. He's *Moses*! Mick thought. The thrilling music flushed away all thoughts except those of himself posing. It was the music to which he displayed the moving symphony of his muscles.

They entered the private gym. It looked like a theater set representing a gym: The gym equipment—weights, benches, pulleys—arranged neatly, like props, on an elevated platform framed by wide drapes. At the apron of the platform were about a dozen theater chairs, upholstered. The large room was lighted brightly, too brightly, with lights that would erase definition. The cold air was either off or it had been lowered in this room.

Mick had of course worn his posing trunks, under his clothes. He took off his jacket, placing it on a chair after removing the small bottle of baby oil, mixed with iodine to create highlights and darken his tan. He began unbuttoning his shirt.

Newman said, "No."

Mick blinked.

Sandra walked in. She was barefoot, and so he wasn't aware of her until her shoulder brushed his as she passed him. Even without shoes, she was taller than he, he noticed for the first time. She sat on one of the chairs facing the platform. Good. Mick wanted her to see him pose. She patted the chair next to her, indicating that Mick sit there. Mick looked in bewildered supplication toward Bob. Newman nodded. Mick sank down, next to Sandra. He felt numb.

Newman marched to a panel on a wall. The lights went out, the music was lowered. Mick felt Sandra's knee pushing against his. Even muted, the epic music swelled within the deep darkness for long, long moments. Longer. The pressed knee asserted itself.

Then the lights rose slowly, dramatically, on the platform, just as they did during the major contests.

Theres stood Robert Newman, stripped to brief posing trunks. His flesh was pale, his body so thin the outlines of his bones showed through. His body was shaved, the way bodybuilders shave to emphasize their definition. The colorless skin was coated thickly with oil.

Mick felt assaulted by an invisible force.

Sandra clapped, the sound unreal and isolated in the large room.

On the platform, Newman raised his arms as if in response to a giant ovation.

"Chest pose!" Sandra shouted.

Turning his body to the left, Newman pushed his chest out like a strutting pigeon's, except that it hardly extended beyond his shoulders.

"Trap shot!" Sandra shouted. Her voice was cool, ordinary, perhaps bored. She merely pronounced the words loudly. Even now, she did not look at Newman. She seemed to look into the outline of darkness.

Newman bunched his shoulders in a pose that would have displayed a squat pyramid of muscles from upper neck to shoulder blades, had there been any muscles to display.

"Lats!" Sandra's strange voice goaded.

Almost stumbling, Newman turned his back to them, placed his hands bunched on his waist and attempted to stretch his narrow back.

Sandra clapped, the sound issuing like an echo without origin. "Biceps shot!"

Newman raised his arms to his sides, tensing the tiny knots above his elbows.

Mick felt trapped in a nightmare in which he couldn't run from the horror lurking just beyond the frame of the dream.

"Most muscular!" Sandra said.

It was Mick's specialty—when all the muscles tensed at once. The audience cheered!—always.

The figure of Robert Newman moved forward and scrunched his skinny body. Now the arranged lights projected two enlarged shadows against the back wall—two giant gangling skeletons flanking the skinny oiled flesh.

Mick touched his arms, so thick two hands couldn't connect about them. He touched his pectorals; they separated into deep mounds.

Sandra's desultory clapping continued, slowing. "You're the greatest, Bob!" she uttered lazy, loud words. "You're the greatest!"

"Who's the greatest?" Robert Newman shouted, body still knotted.

"You are," Sandra uttered.

"Who's the greatest?" Newman demanded.

Sandra turned to Mick and her lips mimed the words:
You. Are.

But they were not addressed to him, Mick knew. He knew
why he was here. He heard his voice, softly: "You're the
greatest, Bob."

"Louder! Who's the greatest! *Louder*!" Newman demanded,
the body strangling in a tensed tangle.

Mick stood up and shouted fiercely, "You're the greatest,
Bob!" He closed his eyes—to pull away from his sudden sense
of an undefined presence—cold, cold; dark, black, terrifying.

The music was reaching its climax, reached it!

Back to them, Newman's body sagged with a sigh of release.
He moved out of the radius of light, into the shadows, toward
the panel on the wall. The lights came down. In the long
darkness that followed, Mick, still standing, felt a cold fever.
The full lights swarmed the large room. Dressed as before, with
his scarf, Robert Newman strode toward Mick.

"The important thing I tried to stress," Newman said in his
usual voice, "is the fluidity of the movements."

"I understand," Mick said. "Thank you, Bob."

"Glad to help." Newman stifled a yawn. "I'm an early
riser—so you'll excuse me," he said. "Good night, Mick. I
think you'll do just fine. Now do stay and visit with Sandra."
He did not look at his wife; he walked up the steps, into the
cold color-splashed mausoleum of his house.

Sandra faced Mick. She had cat eyes; had she outlined them
since dinner? "He meant it—now me, stud," she said. Her
hands slid into his unbuttoned shirt, pushing it off. "Wow!"
she admired his chest. "See mine?" She raised the sweater over
her head. Her chest was bare—no brassiere—her breasts as
erect as when they had been contained by the sweater, that firm,
that round. She rubbed them against his pectorals. Swaying
sideways, back and forth, her nipples kissed his lightly. She
undid her pants, letting them slide down. Naked. "See mine,"
she said. Her pubic hair formed a soft circle. "Now yours."

He slipped out of his pants. He left the posing trunks on.

He put his hand on her crotch. She lowered his trunks. The
heavy nest of thick dark hairs at his groin was the only part of

his body he did not shave. She played with the curly hairs. "Nice cock," she erased his apprehension. His hand remained between her legs, rubbing her cunt with his palm, then with his fingers.

Leading him down by the hand, she lay back on the carpeted floor. He followed her down; he lay at a slight angle from her body. His hand outlined the sensual curves of long limbs; hers floated over muscles, sliding lower, toward his cock. He moved his body farther sideways, and he pressed her breasts together, bunched them. Her nipples were large, bold in their exaggeration. His tongue moved from one nipple to the other, his hands still fondling the moistening circle of hair. Her hand traveled from his sculpted back to his tensed buttocks. He shifted his body again. Now it was almost perpendicular to hers.

"Now me," she said, and she slid under his raised torso and dabbed at, licked his nipples. Her tongue glided lower. Moving his torso away, he kissed her, burying his tongue into her flavored lips. She shifted—their tongues connected—so that their bodies would touch. He pressed his hand over her cunt, forming circles, narrowing them, then sliding a finger into the inviting parting.

Then in a strong move, she thrust her body to one side, freeing herself from the pressure of his lips, and she slid her hand under him, onto his groin. His whole body trembled when she touched his cock because it was soft, not even beginning to harden, soft, limp, cuddling into the dark pubic hair, limp, limp. He pulled her hand away, too late, and rolled over on her, pushing, pumping, pounding as if about to enter her.

She eased him away. She stood up, looking down at his naked body sprawled unflexed on the rug.

Flexing quickly, he stared up at her. Her breasts were even fuller, more assertive, the nipples thicker, like fingertips. He wanted to explain! The anxiety of the whole afternoon! Bob's strange exhibition! The Mr. Universal! Bob's house! Bob!

Naked, she walked to the panel on the wall. Darkness veiled the large room. Then the posing lights rose on the platform.

Mick rose from the floor. Sandra sat on the same seat she had occupied earlier beside him. She crossed her bare legs and waited.

"Double biceps," she hardly uttered.

Mick understood. He jumped on the platform, expanding his chest, preparing a favorite pose. His arms overhead formed a bulging *U*.

He heard her clapping in the darkness. "Traps!" she called.

His body swayed. A glide, a flare, a slide of the hands on the hips—and then the perfect back spread to its awesome width!

"Most muscular."

His whole body became dozens of astonished muscles: trapezius clenched, deltoids rounded, forearms almost crossed, biceps bunched into balls, abdominals hard ridges, pectorals round disks, thighs layered striations, calves oval mounds!

He heard her clapping, softer, more distant—exactly the way the roar of applause always became for him; *his*; private— . . . Applause!

He felt her eyes devouring his nude body, desiring it. His cock began to harden. Hardened. Fully erect now! He cramped his muscles again, his cock pulsing.

Now!

He jumped off the platform. He would push his cock into her sweating cunt, he'd fuck her hard, show her he— . . .

Where was she?

He rushed to the panel on the wall, pushing random buttons. The music from *The Ten Commandments* started. He pushed more buttons, smothering the music, starting it again, stopping it. Finally the room was awash in light. She was gone. Her clothes remained mockingly on the floor. He dressed swiftly.

He ran out of the darkened house and into his car.

He plunged into the freeway.

At home—way past midnight—he was still doing set after set of heavy barbell curls until his biceps were hard as iron, unable to budge . . . except . . . for . . . one . . . more . . . urgent . . . repetition!

The days before the Mr. Universal, Mick worked out—in another gym—with the same determined ferocity. He tripled his intake of steroids—Decadurabolin, Maxibolin, injected, taken orally. At home, he did his posing routine over and over—to the music from *Exodus*. He saw Josie only for short periods. She understood, of course—the contest.

The Contest.
The Contest.
The *Contest*!

"The Mr. Universal!" the electronically amplified voice announced. The scarlet curtain rose.

Seventeen massive bodies stood silhouetted in an arc against the artificial electric dawn of the stage. Reddish lights flooded the cyclorama. A brighter glow invaded the red, tinting it amber. Slabs of carved muscular meat shone like crystal. More light, released, exposed the molded, shaved, oiled, tan-dyed, stripped muscles knotted together by powerful sinews into astonishing individual bodies.

The capacity crowd at the auditorium roared—three, four thousand, more pushing into the aisles. This night's earlier, lesser contests, winners greeted by noisy approval and noisier disapproval, had incensed the fever for the main event, the battle still to rage in the Contest of Contests.

An upset was easily possible this year—that had become apparent earlier in the afternoon during the prejudging display; then, the six probable finalists had been chosen, graded in several rounds—bodies relaxed, bodies in several mandatory poses. During that less formal prejudging, Mick Vale, Herbert Lichtenstein, and the Black Sultan had garnered perfect scores, Ward Elder just one point less. Bo Sanders—a surprising, strong, sudden presence—confident, lithe, bulked—and Chuck Harris—exhibiting the hard cuts of his mature body, splendid beyond considerations of his age, arousing memories of past perfection—both men had pushed into the top with the same score; and one point behind them was an electric youngman whose presence kept arousing the question, "Who is he?" among the avid afternoon audience. All the other contestants were close enough that—a point lost here, another gained there during this evening's decisive rounds—a dramatic upset was not unlikely: A giant might crash, and one of those seemingly relegated at the prejudging to the penumbra of greatness might rush in to fill the place at the massive coronation tonight—*now*!

Now Mick Vale stood on the stage of the auditorium with the sixteen other greatest bodies.

Fans raged, TV cameras zoomed, photographers danced for

angled shots. From the black maw of the audience, cliques shouted their heroes' names:

HER-BERT! HER-BERT!

MICK VALE! MICK VALE!

Ward El! Ward El!

BIG, BAD BLACK SULTAN!

Bo, Bo!

And with recurrent insistence, the utterance of one name only, an accolade in itself: HARRIS! HARRIS! HARRIS!—they screamed for the man whose past memory was so enormous that it might flush away whatever present flaws might emerge.

After hypnotizing seconds, blackness dropped like night on the stage.

The competitors moved away, to isolated corners and cubicles cleared of photographers and interviewers for these tense moments during which they would pull on wet towels to increase their pump or drop to the floor doing pushups, or add more instant-tanning.

Dapperly dressed, Robert Newman scanned the bodybuilders. Mick glanced away from him and saw the Gorilla flexing muscle against muscle. No doubt about it, he was awesome.

On the stage, lit once more, an official of the federation was announcing the beginning of a crucial round, the individual posing.

Applause, cheers, whistles, some heckling from the mercurial audience—these hungry, mean, adoring, fickle fans, many of them bodybuilders themselves.

Body like black ice, the Black Sultan was cool. Cold. He posed slowly, as if he were a king who did not need to wear his crown to prove royalty. He chose defiance, and from his many admirers he aroused defiant demands for his victory.

The Ten Commandments Suite! Mick almost leapt onto the stage. But it was Ward Elder's music now. What a comeback. The audience welcomed him back with screaming embraces. Ward's upper pectorals were not full enough, and so he posed carefully to conceal that, successfully—cheers grew.

Lapping waves of adulation swept Herbert Lichtenstein on stage. Herbert plunged into his routine, without displaying his body relaxed. To the strains of the music from *Star Wars*, he thrust his muscles for adoration by the eyes beyond the lights. He finished with a stunning double-biceps pose and emptied the stage of his magnificent presence, pulling with him a rampage of increased adulation.

HER-BERT! chanted the loyalists. HER-BERT! joined the sudden converts. LICHT-EN-STEIN, CHAMP-EE-ON! a new cry demanded.

Each syllable of the shouted, hated name was a bullet in Mick's heart. Lichtenstein's strategy had been cunning, never to allow a pause between poses, so that his massiveness disguised his middle's thickness. Passing Mick, the Gorilla smiled the smile of a killer.

Bo Sanders might have suffered by going next—too slender in proportion—except that he was young, exultant, handsome— his first time within reach of the highest ranks, and so he moved with the abandon allowed only by the knowledge that merely placing would be a victory—for now, this year. But the steady chanting pursuing him offstage proffered greater hopes.

In between the routines of the acknowledged gods, demigods posed, their ferocious exhibitions giving no hint of abdication.

"Harris! Chuck Harris!" the amplified voice announced.

The name—the remembered magic—brought shrieks. The memory mounted the platform. Harris's body looked even better than at the prejudging. The heavy applause continued—for the legend, for its survival. Harris moved into his routine. His muscles relaxed too soon before others tensed. The applause became automatic. Hearing the change, Harris dared to assume the pose he had made immortal—the pose captured in the classic photograph pinned on the walls of gyms the world over: a three-quarters front pose, every muscle at attention.

Murmurs, whispers slithered through the darkness, the applause became scattered—a noise.

Harris's body wavered, destroying the pose. He almost fell.

Boo! the word spat out of the cruel darkness.

Harris stopped posing.

Boo! Boo! Two more shots were aimed at the ghost.

Boo! *Boo*! BOO!

Harris stood on the platform and stared at the angered darkness.

Oil and weary sweat seemed to melt his body. The lights came down on him like the blade of a guillotine.

Offstage, Mick faced Newman, who was staring at Chuck Harris rushing away from the shrieking enemy. There was a smile of triumph on Robert Newman's face!

"Mick Vale!" the electric voice announced.

The theme music from *Exodus* thrust Mick into the lightening darkness.

He stood almost relaxed on the platform, his body painted with oil and iodine and Sudden Tan. Mick did not move the bronzed flesh. A statue of perfection had been placed before the audience.

Silence collected awe.

Still Mick dared to drain even more stunned adulation—which he must whip into roars at the *exact* moment. One more second. One more! Another! And— . . .

Now!

In what seemed one movement, his right deltoid and biceps tensed into two enormous mounds of vascular muscle, the forearm rose, angled, the fingers clasped, his other arm shot out and up, the deep cut of his pectorals flowed into the shoulders, the lats on the right bunched to display density, and on the left created a sweeping arc proclaiming stunning width, his thighs parted to taper at the knees and release the fullness of cleft calves. Mick's face turned slowly up as if for ineffable inspiration.

The collected silence exploded.

Mick's body joined the flow of the music, which he heard above the roar as if it played only for him, for his body—and now perfect pose followed perfect pose before the eye of darkness, darkness which screamed his name.

Mick swirled, ordered every muscle into his original stance— and did not move until the lights came down.

Applause crashed on the golden statue.

Now the final—fatal and triumphant—round would occur. The six finalists would be announced. Then they would pose freely on the stage simultaneously, all together, for final comparison.

Herbert Lichtenstein! Bo Sanders! Ward Elder! Joe Jones!

Mick Vale! And a new name no one recognized. The new body leapt on stage, discarding Chuck Harris.

The six began their free posing. They were exultant animals celebrating their might, asserting their power over each other and over all the other creatures in the jungle of muscular flesh. Herbert Lichtenstein awed with his sheer mass as muscles formed, re-formed from one magnificent display into another. The Black Sultan remained apart, adored in his imposed exile. The nameless body charged the stage with new energy. Mick Vale waited, his posing subdued for the first few seconds. Ward Elder made his bid; he pushed himself next to Lichtenstein, who annihilated him with a kneeling, back pose. Ward relocated himself next to Mick, still subdued until the moment of Ward's daring intrusion. In one flash Mick performed his awesome most muscular pose, and in that flash he discarded Ward. Bo Sanders performed for the audience—for future contests.

Now Mick began: He posed briefly next to each man, matching whatever pose each assumed, pushing each out easily. Now he stood next to Herbert Lichtenstein. Seeing Mick challenge him, Lichtenstein stretched his tall body, then allowed each muscle its full dazzling exhibition, tensing in a recurrent chain reaction, as if giant muscles were hopping along the limbs of his body.

The audience was on its feet. HER-BERT! HER-BERT! NUMBER ONE!

This is it! Mick knew. Mick exhaled, the wall of his stomach caving into a perfect vacuum, erasing his waist. Angrily, Lichtenstein tensed his left biceps into a balloon about to burst. Still holding his stomach in, Mick flexed his own considerable arm, then dropped it, with the other, fists planted on his sides, emphasizing the slender waist. Then he matched each of Lichtenstein's urgent poses and ended each with a frontal show of his full-ridged, narrow waist.

The screams shifted: MICK VALE! MICK VALE!

The round ended. Darkness. The decision.

Amber lights rose on six trophies and a vacant three-tiered platform.

Sixth Place! "Evan Harrington!" The new body had a name!

Evan Harrington was born, this moment, here, now, young, younger even than— . . .

Fifth Place! "Bo Sanders!"

. . . —who looked at the new—younger—man, and for only that moment lost what had seemed to be his permanent smile.

Fourth Place! "Joe Jones!"

Boos from the Black Sultan's fans indignant because of the low rating. "Rigged!" someone accused. "Fake!" "Rigged!" "White devils!" one voice screamed. "Rigged!"

The Black Sultan did not appear—his place behind his trophy left vacant.

The chant altered: "Bad loser! Bad loser!"

Third Place! "Ward Elder!"

Ward tried to appear enthusiastic as he rushed on stage to take his place on the tier just below the highest. The smile on his face did not match the rest of his set features. Finally surrendering to a ferocious glower, he looked up as if announcing his separation from a vagrant deity.

HER-BERT!

MICK VALE!

HER-BERT!

MICK VALE!

"*Shit*! With that word Herbert Lichtenstein announced his second place and Mick's victory.

"*Mr. Universal: Mick Vale!*"

Victory coursed through Mick's body, the way blood—forcing tissue to grow, muscles to become larger—the way it flowed when he lifted still another, a heavier, weight, and another, another, still heavier—fresh blood asserting *life*!

When neither Lichtenstein nor Elder did what tradition decreed they do, Evan Harrington bounded to the top tier and held Mick's champion-hand aloft.

"EVAN HARRINGTON!" the crowd welcomed a new contender.

Then Mick was alone on stage, enclosed by screams, applause. As always, but now more than ever before, his name, chanted in ecstasy, the thunder of adulation, seemed to come from a farther distance, beyond the audience, the auditorium, from outside, gathering from the very edge of the beach he loved, where he glowed every summer as he ran—one more summer, one less summer; the roar came from the jagged curve of the ocean, yes, and beyond, from the deepening blue of sky, beyond, from the dawn, the dusk, the twilight of evening, and the vast starless darkness of endless water, whose waves washed over him, consuming him, when on certain late nights he stood, alone, naked, challenging the tumult of the crashing darkness.

". . . —President of the Federation of— . . ." the electric voice asserted.

Mick saw Robert Newman walking toward him to present him his check for $15,000. From behind Newman, a banned photographer flashed a bulb. The light smashed Mick's vision. It blurred into a circle that contained smeared figures. Within it, the form of Robert Newman approaching looked like the distorted spectral shadow projected against the wall of his private stage-gym that strange, monstrous night when Mick had felt an invisible cold, dark presence—the shadow of decay, more tragic for *him* because it demanded the surrender of his perfect body, a brutal, sacrificial death. The menacing outline advanced, advanced—*closer*! Mick flexed his huge muscles against the quivering figure approaching him.

Then his eyes cleared on the smiling face of Robert Newman. Newman presented him the check and clasped his hand tightly with both of his.

From the deep darkness, the audience shouted. "Mick Vale, you're the greatest, Mick Vale, you're the greatest! You're the greatest! *You're the greatest!*"

Newman dropped Mick's hand—which was cold, cold—and turned to face the cheering crowd.

Lost Angels: 9

"The fireworks of God," Orin repeated. He still faced the hot darkness through the parted drapes of the motel room.

Instantly, Jesse flung his long booted legs off the bed. He stood next to Orin as if to whirl him around. "How much money did the old woman leave?" his voice asked.

Silence was disturbed only by the humming of the air-conditioner and the scratching of wind outside.

Lisa crouched when she saw Jesse's hand rise ready to fall on Orin's shoulder, to force him to face him and his question. There was no hint of what Orin's reaction would be; his face had remained averting them, scrutinizing whatever he saw within the world of darkness outside the window.

Jesse's hand did not connect with Orin's shoulder. Poised over it for seconds, it fell to his side. His own expression changing to one of surprise or bewilderment, Jesse retreated from Orin.

Because he had seen what Lisa saw now? Releasing the drapes—sealing the motel room and the three of them within it—Orin turned away from the window. His face was streaked with long tears. Or perspiration. He sighed. " 'Yes, Sister Woman will give us proof' —that's what the old woman kept saying." He trembled as if seized by a hot chill.

Lisa sat up. *That woman on television was real!—and Orin believed her*! Throughout these magical days with him and Jesse—and eager to abandon the screaming echoes and twisted shadows of her past—Lisa had moved as if through the radiance of a colored dream in this dreamy city of bright colors. Now—increasingly distanced from past shadows—the props of the dream were transferring into an emergent sharp reality, held in

263

abeyance, jostled now by Orin's words. It was she who studied Orin carefully now.

"When God threw the angels out of heaven, I wonder who wept more, him or them?" Orin was looking at Jesse and Lisa, as if expecting an answer from them. "Always wondered. I know the angels cried a lot because they were lost, and that's not a good feeling. . . . God, see, he was trapped. He couldn't relent, once the fireworks started—nothing could stop them; that's fate."

His cadenced words—that rhythm—they lulled Lisa away from her earlier turbulent thoughts. It was so easy to surrender to Orin's sighed words, to become a part of his present, full of abandoned mystery. That allowed her—and Jesse—to leave behind their own pasts, hidden sorrows and horror; becoming a part of Orin as if in a dream in which they drove and played what seemed at times like games.

But— . . .

But into that dream and those games—reality yanked again forcefully at Lisa, seesawing—three powerful figures were encroaching, figures still not real: the dead woman, Sister Woman, the man in the park—if he was there! Without those three presences, or kept unreal, their—hers, Jesse's, Orin's—drifting throughout the city on daily excursions had seemed endless, wonderfully endless. If those figures shaped, as darkly as they hinted, the games might collide with reality, become rehearsals for that collision.

Sweating. Orin was sweating, though he seldom did—not even, sometimes, in the glare of heat; Jesse saw Orin's streaked face and could not look at it beyond that glimpse. *Sweating*, he insisted. He parted the drapes, looking out, trying to see what it was that Orin had discovered out there that evoked his strange words. Twisted darkness—and swirls of dusty wind blowing about the indigo Cadillac parked in its space. That's all Jesse saw.

Orin's breathing broke—as if he had trapped a sob before it could form. Relenting, the wind exhaled long soft sighs.

That's what Orin had heard, what Lisa heard now, she knew, the sound of angels weeping. And it wasn't sweat on his face. Tears, like those he had shed that night when they were naked in bed. She touched Pearl; the doll and this room extended the safe dream.

"I don't know if God cried!" Jesse crushed the drapes shut. The questions that had rushed his mind just moments earlier—how much money did the old woman leave?—hundreds, thousands, tens of thousands?—where is the money?—in a bank, in cash? in the trunk of the Cadillac!—and wouldn't a crazy old blind dying woman keep her money in cash?—all these questions, deliberations, which had receded as he glimpsed Orin's wet face, pushed forth again now that the moisture—*sweat*!—had evaporated. That beautiful, alluring Cadillac out there; what if it got stolen and the money *was* there?

"What did you ask me earlier, Jesse?" Orin spoke in his ordinary voice.

Strategy! Jesse had to form a plan. But what for and why? "I forgot," Jesse postponed any commitment. Because only this was certain—and it recurred at sudden moments in Jesse's awareness: Orin could simply drive away. One morning they'd look out and the Cadillac would be gone—unless it would turn out to be Orin who would wake up one morning and find it gone.

Head tilted, Orin was facing him closely.

Jesse panicked. He sat down wearily. Could he . . . leave . . . Orin? And Lisa—if she wouldn't come with him?

"I *think* God cried," Lisa said. "Otherwise— . . . Can God be evil, Orin?" Her hand reached absently to touch Pearl on the bed. She discarded all the earlier questions, shoving their reality away.

"Not God—Satan. But maybe Satan's just the other side of God— the mean part. The other one is always sad." Orin shook his head. "I don't know—depends."

And that's what he wants to find out from Sister Woman? —only that? Jesse wondered.

Pearl next to her, Lisa curled in her bed. So tired, tired, tired. She heard the sighing of the wind, like the weeping of angels. Her eyes closed. Her voice was drowsy as she began to fall into exhausted sleep. "Maybe this is where God threw those angry angels, right here . . . into this very city. Maybe they never even fell from heaven, Orin," she said groggily. Her words purled into the rhythm of sleep. "Maybe there never was a God to even care enough to fling them out. And they just . . . imagined . . . that . . . once . . . there was . . . heaven."

Orin turned off the lights.

Jesse undressed to his shorts. He was so exhausted he began to fall asleep immediately, but he jarred himself awake, anticipating the familiar pressure of Orin's body on the other side of the bed. Sleep pulled powerfully. Out of the asserting heaviness of conquering drowsiness, Jesse heard a muffled answer to the question he had asked earlier—and it didn't surprise him, the way . . . Orin . . . had . . . of answering . . . so much later.

"Million. Million dollars. More, Jesse."

Did he ever come to bed during the night? Or did he sleep there on the chair, where he sat now fully dressed—Orin—looking at them? Jesse sat up startled. "What you say, Orin?" he responded groggily to the voice he had heard before dark sleep inundated him last night.

"Didn't say anything," Orin said.

"Must've dreamt you said something," Jesse mumbled. He got up and went to the bathroom.

Lisa jerked against the sunlight bunching at the window. She tried to push away heavy sleep. Pearl rolled over, facing up, eyes fluttering. "I wish you'd been born dead!" Lisa yelled in a deep, deep voice at the doll. "You made me ugly. Look, look!" She buried her hands in her own hair. "Ugly—and that's why they always leave me, over and over—so mean, mean!" Aware of the enraged voice—it wasn't hers!—she sat up and saw that Orin was standing over her, his hand soothing her shoulder. "She said I stole her beauty; I was pretty only because I stole her beauty." She looked at Orin with pleading eyes. The nightmare she had wakened from clung.

"But you didn't, Lisa," Orin said as softly as he was touching her.

"No?" Lisa asked. The nightmare faded.

"No," Orin asserted.

"Awful nightmare," Lisa said.

"Morning," Orin restarted the day. Removing his touch now, he smiled the almost bashful smile of a boy waking up for the first time in the same bedroom with a pretty girl.

Jesse came out of the bathroom. Orin looked too fresh not to have slept in bed. Just got up early again, Jesse insisted.

Yawning, stretching, Lisa took her turn in the bathroom. This time, she took her clothes with her, to dress there. It was as if all of yesterday, that long, long day, that longer night—the dark park, the twisted shadows, the confused tension when the movie heroines she loved seemed to be fighting her, Orin's strange story—it was as if none of that had occurred. None! She felt refreshed by that feeling—and the resurrecting water on her body as she showered. Looking fresh, pretty, prettier each day, she returned to the bedroom. "Hi!"

"It looks like a body!" Jesse was saying excitedly, pointing down at the table. "Look. See? Here are the veins, in red—and all these little yellow arteries— . . . And here's the heart, where they all join!"

Lisa peered over his shoulder. He was looking at a map of Los Angeles. "How can a map look like a body? Those aren't veins, they're freeways and streets. Oh, you!" she said impatiently.

Jesse continued to study the map. It did, too, look like a distorted body, its limbs pulled everywhichway.

Orin studied the map. "It looks like the body of a ghost," he said.

"How could a ghost have a body?" Jesse laughed.

Outside, Orin stopped at the motel office to pay for that day's rent. Jesse and Lisa stayed a distance away. Orin seemed unconcerned by that.

As they approached the car—this time Jesse noticed—Orin touched its trunk, barely, yes, fingers just gliding as if testing to see how dusty it was, but he *touched* it; had he seen him do that other times?

They drove into the hot day. Clearly it would be one of those times—tacitly accepted during breakfast, when no suggestion was made—when their destination would be determined spontaneously. But their reaction to the night journey into the park yesterday precluded a recurrence without Jesse's and Lisa's agreement.

Lisa sat in back, adoring the technicolored splendor of the scenery everywhere. Here and there colored blossoms were so thick it was as if the earth were bleeding. In the distant hills, the giant sign that proclaimed HOLLYWOOD in huge letters continued to thrill her. Yellow, curled flowers, splotched with red, blazed on a lawn.

"Burning birds," Lisa named them. Again? "Bridesmaid's bouquets," she quickly dubbed others.

It was a dramatic day—the wind had swept the sky blue. Leafy, flaring palm trees were able to shake away the still-mild assaults of today's wind.

When they had first arrived in the city, they had heard an announcement on the radio that warned of a "smog alert." A smog alert!—it had sounded strange to Lisa and Jesse. Orin had explained that meant that smog—a combination of fog and smoke, from cars, factories—was so thick on a particular day that people were being advised not to drive unless they had to, that way reducing the dirty fumes. These days, the wind pushed it away. But wads of it would appear at times on the horizon, as if waiting to make a poisonous incursion into the city. But not now, not today—today the sky was blue, blue!

"We've been in Los Angeles several days now, and it still thrills me," Lisa said. "I love it, so much, more and more. And it seems like a lifetime, a wonderful lifetime here, because it's been so full and wonderful," she exulted. "I'm so happy to be with you two!" Impulsively she leaned over and touched Orin and Jesse on their shoulders. She allowed her fingers to rest there for moments.

Jesse's flesh tingled, as if an electric current were flowing, in warm binding, from his shoulder, through Lisa, to Orin. He was sorry when Lisa removed her touch. It would have been good to ride that way, a longer time. "Yeah," Jesse said, wondering what Orin had felt. Orin had changed his life, he realized anew; just simply because at a certain time in the steaming desert he had been waiting for a ride. The wonder of it struck him over and over. "Yeah—it is good."

Happily, Lisa began humming a tune from a movie. "The all-times had beautiful music. Max Steiner—I remember his name; he wrote the most beautiful movie music of all. I don't care if I *ever* see a new movie again, just the all-times, over and over." Yet she thought of the two "new" ones they had seen recently. She pushed them away with her continued humming. "That's from *Forever Amber*!" she remembered.

"I'll say one thing," Jesse James complimented her—but not too emphatically, "you sure got a good memory."

"Yes, I do," Lisa admitted. "I think I'm much smarter than I *used* to think."

"You *remember* real good," was all Jesse allowed.

"Amber loved that Bruce so much—and he took her child and left her for a mealymouth." She sighed. "They were always doing that—leaving them. I cried so much."

"For her or for the kid?" Orin asked.

"Well, of *course* I cried for— . . ." Lisa frowned. She looked to her side. She hadn't brought Pearl along—again. "I cried for . . ." It was suddenly puzzling and important. Whom had she cried for? She touched the place where Pearl would have been. *Whom*? Lisa jerked her head, looking out, severing sudden memories of the woman who "could have been a movie star"—who blamed her for— . . . being born.

"Sometimes," Orin said, "you've got to cry for yourself." Jesse didn't understand, but he felt sad. Crying for yourself!

The elegant Cadillac purred along Hancock Park, blocks of stately mansions proclaiming old, established—entrenched— wealth.

"Oooo, could we buy a place like *that*?" Lisa pointed to a magnificent house sprawling, the lightest shade of amber, over a lawn of perfect green.

Those words jerked Jesse into last night's dream-filtered memory about money. Jesse heard himself: "Orin could; he said last night he's got— . . ." The certainty abandoned him. "Lots of money, didn't— . . .?"

Orin turned the radio on.

A pang of anger punctured the closeness Jesse had felt when Lisa had touched them both. He shot a slanted look at Orin. It wasn't rare for Orin to manipulate the radio impulsively, not even hear—or seem not to hear—what anyone asked him, but this time Jesse felt sure he had turned it on to avert his question. He hadn't even formed it completely. What exactly had Orin said about the old woman and Sister Woman? Just that he was bringing her money. What if it was a hundred dollars? Jesse's spirits collapsed. The words he thought he'd heard before he fell asleep last night dimmed further. But Sister Woman had seemed to react the night Orin left a message—a note passed on to her from the operator? And if so, there had to be much more than just a few dollars. And in one of her sermons she had seemed actually to be talking about Orin, to Orin—and he'd written her he was coming. Jesus Christ!—was he really—*really*—in touch with her?

"Oh, see that house." Lisa pointed to a magnificent mansion. Mournful willow trees flanked it. "It's a famous one; I saw pictures of it; it belonged to a theater actress— . . ." She was pointing to the house once owned by Karen Stone, murdered in Rome, or so the newspapers posturing at outrage claimed, by a vagrant Italian youngman, whom she had apparently invited into her apartment.

". . . —of civil rights groups protesting the finding that Officer Norris Weston was found to have acted responsibly in the shooting death of the black woman in Watts earlier this year," the radio announcer was finishing. "And on another front, the White House has confirmed that Judge Stephen Stephens III of Los Angeles is one of five men being considered to fill the seat vacated earlier this year on the Supreme Court by the death of— . . ."

"How ugly!" Lisa pointed to a billboard.

They had long left the mournful house and the area of exclusive old wealth, and they were driving now along a section of the city of squat hardware shops and stucco bungalows colored desperately. These blemished patches of city recur with jagged regularity among the flowers and trees.

Orin slowed down to see what Lisa had pointed to.

"LOS ANGELES DESTROYED HOURLY!" the billboard screeched.

A drawing depicted a terrified man running, open mouth petrified in a scream. Behind him, a traumatized woman stood on a cracking sidewalk split by earthquake. Beyond, other figures fled from an avalanche of lapping water. Waves of orange fire raged, palm trees crashed.

"See It All Happen On The Universal Studios Tour," words at the bottom of the poster invited.

"That's in my guidebook, remember?" Jesse connected.

"But not *that* ugly. Drive away quick, Orin," Lisa said.

". . . —extending the Santa Ana conditions," the weather announcer said. Then another announcer on the radio introduced "Social Notes from All Over." "European Solidarity workers, American factory workers, and even Italy's Red Brigade terrorists," a woman's easy voice was declaring, "will have roles in shaping women's and menswear this season, according to designer Brian Lorring, whom I interviewed recently in his ultramodern home. Thus an industry that built its reputation on beachwear and jeans has discovered life beyond leisure. Brian, what do you foresee?" A man's voice followed: "Darling, we're going to see a look dominated by—well—industrial and military influences." "Among your rich clients?" the woman inquired. "Darling," the man said, "the whole point about being rich in our time is that you don't wear rich *out*. The radical-worker look will— . . ."

Orin shifted the radio to— . . .

"The Western and country station—wowee!" Jesse James welcomed, claiming a victory for himself. Or had he been allowed one? he revised more soberly.

Whatever. Soon the radio was singing about destinations to the land where broken hearts are mended.

They ate at a Howard Johnson's restaurant—incongruous pseudo–New England facade and, inside, neat rows of orange and blue booths; they ate hungrily as if to fill the drain of yesterday's events. Still there were no suggestions or questions about how they would spend the rest of the day.

"Does it seem like you're driving inside a body?" Orin asked Jesse only minutes later when they glided into a freeway. "Like when you looked at the map?"

Jesse pondered his feelings. "Not when you're on it," he said, disappointed. Less so when he consulted his guidebook and learned that: "There's six hundred miles of freeway within the city, and if you stretched them all out end to end you'd get from here to Phoenix, wow!"

Not yet mid-afternoon, the traffic flowed. Chrome captured slivers of sun in blades of flashing silver, like bullets.

Orin moved the car swiftly out of the freeway.

The wind had begun to push with growing force. Leafy crowns of palm trees shook.

Orin stopped the car on a side street, adjacent to a series of vacant abandoned lots. Pretty purple and yellow weeds crept throughout the tenacious remains of the dusty foundations of houses long ago cleared away for the nearby freeways.

Orin got out of the car, looking toward the slope adjacent to the lanes of freeway. He stood over the concrete network as if from this distance he could untangle it into discernible order.

Jesse got out of the car. He traced Orin's gaze—he saw only cars beginning to slow in the stases that are part of the city's freeway rituals.

So intense, Lisa thought inside the car. Jesse is getting to look like Orin sometimes, that intense. Or trying to. Automatically she walked out. The recurrent *whoosh!* of cars and the surge of wind created a sound like that of the thrusts of the ocean, turbulent water shoved against the edges of the land.

The three stood overlooking a section where almost all the freeways of the city, or their extensions, crash into a twisted star. Arcs of concrete sweep over streets at that point in intricate interconnection. Cars move in every direction, in long, long files. Untangling from the tight noose of traffic here, they scatter into the vast city, its myriad destinations.

High above this point—to the side of the crushed fields—a rise of land furry with grass and brush and thick trees grows into an uncultivated hill, right in the midst of the city and over the freeways—a patch of forest. Now shaken by the wind, leaves ahead changed periodically to silver green, then dark green, their two sides.

Jesse and Orin moved closer to the slope over the freeways. Flowered vines crawl thickly to the very edge of the concrete many feet below.

Lisa saw the two men on the viny grass, among tiny eruptions of white and orange flowers like expiring miniature stars.

Growing nervous and impatient, the traffic below became thicker on the freeways, cars shoving into slowing lanes. Lisa could feel the reverberations of stalling motors, as if the earth were trembling. Moving closer—but still away from Orin and Jesse—she stared down into the quagmire of metal, chrome, and concrete. Her ears were assaulted by the mechanical roar competing with the growling wind. As if wiped away by a giant hand, everything blurred before her. Dizzy, she closed her eyes. Her breath came in sudden pants, her heart pulsed against her ears, and she felt panic.

When she opened her eyes again, removing her hands from her ears, she saw Jesse and Orin running toward her. They seemed exhilarated.

Although he had to shout to be heard over the wind and the roar of cars, it was as if Orin had whispered the words, he spoke them so evenly over the clashing sounds:

"You'll stay with me, both of you?"

Stay with him? Could they leave if they wanted? Jesse wondered in a moment which would certainly change. *Trust me.* . . . Had a decision already been made?—as far back as the Texas desert? Jesse allowed himself to feel what he had pulled away from at the sight of Orin's moistened face last night: Orin had been *crying*—not sweating—but that was all right because Cody cried, too! Jesse felt now that Orin had been crying for all three of them. "I just about guess we've *got* to!" he shouted, feeling a sweep of joy.

"Will you, Lisa?" Orin repeated. The reddish blond hair whipped across his face, then back, leaving imploring sad eyes.

Trust me. Despite last night's anger and doubts—which she had buried today—Lisa nodded. Yes, extending the idle dream, the aimless journeys.

Jesse laughed exultantly. He ran toward the green forested hill over the freeway. He thrust his laughter against the roar of the wind and the cars battling beyond, below.

Orin threw his head back and joined Jesse's laughter.

Lisa drew away from them. She ran across the barren field, back to the car—away from this game. *A dream, a game!*—the edges of reality stabbed at her.

Jesse continued to climb, higher, concealed now by the green thickness of the hill until he emerged near the rusted remains of what must have been a water-supply tank, a tall cylinder long abandoned, oxidized dusty orange. A metallic ladder clung to its side. The ladder was flimsy. Jesse's boots were aware of the give in the rotted rungs. Locating the firmest part of the railing, he held on to it and thrust out his body at a slant from the top. White heat embraced him. Whatever Cagney—Cody—had yelled, he had yelled it triumphantly as bullets zinged and white flames exploded like a huge black and white orchid.

Still laughing, Jesse shouted at the wind, *"Come and get me!"*

Carla: "Roses in Hell"

Her sweat saturated the newspapers and rags on which she lay. She welcomed the moisture. It cooled her as she slept, or tried to sleep. "Sleep" was a glazed limbo of subdued awareness kept alert for assault.

A foot kicked her bare legs. Farther into the hollow made permanent night after night by other bodies that hid in the maze of ledges, she forced her bony frame—which hurt more than its forty-nine years should allow. Aroused by the connection with hurting flesh, the foot kicked again more forcefully.

Carla reached back to protect the shopping bag, which contained everything she owned this moment—a mirror pressed between cardboards, an almost toothless hairbrush, maybe a skirt or even a dress, a stolen tube of lipstick, a perfume bottle—and the ashes of long-dried roses.

Icy light stunned her eyesight.

"This one's a woman!" said the man's excited voice from behind the frosted flashlight.

A stick explored intimately between her legs. "Yeah," another voice affirmed.

Standing up, Carla clasped the cloth bag against her thighs. Her sight struggled to recover from the assault of white light encircled by the blowing night. She saw electric smears of white, orange, green, blue; distant blurs. Two dark-uniformed bodies came into focus before her.

The stick outlined her dried breasts. "Get outta here, dirty bitch!"

The cops moved on, rousting scraggly living ghosts concealed throughout the many levels of these lawns.

Where was she?

The beach! No. . . . A railroad station? A hospital room? *A clean one, a filthy one, one bellowing with invisible pain.* A bus depot? A storefront? A subway tunnel warmed by gasps of steam? *Against shadows? Cringing from advancing feet bringing roses?*

Carla studied the night. The electric smears shaped into lighted signs radiating on top of encroaching, sleek buildings. Orange and green on white: UNION 76. Cool, illuminated blue: ATLANTIC RICHFIELD PLAZA.

As bodies shuffled to other hollows, Carla crawled back into the same cove, rearranging the papers and rags left there from an earlier occupancy. Her fingers touching the brownish bag, the dusty roses, she floated again within the limbo that replaced sleep, floated until the rusted sun burst through the tarnished horizon and she heard the urgent rustling of leaves coming from the body-carved cove nearest her. The cops were back! She knotted her body so that when they kicked this time, the lunging feet would connect with her buttocks, still the softest part of her emaciated form. Both hands hugged the shopping bag.

She heard ugly aroused laughter and the beginning of a scream, throttled as it began to rip the hot dusk. Rushing feet carried away the sick laughter. Safer to remain hidden, she knew. She shoved the bag between her legs. Silence extended. She peered out.

On the sidewalk—and against distant palm trees pulled into reality by the beginning morning—stood a tiny man of perhaps seventy years. He looked like an aged doll—frayed clothes; long white hair; delicate, almost fragile features. A garish red bandanna decorated his skinny neck. No—not a bandanna! The red line across his neck broke into the flowing anarchy of astonished blood.

Dragging her bag, Carla clawed her way with one hand into the thicker part of the ledge. Twigs cut her skin. She forced her body through to the other side of the lawn and emerged onto exposed grass. Responding to a new ambush, other tattered bodies crawled out of leafy pockets.

Carla stood a safe distance away, on the sloping lawn. She saw the whirling colored lights of a police car, heard the siren screaming into her ears coming for her, wailing its accusation:

Your fault, it's your fault! Now two cops hovered over the fallen man. Then an ambulance came and took the body away *and she was on a stretcher, her hands tied over her as if she were dead.*

Carla looked at her hand. Drying blood. *The long-haired old man with the slashed throat stood before her; huge drops of his blood spattered her hand red. She didn't withdraw it until he collapsed.* She blew anxiously on the blood.

From her bag, she pulled out her perfume bottle—ornate designs like glass veins. She drank the cheap wine or liquor she tried to make sure she'd have for morning, filling the vial early, counting on forgetting she had it. Her tongue searched out the last drop of the liquid—not enough.

Day flooded the world. Behind her, the aged library rested in squares on the lawn. Over it and her—beyond—were tall, lean muscular buildings of unyielding concrete, shiny glass and plastic. LLOYDS OF LONDON, BANK OF TOKYO, LINCOLN SAVINGS, PACIFIC FINANCIAL, CROCKER CITY, NA-TIONAL, WESTERN FEDERAL, CANADIAN BANK, WELLS FARGO, BANK OF AMERICA. The three enormous cylinders of glass—the Bonaventure Hotel—shone like black mirrors at dusk, changing to silver in daylight—now.

Across the street from the library and flanked by careful regiments of flowers, a fountain cascaded in silver ribbons of water. RICHFIELD PLAZA. Its twenty storeys soared before an orange free-form sculpture of steel bands ascending like curved ladders to nowhere. Beyond, on rising hills, new condo-miniums captured the first rays of the sun.

Carla prowled the grounds of the old library until it opened. Stairs hollowed out by millions of footsteps lead to cavernous musty rooms. Her own footsteps—she was wearing shoes now—always fascinated her; here, the hallways captured echoes, then released them in huge rooms.

In the lavatory, she slid under the opening of one of the cubicles, not bothering to notice whether it required coins or not. Setting her bag carefully behind the toilet and away from the adjoining partition—once, hands had reached from under to snatch it away, but she kicked at them—she flushed the toilet until the water looked fresh. Then she bathed her feet in it, cooling the open sores. Carefully, she washed her lower body. She forced the grudging roll of tissue off its container to dry herself.

When she came out, several youngwomen, students with books, stopped chattering. Two women stared at her—then pretended not to see her as she lowered her dress and washed her breasts, then her face. Her clothes adjusted again, she untied the string holding the two pieces of cardboard that protected the small mirror. She peered at herself, applying lipstick to her lips, spreading one dot of it on each of her cheeks; another dot, flushing them. With the brush, she smoothed out her soiled white-and-brown hair. She felt refreshed, shedding last night's crushed sleep.

Traces of a good-looking woman—a pretty woman—remained under the roughened purplish-tanned skin seared by sun, cauterized by wind. She had strange gray, brown-rimmed eyes. *Deer eyes*.

She reached for her perfume bottle containing the wine from last night. Empty.

In the library, she walked from room to room, stirring hollow echoes.

She sat on a bench on the lawn of the grounds. The police and the ambulance were gone. Her fingers roamed the seams of her bag, touching the familiar ashes of roses. Reassured, she walked away from the Los Angeles Public Library.

She entered a long tunnel. Its rounded walls were glossy, like melting ice. Cars rushing through it in both directions made liquid reflections. From the other end of the tunnel, a man advanced toward her, his shadow borrowed from the night. She turned away, running from the sound of her own pursuing footsteps.

Out of the tunnel, she heard the soft roar of the ocean. She was near it! She followed the recurring sound—along the hot concrete block. She heard it, closer! She was there! She squinted her eyes; she would open them onto the blue expanse of silver water Emmett had promised her would be at the shore's end. Under her patched shoes, she felt a softness. Sand!—but not the cool breeze Emmett had offered. She opened her eyes to speeding traffic just feet ahead. She was standing on a wide incline of grass bordering a freeway. It was the whooshing! of cars she had heard. To resurrect the triumphant sense of discovery, she closed her eyes more tightly and leaned forward, determined to conjure up the sound of water lapping at a peaceful shore. She jerked back, feeling herself slipping toward the crushing traffic. She turned back, walking up, toward towering buildings.

She reached Pershing Square. Emmett had told her about the fiery preachers, the hustlers, the transvestites. The park was denuded now. Trees and benches rationed, to keep the drifters away from the scurrying clerks and bankers moving in and out of the parking lot below. In the center of the park, a building of giant globes like the eyes of a fly enclosed a travel agency, with photographs of brightly colored cities.

"Where is *this* one?"

"Get out of here, get out!" the woman cringed from Carla.

"I want to go *here*!" Carla pointed on a blue poster.

"I'll call the police," the woman warned.

"They'll poke me with their sticks!" Carla shouted at her.

Then she was on Broadway. Then she *hadn't* left after all. *Along its yellow-grassed median, they sat in the sunless days and held small brown envelopes full of pretty pills and instructions about when to come back to get more.* Oh, *another* Broadway. Electric dots chased each other on the marquees of three-feature movie houses and Spanish-language theaters. On the hot sidewalks, Negroes and Mexicans waited for buses while others got off them.

She was so thin she slid through iron gates and into a small triangle of grass and shade. Into— . . .

". . . —can't sleep here!"

Candles glistened like tiny red jewels in truncated bottles. There were roses at the feet of the statue of a woman whose hands were clasped, her body draped in colorful folds.

"I said, you can't sleep in here!"

Carla sat up on the wooden bench. The flickering flames needled her eyes. *Deer eyes.* A priest stood over her, nudging her to get out.

She was again in the churchyard surrounded by iron gates.

Spring Street. She expected many trees—but there were only old buildings, solid gray walls like fortresses. Tombstones.

Main Street. Hock shops, gaudy clothing stores, cheap fried food, stores with magazines displaying colored pictures of organs devouring each other. Tough bars vomiting music and smoke and disinfectant. Black pushers; cheap hookers: women in pants so short their buttocks looked naked; extravagantly coiffed Mexican, Negro, and some really blond transvestites with faces drawn on flesh. The yellow lights of police cars blinked near fallen bodies.

Los Angeles Street. Beyond.

Along pockets of heat, she entered the world she searched through in city after city. Squashed hotel corridors and squat bars were bathed in light the color of weak urine. She moved deeper into the ulcerated zone. Men and women leaned like breathing corpses against fuming walls. Old, younger—and some very young; youngmen with headbands like Indians, their faces already purple-tan. And youngwomen with matted hair. Bodies roamed the streets and alleys in small groups or alone. They sat, stood, staggered, surrendered to barren ground, vacant lots littered with bottles, wire, rags—and other bodies.

In the skeletons of apartment buildings blackened by smog— she knew their gray corridors, coated with soft grime she used to touch, pretending it was velvet—skinny men without shirts, women in slips or brassieres or bare-chested stared out of the windows at nothing. Where there were curtains in the windows, they were knotted into X's—like warnings of plague; windows begging for a breeze—but only heat shot in.

Carla gasped. She was in all those rooms. They were cold and hot, often at the same time. *On the box papered to look like a dresser, she spread out the contents of her bag, careful not to disturb the reddish dust of flowers, which she touched delicately. Then she replaced the contents and looked down onto the fetid street where live corpses scavenged into the alleys. "Tramps!" she yelled.*

Tramps. She locked the word in her mind. Finding his bottle of liquor empty, a man flung it in angry betrayal. It smashed on the street at Carla's feet.

She backed away and saw a man and a woman entering a hotel; they were laughing. *The man shoved the knife into the woman and she moaned, but why did she laugh?* In the ashen

light of the lobby, which smelled of Lysol and piss, a television
set was on; gray outlines talked to each other. Behind a wired
counter, the clerk looked like a caged shrunken hawk; his hair
grew in a peak, his eyes were black dots, his nose was beaked.
He stared fascinated at the television screen before which other
bodies sat on linoleum-covered couches.

The voice on the television said: ". . . —exploration into
'*The Lower Depths.*' On tonight's news she'll introduce you to
a tragic life of waste, danger, murder in an area the size of a
small city, where from six thousand to fourteen thousand of the
chronically homeless wander. You will learn shocking facts:
The denizens used to be middle-aged or older men; now there
are an increasing number of wandering women, and young
people. You will meet them tonight, lost souls, alcoholics, men
and women with nothing to hope for except a bottle of wine and
welfare— . . ."

Welfare!

"You don't have a social security number?"

"Yes, and I've memorized it. It's three-three-three-three-three-
three-three-three-three-three-three-three-three-three-three— . . ."

"Place of birth?"

"I wasn't finished. There are three more 'threes.' "

"I *said*, Place of birth!"

"The Dust Bowl."

"Look, unless you cooperate— . . ." Incomeinthepastsix-
monthsrelativesapartmentaddresslastplaceofemploym—. . .

"Fuck your welfare!"

"What did you say to me?" the clerk demanded from behind
his shelter of wire in the rancid lobby.

Carla laughed uncontrollably. "Did that man on that television say all *that*? I think I read it somewhere. In the library—in
the newspaper section. Yes, I read it there, this morning."

"What do you want?"

"Want a room," Carla said.

"Show me your money."

"I'm with those two who just registered," Carla said. "They're
expecting me, I'm always there."

"Like hell they're expecting you," the man said.

"Ask them," Carla said. Her voice became urgent. "He's

going to stab her, and then they'll bribe me with roses—I want
to give them back!'' *He shoved the knife deeper, grunting,
pushing it, his tongue licking her neck. She could smell the
sweet and rancid odor.* ''I *have* to thank them!''

''Get out of here, we don't rent to loonies.''

''They just work here.'' Carla moved out of the sick hotel.

She walked past the Greyhound Bus Depot—an island of
tourists and frantically gay shops surround a square building;
cabs wait to whisk tourists away from the contaminated area. A
bus brought her here. The man panhandling told her to go to the
park outside the library.

''Where can I sleep?'' she asked the panhandler.

''L.A.'s got no shelters; mission's got a few beds for women,
though.''

''I'll sleep in the lobby,'' she told the man who came to the
glass door but didn't open it.

''The lobby's filled, too,'' said the man. ''You've got to get
here early—very early. Sorry. God bless you.'' He seemed sad,
really sad.

Carla stood under black fire escapes, which climbed up the
walls. Beyond the window, bodies slept on the floor. She
nodded, pretending she was inside, dozing on a couch.

''If not, try the park outside the library—cops come around
every few hours, though,'' the panhandler said. ''It's past Main,
Broadway, Hope Street—you'll see it.''

Her sweat saturated the newspapers and rags on which she
lay. A cop's stick explored intimately between her legs. *Deeper—*
. . . A garish red line across the old man's neck snapped into
huge drops spattering her hand red. She walked away from the
Greyhound station.

A windowless fortress loomed gray. On one of its walls was a
mosaic mural of faces and black cars. A sign said: TO PRO-
TECT AND SERVE. Out of the barricaded police station emerged
young, shaved, laughing cops.

Deeper— . . . She felt a terrible pain where the cop had
poked her with his stick last night. *She clawed, tearing at the
tall black boots, burying long sharp fingernails.*

As the cops drove away, she spat at them. ''Tramps!''

At the mouth of an alley, Carla smelled food. She remembered she was hungry. Some restaurants arrange leftovers neatly in boxes on top of the garbage, others mix them with filth, even roach poison. In the alley, heaps of rags stirred, bodies strewn on the ground like the wounded left to die on a devastated battlefield. Ahead, were red and white fried-chicken boxes. She hadn't eaten for days. As she moved toward the food, a bold body shoved its way into the other end of the alley. Now two others flanked it. She froze. The three rushed at her. They were young, in their teens, two dark, one blond.

She knew what to do. Emmett told her when they lived under the subways in the maze of metal tubings, warm pipes, criss-crossed, creating small units like rooms under the city. It was the day he found the beautiful roses, yes, that day, that day, the same day they saw the punks waiting with sticks at the station where they crawled under the bitter city. "Act crazy, like an epileptic; stagger past them, scare *them*!"

She did now, in the alley, she allowed her body to lose control, she quaked, howling, letting spit run out. Bodies lying in the creases of the steaming alley did not stir, merely curled inward, to shelter themselves from whatever was happening but not yet to them.

The menacing young bodies danced about Carla.

"You a crazy?" accused the Mexican.

She backed away—and ran into the Negro. "She got lots of bread in that bag, see how she holdin' it?"

The blond boy had pimples like pox on a white bloodless face; he was so skinny his arms were knobby. "You got something real good in that bag?" He poked at her with a finger.

"A bomb," Carla said. "I got a bomb. Boom!"

"Maybe it'll bust your dirty face, filthy scumbag," said the Negro. No, the blond one. No, the Puerto Rican. No, the—. . .

"How'd you like *this*, hag?" The Mexican groped himself.

The blond boy advanced, his hands reaching out tauntingly toward the bag. "What you got in the bag, ugly bitch, huh? Whatcha got there?" Whatcha got there? Whatcha got there?

My life. My father gave me the roses. No, he gave them to my mother and she gave them to me. Then he took them. I found them abandoned in a trash can. Someone left them for me in a train. Emmett brought them to me when we lived under the subway. They were wrapped in delicate green tissue. They grew in my mother's garden; I took scissors and cut them, but those weren't roses. After I cut them, the wind and the dust smothered everything—yellow, gray wind, yellow, gray dust—and I could see the men and sometimes women jump off the freight cars, once I heard shots. They would run hopping over the tracks and came asking for food before they jumped on another train when it was night, into a dark boxcar, bodies pressed tightly, smelling rancid and sweet because a woman wouldn't throw away the roses, which had begun to smell. Someone brought them to me in one hospital, and left them there. No, I went to a funeral, and I gathered them from a grave. My father's. My mother's. They were not my real father or mother, they were people in the freight train calling me in. Maybe my father was there. Or a woman, terrified. I held on to the shadows. So many feet, so many legs—the stick, and the policeman's boots! But they had to let us all out because the law said so. We sat on benches from summer to winter. I held my bag on my lap; the flowers were in it then. "That's what's in the bag!" she screeched at the blond boy.

Where were they? Had she scared them away? They hadn't taken her bag—it wasn't even torn or soiled.

The sleeping forms of ragged men hadn't stirred. Beside one was a bottle. She picked it up. A dirt-caked hand tried feebly to protest. The rags sighed. She took the bottle and drank the remaining liquor, real liquor, not wine—and a lot. It was warm, almost hot, but her body welcomed it with a jolt that reminded her she was alive—and made her realize that she had been shaking, trembling. She forgot she was hungry. She threw down the bottle and walked out of the alley. She felt scorched inside and outside by the liquor and the fired wind.

". . . —another slashing." Under the iron webs of fire escapes men clustered by the mission, talking, already lined up for breakfast, lunch, dinner, beds? The line grew. "Just one more hour," the man said, and went on: "Happened this morning, near the library—the fifth throat slashed."

"I was there," Carla said.

"Not safe at night," another man said.

"One punk's doing it all," an old man asserted.

"A gang," said a youngman; he had a brown-dyed face, matted hair, a beard; a girl with blank eyes was with him.

"Tramps," Carla said sadly as she walked away. To another street, which stretched like a block of colored broken glass. "Tramps," Carla echoed her sad sigh. Then a knot of anger choked. *Tramps! Hobos! Tramps! Tramps! Tramps! she screamed when she saw them running across the desolate tracks. Tramp! the word and hand slapped her face, branding it with heat.*

"How much for this one?" She pointed to the picture of two intertwined roses. Framed drawings of tattoos decorated the walls, every inch of them, in the small shop. Butterflies, flowers, vines, birds, ships, flags, torsos, warriors, faces, stars.

"Thirty dollars." The man with the braided hair did not look up from the lighted magnifying glass under which his needle drilled into the arm of a youngman with dark short hair blackened deeply with dye. His eyes were so pained Carla couldn't look into them. She watched the tattoo forming. There was a skull, and under it, "DEATH BE." Now the needle made an *F*.

Carla said to the man with the braided hair. "I want a pink rosebud and a red blossom."

He glanced at her skinny arm. "Not enough flesh for *one* rosebud. Wait your turn, though, and I'll try—money first."

"I *got* roses." Carla's anger rose. "I don't need your fake ones—*I* got real ones, here!" She pushed her bag toward him and drew it back quickly against her thighs.

Outside, police were kicking at the bare dirty feet of a body on the sidewalk. Another body faced a broken wall.

"What they do?" she asked.

The cops were about to handcuff two men.

"You wanna come with us and find out?" the young cop said.

I did!

She heard the handcuffs click—loudly, like bolts, like iron-barred doors.

That's why Emmett never came back. They chained him while I waited for him under the subways. Then I couldn't wait anymore—but I did anyway, in the green-walled hospital taking pills.

Near padlocked warehouses, bodies lurked. Windows had

been gouged, covered over with nailed boards, the boards had been torn apart, to create shelter inside. But now the heat rotted the waste within, releasing fumes of decay, and so the bodies floated into the hot but cooler shade outside.

"The attacks began right after winter," a man was telling her. They were sitting on the steps of the abandoned building. The late afternoon stretched its shadows, and the distant tall buildings shed theirs, shortening the day here. The man had long disheveled brown hair, his feet were sockless. He wore a jacket—but no shirt. His ribs cut his torso into brown slices. "They come in a car and rush out. First they just beat up on people, now they slash. This heat don't help, either. Saint Moses got it in the library park."

"I was there," Carla said. "I bled on him." She held out the hand he had bled on.

"Eight murders in three, four months. Used to happen far in between; you could rest nights when you didn't get to the mission before it filled. Then two, slashed in one day. No women, though. Ain't killed no women yet," he assured her. He touched his beard, throat.

He smelled sweet—of sweat and booze and urine and flowers. He took a secret drink from a bottle hidden under his coat.

"Give me some," she said.

"No." He tucked the bottle back into the coat. "They burned a man."

"I was there," Carla said.

"I was in a hotel that night," the man went on. "Looked out the window, saw an orange glow, alley lit up. Heard the groans, and I seen him burning, trying to lift himself from the papers he was sleeping on."

The sound of drunkenness, pain, despair, rage—she heard that from then and now. She laughed, but that did not block the louder roar. "They tried to kill me earlier," she said. "I kicked at them, acted crazy, like Emmett taught me, they disappeared."

"Saint Moses—he didn't get killed," the bearded man revised. "It was Sam, Sam got it; he and Saint Moses were sleeping in the same place; used to be together all the time— . . ."

"My mother and father were like that," Carla said, "until he killed her; she killed him first. When they were gone, they'd leave flowers for me, so I knew they were with me." In the hospital she demanded them, screamed into the night. They tied her. When they had to let her out, she said to the nurse, a hairy man, "You stole them, bastard!"

The wind whined against the reeking building. Beyond the tracks, the orange sky bled smoke; but directly above, it deepened into clean purple.

She had been talking to this man for limbo days, empty or full, an hour and a lifetime. Time was the color of the sky, early morning and early night were the same color, so you didn't know whether to try to sleep or try to wake up.

She walked along the row of the bars on 5th Street. Some open wall-less into the street. A television set was on. A woman said from the screen, "I asked a man how he had come to allow himself to sink so low, Ken, and he couldn't give me an answer."

She was still standing in the lobby of the hotel looking into the television. She had to get upstairs before the man stabbed the laughing woman he was with. "If you don't get out of here, I'll call the cops," the man like a hawk in a cage said.

"You already called them just because I looked at the blue poster," she told him.

On the steps of the abandoned warehouse, the bearded man took another hidden drink when Carla bent to loosen her shoes, her feet swollen with heat. "Saint Moses says he's a priest, sometimes claims he's a minister, changes his religion depending on the congregation," he laughed a phlegmy cough. "Had his own church once."

"But he left because he was so angry when he saw that priest run me out," Carla said.

"He was the best preacher in the Square. Didn't preach damnation like the others, no, sir, Saint Moses, he preached *salvation*!" Again he tried to drink secretly from his bottle. This time, Carla pressed her cheek against his, to force some of the liquor into her mouth. He allowed a few drops to dot her tongue. She grasped his hand, tilted the bottle, and took a full, long swig. He wrenched back the bottle from her. "Saint Moses made a miracle in Pershing Square, I seen it. Cured a man with a twisted leg. Saint Moses prayed all day, called on God, lay hands, and the man walked straight as you and me.''

"I remember," Carla said. "The man walked straight."

"He tried to preach at the mission the other night, and they wouldn't let him."

"I was there," Carla said. The sun festered on the smoke-scratched horizon. Carla felt hot; the heat of her body radiated into the heat of the windy night.

"What the hell you doin' on Skid Row?" she asked the youngman sitting next to her in the bar that opened into the naked street; the woman was gone from the television. The youngman next to her was in his twenties, tall, skinny, wearing a sleeveless shirt, his arms tattooed like blue maps; he had dark, weather-lashed skin. "Still got youngblood," she heard her voice, "lots of fight ahead, save giving up for the last, this is the last stop before— . . ." *Before the beach. She looked up and saw only the sky, then the stars, dim but there; she couldn't see them till Emmett told her to look.* "You're not due yet," she told the youngman.

"Shit," he said, "what's it to you?"

His name was Tattoos. He was in his twenties.

"I'm Carla," she told him. *"I'm Emmett. You can't panic like that, you're too young, still got youngblood, lots of fight— and eyes, strange eyes, like a deer's." He held her; they sat on the rotting piers. Behind them, the city was rancid despite the sprinkles of distant lights. She could still hear the roar of the subways she had been riding for days when he joined her, made her get off—but he told her it wasn't the subways she heard here on the piers, it was the ocean. "There's no beach," she said. "Miles of it in— . . ."* "And that's why I'm here, smartass," she told Tattoos, and she walked out into the world she had forbidden him.

She sat in an alley. She had a full bottle of wine with her. No, she had already drunk half of it. She bought it in the liquor store, waiting outside until no one but the clerk was there; she hid the bottle while she paid for it—so no one would see her, follow her, take it from her. She didn't open it until she was in the alley. That's when she drank half of it. In her bag she still had much more than a dollar.

The steps of the warehouse were darkening. The orange sky tarnished into gray. New shadows lurked about in the heat.

Suddenly the bearded man shoved her against the bolted door of the warehouse where they had sat for days talking about Saint Moses and Sam and murder. She pushed her bag behind her. "I don't want your bag," he said. "What do I get for all the booze I gave you?"

"Couple of swigs—and I had to take them," she said, and raised her knee, thwarting him.

"For another one?"

"It's all gone, you threw the bottle," she reminded him.

"I'll get another, give you half."

"Get it first," she said. Her knee became firmer. "Or give me the money and I'll get it." He was much drunker than she was, weaker, and he knew it. She could knock him down the steps by straightening out her leg—he knew it. "I got a dollar," he said.

"Two," she upped it.

He searched in his pocket. There was a crumpled bill and some coins. " 'Bout fifty cents and a buck," he estimated.

She snatched the money from him, put it in her bag, replaced it behind her, and lowered her leg.

"Give it back," he said—but he raised her dress, opened his pants, and pressed his soft cock against her cunt. He rubbed against it, pushing with his hips as if he were inside her—pushing her against the bag behind her.

She closed her eyes and breathed in, collecting smells, rancid, sweet, rancid, *rancid*!

She shoved him against the wall.

"Gimme back my money!" he yelled.

She squeezed past his pressing body, lowering her dress, not bothering to run, knowing he could not catch up with her. In the liquor store in light as white as bones she looked at the crushed bill when she paid for the bottle. It was five dollars!

Soon she would fill the perfume vial before the wine was all gone, and then she'd forget she had it, until morning.

Tattoos asked her why she was in that bar and warning him to stay away. "Because I'm *looking* and you haven't even started!" she said and walked into the sphere of hot night.

She heard the sobs of an old man. Several bodies gathered about him, black, white, emaciated, shirtless bodies. A black bony woman in a slip kept saying, "Amen!"—raising her trembling hands, closing her eyes. Nearby a youngwoman kept squeezing her own arm; she sat on the curb of the street, trembling, perspiring.

"There were three of them, one slashed Sam's throat, the knife ripped past his neck to here on mine." Saint Moses pointed to the edge of his neck, right under the earlobe. "I rolled over on the ground, and I wish I hadn't, I wish they'd slashed mine, too." He sat on a littered curb.

She peered out of the leafy pocket where she'd slept on wet papers. Behind the bleeding man, Saint Moses touched his own neck. With the blood-smeared hand she clawed her way into the thicker part of the ledge, and on the other side they waited for her because she had seen it all. One held the bloodied knife. She felt it like a lit match searing her flesh. The man died over her, killed by his own knife.

"I'm going to sleep outside, in the open," Saint Moses sobbed, "until they find me and slash my throat like they slashed Sam's."

One of the men offered him a drink. He took it thirstily. Another man cursed him and walked away.

He needs to make another miracle! Carla remembered when he had cured that cripple in Pershing Square. He'd prayed and prayed, laid hands, and the man walked! She slid through the sweaty bodies about Saint Moses crying on the curb. She protected her bag and the bottle in it. She went limp, quivering, "*Cure me!*" she moaned. The men began to laugh.

"You're mocking me!" Saint Moses rose up wrathfully.

"No, no, I want you to cure me like you did that man in Pershing Square. I was there!" Carla pled.

Laughter!

"You're trying to rob me of my miracle, even that." Saint Moses shook before her. "You're not sick, *he* really was, and I cured him!"

Carla began to cry, urgent gasps and tears hurled against the growing laughter. No, she protested silently. *It's your fault*! "No!"

He pushed her away, she toppled back. Her bag fell beside her. One of the men lunged for it, but he slipped because the bottle in it broke and spilled the liquor. She clutched for her bag and fled.

Hidden in the jungle of steamed shadows in the alley, she removed the pieces of the shattered bottle from her bag. The remains of roses would be wet. That was all right. Like watering them. She licked the wine, which moistened her probing fingers. She still had the money the man had given her, rubbing his prick against her, rubbing his soft prick against her and pushing her against the door of the warehouse.

"That's enough!" she told him.

"I'll come like this."

"Not even hard."

"I can come, though."

She felt moisture on her thighs. "No!" she screamed, pulling away from him. "No!" Her vision erupted into brutal redness.

Saint Moses shoved her into the street. She fell into the liquor-and-urine-spattered gutter. She grabbed her bag. Night blew heat on her, into her eyes, drying all moisture. She closed her eyes.

When she opened them, she was peering into the tattoo shop. It was washed in light but it was closed. An iron-grilled gate blocked it. She heard sobs. Next to her, a Mexican youngman was crying, crying. He moved away along Main Street. Carla looked inside the tattoo parlor. She saw the drawing of a naked woman. Then she searched out the framed roses. She clenched the black bars—*the iron bars of the jail*—and the bright light forced her to blink. "Don't cry," she said to the Mexican youngman, but he was gone. Don't cry. She leaned against the bars. Don't cry. She closed her eyes and opened them— . . .

. . . —*in an exposed bright room. She stood before rows of youngmen and a few women, all in white. An older woman also in white was standing with her. ". . . —give my permission, in exchange for professional care— . . ." She signed the paper. A young hand in the room shot up: "In this stage, then, is chemical treatment a pos— . . .?" The older woman next to her said to the seated young people, "No—all of it is buried forever in her mind, scorched in by pain. Whatever brutality she was*

*exposed to was so enormous she's collected all memories into
one deep, unhealable wound. Perhaps there are two overwhelming memories, perhaps many; perhaps one was joyful." The
woman looked at her and said; "I hope so, my dear, I hope you
have at least one beautiful memory. You have beautiful eyes,
you know. I've never before seen eyes quite that color." Carla
rested her head on the woman's shoulder and closed her eyes.*

When she opened them, her head was against a pocked
paint-spattered wall in an alley, the three muggers were trying
to ambush her. The blond one with the pitted white face and
skinny arms kicked at the back of her legs, and she dropped
kneeling to the ground. There were two blond ones—twins. The
Puerto Rican danced excitedly about her. "Tramp! Hag! Bitch!
Cunt!" The blond boy lifted her dress, exposing her naked
flesh. Then he turned her over, face down. "Look at that," he
giggled. The Negro rolled her over, face up. "Look at *that!*"

"It's too dry!" The blond boy spat on her.

"Can't shove nothing in it!" The Puerto Rican added phlegm.
"Try *this!*"

She tore at flesh. In the shadows of the alley, *the shadows of
the freight car, the crouching shadows of the jail, she screamed
a scream wailing up and down like a broken siren.*

She screamed a scream wailing— . . .

It was Saint Moses who had screamed. Three bodies tore
away from him. They had pressed him against a leprous wall.
They ran into a parked car, then raced away into darkness.
Throat sliced open, blood blooming from his mouth, Saint
Moses sank onto the blemished ground.

The blade of a streetlight cut the darkness of the black
bludgeoned alley she fled into.

"What you got in that bag?" a voice came from the dark.

"My life," she said.

Feet advanced.

Carla closed her eyes, to push this assaulter into invisible
blackness. But this time when she opened them again, the
shadow had become a man facing her. "Give it to me," he
demanded.

She tried to run. Two strong arms grabbed her. Growling, she
fought fiercely. The man yanked the bag from her. She felt the

handle tear. In a puddle of invading light, the man turned the bag over, shaking it. Her cardboard-protected mirror, the unfilled vial of perfume, the aging brush, some cloth, the lipstick tube, shards of the wine bottle, the money—all spilled out. He took the bills and the change. Then he shook the bag over and over, to make certain there was no more money.

Shaking out the ashen roses!

"No!" she screamed.

"No!" she screamed.

He flung the bag at her. She knelt over it. It was ripped, still wet from the spilled liquor.

She would get another bag. She had had many. All that mattered was saving the roses.

Her fingers traced the seams of the bag, searching out the dried, flaky petals. They were gone! But maybe along the upper seams— . . .

A finger stung, she pulled it out. A piece of glass had cut it.

In the severed light, she looked at the red blood. It would dry, the way blood always did. She lowered her finger between her legs. Yes, the blood would dry into flakes and then she would transfer them into a new bag.

Standing, she pressed her bleeding finger between her legs, and with the blood, she drew there the outline of a rose, another, then another, until there was one huge scarlet blossom.

Lost Angels: 10

"White Heat," Lisa said coolly when Jesse, shirtless and soaked with sweat and exhilaration, returned to the car. Orin had waited for him outside in the whipping wind over the entangled freeways. "You were trying to do *White Heat*, Jesse. That's easy to guess because that's about the *only* movie you *ever* talk about." She took advantage of the fact that Jesse couldn't answer her because he was panting so heavily. They had frightened her, with all that yelling and laughing in the wind over the howling freeways.

Crashing from the soaring elation of the earlier moments of aimless defiance, Jesse lay back in the seat of the car and closed his eyes as Orin drove away from the area.

Cody Jerrett! Cagney! Jesse could see the bulldog face, tough and sad; yes, even Cody was sad sometimes. Clinging to the rusting ladder earlier, Jesse had felt an invasion of sharp memories of that favorite film: scenes of dark wind outside the motel where the gang stayed—like *them*, in a motel—and the money—hundreds of thousands in a suitcase—was in the trunk of the car! And Cody had this "red-hot buzz saw" inside his head—because as a kid he'd faked headaches to get attention from his father, who soothed him, the only one who could until he died, or stopped, or Cody's mother took over, tried, but— . . . The events of the film began to blur. When they told Cody his father died, he went crazy, in prison—no, that was later when Ma was killed by Big Ed and sexy Verna, the two-timers. And most of it happened in *Los Angeles*! Here, in *this* city! They might be on the very same street Cody drove on, on his way to that plant they went to rob: Huge metallic spheres and columns, and Cody climbed a steel ladder. All the others in his gang abandoned

him, of course, surrendered. Not Cody!—he *wouldn't* surrender
even when the cop said he didn't have a chance. Cody said—
. . . shouted— . . . "Top of— . . .!" No, that was when he
talked to his dead Ma on a black, windy night.

Now they were driving past an area of Wilshire Boulevard
that had once been glamorous—like so many now seedy sections of the city: MacArthur Park was dying, the cultivated lilies
gone from its ponds, unruly grass inviting weeds; and Lafayette
Park with its colorful rows of flowers still holding on, stared
ominously at the intruding waste and poverty; carelessly aging
houses, now separated into apartments, rooms.

Farther on, Wilshire Boulevard glittered as it prepared itself
for Beverly Hills.

After dinner at a Sizzler Steak House—and Jesse's mood
lifted when Orin encouraged him to have the steak and lobster
combination—Orin told Lisa she could choose a movie from
the newspaper listings.

"Casablanca!" she drooled, not believing the good luck.
"And *Now, Voyager*!"

They were playing in the old Warner's Theater in Beverly
Hills, an enormous, lavish shell of a theater, being allowed to
disintegrate in cruel humiliation: worn faded carpets; chunks of
walls unrepaired; broken mirrors removed, squares left gray.
And yet the remnants of its resplendent Art Deco excesses shine
through defiantly: prisms, arcs, layers of once-bright colors,
geometric bursts of glass. It flaunts its tattered presence—knowing
it will soon be crushed, replaced by the sinister levels of still
another parking lot, or the concrete slabs of a rectangular building.

Lisa cried, again, through *Casablanca.* But an intrusive,
unformed thought pushed her away for moments from the story:
Ingrid Bergman looked very much like that woman in that odd
movie Orin had chosen that other night—*The Conformist*, that
was the name. She startled herself when she realized her mind
had wandered away while Ingrid Bergman was crying in the
man's hotel room. So mean to her, so mean.

Jesse liked Bogart a lot—but not all that much in *this* movie;
he wasn't really tough in this one.

Orin sat as if he was scrutinizing the movie.

Lisa pled to stay for *Now, Voyager*. Jesse hated it immediately and fell asleep. Lisa cried through it again, too—and this time her mind didn't wander from Bette Davis. Orin sat stiffly, as if deep inside himself.

In the lobby Lisa caught an unexpected reflection of herself in a long mirror. She paused. "Here's looking at you, kid," she repeated from the first movie. "Don't ask for the stars, we got the moon," she mixed from the second.

"Awright, kid," Jesse asserted his own line. "*Cody* said *that*: 'Awright, kid.' "

Lisa continued to study her reflection. Yes, she could have been a movie star—but only *then*; the *very* time her *mother* had been young. She thought of Pearl; fading. Makeup. She'd use some makeup on her when they got back.

Outside, the heat waited. Orin brought his watch to his ear.

Making certain he has the right time, Jesse felt sure, as they walked toward the car. That meant they would watch Sister Woman tonight; they hadn't last night—too late when they returned from the park, or was Orin making *her* wait now? Last night had been so full of turbulence that Jesse realized only now that, no, Orin had not even turned the television on!

Although it was out of the way, Orin took the Hollywood Freeway; traffic was fast and smooth. He always slowed down when they approached a giant mural beyond a grassed slope and on a tall wall. It was an enormous painting of an old woman, graying, beautiful, with brilliant eyes. There were murals all over the city. Another painting, on a long wall off Santa Monica Boulevard, showed Los Angeles crumbling under water released by a giant earthquake, a freeway toppling into raging water.

"Movieland Wax Museum!" Lisa read aloud. Signs on bus benches all over the city advertise it, almost as often as they advertise mortu-aries. Each time she had seen it before, Lisa forced herself into silence. The Movieland Museum was too precious a venture to risk wrong timing. She had waited for the right moment, which she decided impulsively was now. "Please, Orin, we've got to go to the Movieland Wax Museum!"

"Sure," Orin said.

So quickly. He kept acquiescing to Lisa, or so it seemed to Jesse. But then, Orin seemed to be acquiescing to them *both*, perhaps because of Lisa's—*their*—anger after the journey into the park. "Sure," he echoed Orin, as if his approval were required equally.

They *were* becoming alike—no, similar—in a way she didn't understand, Lisa thought, hearing Jesse echo Orin.

On Western Avenue, Lisa was relieved when Orin took Sunset to the motel. There was still the implicit hint that at any moment he might want to return to the park.

In the motel room Lisa insisted Ingrid Bergman should have been allowed to stay with Bogart. "She loved him, and he only *pretended* to love her—she sacrificed so much for him; he was mean to let her go—and"—this occurred to her for the first time, with doubled horror—"he *forced* her to go with the *same man* who left Bette Davis in the *other* movie. Oh!" She went immediately to Pearl Chavez on the bed; she would make her beautiful again.

In the bathroom with the door open, Orin was washing his hands, slowly, methodically; he did this often after a long day.

"I bet your favorite movie is *The Wizard of Oz*," Jesse teased Lisa, paying her back for deriding him earlier about *White Heat*.

"*The Wizard of Oz!*" she blurted in indignant disbelief. She had begun to apply makeup to Pearl. Rouge first. That really helped, she told herself. After all, the real Pearl Chavez had been a half-breed. "No, that is *not* one of my all-times, not even a half-favorite. It's too *real*."

"Real!" Jesse couldn't believe her. "Real?"

"Yes," Lisa said. The makeup *was* working. She applied lipstick to the tiny lips of the doll; more, thicker, more— . . . Her finger moved unsteadily and it smeared the doll's lips; they looked bloody. With a tissue, she cleaned the smudges. She added more of the waxy makeup.

"Hey, Orin," Jesse called into the bathroom. "Can you believe Lisa thinks *The Wizard of Oz* is too *real*?"

"The reason it's real," Lisa said with conviction, "is that it's too much like life would look like if you looked *inside*." She paused, reasoning it out carefully. "Not the singing and the funny parts—although I'm not so sure there really *were* any. All those scared people— . . ." She outlined Pearl's eyes darkly.

"You're not making sense," Jesse derided.

"I know exactly what I mean," Lisa said firmly. "And sometimes Orin doesn't make sense either," she said tentatively; then boldly: "But you sure do listen to him, yes sir. And I bet *you* liked those ugly evil flying monkeys in that *Oz* movie and the— . . ."

"*I* don't make sense?" Orin stood calmly wiping his hands as carefully as he washed them.

Jesse marveled: Orin wasn't angry; he was smiling!

"I guess you do make sense," Lisa retreated somewhat, but only because it was true. Even when he didn't make *strict* sense, she *understood*. But not always. And she was beginning to listen much more carefully. "I take it back, Orin," she said faithfully. "At first I didn't understand you, but now, when you talk such beautiful words, I do understand. Sometimes," she heard herself add. With scissors, she cut the doll's dress, making it jagged, short; she lopped off the sleeves, formed a *V* at the bosom. With her finger, she forced a rip into the dress, near the thigh. "And sometimes, Orin," Lisa went on, "you look like an angel, you really do, with that beautiful reddish hair and blue eyes; other times, even though you're so fair, you get that dark stare— . . ."

"How do I look now?" Orin distorted his face at all angles.

"Ugly!" she said. She stared at the doll.

Jesse laughed at the faces Orin was making. So happy. But in another moment he might become all solemn.

Orin turned on the television.

". . . —attributed to the purported damaging effects of Agent Orange, a chemical used by the army in jungle warfare." Kenneth Manning finished. Now Eleanor Cavendish was saying, "Sporadic brush fires continue to cause grave concern among firefighters and citizens of threatened areas. Winds up to fifty miles an hour in the canyons are fanning fires at— . . ."

Lisa dabbed rouge on Pearl Chavez's cheeks, pushing the color up and back toward her ears.

Orin shifted channels.

Brother Man faced Sister Woman on her throne against the imitation sky. The telephone number to call for witnessing and pledging was on the screen. "Fire burns on the lips of sinners— and only *he* can quench it. Come." Sister Woman's hand beckoned, the chiffon sleeve a blue ghost. "Surrender to the Lord, let Him unburden you of the weight of your grievous sins—*and the sins of those departed!*—sins which are not buried with them but which extend deep down into hell and out— . . ." Her hands burst open, fingers thrust outward. ". . . —to you, who have the power to bring them peace."

With the edge of her comb, Lisa frizzled Pearl's hair, thickening it into a bushy halo. She was forcing herself not to listen to that woman. She threatened her—them; aroused intrusive doubts, like last night's.

The sighing chiffon flowed to Sister Woman's shoulders as she raised her hands as if to bring down heaven to purify hell. Her exposed arms were white. Her soft voice stumbled on a sob, resumed in anger: "But! If you wait too long, the beast will grow stronger, roaring out of the abyss—strengthened by sins captive in hell!" Her head turned away as if from a vision of the burning holocaust of perdition. The colorless eyes faced ahead now. "And then the beast will rise to lure you into the flames of hell, heated beyond comprehension by sin—the tinderwood of hell!" The arms and hands crushed down. *"And I have known him in hell!"* Her eyes closed. "I see four lost angels," she barely whispered, as if to herself.

Lisa heard, ". . . —four lost angels." She looked at Orin, who nodded.

Sister Woman's voice purled again. "Escape, now, oh, the deceiver is powerful, so powerful and cunning that at times it is difficult to tell the demonic angels from those of the Lord."

"Then how shall we know the difference?" asked Brother Man.

Sister Woman's lips smiled.

Jesse's eyes shifted to Orin, who watched, watched.

Sister Woman reached out with her hand. "How shall we know the good from the deceiving evil? you ask. By calling on the Lord. And *he*— . . ." The wings of chiffon spread outward, up. Then her hands fainted into delicate crucifixion on her lap. "And *He* will tell us! *He* will give us the radiant proof of His righteousness!"

"No," Orin said softly to the figure on the screen. "*You* will tell us, just like you promised her." He turned off the television.

He reached for the telephone, pressed it tightly to his ear, his fingers on the dial.

Lisa looked in surprise at the doll, what she had converted her into. The doll looked savage, cruel, brutal, grotesquely sexual. I made you that way! she thought triumphantly and heard similar words aimed at *her* from her past: *You made me ugly*! . . . When she heard Orin dialing, she looked up in fear.

Holding the receiver so tightly to his ear—Jesse noticed—to drown the sounds that would reveal no one would be on the other end? He'll put down the phone, Jesse thought, and then his face will be the little-boy one and he'll laugh and make us laugh at his playacting and for letting him fool us into thinking— . . ."

"This is *Orin*! . . . I called, left a message— . . ." He repeated the identifying details he had left the earlier time. He reached for a piece of paper, wrote down a number. "No, not tonight. Tell her tomorrow—*after* I hear her sermon." He repeated the telephone number. He hung up.

"Stop pretending, Orin!" Lisa was desperately washing Pearl's face with a moist towel. "You know you weren't speaking to anyone!"

Billy and Stud: "Bitter Street Love"

Billy fell in love with Stud the moment he saw him entering Coffee Andy's on Highland Avenue. Coffee Andy's is a restaurant where malehustlers gather throughout the day before scattering along Santa Monica Boulevard a distance of perhaps a mile, an ugly gray stretch from the tip-end of Hollywood to the beginning of West Hollywood long before the boulevard turns chic in the area of mutual cruising, unpaid homosexual encounters.

Billy heard Stud before he saw him, heard his motorcycle have a fit outside before it passed out. *"The Wild One,"* Billy looked out the restaurant window and said to Ed, a middle-aged married client of Billy's; he drove in from Pasadena once or so a week to see Billy, and paid him $30, the amount Billy had asked for when they met—and then Ed would always add more. He would also take Billy to dinner— like now.

Stud walked in shirtless, showing off his gymnast's body, pushing the time before he would have to put his shirt on—a waitress was charging at him; he peeled on a sleeveless t-shirt with a slight tear that showed a part of his chest. He was frowning because the motorcycle had hinted of a death rattle.

Seeing him approach, Billy lowered his long, dark eyelashes, assuming a look he knew was among his very best, and then he flashed his beautiful green-speckled brown eyes at Stud and allowed a strand of sun-lightened blond hair to fall over his forehead. Billy was eighteen.

Stud stopped before Billy. His mouth opened.

Billy pushed away the strand of hair, counting on its falling again, and splashed a dazzling look on Stud.

"I saw you on TV!" Stud said excitedly.

Billy was crushed. "Oh, that thing," he said. Ed had been consoling Billy about that.

Recently that woman announcer and her busy crew had invaded Santa Monica Boulevard with vans and wires and lights and cameras, doing, they said, a feature on "street life" that would tell "the truth." They interviewed several hustlers; Billy was featured. Yes, he'd looked great—his eyes even greener, mistier. It was only when he saw the news program—as he sat about the TV set with several of the other hustlers who shared the two-room apartment in a building that would be demolished at the end of summer—that Billy realized he'd been used. The female announcer had kept saying, "You're *very* beautiful; certainly you make a *lot* of money." She kept reminding him all his friends would see him on television—along with prospective rich customers, even a movie director. So Billy told her he made $1000 a week hustling the streets. In the segment, none of that Mandy Lang-Whatever's pushing had been included; just the figure—which a vice cop who followed in the program used as evidence that there were a "lot of perverts out there buying young bodies." The program had ended with a long shot of other street hustlers, idling along the trashy blocks, peering into slowly moving cars, malehustlers searching that night's cheaply paid contact. "They peddle their bodies for high stakes—to the highest bidder, these young prostitutes, coming here to make their fortunes on the erotic streets, the way others in yesteryears came to find fame—legitimately—in the movies," the woman's voice-over had throbbed. Billy had felt dirty—the way he hardly ever did hustling the street.

"Yeah, I thought it was you," Stud said. He strutted to a table in back, pulling several pairs of eyes after him.

Including Billy's. ". . . —and that woman said I was effeminate—I'm *not* effeminate," Billy protested to Ed.

Ed soothed him. "She said you were very *beautiful*, effeminate or boyish, depending on how one viewed you," he reminded Billy. "My wife commented on what a beautiful youngman you are, Billy. You do have a *boyish* beauty," he emphasized.

Billy *was* beautiful. He had a slender blond body that turned golden instead of tan, eyes so misty at times they looked painted with water colors, and long dark eyelashes. It was true he was not effeminate—he was gracefully boyish, looking radiantly younger than his eighteen years. Tonight he was wearing the familiar Levi cutoffs, which showed off his proud round buttocks, and a powder blue shirt, chopped at the stomach to exhibit his gold-tanned waist hardly 27 inches. He was from Louisiana, from "a city with a French name," he would say, not wanting to evoke it further. A southern accent filtered his speech.

"That youngman who just walked by thinks you're very beautiful also," Ed said, tracing Billy's gaze on Stud.

Billy *did* notice him looking his way. "A lot of people stare at me since I was on that TV show and said I made a thousand dollars a day," he said ruefully. "I could kill that Mandy Do-Shit!"

Stud looked away when he realized the two were talking about him. He was good-looking, eighteen years old; he hadn't had a haircut since long before he'd left Bozeman, Montana—*empty fields, frozen winters, poverty, anger*—and so it curled in dark loving licks at his neck and about his ears. He had a muscular body built by hard country work and improvised gymnastics. He'd been in Los Angeles a night and a day and had made $30 hustling. Like other restless youngmen of his age and meager background, Stud learned from scandalized newspaper and television accounts about malehustling in large cities. These reports were always breathless in their denunciations. Like the others, Stud heard only the huge amounts of money to be made "out there." That message became an insistent beckoning away from a drab life and angry shouts.

Last night, with his satchel containing his possessions, he had walked to Santa Monica Boulevard; he saw dozens and dozens of youngmen on the streets, semi-exposed bodies, some masculine, others effeminate. The pretty ones sometimes called each other "she" and the masculine ones called them that, too, at times. Some were not effeminate, but pretty in a way Stud found confusing. A man stopped for him. Stud asked for "the usual." The man offered $30. Stud wondered whether he should have asked for more. At the man's pretty home—as pretty as any Stud had ever seen before—he watched the segment in which Billy starred on television.

Ed gave Billy an extra $20 today. "Go over and talk to that kid." He paid at the cash register and left. There were mean clients and sweet ones—just as there were good hustlers and the criminal types who beat and robbed their clients—and hustlers sometimes got beaten up, too—and Ed was one of the sweetest clients—giving Billy an "emergency telephone number," even trying to talk him into leaving the streets, offering to help him get a job, or go to a trade school—even though they didn't have sex at all sometimes. But Billy hadn't even finished grammar school and had already been busted for prostitution.

"Can I sit down or you wanna be alone?—you look so moody." Billy went over to the youngman with dark hair.

A smile broke Stud's scowl. He had a chipped tooth on one side of his mouth. Maybe that's why he smiled crookedly, to disguise it. Whatever—it made him look very sexy. "You really make a thousand bucks a week?" he asked Billy.

"No!" Billy said. "That woman made me say that—and *she* knew it was a lie. What's your name?"

"Stud," Stud said—he called himself that now; the man he'd gone with last night had called out to him, "Hey, stud!" "I figured she tried to get you to say that so the cop could say what he said," Stud said knowledgably.

"Thank you." Billy was grateful for the understanding.

An effeminate young waiter breezed over. "Well, aren't *we* everywhere!" he said to Billy. "First we were over *there* with the sugar daddy, and now we're over *here* with the macho man. And, honey, you haven't made a thousand bucks since you began hustling your buns at the age of ten."

"Leave her alone!" Stud barked.

Billy lowered his head toward the table.

So Stud strengthened his defense. "Fuck," he said to the waiter, "you would've done the same thing—*I* would've."

"Take your order, *sir*?" the waiter frosted over. Stud ordered a hamburger and fries—double hamburger for the protein to keep his muscles firm. He looked at Billy, expecting to be thanked for his defense.

Instead, Billy said quietly, "I'm not a 'she,' Stud. I'm a 'he'—just like you."

Stud was flustered. When he saw Billy on television, he'd

thought Billy was a girl—not because he was effeminate—he wasn't—but because he was so *beautiful*. Within his experience, he couldn't think of anyone being that beautiful and not a girl. Sorry, he wanted to say. Sorry, he tried to say. But he couldn't.

Billy brightened. "Where you staying, Stud?" he thickened his Southern accent.

"Here and there," Stud said.

"I—we—got an apartment around the corner. Have a recent vacancy, too. Everybody gives a few bucks."

"Sounds good," Stud said. Billy's eyes were actually as greenish gold as they had appeared on colored television!

Outside, darkness was inking the sky. Billy suggested they walk to the apartment. Billy said he didn't want to leave his bike there. The bike leaned forlornly against a pipe at the edge of the coffee shop. Even the chain with which he had secured it looked weary. It was a skinny motorcycle, eager to give up. Billy told Stud where the apartment was. Stud suggested Billy ride there with him.

Billy's heart leapt—but he also eyed the motorcycle and wondered whether it would hold them both even that short distance. Stud was undoing the chain, making motions that would flex his biceps. Showily, he removed his shirt. Billy decided he *would* ride with him even if the rickety machine *collapsed*.

Stud stood up, ready to mount his bike. He and Billy were the same height; then he noticed Billy was wearing sandals and he was wearing cowboy boots. He straddled the machine, hopped down on it. The machine made not the slightest announcement it intended to start. "Motherfucker." Stud tried to control his anger.

Billy wanted to reassure him, but he felt that might aggravate the situation.

Pumping away at the silent machine, Stud was sweating rivulets. He was becoming angry. "*Fuckin' cocksucker!*"

Billy's agate eyes shot a reproving look at him.

Stud pumped more—and with one foot he kicked at the side of the machine as if spurring a horse. The machine jangled to life. "Quick!" he called to Billy, who hopped on.

The machine bucked, bucked once more, and then rolled on

as smoothly as it ever would again. Billy put his arm on Stud's moist stomach, and he leaned his head against Stud's shoulders; only the blond, golden-streaked hair touched the brown-tanned skin.

The machine made it around the block. In front of the apartment building, it died, died—they both knew—forever. Stud looked down at it. "It brought me all the way from Montana."

"You can chain it in the courtyard," Billy said.

Carrying his satchel, Stud started pushing and pulling it toward the building, thinking he might be able to sell it as scrap.

The building was the last on the block. Two others had been abandoned. The one on the corner was only slabs of concrete like upright pieces of discarded jigsaw puzzles. The other had not yet been demolished, but its windows had been knocked out. That emphasized the desolation of the building left standing.

One side of a double swinging iron gate had become unhinged, so loose now that even a breeze threatened to topple it. The grass was a bristly mat of yellow. A fountain in the courtyard was a dry pool of debris. Trees still struggled for life. Valiant flowers—gray—managed to grow.

To the side of the courtyard, several open stairways led up to the second and third storeys of the building so decrepit no one cared who moved in or out—mostly hustlers. Before the new season, concrete demolition balls would attack the morose structure.

Stud chained his dead bike around a tree. He followed Billy up one flight of squeezed steps. They walked along a corridor that would be dark no matter what time of day it was.

Billy didn't even think to wonder how Stud was reacting to the crumbling building. The hustlers who took their nightly posts along the boulevard slept from place to place, or in garages, parks—jumping over wired gates and past warning signs. Sometimes they slept in doorways. Having a place of your own—a rented room, an apartment—that was *something*!

The door was unlocked. Stud and Billy walked into a two-room apartment littered with hamburger wrappers, fried-chicken boxes, cans of soft drinks, beer, milk. There was one large window—and a small one in the open bathroom. Several mattresses were scattered about the floor. Doorless closets revealed shaggy clothes. A small color television—on—was chained, tightly chained, to an exposed pipe. A stunted stove, a refrigerator with coils. Heat squatted in the bare rooms.

Billy extended his hand, welcoming Stud.

"Looks just fine." Stud meant it. He put down his satchel and looked at the others in the room—two youngmen and a girl, all about his age.

"This is Dianne from— . . . .God knows where," Billy introduced. "She just appears." He hugged Dianne fondly; she let him.

"Like a mushroom, overnight," Dianne growled in a surprisingly rough voice. She was a small, frail girl with an acne problem.

"Gary from— . . ." Billy was proceeding.

"Sedalia, Missouri; know where that is?" Gary had just turned seventeen—a veteran of two weeks and still making it, a slim tough-looking youngman with the angular features popular on his type; he had a flowery tattoo too large for his biceps. He lay on a mattress and in his shorts with Valentine hearts. His eyes were tied to the television set.

"Tim from Albuquerque, New Mexico," Tim announced himself. He was pretty and more than slightly effeminate. He wore subtle makeup. Unlike Billy's, it was not the sun that had bleached his hair.

"And this is Stud from— . . ."

"Bozeman, Montana," Stud smiled crookedly.

"*Stud?!*" Dianne blurted incredulously, clearly hinting she might just laugh aloud. "*Stud!*" she rasped in her tough voice.

Stud almost retreated to his real name. Instead, he dug the heels of his boots firmly into the mushy wood of the floor and challenged, "Yeah, *Stud!*"

"Shee-it." Dianne swigged from her beer can. She straddled a chair and leaned her elbows on its back. "You gonna tell me you're straight?" she tossed. No one knew where she came from or what she did. Almost every day she'd just turn up from nowhere in her old Toyota and go back wherever. Though she never stayed, she brought food. If, especially on weekends,

someone had left without paying a part of the rent, she'd
contribute a few bucks. She was just there among exiles.

"I *am* straight," Stud said.

Gary looked away from the television screen, Tim blinked.
Dianne said, "Shee-*it!*"

"I've never kissed a guy or done stuff like that. I never
wanted to do a guy or get fucked," Stud offered in evidence. "I
never fucked a guy, but I fucked lots and lots of girls in
Bozeman." Two. "And that's how it's gonna stay."

"Straight as a bow—sorry, arrow," Dianne derided. "And
what's so fuckin' good about *that*?"

"Leave him alone, Dianne," Billy defended softly—but he
felt a pang of apprehension about Stud. "He's just Stud. Period."

Gary said, "Hell, man, as long as you charge, what difference does it make what you fuck?"

"Or get fucked by," Tim extended.

Ernie, a Mexican youngman, older than the others, maybe
nineteen, with dreamy soft eyes and brown velvety skin, walked
into the apartment. "You the new tenant?" he asked Stud.

Stud nodded. Ernie walked over and kissed Dianne, who
turned her cheek: "Ugh!" Then he kissed Billy on the lips.
Stud frowned. "Hey, you looked beautiful on TV," Ernie told
Billy. He opened himself a beer. "You contribute yet?" he
asked Stud. He went to a drawer, took out a box with some
concealed rolled joints he'd come back for.

Stud grandly pulled out a ten. "This enough?"

Dianne collected it. "The man's been coming round," she
rasped.

Ernie said it casually to Gary in order not to sound uncool:
"Heard you got real low on downs yesterday. That shit's a
killer, especially when you switch to uppers." Then quickly:
"I'm on a roll," he said, combing his slick hair, "gotta keep it
going when it's hot." He groped his groin.

Gary had lowered his head when Ernie mentioned the pills.
Now he reached up playfully and grabbed Ernie's ass. "That,
too?"

"Whatever's hot," Ernie said.

Dianne mimed the word: Shee-it.

That night Stud went out with Billy into the world they called "the street."

It was another world, ugly and beautiful. Like no other. When things went right for Billy, he would not trade it for any other. When no one but the cops and "queerbashers" stopped, he *did* wish there were something else. There wasn't.

Most of the hustlers on the street could do nothing else, with hardly any education or skill, families relieved by their disappearance, some with records of petty truancy, options all but shut at a time when they were just opening for others their age. Most abandoned their brief turbulent pasts when they came to Los Angeles. Some on the street were there because they had to be, and resented it—those were mainly the ones who robbed, beat up clients; others came to love that world—at times—because it contained a tacky glamor available to them in no other way.

Otherwise thrown away, discarded, they had only their youth and beauty—sometimes only their youth—to unlock doors to worlds they would never peek into otherwise except for those moments of sexual importance when they shone like stars.

They did not know it, of course, except as a shapeless anger mixed with fear, which recurred without pattern, that they were doomed; youngmen who would live out most of their lives as ghosts of what they had been, briefly, one summer, one season.

With variations in between, there are two main types of malehustlers: the overtly masculine and the pretty-boyish. Like Stud, there were those who claimed to be "straight" and "did nothing"—just got blown, masturbated for or were masturbated by someone; posed, flexed. Just as masculine, the self-proclaimed "bi's" might allow themselves to be fucked but would not go down or would go down but not get fucked—or do any or all of the variations, depending on price and the client. Most of the customers of these youngmen were middle-aged homosexuals (although there do exist the young exceptions); men, often married, discovering their homosexuality probably latently.

The pretty-boyish hustlers were not necessarily effeminate; like Billy, very often not at all. In others, the boyishness might veer toward girlishness, finally painted effeminacy—or they might turn toughly masculine. Usually they got fucked or they sucked the client. Like Ed, most of their clients were married and, quite probably, heterosexuals who had problems with the women they would have preferred and so turned to unthreatening youngmen.

The hustling strip along Santa Monica Boulevard was created a few years ago when developers decided that the then-hustling area on Hollywood Boulevard and the side streets off it was ripe for profitable "renovation." And so began the vast raids against "undesirables." The lucrative real estate campaign was pushed as a campaign for morality. Daily, the police rounded up the loitering young people—cruising or hustling homosexuals, Negroes, Mexicans, and others who came to the crushed boulevard because there was nowhere else to go. As repeated arrests bludgeoned the area, the survivors of that powerless army scattered to Santa Monica Boulevard, the blocks at the end of Hollywood, the beginning of West Hollywood. This new strip had one clear advantage—on this street hustlers could linger, pretending to hitchhike, while the clutter of Hollywood Boulevard had not allowed that pose. The bruising "clean-up" accomplished, the renovation of Hollywood Boulevard proved more costly than profitable to the politicians and building interests, and so it was abandoned. Especially on warm afternoons, some of its earlier inhabitants still return in desultory bands; but late at night, the long famous street dies, a few feeble arcades remaining doggedly open, in mourning.

The hustling area on Santa Monica Boulevard is one of the ugliest stretches in the city—one of the few where, for blocks, there are no vines or flowers, just weeds; row after row of mostly one-storey moribund buildings; warehouses, garages, spotty bars, auto-body shops, second-hand furniture stores, a mortuary, abandoned stores with no vestiges of identity, a sloppy food stand—and one small park commemorating a historical incident long forgotten. The street is flanked by dark electrical posts, the remains of a streetcar system. Thick black wires linking one post to the next enclose the shabby street.

That was the world Billy and Stud inhabited.

"He wants you," Billy said quickly when a man stopped around the corner after having eyed them where they stood on the street. Cockily, Stud began walking toward the man. The man shook his head. Stud felt awful. Billy knew it. "I don't think I wanna go with him. Probably just stopped 'cause he recognized me from TV," Billy said. "Go on," Stud understood, "I'll make out."

Billy did not hop into the car, just chatted through the window while casting a spell over the man and sounding him out. If anyone was too immediate about stating a price and a sexual act—the two requirements for a prostitution bust—stay away. Reasonably assured otherwise, Billy would get in, wishing aloud that "there was some way you wouldn't have to be nervous about who's who on the streets these days," inviting a signal—like having the man reach over and touch him intimately. Cops are forbidden to do that, although there are many stories otherwise.

Looking back now, Billy thanked God when he saw a man stop for Stud.

"You got a beautiful body," the man said to Stud. The guy was okay, Stud determined. He laid it on the line: "Thirty-five dollars—and I don't do anything." "Fine by me," the man said, "but all I got is twenty dollars; maybe we can do something in the car and you'll be back soon enough for someone with thirty-five dollars," he coaxed. Stud didn't want Billy to see him get out of the car. He figured he'd be ahead anyhow. In a parking lot surrounded by vacant cars, darkness, swirling wind, Stud lowered his pants to his knees and the man blew him and jerked himself off.

"First *really* slow night I've had," Gary complained when Stud was back on what he was already thinking of as "his"— and sometimes Billy's—corner. "Had five rides up and down the street; everyone just wants to talk tonight."

Nearby, that swarthy Ernie leaned so tough against a wall that Stud took off his shirt.

Stud was new, good-looking, muscular, and so he stood out; he made it again that night, for $30 this time. The man who picked him up took him home, dressed him in cowboy clothes and jockstrap.

When Stud returned to the apartment, Billy was back, too; he was wearing only his cutoffs and getting ready for bed. On the mattress next to him, a barely covered velvety brown back and a heavy-haired, curved leg sprawled. Ernie! Billy reached over and pulled a small mattress, locating it closer to his than Ernie's was. Pretending to be choosing where to sleep, Stud chose that one.

On the street the next night, Tim, with bolder makeup, gasped at Stud, "Billy's talking to a pig around the corner. I saw him bust someone earlier."

When Stud got there, Billy was leaning into the car window. The driver bent over and opened the door. Just as Billy would have got in, Stud yelled at the driver, "You trying to pick up my kid brother, huh? I'll punch you out for that, I oughtta call the cops!" He looked over at Billy and barked, "Get away!"

Understanding, Billy ran.

Stud looked at the man behind the wheel—a cop, for sure—and with deep anger Stud said, "Fucker, you goddamn fucker." The frozen face stared at him.

Billy was ecstatic that Stud had saved him. He treated Stud to a steak at Coffee Andy's—and they started with a fresh, water-sequined salad. Stud treated Billy to a first-run movie.

Back at the apartment, Stud realized he hadn't gone hustling that night. Billy laughed—but it was suddenly very important to Stud that he go out.

Largely because of mutual—and rampant—threats and dangers on the streets, a close warmth may develop among hustlers. That is compounded by their being exiled exiles—shunned by "straight" homosexuals—the vast majority, pursuing careers and unpaid sex encounters and affairs, looking on hustlers as a puzzling blight on their horizon.

At night, hustlers band together, warn of that night's new danger—and always, always exaggerate their earnings even while cadging a cigarette. No one will ever admit to going for less than $35—but all will, and for much less in the deep, desperate hours of crawling nights.

Often, in the afternoons, especially in the lot next to the closed Bank of America building or near Big Boy's Hamburgers across the street—and when the cops don't run them out—the camaraderie overflows among the masculine youngmen and the pretty boys, all gathered, jostling each other, clowning, playing, wrestling showily.

Today, several of the youngest were skate-boarding. Others rooted or jeered. A blond boy carved out a dazzling series of *8*'s on his board. Another wove perfect *S*'s about him. Challenged, the first one somersaulted onto his board, knobby knees held rigidly, bare feet poised. The other tried to best him—balancing himself on one hand. He fell. Glee broke out as the two began wrestling. Others joined the pileup of flailing, laughing bodies.

Ernie saw Stud standing with Billy. The Mexican youngman showily tied his shirt about his waist. He jumped, grasping the protruding part of a billboard announcing a movie about the end of the world. He began chinning himself, counting aloud until he had drawn a growing crowd, who took up the count. Numbers rose. Ernie's straining back was a smear of brown sweat. He forced one more chin, another—101!—dropped himself easily, and accepted cheers.

Stud grasped the same board. They all counted aloud. Billy looked on, both proud and apprehensive as Stud, dripping sweat, approached Ernie's record—but everyone could see his lats beginning to quiver, resist: 97! 98! 99! 100! 1-01! 1 . . . 0 . . . 2! The record toppled. One more chin and Stud let go. Ernie came over bigly and congratulated him. The clasped congratulations turned into a hand-wrestling contest—which Ernie won. Now others swung from the billboard—12 hard chins, 5, 3! Heckling, laughter. The skate-boarders tried new tricks, falling deliberately, all laughing, romping—and then two squad cars came, scattering these male prostitutes.

Ernie and Stud walked away with Billy. "You both won," Billy congratulated the two. That didn't please Stud. He suspected there had been something between Ernie and Billy. Among hustlers sex may occur—unpaid, of course—affairs unaffected by each other's hustling. That morning when Billy was in the bathroom, Stud had pushed Ernie's mattress a few inches away from Billy's. Billy saw him. "Cleaning up," Stud said.

Dianne came over one afternoon when Billy and Stud were watching the chained television. She laid down a sack of groceries. She sat in her familiar way, arms crossed about the back of a chair, legs straddling it. It was the afternoon movie, about a soggy creature who appears out of a murky pool.

"Who'd be afraid of *that* seaweed?" Dianne said. "I can show you a thousand scarier things just outside the door."

Stud watched rapt. Billy leaned over on his bare shoulder and rested his head there at the same time that he reached for Stud's hand. Stud pulled away as if he had been scorched by fire. Billy's head jerked from the sudden movement. Dianne shoved the chair away and stood up, glowering down at Stud.

"What the fuck's the matter with you?" she demanded.

Stud said, "I'm not doing nothing to you."

"Not to me—to Billy."

"Not doing nothing to Billy, either," Stud said firmly.

"You're encouraging him—and you keep insisting you're fuckin' straight."

"I *am* straight," Stud said. He faced Billy, knowing Billy would tell Dianne to mind her own— . . .

"Let's go for a drive, Dianne," Billy said.

"Asshole!" Dianne thrust back at Stud.

Stud was still staring incredulously at the shut door when it opened and Gary staggered in. He acted jittery, glanced at the food Dianne left but didn't touch it. He nodded at Stud and lay on a mattress and fell asleep. Stud noticed he was wearing a flashy new watch.

Angered that Billy had gone out just like that, Stud went to Coffee Andy's. Ernie was there. Now that they had both won a physical contest—a "shoot-out," Ernie called it—they were friends.

"Everyone's on a downer, man," Ernie said. "Big raid coming down. That TV program really got people all fucked up about perverts and shit, and the vice is moving in. . . . Hear all about those hustlers robbing johns?—that ain't gonna help either, man. This rich guy got beat up in a motel the other night, robbed, maybe got killed—heard it both ways. You never know."

The street was a cauldron of rumors, often exaggerated, embellished. A robbery became a wave. A rape became an epidemic. There were the recurrent rumors—a heterosexual who hated hustlers was going around beating them up, then it was a closet homosexual, then a cop on the force, on-duty, then an off-duty cop, a retired cop. Most rumors signaled a dangerous new truth in that forbidden world where anonymity invites violence. Youngmen with little identity beyond the outlines of their bodies were rendered vulnerable to others, just as others were vulnerable to them.

". . . —heard two, but Tim said three or four and only to
femme guys, or the pretty ones, but I heard they picked up only
masculine dudes, so watch out, man," Ernie was going on.

"What?" Ernie's words pulled Stud away from his thoughts
about Billy walking away like that.

"These guys, man," Ernie repeated. "They drive a van or a
pickup; Gary said he saw them in a long limousine—same guys,
though. Maybe they shift around, you know? They pick up
hustlers, man, rape them real ugly, like with their fists and
weird dildos. They're supposed to be straight, hate gays, especially hustlers. Cops ain't doing shit about it. . . . Hey, look at
that Gary!—he's shooting up hard now— . . ." Gary didn't
even nod back when they left.

Outside, a smoky dusk pulled at colors. Smog was making an
urgent incursion before the wind pushed it away. Around the
city, the foggy smoke gathered like enclosing barbed wire.
Scenery seemed sketched on a gray screen. Gray, starless night
descended. Hustlers lined the streets at their posts.

Suddenly an army of squad cars invaded the boulevard. Up
and down the street, the hated angered glow of cop-lights
filtered into the night. Cops rushed at every hustler in the area,
shoving them against the nearest wall.

Billy! Stud thought. A brutal white light flashed in his face.
"Put your fuckin' hands up and move to the corner," the
amplified voice ordered Stud and Ernie. Two cops jumped out
of the quivering car and corralled other youngmen. One of the
cops was a redneck with the beginning of a beer belly and
broken veins on his nose, although he was hardly thirty. The
other cop was an oval-shaped blond woman with a mean face.

Ernie winked reassurance at Stud. Stud winked back. The
thought of Billy persisted. Billy, shoved against the wall! Billy,
mauled! . . . The cops made them face an abandoned hot dog
stand—palms against it. "Feet out farther," the woman cop
ordered. Ernie's arm slipped.

Both cops drew their guns.

"Smartass!" the male cop wrenched one of Ernie's arms
behind him.

Rage gripped Stud. But he had to stay like that, powerless.
One word, and they both would be handcuffed. Another squad

car drove up; two more cops jumped out. Stud felt hands
exploring his lower body, for "hidden weapons." He kept
thinking of this happening to Billy. No!

The woman told them to turn around. Stud blinked in disbelief.
All the cops had their guns out. The redneck said, "Whattayasay
we book 'em all?"

"Sure," the woman tried to match his tone.

The two other cops drove away, to other rousted groups on
the street.

The redneck went back and radioed in the squawking car.
The woman moved her gun in an arc covering them all.

The jumbled cop-jargon came back in broken snatches on the
radio. "Compound's booked solid; no more buses," the cop
said.

"We see you again, you go to jail," the woman said.

They got in the car and screeched away.

"Pigs!" Ernie spat.

"What did they mean about a compound?" Stud asked.

"They set one up in an alley nearby, take everyone there,
then to jail in buses," Ernie said. "They just ran out of buses,
that's all. Hey, where you going?"

Stud was walking into the red-glowing battlefield ahead.

"Gotta look for Billy," he said.

"You walk over there and they'll stop you again and this
time they'll have a bus," Ernie said.

"Fuck it." Stud continued on his way.

"Hey, I saw that old guy Billy sees—waiting for him when
we left Coffee Andy's; I bet Billy's there—I'm sure."

Billy was there, with Ed. Billy rushed up to Stud. "Ed drove
me up and down the boulevard to see if they'd stopped you."

"I worried about *you*," Stud sulked.

"Join us," Ed called.

"Thanks. I'm going home." Stud looked at Billy in signal.

Billy walked in just minutes after Stud entered the apartment.
"You really went looking for me?" Billy asked him.

"Yeah." He tried to sound indifferent now. He felt Billy's
hand like burning iron on his shoulder. This time he didn't push
it away.

Gary walked in. Stud pulled back. "Feel like I'm thirty years old and just turned eighteen,'' Gary said. The garish watch was gone. There was another one on his wrist. His face was white beneath a layer of tanned skin. He sat on the mattress, counting out some money from a wallet, discarding cards and papers, keeping others. "I'm not asking for money anymore,'' he said to no one, "I'm *taking* it!'' He started to light a cigarette, but his fingers were trembling so erratically that the match kept blowing out. Billy lighted the cigarette for him. "Shit!'' Gary threw the cigarette on the floor and walked out.

Billy gathered the discarded cards carefully. There was a driver's license with the photograph of an older man. He didn't look like Ed, not at all—but Billy thought of him. He decided to put the cards in an envelope and mail them to the address on the license.

That night, Billy woke up startled. Stud was asleep beside him. Billy leaned over and outlined his shoulder, his arm, his hip. "I love you, Stud,'' he whispered to the still form.

Stud heard, but he didn't move.

The next night heat gathered. More young bodies were bared on the street. The streets were inhaling the heat in the day and exhaling it at night.

Two happy middle-aged men in an expensive Mercedes stopped to talk to Billy and Stud. "We want both of you. We're having a grand party, and we want to liven things up with pretty, fresh faces. We'll pay you for the night, and then you can just have a good time.''

They got in. The two older men, still attractive, were lovers. "Together twenty-five years—so, you see, it can work.'' "With a little bit on the side,'' the other said naughtily. "And we're celebrating the anniversary of *another* couple—*thirty* years together!''

There were about twenty men in the beautiful old home. Most of them were of the same age as the two, also well-dressed, attractive. On a long table, food was spread like a chopped rainbow.

Sounds of approval and applause greeted the entrance of Billy and Stud when they walked into the dining-room. "Have you ever seen two more beautiful boys?'' one of the men whose anniversary this was asked his companion of thirty years. "Well, *we* were rather pretty in our time," the companion remembered, to happy applause from the other men. "They *are* adorable," the first man said. "And so obviously in *love*," the other added. "They'll last thirty years, too!" one of the men who had invited them said, to more responsive applause.

Billy looked apprehensively at Stud. His shoulders squared wider.

But everyone had a great time. No sex. Billy and Stud were star presences. At midnight they all toasted champagne to the couple's thirtieth anniversary.

That night in the apartment it was Stud's turn to look at Billy asleep. The moon did not enter this side of the building, blocked always, but on bright nights its light filtered in—so did the gray morning. Stud watched Billy intently. Billy's body was not softly formed; where had he got that idea? It was slim, yes—but very solid-looking. Stud leaned back and had trouble falling asleep.

The next day when he returned to the apartment in the afternoon, Billy was sitting on a mattress sewing a shirt.

"Whatya doin'?" Stud wanted to emphasize the obvious.

"Sewing my shirt," said Billy.

"Sewing!" Stud laughed, felt pleased, and liked Billy a lot.

"Got a mighty fine body there," a man called out of a car window to Stud that night. Stud flexed, as he did always to that remark. There were hustlers on every corner. So Stud got in. "How much you go for?" the man asked, "and what can I expect for it?" Stud knew instantly the man was a cop.

"Not hustling," Stud said firmly. "Let me off at the corner." At the corner, two arms reached in through the open window on Stud's side and pulled him out. The driver of the car handcuffed him. He and the man waiting at the corner said, "Los Angeles vice officers." "You're under arrest," the man who had propositioned him said easily.

"For *what*?" Stud said incredulously.

"Prostitution," the cop said.

Stud protested. "I told you I wasn't hustling." He couldn't believe he was actually chained.

"Guess I didn't hear that part," the cop said. "All I heard was when you told me you'd blow me if I paid you twenty bucks."

The enraged heat rushing out of Stud's body made the night's warmth chill his flesh.

"Fuckin' liar!" Stud yelled.

They pushed him roughly into the back of a waiting squad car.

In the cop station flooded with hideous white light like in hospitals—but colder, uglier than that—Stud was booked for prostitution. All about were other chained, crushed presences, mostly Mexicans and Negroes, and youngmen like himself— and women, most in short skirts.

Stud felt himself drowning in a stagnant ocean of indifference. He could disappear, just disappear—because a cop had lied— and no one would know where he was.

"You can make a phone call."

Call whom? He shook his head. An iron door opened with a grating electric buzzing. Beyond it were rows of iron-barred cells. Years ago, Stud had gone to a zoo. He left, crying, so sorry for the pacing animals locked up like that, like him now in this nightmare that was proceeding. He was put in a cell with four bunks suspended by angled chains. An uncovered toilet. There was a youngman sitting on a bed.

"Hustling?" he asked Stud.

"No—the pig just said so."

"Happens," the youngman said. He looked haunted. "I called my father; the bitch said he's not coming for me."

"What . . . happens now?" Stud asked, his heart a frozen fist of anger and fear.

"Wait. Eventually they'll take you to a judge; you can't pay the fine so you'll go to jail."

"But I didn't do anything, I can prove— . . ."

"Can't prove anything," the kid said knowledgably.

The nightmare pushed deeper. Stud felt his body trembling inside, but the outside was rigid. The world was outside and he was in a cage. Would Billy think he'd just gone away, just like that?

Billy heard about the busts. A real raid was going on, not like the routine harrassment every night, the news was flashed to Coffee Andy's. Stud! "Yeah—I saw him, they busted him," one of the skinny skate-boarders said.

Billy dialed the "emergency number" Ed had given him.

"Hello?" a woman answered.

An answering service. "I want to leave a very, very urgent message for Mr. Edward— . . ."

"You don't have to leave a message," the woman said. "He's here. Is this Billy?"

Billy couldn't believe it. "Yes!"

"I hope you're not in trouble, Billy," the woman said.

"I am! No, my friend! I— . . ."

"I'll call Ed." Billy heard the woman's voice: "Ed, it's Billy, I think he's in trouble."

Before Ed came to the telephone, Billy's anxiety burst, and he was crying.

It had been so long since he'd heard his real name that Stud didn't respond at first when a cop yelled it out. "Bailed out," the kid in the cell with him said. Stud merely accepted it. "Can I call someone for you?" "That bitch? Fuck him," the kid said.

The buzzer hissed. The iron door parted. There stood Billy, in his cutoffs and blue shirt chopped at the middle. For all the cops to see, Billy hugged Stud. Ed was talking to the bondsman. Billy's description of Stud, the location of the arrest, and "Bozeman, Montana" had identified him.

As they were walking out of the cop station—and making sure the cops' attention was on them—Billy stopped, looked around. "You ever noticed?" he asked. "You ever noticed that cop stations are lighted the color of weak piss?"

Even in the deep depression he was in, Stud was able to look at Billy with a lot of admiration.

As Ed drove them to the apartment, Stud felt more fear than when, at ten, he had run away the first time—a distance of ten miles.

At the loose iron gate to the building, Billy told Stud to go ahead, he'd be right up. Stud thanked Ed, promised to pay him back, really, really. Billy got back in the car with Ed.

"He'll have to go to court; they'll reduce the prostitution charge to disorderly conduct. A fine. I'll take care of it." He gave Billy money.

Billy remembered his own arrests: the miserable days in jail, the ugly man who called him a queer and tried to fuck him—but

Billy fought and fought—the odor of urine, the spotted food.
"What did the cop report say?"

"That Stud offered to go down on the arresting officer for
twenty dollars," Ed said softly.

Billy winced in anger and pain for Stud. "You know it's a
lie," he said to Ed.

"Of course," Ed said.

Billy kissed him. "Thank you, really. I love you, too. Really."

"In a different way," Ed said, "yes."

"Your wife— . . ."

"She knew before I did. We love each other, too—in a
different way."

In court Stud was fined on a reduced first offense of disorderly conduct. "The cop lied," Stud said to the judge, perched
over everyone like a humped hawk. That was the only moment
the judge looked—glanced—at him.

Not even the steak that Billy treated him to could bring Stud
out of his dark, dark mood. "Fuckin' liar cop!" he kept saying;
he seemed more depressed by the cop's report than the fine or
the arrest; the cop had deliberately humiliated him further, that
was clear—had known how to do it.

As they walked on Santa Monica Boulevard—all gray, closed
buildings—a car came to a sudden stop ahead. Two youngish
men yelling, "Fags!" "Queers!" started shoving Tim and another equally effeminate boy around near the pizza parlor.

All the accumulated rage erupted in Stud. He ran across the
street, Billy followed. Stud's knee connected with a groin. He
felt a fist on his cheek, and punched back. Tim and the other
effeminate youngmen were flailing with small hands. Billy
rammed his fist into the face of the other attacker. Stud looked
at Billy in surprise when he heard the crunch of teeth.

They all scattered.

Stud felt good, the anger shoved out. *"Now* I'm hungry," he
said.

"I love you so much, Stud," Billy said.

Stud held his breath and pretended not to hear.

He had been in Los Angeles a week, less.

Then another of the nightmares of the street happened. He
was walking along the boulevard. A car slowed, and then it

moved on. "You're not worth thirty-five dollars," a man said to him. "I'll pay you five bucks." "Fuck you!" Stud slammed the car door. "You want me to pay you and you do nothing?" another man was indignant. Stud said Fuck you, again, got out. Another man agreed, and then he noticed another youngman, new on the streets. "I think I'm looking for something else tonight," the man said. Stud saw him pick up the kid who had just walked by. A nervous middle-aged man said yes to everything and couldn't keep his hands off him as they drove into a dark residential area. Before a small house, the man stopped, opened the car door for Stud to get out—and drove off leaving him stranded. Humilated, Stud walked back to Santa Monica Boulevard. He didn't want to know what time it was—but he knew it was at least midnight. A squad car flashed a light in his face. He walked on. A car stopped. As Stud approached, the man appraised him and drove off. Stud knew he must look very tired. He began counting the numbers of hustlers still out. Dozens. He saw older ones, in their twenties—the old-young who haunt the streets, knowing death can occur at twenty; the ones he didn't hang around with. What would happen to Billy when he was twenty, twenty-one? Stud stopped himself when he realized he was doing what he'd never done before; what others did—peer anxiously into slowly moving cars and grope himself. It had to be three o'clock. Shadowy bodies soon to be trapped by the threatening, accusing dawn. Finally Stud surrendered, started waking back to the apartment. Then a car slowed as it turned the corner. Stud heard it stop, and his heart raced in gratitude as he walked quickly around the corner, only to realize that the driver of the car had stopped for another youngman, slouched against the lightening shadows. Feeling very, very, very tired, Stud walked back in gloom to the apartment, with the dark knowledge that for the first time he had not been able to make it on the street.

The next day, to assert his identity, he had STUD tattooed on his arm. And that evening everything was different! Everything changed, as it has a way of doing, and he made it several times. The one disappointment of the day: Billy had frowned when he saw the fresh tattoo on Stud's arm; then quickly he told him how wonderful and tough it looked—but Stud remembered the first look. He told himself Billy had reacted only because the tattoo had not fully healed. Yes! That was it.

He and Billy were standing on "their" corner when a round-faced man got out of his car and offered to pay them both a "modeling fee" to let him photograph them nude. Billy said yes, Stud shuffled his feet.

Of course, Stud and Billy had seen each other naked—on their way in or out of the bathroom, or at night, lying without a sheet in the hot beds. Here, in the man's house, they both stripped awkwardly, though. While the man fussed with the camera, they stood on the floor at opposite sides of the room. Then Billy looked at Stud and could not take his eyes off him—he was the most beautiful person he had ever seen. Stud glanced at Billy and noticed he was becoming more masculine all the time, but strangely just as pretty.

The man photographed them separately. Then he offered to double their "fee" if they would pose for "sex pictures." "Nothing kinky," he emphasized. "Just you— . . ." He pointed to Stud. ". . . —going down on him." He pointed to Billy.

"No!" Billy protested for Stud.

"But your cock's bigger than his," the man said.

"It's not!" Billy said, putting on his pants.

The man drove them back in silence.

Near the chained motorcycle, Stud said to Billy, "It is true, Billy, you're bigger hung than me."

"No," Billy soothed. "It's just that I was more excited than you, so I looked bigger."

"No," Stud said, "you are bigger hung. But I'm not small, either!" he emphasized.

Tim was walking out of the bathroom. He was in full drag. "I am now Tina Louise," he said. "And I am hustling Western Boulevard with all the other ladies—you boys can have Santa Monica Boulevard."

The next day at Coffee Andy's there were no new rumors; just the news that Gary was dead, found in a park overdosed on uppers and downers. The death weighed over them all. Another intimate unknown presence had disappeared. They did not even know where the body would be, where they might go and at least say good-bye. Only the hated cops would know, and not care.

In the apartment, Stud folded Gary's mattress until a new tenant would claim it. "Shit," Dianne kept saying, "shit, shit, shit, shit—it's *all* fuckin' shit!"

The next night there was a bright moon. Billy and Stud could tell from the silvery shadows in the apartment. Billy in his cutoffs and Stud wearing only his jeans, they sat watching television. The air was breathless. Billy lay back. In the spill of glowing colors from the television screen, his face looked like that in a painting. Stud turned off the sound, not wanting to change the glow on Billy, and leaned back on the same mattress.

Billy bent over him and kissed him on the lips. Stud felt his cock harden more quickly than it ever had before; he felt Billy's pressed against his and just as hard. Stud's legs curled about Billy's hips. Billy reached for the buttons on Stud's pants, opening them, pulling out the eager cock. He felt Stud's fingers pulling down the cutoffs. Both of them lay naked on the narrow mattress, the electric colored glow brushing their limbs in changing hues. Their erect cocks kissed. Billy slipped down, licking Stud from his lips to his chest, to his waist, down. His lips swirled about his balls and then enclosed his cock, licked his balls again, enclosed his cock, and sucked. Stud sighed and leaned slightly to one side, to see Billy's body, study it openly for the first time—the sculpted buttocks, the golden down. His own limbs were brushed over with darker hair. The meshing of their bodies looked beautiful and right. He shifted farther and took Billy's cock in his mouth, sucking him in the exact rhythm with which he was being sucked. Stud felt the strange, full organ in his mouth. He didn't know whether he was about to come in Billy's mouth or Billy was about to come in his, the excitement was so totally fused. He pulled his head away slightly and studied Billy's cock and balls cupped in his hand, the knot of the heavy balls, the round firmness of the cock; he licked it, and the balls, and felt Billy's tongue slide along his. Stud swallowed Billy's cock, deep, deeper, astonished that it slid into his throat, as deeply as his slid into Billy's! Their buttocks thrust. Then they shifted their bodies and kissed and kissed, their mouths parting only for seconds in order to connect again.

Billy lay back, opening his legs. The light from the television brushed him in gold, the hairs on his legs gleaming. Stud spat on his hand and touched the knot at the parting of Billy's buttocks. Billy widened his legs, his ankles on Stud's broad shoulders. Stud rubbed the spittle on his own cock and into Billy's ass, entering it slowly. He held Billy's legs. Then he arched his body and pushed in as he lowered his torso so they could kiss to the rhythm of his pumping strokes. Billy came against Stud's rubbing stomach. Feeling the moisture, Stud pushed his full length into Billy's ass. His lips and tongue roamed eagerly over Billy's mouth and face. Stud came—came, came, came.

Then he rolled over, onto his own mattress, out of the spill of the television's soundless colors. In the grudging moonlight, Billy noticed, Stud's look had changed.

In the morning the mattress beside Billy was vacant. A note was there, in his place:

Deeres Billy;
   Life is strang in't it?!!! You think you no everythin ther is to no an you fine out you dont no anythin atall—life is shor strang!!! I cain love a guy an stil be my self Stud—you heer bout goin away to cleer yor hed—well—thats wat I am doin—to much hapent to soon an Gary dyin like that to— Billy I got-a cleer my hed then maybe life wont be so dam strang—I hop you unerstan???? You ar a boy like me an thats the dam problum!!!! Who nos what tomoro will bring???? Heers wishin you the besta helth—

                                    You truly—
                                         STUD

Billy's face was drenched in tears.
Dianne snatched the note from him, read it, dropped it.
Billy couldn't stop crying—frantic, lost, desolate. Stud's satchel was gone.
Dianne stormed out. In her Toyota, she drove up and down the boulevard, into Hollywood, back to Coffee Andy's asking everyone whether they'd seen Stud. She even went to the Greyhound depot in Hollywood and circled the Y. She saw his

satchel before she saw him in a small park where hustlers slept when they didn't have a place; it was only five blocks from the building where he'd lived with Billy. Dianne parked in a no-parking zone and went to where he was lying looking up at the smoky sky.

"Asshole!" Dianne shouted at him.

He sat up in the ashy wind.

"You fuckin' asshole," Dianne said.

"Leave me alone, Dianne."

"Life is strange, and you're trying to figure it out while it just stares you in the fuckin' face! You don't wanna be gay, huh?"

"Nothing wrong with it," Stud said.

"Then what's the fuckin' problem?"

"I don't know," Stud said truthfully.

"Asshole," Dianne said. "Look, there's nothing wrong with liking certain sex things and not others—that's where everyone's goofy saying *everybody's* gotta like *everything*! Some of us don't like *anything*!" Dianne sat wearily next to Stud on the grass.

"But I *did* do certain things," Stud said, "last night, with Billy. *Everything!*"

Dianne looked at him in surprise, and then she sighed, relieved. "Well, it's better than I thought. Did you like it?"

"Then, yeah. Later, no." He shook his head. "I'm not sure; I mean, Gary dying, just never coming back."

"So each moment matters—that's all you got!" Dianne was very serious. She pulled back quickly. "You wanna know something, asshole? You just about killed Billy. I've never seen him crying like that—like he could just fall over and die."

"No!" Stud stood up. Sticky fingers of wind clutched him. "Don't say that. I'd die if he died! . . . I intended to go back. I just wanted to clear my head, I *was* coming back, I guess I just figured if I told him I was, then it wouldn't seem like I meant it."

Dianne was leading him to her car. "You're so blind, Stud; you never see that Billy's got problems, too—not like yours, other ones. He might've just rushed out and gone hustling cause that's all he's got. . . . Well, you wanna go back or not?"

"Yes!" Stud said.

Dianne relented. "Look—can you drive?"

"Sure!" Stud was indignant at the implied blemish on his masculinity.

"When you and Billy make up, I'll lend you my wheels, okay?—and you two can go to the beach, get some sun, get away from these fuckin' ugly streets."

"Yeah!" Stud longed for that.

"You *can* drive?" Dianne insisted.

"Better than *you*!" Stud tossed. Then: "And, Dianne— thanks."

They were driving along Santa Monica Boulevard. As if she couldn't cope with the emotional gratitude, Dianne merely said, "Fuck it, it's just— . . ."

"*Billy!*" Stud yelled out the window. He had seen the unmistakable lithe figure of Billy, in his cutoffs and short shirt, getting into a van with painted swirly fingers lapping like flames. Stud felt his heart sink.

"Don't worry, he'll be checking for you back at the apartment." Dianne left Stud at Coffee Andy's. "Asshole," she called back at him.

Stud hung around about half an hour. His emotions bunched tightly. He went back to the apartment. It was emptier than he had ever seen it. Ernie came in. No, he hadn't seen Billy since he ran out in a hurry this afternoon early. "Strange about Gary, huh?" Ernie said. Yes, it was strange, very strange, and it compounded the feeling of physical absence Stud felt about Billy. He went back to Coffee Andy's. Back to the apartment. Each time, the apartment seemed emptier. He noticed how really ugly the building was, really ugly, waiting to die, resigned, everything dry and dead, like his bike—which no one had even bothered to steal.

He walked the length of Santa Monica Boulevard, the hustling stretch. In the lots, nobody was clowning or jostling or chinning. It was so hot everyone lay on patches of grass, like a recuperating army. He waited around, talking to some of his friends and trying to stay away from the apartment, sure that if he did, when he went back, Billy would be there.

He wasn't.

Stud went out again, feeling cold in the heat. It would be one of those nights so hot that the heat seems to color the sky a blackish orange. Maybe a distant fire was raging. This was the season of canyon fires.

. He milled around Coffee Andy's. Back to the apartment. It was night. Stud had walked miles. Ed! He looked throughout the room, found nothing, nothing but the traces of Billy's existence—several cutoffs, several shortened shirts. No telephone number.

He lay on his mattress, then slipped over onto Billy's. He was so exhausted he fell asleep. When he woke, there was either a very bright moon or it was the beginning to dawn. Had the wind blown all night or had he dreamed it? The heat was like a scalding rock radiating waves in the room. Ernie was asleep. So was Tim. Gary's mattress remained rolled up in a corner. And Billy was not there.

Stud went out. The dawning sun was already burning through the morning smog kept distant by the wind. Coffee Andy's was open. Only when a waitress told him he couldn't come in without a shirt did he realize he had left without one. He walked in anyway, looking for Billy. He lingered outside. He felt a coldness in the heat, as if it had chosen only him. He returned to the apartment, went back to Santa Monica Boulevard through sickening heat.

He saw the slender form coming toward him against the sky, which glowered an angered orange. But it wasn't Billy.

Heat saturated the air and his body. Panting, he sat down on a patch of grass by a closed playground. He let all the apprehension, shackled fear, isolation, loneliness crash on him. He faced that something terrible had happened to Billy. He remembered the flashy van— . . . Maybe he'd been busted!

He took a deep breath and walked into the Hollywood police station where he had been booked. "I want to know if someone by the name of Billy— . . ." He didn't know Billy's last name! ". . . —is here," he said to the fat cop behind a desk. The balding cop looked up at Stud. "You what?" "Billy—that's his name," Stud said. "I don't know his last name—we just call him Billy, but you couldn't mistake him for anybody else because he's— . . . very beautiful." He felt sweat gathering under his arms, streaking into his pants, down his legs. "He's very handsome," he corrected.

The cop looked at him as if he wanted to bust this shirtless sweaty boy. "Beautiful!" he seized, alerting other, milling cops to listen to *this*. "Is he a girl?"

Stud saw the smirking faces. "Billy's a guy, like me," he said firmly. When he had been arrested, he had thought he would never again feel that helpless, that little, that insignificant, that lost. He knew that was not so. That was nothing compared to now. Seeing the contemptuous faces of the cops, he knew how thoroughly unimportant he and Billy were to everyone else except in those moments when someone desired them. *And except to each other*. He wanted to shout and be heard, because he knew that none of them, not him, not Billy, not Tim, not Gary, not Ernie, not one of them mattered—not to the cops nor to those TV people nor the ones who had looked at Billy like a freak on that program—not one of them mattered one fucking goddamn bit. He walked out into the melting Hollywood sun.

He went back to the apartment. Billy was not there. Was it possible that somebody could just disappear, just like that? What if he never saw Billy again? What if he'd never know what happened to him. He couldn't stand that. He'd— . . . He heard the door open, and he closed his eyes. If it wasn't Billy, he didn't want to know right away, he'd keep hope locked in blackness behind his eyes. He heard slow footsteps, forced breathing.

"Billy!"

Billy's body sagged into Stud's. Stud would remember that always—and how Billy was covering his face with both bloodied hands. He wasn't wearing a shirt. His cutoffs were brutally ripped. There was blood on his stomach, on his legs— . . .

Stud held Billy and saw his bared face, black with bruises, one eye closed shut and puffy, the upper part of his lip bloated purple from bleeding. Stud thought, If he dies, I'll kill myself, I'll die with Billy. He felt Billy's tears squeezing only out of one eye. Or was it sweat? Or was it blood!

Stud laid Billy on the mattress. Trembling, he brought towels, as clean as he could find them—towels, water, ice. As the caked blood cleared, Stud knew the bruises had been made by pounding fists. Gently he tested for broken bones. None. He was aware of Ernie but only vaguely—aware that Dianne was here, too. He heard himself asking Billy, "Are you all right, are you all right?" He kept checking his breathing.

"We gotta call the cops, they'll take him to the hospital."

Stud didn't know who said that. He only knew the words untapped his rage. "They'll just smirk at *us* and shove *him* around." If Billy got sicker, they would *have* to call the cops; but he didn't want that, didn't want the cruelty, the cold indifference. And they wouldn't allow him to stay with him. He didn't want to let Billy out of his sight.

Dianne leaned over to Billy and whispered, "Billy, we might have to take you to the hospital."

Billy uttered one word through his bloated lips: "No."

Hope shot through Stud. He can talk—he'll be all right, he'll be fine— . . .

Dianne left and came back, with bandages and everything she had ever heard was used on someone hurt. She and Stud patched Billy, dressed the wounds. Stud cooled him with a towel. He wished there were clean sheets, but there weren't. Gently, he tore the ripped cutoffs entirely. The back of them was soaked in blood. He threw them away fiercely with a cry of anger and despair. He watched terrified to see whether more blood would come from Billy's rectum. No. He waited. No. He waited. No more blood! He felt the heat now as if it were something artificial that had attached itself to him forever.

Through the window and over the rooftops, Stud saw the shaggy palm trees of Los Angeles bending in the wind. The glow on the horizon deepened to orange—the glow of sun and wind and fire.

Stud nestled next to Billy, careful not to shake him. "I love you, Billy," he said.

Billy heard. He tried to open his eyes. Only one opened as wide as it could. It was the most beautiful, cruelest green-speckled color Stud had ever seen. Hope embraced him. Stud's hand closed over Billy's. He felt Billy's fingers press back with determined strength, promising to live.

Lost Angels: 11

Marilyn Monroe breathed, "Hi," in that way she had of whispering words that was like blowing pink bubbles which burst softly. "Hi," Lisa whispered back.

Against folds of bleeding red velvet, Marilyn stood dressed in clinging white satin, sequins like bits of ice, white furs like pure snow.

"The figures are *wax!*" Jesse James laughed at Lisa.

"I know they are," Lisa said, "but what if a piece of her soul crept inside it and I didn't say Hi?" She thought she said it under her breath, for only Marilyn to hear—until she saw several tourists studying her closely. She had said, "I could be Marilyn's daughter."

"Well, you know, you *just* could," said a fat jolly woman past middle age, her hair had just been tinted and set—not a wisp moved. "Well, you know," she informed everyone, "they do say she had a secret child."

"I know," Lisa said as more tourists continued to study her.

"Well, *doesn't* she resemble Marilyn?" the happy woman asked her husband, who nodded. "Well, my goodness, you're the same remarkable people we saw outside the Chinese Theater!" she discovered joyfully. "Well, you certainly have become *much* prettier!" she told Lisa. "Well, you know, they *do* say Los Angeles does that!"

This morning, Orin had wakened Lisa by barely touching her shoulder and whispering they were going to the Hollywood Wax Museum. She heard it in a dream. Orin repeated it. Lisa jumped up!

Cagney! Bogart! Robinson! Jesse sprang from the bed.

Last night after Orin had hung up the telephone and Lisa had

331

accused him of pretending, she quickly forced laughter—which Jesse eagerly joined. Then Orin laughed, too, a strange sound they preferred not to notice. "Oh, you!" Lisa had said, *"always* pretending!" She and Jesse were glad to allow today's excitement to bury the matter, for now.

They had taken the Santa Ana Freeway to the Wax Museum, which is near Disneyland, Magic Mountain, and Knott's Berry Farm. In the back of the car alone, Lisa had let the hot air dry her hair, which she had cut shorter, just washed, wanting to look gorgeous. And she did, in a light blue dress that deepened the azure of her eyes and the tan of her glowing skin. She had deliberately "forgotten" Pearl; it was important that Marilyn not feel "betrayed."

When they had reached the museum, there were bunches of tourists. In the crowded lot, each parking space is named for a movie star. "Hedy Lamarr!" Lisa gasped. "Greta Garbo! Merle Oberon! Ugh—Sinatra, too?" She was chagrined because the first parking space they found was one named after La Wanda Page, and she had not heard of her.

At the entrance is another huge naked David. "The other one at that cemetery was sexier," Lisa had said, "and *he* wasn't wearing that silly leaf."

When Orin paid for their tickets, Jesse had lingered close by. The grouping of money in Orin's wallet had slimmed. He was not replenishing it; there had to be more, that was for *sure*.

Inside, the museum is filled with angled mirrors so that at times the figures seem trapped in geometric designs of glass. Some of the wax statues stand alone in the niches, others are grouped into scenes from a particular film. The figures are carefully lighted, so that the wax may look like flesh, the wigs like real hair. At times, though, they look only slightly more real than store manikins, at other times less real for the attempt at deception: petrified figures. But the tourists—many, many, young and old—had come to be thrilled, and so they exclaimed, "They're so real, aren't they real?—you expect them to talk any minute," before the figures propped like painted corpses in an adorned, noisy mortuary. Then Lisa had found Marilyn Monroe in icy satin and sequins, snowy furs.

Now the fat lady was going on happily: "Well, it's a pleasure to see you again, we seem to be visiting the same wonderful places; you're touring the sights, too?''

''I just *had* to see Marilyn,'' Lisa said quietly.

''Well, I think it's important to have a goal; and, well, *you're* certainly remarkable young people. . . . Well, good-bye now, we'll probably see you at Magic Mountain.'' She moved along jovially with her husband and clusters of other tourists.

Lisa squinted her eyes and looked again at Marilyn in her velvet enclosure.

They wandered from figure to figure, scene to scene. Lisa's mood fluctuated. At times she would ''Oh!''; other times she'd be silent. Then she became bewildered, as if unexpected feelings were battling within her; her voice veered toward hysteria—she'd name a star, explain a scene. Orin studied her, and the figures, without a word. Jesse sought out cowboy and gangster figures.

Lisa glided past Mae West and would have lingered longer before Jean Harlow—reclining on a white divan and wearing a white dress like a slip—except that she knew that, somewhere, Marilyn was looking on. ''Hedy Lamarr and Robert Taylor in *Lady of the Tropics*—she was *so* beautiful. You know, she's alive—somewhere; imagine that: Hedy Lamarr is *alive,* this very moment, doing *something*! Oh, Garbo! Look! Joan Crawford was not, not, *not* a mean mother! . . . Gene Tierney!—she *had* to kill her child because *he* made her do it, drove her to it—and *he* left Amber!'' She stopped, aware of her fevered frenzy. Again, it pitched: ''Look, Jesse—Tyrone Power, but *not* as Jesse James; he's the bullfighter who left Linda Darnell *and* Marlene Dietrich in that other movie, when she sacrificed everything for him! They just kept doing it, being so mean to them, over and over!'' Mirrors thrust her into a hideous wreckage of spilling water, steam, tangled pipes—the recorded sounds of fear and panic! Lisa wiped her reflection from the reproduced setting of a disaster movie. She rushed away from the simulated horror.

Orin paused in a spooky cave of ice, studying its crystals; where Superman lived. He paused two more times: before Spartacus—Kirk Douglas, assertive jaw and teeth, wears a loincloth and prepares to fight a muscular gladiator; and before

Ben-Hur—the fallen charioteer lies bloodied on the ground near four white horses and Ben-Hur stares on in— . . .

Pity? Regret? Satisfaction? It could have been any of those, Jesse thought. But not loyalty.

Sissy cowboys! Jesse was angered by that silly Tom Mix— whoever he was—in an ornate costume with *flowers* on his shirt; the gun didn't help one bit. And Alan Ladd—one of his semi-favorites—why did they choose that frilly frontier costume?

"Jesse, stop that! I know what you're doing!" Lisa admonished.

Mounted on a motorcycle, Nancy Sinatra wears a short white skirt and boots. The floor was a mirror. Jesse was angling himself to catch more of Nancy's flirtatious, winking panties.

"Some of them are real sexy," Jesse acknowledged; his cock was responding. And *there* was Brigitte Bardot, the unbelievably curved body stripped to the lower part of a polka-dotted bikini—no bra, her hands covering her bare breasts! Jesse's was a full hard-on now.

Lisa wouldn't glance at Brigitte—Marilyn would "know."

Jesse groaned silently. "Look at that silly fringe and those decorated boots on that awful, awful Roy Rogers." The happy gathering from *Bonanza* didn't help—and neither did *Butch Cassidy and the Sundance Kid*, which he liked a lot, but not *this* smily scene, which never happened.

Lisa froze. In torn—ripped—clothes, Sophia Loren, hair disheveled, face anguished, kneels crying, holding a youngwoman—her daughter—who is bleeding from the mouth, her eyes imploring her mother to— . . . *What!* Orin eased Lisa gently along—to Fred Astaire and Ginger Rogers! Top hat! Sequins! Lisa looked gratefully at Orin for having led her away from that other scene; sometimes he seemed to think *with* her.

Bogart! Jesse was indignant. They had him old, pulling on a sinking boat with that woman. Things got better, though—when he pushed himself away from *that* Bogart. Chuck Connors wasn't bad, his rifle cocked. John Wayne— . . . He'd always looked phony to Jesse, and he strutted like those hard-boiled frontier women in red feathers.

Robert Stack held a machine gun. Jesse studied the man, the weapon, the setting. He didn't like him. Stack would be *against* Cagney and the *real* Bogart—the *tough* Bogart. Stack even looked like the man who shot Cody, that two-timer cop. Even went to prison, to get Cody's confidence. Jesse shot Stack a challenging look. Gary Cooper in *High Noon*. That was good— but in the movie, Cooper didn't know which side he was really on.

"Hey, Lisa—look!" Jesse teased. *"The Wizard of Oz!* There's ole Dorothy and the three— . . ."

Nose in the air, Lisa walked past them, and him. *"You* look like Roy Rogers," she shut him up. She ignored *The Phantom of the Opera*, hurried past Dracula in a coffin, Frankenstein on a stretcher. "Too real, too real, too real," she protested in disgust. "Oooooo! *Gone! With! The! Wind!"* she gasped out each word at the full scene of Tara. Scarlett, Rhett, Melanie, Ashley, *and Mammy*! She loved Mammy, and always wondered why Scarlett didn't free her. Now she said; "Scarlett was so brave! Even when everything was burned around her and she stood among black ruins, blackened stones! Even then she— . . .!" Suddenly Scarlett threw her into a *clear* confusion, because, no, *they* weren't that mean to her; *she* survived, unlike— . . . *"That Hamilton Woman!*—Vivien Leigh played *her,* too!" she said urgently. "And they were so mean to *her,* put her in debtors' jail—*and* in *Waterloo Bridge* she threw herself under a truck! And *then* she was poor Blanche—so very much like my—. . ." *Where were Maria and Pearl Chavez!* Agitated, she looked down at her hands, for a second thinking she had brought her doll with her, wishing so. She hurried along the groupings of frozen movie stars.

James Cagney!

In a tuxedo, Cagney holds a gun to Pat O'Brian, the white-collared priest. Jesse had not seen *Angels with Dirty Faces*. The priest must've been a fake priest, like those FBI guys, treacherous. The cop *locked* himself in prison to get Cody's confidence— Jesse's mind kept pulling to that—pretended to love him and then betrayed him—boy, did he!

James Cagney!

In profound respect, Jesse James tipped an imaginary hat at Cagney. It wasn't *White Heat* there, but it was Cagney and he was Cody, tough, tough! And yet like a little boy, too. Jesse's hand reached out, to touch the figure in tribute. A terrible

electronic hiss spat at him. Dozens of tourists looked reprovingly.
An amplified voice ordered, "Do not touch the figures!" Jesse
James had withdrawn his hand. He smiled crookedly at Cagney;
he'd understand, *yeah!* Jesse felt good, loyal.

Edward G. Robinson!—and the figure moved! He's shot in
the arm, but he still holds a stub-nosed gun. Jesse had seen
Little Caesar. With tan coat, bowler hat, Robinson moves in an
arc. Jesse liked Robinson, sure—but he wished they'd done this
with Cagney as Cody Jerrett, made him move, and had a record
of his last words before white flames mushroomed— . . . He
couldn't believe it! Right next to Robinson was *Shirley Temple*
with those crazy curls. He moved away before Lisa could say
anything about that.

Noticing him acting sheepish, Lisa thought it was because she
had told him he looked like Roy Rogers, and so she made up.
"Actually, you look more like that sexy Big Ed in *White
Heat*," she soothed him.

Jesse James squared his shoulders; he remembered the tough,
good-looking man with incredibly wide shoulders. But! He had
been the dirtiest of the two-timers—betrayed Cody and Cody let
him have it in the back, like Big Ed had let Ma— . . . Ma?
Come and get me— . . .! Jesse's memories always jumbled at
that point. Every day he looked at what was playing in those
theaters that showed only old movies, hoping it would be *White
Heat*—they would *all* see it together!—but it was always one of
Lisa's "all-times" they were showing. He turned around to tell
Lisa he didn't want to look like the man who two-timed Cagney,
but she had disappeared among the glittering wax figures and
the angled mirrors.

" 'Bye," Lisa returned to say to Marilyn's soul.

Paths and arrows guided the visitors through a curio shop and
into the Palace of Living Art. It is an extension of the Museum.

Lisa, Orin, and Jesse passed wax-figure reproductions of
famous paintings—the Grand Inquisitor of Spain; a princely
priest in a purple cape; Cardinal Richelieu in brutal red; an
opulent, sated Louis XII. Corrupt, disdainful.

Jesse's attention was quickly diverted by the many naked wax
women in this section of the museum—Leda and the Swan, a
naked woman on a couch. Salome with a severed head on a

tray, three naked female bodies—one exhibiting her back, the other teasing in a three-quarter pose, and the third boldly facing the front. A naked golden woman holds a dog on a leash! A nude Venus has arms. There are male bodies, too—naked wrestlers, a sissified David with a thick figleaf held God knows how. "The Captive" writhes in a loincloth and chains.

Then they passed an alabaster reproduction of the Pietá— Christ in the arms of his looming mother, his thin limbs flowing into the giant folds of her shawl. A recorded voice intoned, "The hands execute, the heart judges."

Wandering voices hushed as recorded thunder pulled them to a crucifixion scene. Crowned with thorns, the waxen figure of Christ waits to be murdered. Muscular Romans cast lots for his robe while clustered women weep. The sky changes shades, light, darkening, dark. A recorded voice pleads, "Father, forgive them, for they know not what they do." In answer, thunder pounds.

"I don't know what *that's* doing in the Movieland Wax Museum," Lisa said, looking at the spooky man preparing for radiant martyrdom; the dazzling, indifferent soldiers; the eagerly resigned women huddled weeping.

Jesse didn't know what do to here; Orin just stared and stared.

With a gasp withheld since she first saw the waxen movie stars, Lisa separated herself from Jesse and Orin; she pushed her way urgently through the lines of tourists, looping in knots before a particular favorite figure—and she hurried past the curio shop—and back into the Movieland Museum.

She saw herself in various mirrors among the dead polished wax figures. She felt hot—disturbed. She found her—the figure of Marilyn Monroe—and stood before her. This time she didn't squint her eyes. She looked at the artificial face, the wax skin. She turned her back abruptly.

"Good-bye, Marilyn," she said aloud. *Good-bye, Bette Davis, Joan Crawford, Ida Lupino, Linda Darnell, Paulette Goddard, Olivia de Havilland, Gene Tierney! Good-bye!* And walking away without looking back, she added, Good-bye, Cathy, haunting the moors for Heathcliff; good-bye Amber, searching Bruce in the wilderness of a new country; good-bye Leave-her-to-heaven demanding love beyond death; good-bye, Miss Julie—

Jezebel—facing her fate in the wagon taking her and her sick lover to the island of death; good-bye, Cassie, abandoned to her murderous father; good-bye, Now-voyager, longing for moon and stars; good-bye, Casablanca, flying away to unhappiness; good-bye Maria, pulled by horses— . . . Pearl Chavez— . . . Pearl— . . . Maria— . . . Pearl— . . .

No!

She withdrew the last two farewells. She ran out of the museum. She could not say good-bye to Maria or Pearl Chavez.

Mandy Lang-Jones:
"The Lower Depths"

Mandy Lang-Jones is fucking the brains out of Tommy Bassach!
Tom Bassach thrust his hips up, drilling his cock in deep. But Mandy, straddling him upright, raised herself on her knees, just enough to control his shove and keep his cock at the lips of her cunt.

Mandy Lang-Jones is fucking the hell out of this dumb television grip!

"Shove down, shove *down*, goddammit, I'm about to come!" Tom Bassach sex-groaned.

"Not yet!" Mandy raised herself another essential inch and abandoned his despondent cock; a tear appeared on its tip.

He jabbed at her. But she put her hand over the fluff of her legs, feeling the warm moisture—and shut out his straining cock. With her other hand she slapped his readied erection.

"Ouch!" he said; his discouraged cock surrendered to the smarting slap.

"Don't come yet."

"Where'd you learn to do that?" he asked her, watching his deflating organ. "I was about to come. *You* already came," he accused.

"Once," she said. "But you weren't ready then." *Mandy Lang-Jones is going to fuck the cocky fuck out of Mr. Hotstuff!*

She lay back beside him on the unadorned tanned sheets she preferred, her hands behind her head.

She was even prettier than she appeared on television. When she did her special reports, she insisted on makeup that added seriousness to her face; then—and only then—she had her lips painted thin, to subdue their sensuality and increase the grave concern she needed to project to her growing audience—"fans," they were beginnng to say at the station—and the show's sponsors. She had large, dark brown eyes, and a nose that seemed just about to tilt and didn't. Her brown hair was straight except for a sudden assertive inward swirl at each side of her neck.

She was thirty-four, and her body was superb, with curves that flowed like a series of linked S's; firm curves unmarred by fat; thighs that arched to a lithe taper. For Mandy the "ideal" woman's body was one that strengthened "femininity," not one that altered it; she disapproved of women weightlifters, who were increasingly converting their bodies into ugly knotty muscles parodying men's—the way some women, but not her, thought transvestites parodied women; she herself admired their gutsiness. In action—roaming the city for her "specials," or swimming—firm arms and legs creating a sinuous flowing line—or playing tennis, jogging, fucking—in all of which she excelled—Mandy's body moved in feline harmony with her limbs; her flesh did not sag or bounce. The nipples of her round breasts remained boldly pointed, proud to be there and asserting that pride.

Now in bed she stretched her body, displaying its radiant sexuality. Light wisps—silky breaths—of hair curled between her legs and glistened with sequined moisture in the reflected light of the hot moon flooding in through an invisible wall of glass.

Tom Bassach, too, stretched his body, emphasizing his greater length. He was twenty-seven years old and on the thin, wiry side—a lanky, long, hairy body; strong slender limbs and impressively ridged abdominals; a basketball player type. He had a thick, dark, aggressively prominent moustache. It was like a patch of his pubic hair!—that's what Mandy thought when she saw him naked and touching it and his groin at the same time.

She reached over his chest and retrieved two cigarettes from a package on a table on his side. She inserted one in his mouth, held the other in abeyance for herself, and proceeded to light his. "I don't smoke," he told her. He took out the cigarette and inserted it between her lips. His fingers patted the possibily ruffled moustache. She smiled, an ambiguous smile. She lit the cigarette he had handed back to her.

"I smoke only between orgasms," she said.

For about two weeks, she had seen Tom Bassach at the
television station or on location, always coiled in electrical
wires or pushing equipment; he was a cameraman's assistant, a
grip, something like that. His shirt was always open at least
three buttons, showing off puffy dark chest hair. He flirted
constantly with the giddiest girls—secretaries, assistants; they
obviously welcomed his attentions. "A skinny John Wayne,"
Mandy had heard one of them describe him. Mandy fixed her
with a petrifying look. Soon, Tom Bassach started coming up to
her and asking seriously whether he could be of any "help"—
never defining the area of aid. Obviously he wanted to
approach her more directly, and personally. He was not shy—
that was clear from the way he acted with the other females. So,
Mandy assumed, he was reticent with her because, after all, she
was a star—a demistar, for now; not the star Eleanor Cavendish,
the regular coanchorwoman, was, but getting there, getting
there, and *soon*! He had been holding a coiled orange electrical
wire when he asked her, again, whether he could "help."
"How about coffee after the show?" she suggested. Her direct-
ness caused him to tangle on the long wire. "Better still," she
said, "if you can get out of that coil, why don't you come over
to my house for a drink after dinner? Tonight." She gave him
one of her private cards.

Here he was!

On Mandy's queen-size bed.

"You've got a great body," he said to her. He felt his cock
preparing for a new incursion; it gave a shivering flutter. He
began to play with the hairs between her legs.

"You're not half bad yourself," she said. She was proud of
being able to "relate" to all types of men—poetic types, intellectual types, jocks—once she'd made it with a Mr. Universal—
who actually flexed his biceps when he came. A bad fuck.
"You cooled off now?" she asked Tom.

Okay—so she was enjoying it so much she wanted to extend
it. Nothing wrong with that. And she'd already come—he'd
already *made* her come, Tom revised.

Now Tom was a popular man with women. He had one main
girlfriend of several off-and-on years' duration, Liz, who called
him "my cat's meow." But for all his sexual experience, he'd

known this encounter with Mandy Lang-Jones would be "different" the moment he walked in earlier and she asked him what he wanted to drink— "Wine?" "Bourbon?" "Beer?"—and added: "before we fuck." That aroused the hell out of him. Yes, he was impressed that she was a star—well, almost, actually very close—but he would soon start the necessary leveling process. He was younger, but with a woman like Mandy that could turn into a plus or a minus. Maybe—this had been at the back of his mind, perhaps midway there and now it moved forward—there might be more in this for him than just a good lay.

Mandy Lang-Jones lived in an attractive rented house in a cul-de-sac off Sunset Boulevard. One of two bedrooms, the room they were in opened invisibly through sliding glass doors into a very green garden. No flowers. A long swimming pool shimmered under the sweaty moon and, when the wind floated over the water, it crinkled like tinfoil in the silver light. Large, comfortable, the house did not bear a trace of Mandy on it— except by the very fact that it did *not*. The owner had had it decorated, and she had moved in and left it exactly as it was, with one exception: she had hired a gardener—a horticulturist, he called himself—to remove puddles of cute flowers about the pool and in pretty bunches about the lawn; they had reminded her of the beribboned tufts on quivery little poodles. Mandy didn't like to be "owned by things," especially anything living, like flowers. Grass was different—it was mowed down regularly.

"Tommy," she said intensely, "do you— . . .?"

"Tom," he interrupted her. The moment he corrected her, he realized he hadn't really minded the endearing dimunitive—hardly anyone ever called him that, not since he was a kid.

She didn't revise her designation. "You know what Tantra Yoga is?" she asked him.

"Yoga? Sure," he said proudly. "I was into it for a while. I still practice it, but only to do vacuums for my stomach. Keeps it flat," he pointed out the obvious. "Like this."

He stood up, on the floor, at the edge of the bed.

Mandy leaned on one elbow.

"You exhale, every bit of air." He blew out in profound puffs. Then he placed his hands on his upper thighs—and exhaling audibly once more, drew in his stomach, so that it almost touched the wall of his spine. He worked the isolated abdominal muscles like moving knots. He inhaled a great gush of air. "Like that," he said. He pushed his hair—but not too seriously—from his face and did another vacuum.

"You're a vain little thing, aren't you?"

He puffed the air out. There it was again—the enigmatic smile of hers. "I've never been called *little* before," he said.

"What I mean is *sex* yoga." Mandy Lang-Jones patted the pillow next to her, so he would join her back in bed. He did. "Orgasms," she clarified.

"Oh, I—uh—have to admit that—well, I don't— . . ." He hated to admit he didn't know what she was talking about— because he was a sophisticated man, knew how to relate to women, especially "the new woman." With Liz he had gone to a women's meeting once—he was by far the sexiest man there, most of the others were kind of small and squishy—and he got hearty applause when he agreed that, hey, men *had* given women a "bum deal" for too long. Liz was very proud of him; but that was the same night that he tried to— . . . "I know about the vaginal and clitoral orgasms," he offered in substitution.

Dumb grip. "In Tantra Yoga, there's the valley orgasm as opposed to peak orgasm," she said. "When you have a 'valley' orgasm, you go slow and easy, you relax, stretch it all out, *flowing* into orgasm, nothing urgent about it, just flows— . . ."

Was she making a judgment on his style? He listened attentively; it was important to let women know that a man listened.

"A peak orgasm—that's what accounts for premature ejaculation."

He winced. "I didn't ejaculate pre— . . ."

"You didn't ejaculate at all," she said. "But I don't mean you. I mean, men in general; it's especially important for men to learn to relax, otherwise it's all over—wham!"

Hell, he could come *three* times in a short period. *That* certainly impressed Liz, especially since she never came—though they definitely had a good—a *very* good—sex life; she said it wasn't important, her coming. He was about to tell Mandy about his orgasmic ability. Instead, he said—starting the leveling, "I don't think I'd like meditating while my cock's in— . . ."

"Tantra Yoga makes you learn how to *really* enjoy sex." Mandy disregarded his remark. "Great for men because a woman can have multiple orgasms, a man can't."

His cock lay limply in its dark nest.

"Actually," she said, "there's no such thing as a vaginal orgasm and a clitoral orgasm—just good and bad ones; it all depends on the fuck."

"I think for too long men have told women what women feel," he said in a deep, serious voice. That's what he'd said at the meeting with Liz, when he got another round of applause. He was proud of his liberated observations. His hand between her legs, he touched his moustache—which was *much* thicker than the hair on her crotch.

She stroked his cock. Turning sideways, he curled one long leg over her thigh. She thrust her lips against his and pushed her tongue in. He shoved it back and pushed his into her mouth. She thrust it back and continued her incursion into his.

Mandy Lang-Jones is just getting ready to ball Hotstuff so the giddy secretaries won't even recognize him! Forming her thoughts into precise words excited Mandy when she was having sex. It was like in a documentary, where the voice-over enhances the action—her own inner voice commenting, complimenting, goading.

Tom Bassach made a surprise attack—one rough stab of his hips. But Mandy intercepted it. She reached under and guided his cock so that it slid from her crotch and up on her stomach. "Slo——ow," she reminded him. "Tan-*tra* Yo-*guh*!" she said as if pronouncing a mantra.

Okay. Slow. He moistened his fingers and drew narrowing circles on her breasts, until they enclosed the nipples.

"They're dry now," she said.

"What!"

"Your fingers—they're dry now, and it felt real good when they were moist."

He moistened them again. This time he concentrated on the nipples. With one hand, he grasped her left buttock—so firm! —and located the bud of her ass—so sensual! Pulling her lips away from his, she aimed the enigmatic smile at him. She retreated just enough so that his cock poked at her belly, the moving causing his hand to slide off the opening at her ass. She clasped his cock between her legs, letting him pump that way. Then she released it, and it slid on her silky flesh, up, down, up, down, moving from between her legs toward her navel. "Floooow— . . ." she said. His sliding movement increased.

He could come like this, and— . . .!

"That would be a waste." Her hands, clamped over his back, stopped his motions.

"Sure would," he said. He rolled over, facing up. Another drop of moisture had gathered on the head of his cock. She glued it to the tip of one finger, and tasted it. He thought he read her signals—and he reached for her neck, rubbing it, encouraging it downward, his fingers gliding over her fleecy crotch, inching lower, toward her buttocks.

"I'm really hot," he said. "Could keep going." He was about to tell her he could come three times, easy.

"I've had up to fifteen orgasms in one night, and I could have gone for more, but the man I was with— . . ." She made a face, reached again over him for another cigarette, the first had mummified in the ashtray, puffed on only once.

He was glad he hadn't told her he could come three times.

"Encounter groups, est, primal, Rolfing, going sane, psycho-analysis—I've been through all of them," she said. "You?"

"Never felt I needed any of that," he parried. Yes! Oh, *that* tone sure changed the smile on her face.

"You know what they're all about?" she asked.

"Getting to know yourself," he recited. "Hey, that's what it's *all* about, sure."

"No—it's all about good orgasms or bad orgasms."

He pondered that. Nodded. He started, "Hey— . . ." and didn't know what to add.

"It makes you creative—and it sharpens your humanity."

"Huh?" He wished he had uttered something other than that sound—which annoyed him when Liz made it.

"Did you see my series, 'The Lower Depths'?"

"I worked on most of it with you, remember?" He felt

chagrined; was she pretending? It was true that when she worked, she *worked*!

"You think I could have so much empathy for the people I interview on my specials—really get to know what they're all about—if I was worrying all the time about sexual fulfillment? Did you see the segment on those street kids—the malehustlers on Santa Monica Boulevard?"

Tom remembered that vividly—and the interview with an incredibly beautiful blond youngman in cutoffs.

"You know what made that a great show?"

"A good orgasm," Tom tossed at her. Oh, he was moving on, *moving on*! He'd allowed her too many. He had to catch up—getting closer to that needed balance, then a slight tilt in his direction, and *then*! His cock began to stretch.

Mandy leaned confidentially on her elbow. "When I kept asking that kid how much he made hustling the streets and he wouldn't tell me, I knew why right away—because he'd go for whatever he could make." Her breasts didn't even tilt, not even slightly. They were so close to Tom's mouth he reached out and dabbed at each of them with his tongue.

"Ooooo," she said. And went on: "I *got* him to say he made a thousand a week; remember when he said that?"

"Sure—and that's a lot of money for a kid."

"I knew it wasn't true," she said. "So did the cop who talked about those kids afterwards on the show, he told me; sometimes they don't even have a dime to call anyone when they're busted. But I *understood* that kid. All his friends were standing there. He wants to be a big star; this is his one big chance to be noticed—maybe by someone big. I'd driven up that street; I saw some of them—real cute, too—waiting for hours. I knew how little they'd go for. If that kid had told the truth, he would've been just a little chippy. I gave him an opportunity to triumph!"

For a full week radio and television spots had shouted, "Young boys earning one thousand dollars a week selling their bodies to older men; watch it all on the news with Mandy Lang-Jones."

"You knew it wasn't true, and yet you used it?" Tom was surprised by his uncool eruption.

"What is truth?" Mandy repeated the famous viceroy's

question. "You know what truth is? Truth is what we put right *there*." She pointed to the large, blank television screen a few feet away. *"That's* what *makes* reality. You think anyone would care about a kid making five bucks a night selling his body? Cheap stuff. *Figures! Lots* of kids, *lots* of customers, *lots* of perversion, *lots* of corruption, *lots* of bucks—*and lots of viewers!"* Again she pointed to the dormant television. "Truth is in *there,* the moment I turn that set on, it pours out truth, it *makes* truth; and if no one sees it, it's *not* there. Like the tree falling in the forest; nobody hears it, there's no sound." The passionate asseveration cooled. "Besides, it was a public service; it brought lots of attention to those poor street kids—how else would they get that kind of attention?"

He wasn't sure what he felt. She had coaxed that kid to lie.

"Now you take child laborers in the fields—right here in the groves of California. Good story, right? Lots of pathos, lots of human interest, pictures that would break your heart. Great story!"

"Right!" he said enthusiastically. He'd work on it with her. Associate producer— . . . And on location he'd give her all the good orgasms she needed for empathy. *"Great* story," he underscored. "You could even start with— . . ." he started to contribute.

"No story at all," she said. "Sure it tears you apart, right? —kids doing stoop labor in the fields—and illegally—but that doesn't make a story *there."* She addressed the television. "People who watch TV, *really* watch—the ones who give us our ratings or turn us off—*their* kids could run away, end up on the streets peddling their asses, and if it's for a lot of money, there's *got* to be a lot of *threat.* Great story. Now those same people's kids—they're not going to end up in the fields doing stoop labor—so, no story!" She mused, "I learned that right away when I did my first special—on the Mexican women, mostly illegals, who work in the garment district sweatshops, sewing. Exploited? Damn right! By the employers *and* the Immigration. And I had no ratings at all. Nothing for the TV viewer to relate to. You know the ratings we got on 'The Lower Depths'? Wiped all the others out. *And* we accomplished *good,"* she insisted. "Some people really cared about those kids on the street. Who knows?—that one kid might even be able to charge one hundred dollars a trick now." She paused intently. "I might win a prize for that series. . . . Ready?" She faced him sexily and cuddled his cock.

"Always." He crooked his smile. A hairy leg hugged her.

"Lean back," she told him.

He did.

Her tongue drew a *T* on his chest, extended the lower part downward, curved the line into a circle enclosing his cock and balls. Then she sucked his cock into her mouth.

When a woman went down on Tom, he liked to push her head down, rumple her hair, pretending force. Liz hadn't wanted to go down at first, but he'd persuaded her and that excited him; now she did it routinely when they first started having sex. Not that he'd tried, but she'd told him she didn't want *him* to go down on *her*—she knew it would "tickle uncomfortably." That was all right with him, because he wasn't really into that.

Depending on whom he was with, Tom liked to think or even say words like "cunt," "pussy"—he'd stopped saying "bitch"; that was risky. With Mandy now, his usual routine floundered. Only tentatively, he put his hand on her head—not pushing, not rumpling. She raised her hand, removed his from her head, and held it pinioned at his side.

The smile again. "Relax, Tommy, I'm doing it." She looked up at him. *Mandy Lang-Jones has your cock in her mouth—but she's in total control!*

He felt the cum gathering. His breathing began to knot. He'd prefer to come in her cunt. *Shoot my fucking wad in Mandy Lang-Jones's fucking cunt-pussy!* But if he broke the connection, she'd withdraw again, and so he would ride— . . .

He tried to slide sideways so he could play with her cunt while she blew him, but she did not allow the movement, kept him pinioned. One more stroke of her mouth and he would shoot! She pulled her lips away. "Okay, I'll fuck you," she said.

That fucking smile of hers!

Straddling him, she spread her great legs, pulling in his cock as he pushed. Up and down, up, down. His hands grasped her breasts. She felt his spilling orgasm, hers reached for his, he thrust his head back, she flailed hers to one side, both came.

His long body quivered, relaxed, rested. He waited for her approbation. She reached over him. "Fuck—no more cigarettes," she discovered.

"That was great," he said. Now he waited for her to echo him.

"You know Freud's bullshit about penis envy?" she said.

"Hey! That's been disproved entirely," he knew to say.

"No—he was right."

Tom felt as if he had rejected a victor's laurel, without knowing he'd won it. "Well, I *have* always, maybe deep down, felt that he might have had a— . . ." he started.

"But not about women he wasn't right," Mandy said. "Women don't envy men's cocks. Men envy each other's cocks. Size doesn't matter that much to women; it does to men."

He squinted at her. He was no Jimmy Steed, but he was *much* more than just adequate.

"Don't worry," she assuaged him, "you're fine; just fine. It was just a general observation." She got up and left the room, to search for cigarettes. She returned with one between her lips. She stood near the sliding glass panels. The reflection of the moon in the pool hugged her lovingly, the curves outlined in luminous kissing light. A mirror captured the silver silhouette, front and back at the same time.

She really did have a sensational body! Tom Bassach knew he'd be ready for her again.

Still standing there, "You ever tried anal sex?" she asked him.

When he had tried—with Liz—not even telling her, just letting his cock slide away from one opening and toward the other—she cried when she discovered what he wanted. He denied it, said he hadn't meant to push hard, there. He *had* fucked one of the receptionists at the studio that way, and another time he— . . . "Yeah," he said, man of the world.

"Did you take it or give it?" Mandy asked him.

"*What?*"

"Did you take it up the ass or put it there?" she enunciated as if he hadn't heard.

"Listen," hysteria tinged his voice, "I just fucked you, I made you come twice, so I assume you know I'm not a fag." He had thought her strange smile was gone permanently. But it either returned now or never left.

"I know you're not," she said. She shrugged. "I've tried it; mostly a man's trip, though." This time she took a third puff from the cigarette. She continued to stand, as if trying to decide something important.

To let him try? The tip of his cock stirred. And to ask him to spend the night? Go for sixteen orgasms! he thought with amusement, excitement, and apprehension. Or would this be a one-night fuck? Whatever her new TV special, it would have to be spectacular to top "The Lower Depths." He wanted to be a part of it. Christ, she could help him, especially if she did replace Eleanor Cavendish—and he'd heard a lot of criticism about Eleanor. Her makeup took one hour each day, and she was always arguing with the lighting men. And Kenneth Manning wasn't getting any younger, and so— . . .

"Suck my cunt," Mandy growled. She stood at the edge of the bed, near his head.

"What?"

"I said, Lick my cunt," she growled again even more sexily.

"I just came— . . ."

"Squeamish?"

"It's just so soon after."

She lay beside him, and buried the cigarette with the other dead ones in the ashtray. She reached for his head. Resisting its pull, he burrowed it between her breasts. His hands slid under her buttocks, spreading them, and he felt excited again, yes. Actually, his orgasm had been one of those strange long ones when, finally, he didn't *fully* shoot; that happened when he waited too long. But: "Let's wait just a while," he said, to avoid the push of her hands on his head.

"Okay," she said. Each time she smiled—"that way"—he felt she was signaling a private victory, hers, unknown to him.

"Where did you learn so much about women, all about vaginal and clitoral orgasms?" she asked him.

"Hey, you know, I like to be up on things; read a lot—stay current. Opens you up, you know? I went to a meeting—a women's meeting with Liz—just a girl I know; we signed a petition for equal— . . ."

"Does she come—Liz?"

He coughed. "Sure." He was about to touch his moustache, but didn't.

"Good orgasms?"

"Sixteen peaks, sixteen valleys," he sparred with her.

"Gotcha," she said. "You pick up quickly on the raps, don't you, Tommy?" She didn't wait for his answer; she said, "I'll tell you something you won't learn at those meetings, something about real liberation—something those chanting women at demonstrations don't know: Liberation is *inside*, deep, deep inside— . . ."

"In the lower depths," he tossed.

Her sudden look bored into him. "And in men, too," she said. Her words were carefully enunciated; tinged with vague warning? "Mass killings," she said.

"Huh?" That hated sound again; it just flew out of him. He never used it—*Liz* did.

"Mass killings—my next special," she said.

"The Nazis— . . ." he started, trying to move ahead of her.

"I don't mean war," she said. "You get into all kinds of problems there, issues—the right, the left, the up, the down. Nazis, Viet Nam, Hiroshima—stuff like that, that's *war*. I'm talking about *mass* slaughter—Starkweather, that guy on the tower in Austin, Manson, the Skid Row Slasher, the Lovers' Lane Ripper, the Hillside Strangler; explore what makes— . . ."

"Could be terrific!" And it could, he knew. "You could start with an overview of— . . ."

"Right," she dismissed him. She reached for the remote-control device on the table on her side of the bed. She turned the television on with a click.

There was Eleanor Cavendish. Mandy propped herself on a pillow and stared at her. "One more good story and you're *mud*, Eleanor," she said, "and then I'll go after Ken." Eleanor was telling Ken about the growing danger of fires as the Santa Ana winds increased. Yes—and a potentially major fire had already erupted in one of the outlying canyons, Ken told her. The screen showed red flames pouring down a hill. "Sam

Bernheimer has a live report— . . .'' Sam Bernheimer appeared among firetrucks and smoke-smudged people evacuating the area but pausing to be seen by the camera.

"I'm not doing fires any more," Mandy said victoriously. "No more fires, I told them, unless it's the whole city! And I mean it. . . . I'll have to go a long way in my next series to reach 'The Lower Depths.' I know that, and so does Eleanor."

"That mass murder idea could be great if— . . ." Tom started again.

She held her finger on the remote selector, sliding over images of faces, fires, cowboys, a man falling, a can of beer, a girl skating, a child eating bread, a ballet dancer, police surrounding a house, a woman chauffeured to— . . .

". . . .—four! There shall be four! And on the other side: *There!* will Satan face them!" Sister Woman gasped.

"Those fake evangelicals and their bullshit," Tom Bassach said.

"It's not bullshit," Mandy said, watching intently.

Tom sat up, startled. "Cummon, you don't really believe— . . ."

"Of course not!" Mandy snapped, watching the screen. "But the *following* she's got, and her *power*—that's not bullshit. She knows television better than any of us. I learn from her, a lot—no, I'm serious. About how to convince. You know, she actually makes up scripture, quotes it as her own—or just mixes it all up so she's got her own 'word of God'! And those idiots don't care."

"At the Great Gathering of Souls Sunday, I promise: something awesome!" Sister Woman covered her eyes, as if momentarily blinded. Then she removed her hands; the colorless outlined eyes stared forward. Now they were black, reflecting black.

"Notice how she creates suspense," Mandy said. "Four— that's her secret number. Never explains, uses it over and over; and then it's 'something awesome'—mysteries and secrets and vague promises, to get all those creeps to call and— . . ."

"And send 'love donations,' " sneered Tom.

"Nine million dollars' worth—that's how much she raised; she's aiming for ten. People leave whole estates to her, instructions in their wills."

"Shit," Tom looked at his cock. That spooky Sister Woman wasn't going to help this situation.

"And *nothing* can touch her, not criticism, not ridicule, not scandal. *The Enquirer* ran what it claimed was documented *proof* that her rich mother and father were brother and sister and committed suicide together—and their readers, who love to read that stuff, threatened to boycott the paper even though there were no threatened suits or rebuttals from Sister Woman. Now *that* is power!" Mandy said admiringly.

"But will they surrender to Satan, Sister Woman? Though his power is temporary, it is terrible to behold, terrible in its mighty persuasion!" Brother Man bemoaned.

"He looks like a fag." Tom cupped his groin securely.

Sister Woman shook her head. Her eyes seemed to melt into tears. "God always wins. It is sinners who lose."

"Cummon, Mandy, turn the fuckers off." Tom reached for the remote control.

Mandy grasped his hand, stopping him. "Just *look* at her!" She shut off the sound. In pale lavender chiffon, Sister Woman wove her invisible web with her hands. "Great! She's just great!"

Tom looked from the face on the screen to Mandy's. "You're really serious about learning from her?" He tried to make it both question and statement.

"I told you—yeah." She clicked off the television. "She knows mass communications." She faced him in bed. "Have you ever thought about what that means? Hear it: mass . . . communications. Mass— . . ."

"Religious, too," he said. "Lots of resonance. Mass communications," he repeated.

"You'd make a good weatherman," Mandy said.

This time, one hand touched his moustache and the other connected it to his crotch. For a moment he liked the outlaw image she had evoked of him—the way she saw him—but then he had second thoughts, "Look, I'm a liberal guy, but not a radical. I hope I haven't said anything that gave you the idea that I'm— . . ." It wouldn't help for it to get out at the station that he was an extremist, for God's sake. "And I was just a kid when they— . . ."

"I didn't mean *that* kind of weatherman." She laughed. "I meant those cute guys the stations hire now to tell the weather. Even if it's going to *flood,* there they are, all sunny smiles."

He liked the outlaw better. "I sure the hell don't see myself that way," he said.

"You're not. Believe me, you . . . are . . . not." She spread her legs, offering them to him. "I've got some sweet honeydew for you, stud, just for you," she said.

"Honey dew melons." He cupped her breasts. Oh, he was ready—and astonished and turned on to hear her talk like that, actually kittenish.

She guided his mouth to her breasts. He licked. She moved his head until she located his tongue on the exact spot she wanted aroused, just slightly to the left of her right nipple. "Stay *there*," she said.

His cock was erect; he was hotter than before. Now he would do this—on his own—wouldn't really do it, just tease her. . . . *What a body!* He slid his head right to the edge of the triangle of pubic hair. He held her thighs closed, pretending to caress them. She flung her legs open. "Eat it!" she commanded, and he dove hungrily into the lightly furred moist opening. She held his head firmly down, but he was not resistng, not at all. He was licking willingly, lapping at the opening, tongue dabbing, darting, exploring, entering, pushing into the dewy folds.

Then she raised his head. "Let's fuck," she said.

He was *hot!* And *she* was waiting for *him* now! Look at her! —leaning down and forward! her hands propped on the bed! her ass toward him! He knelt behind her. One of his hands grabbed one of her breasts, the other grasped her slim waist. His cock brushed her ass. She squirmed. Holding his cock, he moved it down, toward her cunt, rubbing it into her hairs. Tentatively, he returned the eager cock to the nearer opening. Was she inviting, coaxing him to fuck her in the ass? Oh, *yeah!* The head of his cock touched the tight knot. She allowed it to remain there. Now with both his hands he parted the buttocks, he aimed his cock and— . . .

She slid down, flat on the bed, turned her body over quickly, facing him. His body fell on hers. She opened her legs, and his cock slipped into her cunt. Her legs curled about his shoulders, slid down his back. He pushed in, then out, then almost totally out, at the very mouth of her legs, in, out, then again almost, almost completely out, only to lunge back in one hard thrust. Deep! Deep! *Deep!*

Her hands reached over his shoulders, slid down to his back, farther down to his waist, down, down to his narrow buttocks. She grabbed the slender mounds of flesh, spreading them open, kneading them. He pushed in and out of her. She felt his hard cock in her liquid warmth.

Now! She pushed her finger into his ass, forced it deep, deeper, shoved another finger in. *Deep!*

"*Ouch!*" And he came and came and came.

He rolled off her, onto the bed. She had not come. He looked at her. Her smile—that smile—branded him this time. She puffed once on a new cigarette, and put it out, as if not to interrupt the growing smile. In a moment it might issue laughter.

"I think I'd better go." He sat up. That abruptly. Angry.

"Did Mandy wear Tommy-boy out?" she asked. There was a cold meanness in the studied, taunting tone. Where had he heard it before?—that tone of mean triumph? He looked startled at Mandy Lang-Jones. He had heard it in his voice when he was with Liz, when he was with the others, when— . . .

Even more furious, he dressed. Was there anything to gain now from her? He wanted to say something that would crack her hardening smile. He looked at her and said, "With all your bullshit, Mandy, you're not liberated—not in any way, not even in your— . . ." Yes! This was it! He took sure aim: ". . . —no, not even in your very, *very* lowest depths."

The smile didn't crack. It widened, preparing laughter.

He wanted to go on—to tell her she was dishonest, disdainful, cruel in her life and mean in that high-rated precious series of lies she might get a prize for; wanted to tell her she wasn't even honest *about* her dishonesty, still had to rationalize it now and then, call it a public service; he wanted to tell her that she— . . .

But he wouldn't say any of that, and her unrelenting smile told him she knew it, and why—because both knew he would have done—would do—the same or equivalent things in the world they shared. The only difference was that she had been in it—that world of lies—longer than he had. And yet— . . .

And yet what he hated her most for was that she had given him the best fuck of his life.

Smoke from the cigarette concealed her expression. He heard her calm voice.

"Fag-hags—that's what gays call women who pretend to know all about them. Well, I've got a name for men like you, with all your bullshit about women: Tommy-boy, you are a *cunt-runt!*"

Softly—and she knew he would do it that way, softly, and even call out, softly, too, "Goodnight, Mandy, see you soon, huh?" and she might, she just might—Tom Bassach closed the door—softly—as he walked out of her house.

Mandy touched the soft brush between her sculpted legs, touched her flat stomach, her round breasts,—soft, firm. With a sharp stab in the direction of the television screen, she fired the remote control, hopping from station to station as the dark screen unbunched into a soundless picture of Eleanor Cavendish, her lips moving.

Mandy said, "No more fires for *me,* Eleanor—*and* Ken! *No more fires!*"

Lost Angels: 12

"Well, that crucifixion was certainly inspiring!" said the woman with the newly set hair and tint, dabbing happily at her glistening tears.

Rushing out of the Movieland Wax Museum, Lisa waved at Orin and Jesse standing by the naked David outside the Palace of Living Art.

"Well, couldn't you just *see* how He'd die for our sins, right there and then, bless His soul?" the heavy woman continued merrily. "Well, good-bye, you three, lord-love-you." She waved gaily at Lisa and Jesse and Orin.

"You worried us, Lisa!" Jesse smarted. Orin allowed, "You did for a fact."

Lisa didn't say a word. She just walked on to the car. She sat in the back seat. Checking Orin's look for approbation, Jesse lowered the top of the Cadillac. Hot wind spiraled in.

In the car as they drove on the freeway, Lisa was moody, surly. "I haven't had a flavor-of-the-week in ages," she pouted in a child's voice.

"You want one?" Orin offered.

"No!" she snapped.

Traffic was beginning to harden the freeway. They moved slowly, just as slowly when they drove minutes later along Sunset Boulevard. This time when they passed Schwab's Pharmacy, Lisa didn't point out that that was "where they discovered Lana Turner." Missing her observation—which he always greeted with, "You've *told* us and *told* us"—Jesse said wistfully, "That's where they discovered— . . ." He couldn't remember whom, and Lisa didn't remind him.

Orin turned off Sunset, crisscrossing along lawned, tree-

357

tunneled, arrogant streets—onto Wilshire Boulevard and into Beverly Hills.

"Rodeo Drive." That struck Jesse very funny. *"Rodeo* Drive?"

"That's the famous street where the richest people shop," Lisa said curtly.

The famous shops on the street brandished their snobbish names. Limousines parked in front of a striped awning: "By Appointment Only." Manikins there were headless. "Ugly," sneered Lisa. In another shop floppy rag dolls modeled expensive clothes. "Ugly."

Men and women with purple tans walked the streets in aimless determination; they dressed in a special way, like a diverse army, like fleshed versions of the distorted manikins.

Traffic thickened even more as they passed the glassy cubes of Century City—high-rise rectangles, repeated, with trimmed grass at their base sprinkled by arcs of silver water from white fountains.

For minutes the wind had stopped, leaving only heat. But as they moved toward the beach, it sliced at the streets like clashing scythes. Orin had to stop and raise the car's top, trapping unmoving heat. In Santa Monica, palm trees lining the strip of park at the edge of the ocean swayed low, then struggled against the pushing wind.

They could see the palm trees and the restless water through the window of the fancy restaurant Orin chose for dinner—"just for Lisa." Not even that could jar her out of her mood—which was making Jesse nervous. Orin seemed merely to accept her silence.

When they reached Hollywood in the night, dried palm leaves littered the streets. The car's tires crunched as they drove past the park. Lisa looked away.

Then a sudden white darkness fell on the street, the streetlights snuffed out in a power failure. The bright moon plucked out hideous shadows. The wind ripped away the leaves of palm trees. One swept like a fallen eagle against the windshield of the car.

Orin swerved!

The dried branch pressed against the windshield, its dead fingers scratching against the glass.

Lisa screamed, tension bursting. Now another current of wind hurled the fallen palm leaf onto the car's hood, and then yanked it away. Shaken, Jesse leaned back; Lisa's scream had absorbed his own unuttered shock.

Dead leaves floated in the motel swimming pool. The dusty wind created electric-colored puffs of light about it. They parked the Cadillac in its usual place. Orin touched the trunk *again!* Jesse noticed.

Inside, the two men sat the small table drinking from Cokes they had brought back. Lisa would not touch hers.

She rushed to Pearl on the bed. The agate blue gaze was fixed in accusation. "She used to look like *me,* and now she looks like *her,* and *she* said she used to look like *me* until *I* came and— . . ." She shook the doll—and then brought her to her breasts, soothing her. "There, don't you cry, I didn't mean it. I said, don't cry! I should leave you, just walk out and leave you—like *he* did!" Words she tried to forget—tossed at her over and over—bombarded her now.

Jesse stood up. "Honest to God, Lisa. You're like a woman one moment, and a baby the next. Ole Pearl's just a doll," he tried to adjust reality.

"Orin gave her to me!" Lisa said tensely.

"She's what you want her to be." Orin stood up from the table. "She's you *and* her."

Her! Orin understood so much. *Her!* . . . Then the words damming all day flooded out of Lisa: "I *hated* that horrible wax museum! They *all* looked dead, all of them! The only ones who looked real were the monsters! The others looked like corpses. That wasn't Marilyn, and her soul wasn't there! I tried to squint, pretend, force myself to pretend it was her! And everyone was so mean to her. So mean. They wouldn't leave her alone, and it's mean, *mean!* They— . . . !"

"Who's they?" Jesse wanted to stop her deluge, now a deluge of words and tears.

Orin said soberly, "Everybody's got a 'they,' a 'them.' 'They' are the ones who did bad things to you. You know that as well as anybody, Jesse. So does Lisa. And 'it' is what hurts you, what hurts you the worst."

Jesse nodded.

Yes, Lisa thought, calming down, trying to stop the sobs.

Orin brought her Coke, and she drank thirstily. He wiped her tears with his handkerchief. Jesse held her hand. I love you both, so much, she wanted to say. But Orin had already walked away, turning on the television to the presence that waited beyond the glassy grayness.

Lisa looked away. That woman looks like the wax figures, she thought.

". . . —glowing under the light of trees in the grotto along the vined lane, and you stopped in your meditations and looked at me and— . . ." Brother Man's rhapsodic voice changed; controlled: ". . . —you were seized by a vision. What was it, Sister Woman?"

"The word of the Lord came again unto me, saying, Howl ye, woe the day, prophesy and say, the day of the Lord is near, a cloudy day of flaming wrath, and there shall be time no longer," Sister Woman pronounced words.

"The day of wrath!" Brother Man gasped.

"Four fallen angels bruised by the fire of hell!" Sister Woman hurled.

Four. Lisa frowned. Jesse glanced at her.

"But!" Sister Woman's hands ascended, the flowing sleeves like frail, deadly blades. "There is time enough, praise God." She recited memorized words: "For these are they which came out of great tribulation and have washed their robes— . . ."

". . . —and made them white in the blood of the Lamb," Orin's voice recited with Sister Woman.

". . . —but they shall hunger no more," Sister Woman continued, "neither thirst any more. For the Lamb which is in the midst of the throne— . . ."

". . . —shall feed them." Orin closed his eyes, saying the same words Sister Woman whispered, simultaneously. ". . . —and shall lead them into living fountains of water, and God shall wipe away all tears from their eyes," he ended, from the Book of *Revelation*.

Finished with the softly breathed prophecy, Sister Woman pointed her finger like a weapon. "See them! On one side are the fallen angels, and on the other the Prince of Darkness ascends to his black throne, prepared to do battle for souls. Yea, he enlists the black legions. Look! There!'' Her finger sliced to one side. ''And a cloud of evil gathers on the blazing horizon. But God will win!'' she shouted.

The luminous cross scarred the screen.

Orin turned off the set. He took out his wallet, searching the piece of paper with Sister Woman's private number on it. He dialed. Waited, waited, waited.

Lisa and Orin heard their own breathing.

''Sister Woman!'' Orin said. His body relaxed, he closed his eyes.

Lisa accepted what she had thwarted: He *is* speaking to her.

Jesse nodded toward Lisa, accepting the same fact.

''Sister Woman, it's me, Orin. . . . Yes! I . . . am . . . here.'' He pronounced the three words slowly into the telephone. ''Like we promised you. . . . Right after she died, I left. . . . Sins so wrathful, Sister Woman!—sins *you* know! . . . And she cursed— the last moments, her last words! . . . I believe that. That's why . . . I . . . am . . . here.''

Again the long pause between the three words. Now Lisa knew they had a deep meaning not only for him but, mysteriously, for her and Jesse.

''Three of us—all lost. . . . Yes!—and the fourth one, too, just like you prophesied!'' Orin's frantic voice continued.

The fourth one. The man in the park was the fourth one. Afraid, Lisa moved closer to Jesse, who took a bewildered step toward Orin, as if to block the thrust of his words.

''I *always* keep my promises, Sister Woman. . . . It's *you* who know!'' Orin's voice broke an angered sob. ''I have your letters to her: *'beyond death and hell.'* Proof! . . . You promised— you're the only one who knows, Sister Woman! If you can do that, then you'll know the proof!'' He inhaled, as if preparing the next words, which he flung out: ''Tomorrow's Saturday, Sister Woman, the night of your weekly healings. She watched those, Sister Woman, watched until she couldn't see any more, and then she'd listen, Sister Woman. . . . You will give us proof then, tomorrow—and on Sunday in the Silver Chapel, for your gathering of souls, we will come to you, with her gift, with *ours*, and *for* ours. . . . Goodnight, Sister Woman.'' When he hung up, he walked to the draped windows.

Now he will stare out into the night, Jesse knew. Cody Jerrett talked in the dark wind to his dead Ma. His dead Ma— . . .

"You meant us, didn't you, Orin?—you said we were lost," Lisa said. She didn't want to think about the man in the park, not now. In the echoing memories of Orin's beautiful words— but disguised by their soothing rhythms, even now, remembered— there was an angered confusion, which he ordered into his own logic, only his. Lisa heard it in whispering echoes—and that was what was leading them— . . . Where? "You meant us," she repeated, expecting no answer. She felt tired, tired because of the betrayal of the Movieland Museum, tired because again unwanted reality was invading harshly—and soon it might not be possible to push it away—as she tried now. She embraced Pearl. She felt a new sadness as Orin turned from the window.

He reached down and put one hand on Lisa's shoulder, another on Jesse's. "I have to test her—lots of ways; the old lady wanted that, she told me. *Trust me,*" he echoed his words of the day that had led them into the park. "I'll tell you everything, I promise, tomorrow, too tired now, all of us, trust me." His hands on their shoulders became firmer. "Please," he said.

"Yes! Just don't look so sad!" Lisa said.

Jesse remembered when Lisa's touch had connected them in the car. This reaffirmed the same connection. "I trust you, Orin," Jesse said quietly. Tomorrow Orin would explain, he had promised, and he'd just said on the telephone he always kept his promises. Orin didn't look like Cagney—Cody—no, but they both resembled troubled little boys at times. Cody. All he asked for was loyalty. But everyone betrayed him. Betrayal was an awful thing. He, Jesse, was loyal.

Officer Weston: "Internal Affairs"

Click. "Draft of Memorandum of Psychiatric Evaluation in the matter of Officer Norris Weston. To: Investigating Officer, Internal Affairs Division— . . . Officer— . . . Officer— . . ." *Click.* . . . *Click.* "(Miss Burstyn, when you transcribe this tape, get the name and title of the investigating officer from our file and check the correct form for this report—consult the latest evaluation that I conducted for the Police Department; that was in the matter of that man— . . . Cramen or Katoff; also, add Officer Norris's rank—sergeant, I believe—and head this and all other notes and subsequent versions of this report <u>HIGHLY CONFIDENTIAL</u>—in solid capitalization and underlined.) From: Frederick C. M. Krug, M.D., Consulting Psychiatrist. (Paragraph:) Officer Norris Weston was referred to examining physician for psychiatric evaluation and prognosis after several of his fellow officers and superiors complained of serious lapses in the performance of subject officer's duties: bouts of moodiness, apparent depression, irrational eruptions of anger (change that to 'irascibility'; no, leave it—but delete 'irrational'), and persistent tardiness, especially in the afternoons. This behavior did not decline—as expected to by his superiors—after the second (underline 'second') finding concurring with the first from the District Attorney's Office that (quote) 'no prosecutable offense occurred in the shooting death of— . . . of—. . .'" *Click.* . . . *Click.* ". . . —of Emma Lincoln' (close quote) by Officer Norris G. Weston (Paragraph:) <u>IMMEDIATE BACKGROUND</u> (solid capitalization, underlined): Officer Norris A. Weston was on an official assignment to stake out a Central Los Angeles Elementary School (get the name—it's in the referral report)

363

where a man loitering suspiciously had been reported by parents. In his car to observe the suspect's actions, Officer Weston received a Police Emergency Code nine-nine-nine (quote)—'officer needs assistance, all units respond' (close quote). Following accepted procedure, Officer Weston drove immediately to the origin of the distress call, only a few blocks away. (Paragraph:) According to the report of Officer Elton D. Katoff (that is correct, Miss Burstyn, the *earlier* file is on Officer Cramen— with a *C*, and Katoff is spelled K-a-t-o-f-f— umm—yes)— . . . Officer Katoff was driving alone along a street in a high-crime area when he saw a group of black teenagers huddled together in a suspicious manner. Officer Katoff stopped to investigate, suspecting narcotics activity, common in the area. When Officer Katoff identified himself and ordered the teenagers to raise their hands and 'Freeze!' (quote, exclamation mark inside quote), Emma Lincoln, the mother of one of the teenagers, rushed out of her house, outside of which the suspects were gathered, and yelled to the children (make that 'teenagers') to (quote) 'throw them things away and run' (close quote). Thereupon the teenagers threw away the items (make that 'suspicious items'); Officer Katoff assumed that they were discarding narcotics and/or paraphernalia, and he fired twice in the direction of the fleeing youths, hitting none. By then, Mrs. Lincoln had thrown herself on the ground and was apparently looking for the discarded evidence. Officer Katoff warned Mrs. Lincoln to (quote) 'Freeze!' (close quote, exclamation mark inside quote), and to reinforce his warning pointed his gun at her. At that moment, Joseph Lincoln—Mrs. Lincoln's husband—a huge black man (change that to 'a two hundred thirty–pound Negro male') appeared and approached Officer Katoff in a menacing manner, causing the officer to redirect the direction— . . . uh . . . to redirect the pointing position of— . . . to point his gun at the man. Others in the area had begun to gather and allegedly join in the abuse of the officer for being white. Feeling threatened, Officer Katoff sent out the emergency code. (Paragraph:) When Officer Norris Weston arrived seconds later, he observed Officer Katoff pointing his gun at the large black man (delete the description; substitute 'pointing his gun at Mr. Lincoln') while a black woman—Mrs. Lincoln—sprawled on the ground and attempted to reach for what Officer Weston assumed to be a weapon. (Make that 'while a black woman on the ground was searching a hedge for what Officer Weston,' et cetera.) Officer Weston fired four times at Emma Lincoln, wounding her fatally. (Change that to 'killing her.') He fired a fifth shot at Joseph Lincoln, who attempted to attack Officer Weston. Mr. Lincoln was wounded in the arm, handcuffed, and taken into custody. No weapon was found near Mrs. Lincoln's body—only scattered dice. (Paragraph:) SUBSEQUENT EVENTS (all capitals, underlined): After extensive investigation, the Los Angeles County District Attorney's Office found that Officer Weston had reacted responsibly to secure the safety of his fellow officer. As a result of community pressure and alleged discrepancies between the statements of witnesses and the recounting of their statements in the District Attorney's report concerning Mrs. Lincoln's movements and position prior to the fatal shooting—and in response to subsequent heavy coverage by the media— . . . (Start that again:) Subsequently, the head of the Special Investigation Division of the District Attorney's Office ordered the matter reopened when witnesses claimed they had been misquoted in the official report and other groups cited alleged discrepancies. That report had described the attitude of witnesses as (quote) 'biased or prejudiced and marked by a dislike for authority' (close quote). (Paragraph:) Officer Weston claimed to have fired when he saw Mrs. Lincoln reach out on the ground for the assumed weapon. Neighbors of Mrs. Lincoln and others who gathered, claimed that Officer Katoff had ordered Mrs. Lincoln to lie face down on the ground with her hands behind her, and that it was in that position that Officer Weston shot her. Newspaper accounts cited as a discrepancy the coroner's report that the fatal bullet passed through both of Mrs. Lincoln's hands and penetrated her spine, seemingly corroborating the reports of her neighbors and friends. However, a shot which grazed her ear was unreported in the original autopsy report and subsequently was determined to uphold Officer Weston's and Officer Katoff's contention that the first shot or shots were in response to the initial (underline 'initial') threatening action. (Paragraph:) The second report issued by the District Attorney's Office confirmed

the original finding of accidental death and recommended that
no further action be taken against Officer Weston, found again
to have acted responsibly. (NOTE TO MYSELF: Condense the
preceding?—paraphrased from official reports from Internal
Affairs. Necessary to this report?) (Paragraph:) Officer Weston
continues to be the object of vast (make that 'wide') media
attention, protests in the black and left-wing communities (change
'left-wing' to 'liberal'), and renewed demands that further investigations be conducted and that Officer Weston be tried for
murder. Such demands have been rejected. Officer Weston has
been reassigned from field activity to so-called 'desk duties'
(quote 'desk duties') temporarily removed from the glare of the
public attention this case continues to generate. (Paragraph:)
PERSONAL BACKGROUND (all capitals and underline): I
I interviewed Officer Weston in my office on three (N.T.M.:
Check number of times) separate occasions for periods of ap-
proximately one hour each. He is a personable Caucasion male
of thirty-nine years, a veteran of fifteen years in the Los Angeles Police Department. At age eighteen, Officer Weston finished
high school and enlisted in the United States Army, where he
was assigned to the Military Police. Upon his discharge, he
enrolled in (blank, blank) College for a year and a half and
considered a career in electronics. Instead, his military background—and his negative reaction to the (quote) 'dopers and
beatniks on campus' (close quote)—led him to join the Police
Force at age twenty-four. He would have reenlisted in the army
during the Viet Nam conflict, but by then he had the duties of a
husband and parent. The same year he joined the department, he
married a woman named— . . . a woman he calls— . . . uh,
Debby . . . age thirty-six; *now* age thirty-six. (Check the name,
it might be Deborah.) They have two children, a boy, Paul, age
fourteen, and a girl, Laura Marie, age nine. Both are in school
and apparently well-adjusted, average children. Officer Weston
claims that his is a close family unit. They belong to a Presbyte-
rian Church, although, in Officer Weston's words (quote) 'we
don't attend services as often as we should' (close quote). His
performance has been satisfactory and in several instances
outstanding—especially in the area of youth-oriented projects,
including the Police Law Enforcement Scouts, a program which

familiarizes volunteer teenagers of both sexes with law enforcement procedures. That program has been, as he says, his (quote) 'pet' (close quote), along with programs directed to inform youths of the dangers of drug and sexual abuse. He has received commendations in these areas. He speaks proudly about his own children—his boy is apparently an athletic youth—(quote) 'a real boy' (close quote); and his girl—(quote) 'a real beauty' (close quote)—is studying ballet. He admits that he may be (quote) 'a little overprotective' (close quote) because of all he has been exposed to. (Paragraph:) FAMILY BACKGROUND: Officer Weston is one of two children. He has a sister—Bernice (Beatrice?)—two years his junior. His family's socio-economic background is middle-class (make that 'lower middle-class'; no, make it 'middle-class_ish_, underlining 'ish'— . . . oh, I'll adjust that later), his father having been a— . . . a— . . . (here it is) . . .—a pharmacist's assistant in Inglewood, a city just a few miles from Los Angeles and once a white, prosperous community, now predominantly black-populated; it was that situation which put Officer Weston in early conflict with what he calls (quote) 'nigger cutups' (change that to 'Negro cutups'—Officer Weston has a slight Southern accent, apparently absorbed from some of his fellow officers who come from the South, and so he probably said 'Nigruh'—close quote back there). His mother worked briefly as a grammar school teacher. (N.T.M.: Introduce here incident in bathroom— . . .?)'' *Ringgg! . . . Ringgg! . . . Ringgg! . . . Ringgg! . . . Ringgg! . . . Ri*— ''Damn . . . Hello! . . . Oh? Well, I am working late, and I— . . . No, it's *not* the answering service. This *is* Dr. Krug. Wait a minute, I've left the recording machine on.'' *Click. . . . Click. . . .* ''(Miss Burstyn, Mrs. Larkin called; try to give her an appointment as soon as I have an opening—the woman sounds hysterical.) (Memorandum continued:) Officer Weston describes himself as being an idealistic young man when he joined the force; he felt that that was a sure way to do (quote) 'something worthwhile' (close quote). Like most young policemen, he was at first given the most difficult field assignments—skid row, Main Street, Hollywood; all that, he says, (quote) 'initiated him and toughened him up and opened my eyes to the world as it really is'

368 *John Rechy*

(close quote). He is quick to point out that— . . . (N.T.M.:
Insert more of his point of view here or integrate later into my
conclusions? Leave some spaces here.) (Paragraph:) An ambi-
tious man, Officer Weston did what he calls 'stints' as a vice
officer ('stints' is in quotes); he explained that vice officers are
specially selected men who serve eighteen-month (quote) 'hitches'
(close quote). Because of exposure to this unusual experience,
they are regarded more highly for promotion. As a vice officer—
. . . (N.T.M.: Use here or later? Later, when I go into the
interdepartmental tiff— embroilment—matter—when he reported
a partner of his who tried to extort sexual favors from young
prostitutes in exchange for their freedom. Or omit? N.T.M.:
Leave matter of related reprimands for later, or out?) (Paragraph:)
PRESENT CIRCUMSTANCES (all capitals): Until (and underline 'Present Circumstances')—until recently, Officer Weston's
was a (quote) 'happy life' (close quote); his marriage was
(quote) 'successful, having all the good times and the usual
strains and stresses' (close quote). Since the shooting, the
investigations—and concurrent with the lapses in his official
duties—he has developed personal problems. He was reticent to
discuss these at first, but I was able to elicit information that
leads me to believe his marriage has begun to flounder (founder?)
and he is—he admitted—(quote) 'drinking more than I should'
(close quote). This is a problem his mother had. (N.T.M.: Insert
mother here?) Indeed, I believe Officer Weston is going through
a period of impotence (make that 'temporary impotence'). According to him, Debby (Debby is the correct name, Miss
Burstyn)— . . . According to him, Debby (I'll refer to her as
Mrs. Weston)—Mrs. Weston is constantly staring at him as if
(quote) 'accusing me of something' (close quote). Although she
was at least outwardly supportive of him throughout the
investigations, he is convinced this new attitude has to do with
the shooting. The fact that Mrs. Weston has begun to assume
some of the duties he staked out for himself as a caring father—
like driving his daughter to dance classes—he sees as confirmation.
On one occasion she read out in horror a newspaper account that
Mrs. Lincoln has (make that 'had') a daughter of Laura Marie's
age. That troubling domestic situation obviously has a negative
effect on his official performance—one reflects the other. He

equates his transference to a desk job as a reduction of his status; he has, in a sense, been rendered impotent in the field, so to speak. (Paragraph:) He is a man with a strong sense of the family backbone of his moral— . . . uh— . . . spine of morality— . . . The fiber— . . . (Leave a few spaces.) This is illustrated by his keen interest in the activities of youngsters—as described earlier. (N.T.M.: Use here?) This is in partial compensation for childhood traumas. (N.T.M.: Deal with later?) (Paragraph:) Officer Weston feels a deep sense of outrage that he was converted into a (quote) 'monster' (close quote) in the incident that is the subject of this report—although he was (quote) 'fulfilling his duty' (close quote). This syndrome of confusion, not uncommon, is similar to that of soldiers in war. Even when they know they are fighting justly, any criticism of killing sets into motion a whole syndrome of unjustified guilt, not for the official killing, no matter how regrettable, but, more, for child-hood guilts evoked. This has occurred in Officer Weston. (Paragraph:) He points out that (quote) 'after all, Mrs. Lincoln was trying to conceal legal evidence' (close quote) and that she instructed the teenagers—including her son—to 'do wrong' (enclose 'do wrong' in quotes). He resents the accusation in a newspaper editorial that his behavior may be part of what is currently defined as (quote 'a siege mentality—Them versus Us' (close quote) among law enforcement officers. He points out that (quote), 'after all, I have seen horrors that would curdle your blood—knifings, attacks, open perversion, assaults on children' (close quote)—and he says it is simply a matter of (quote) 'answering fire with fire' (close quote; and leave a few blank spaces after that; I may make more of that statement). He describes a growing frustration, shared by his fellow officers, about the lack of respect for law, the collapse of morality and religious values, the coddling of criminals, the leniency of judges, loose morals, the irresponsibility of parents to their children. He thinks children provide (quote) 'the only hope for the future—if they can be reached in time' (close quote). He feels very strongly that society (quote) 'must protect itself, just as medicine protects the body from deadly germs' (close quote; N.T.M.: Condense?) (Paragraph:) <u>GENERAL PSYCHOLOGI-CAL OBSERVATIONS</u> (all capitals): All neurotic compulsive behavior is goal-directed. (Underline 'General Psychological Observations.') When you understand the purpose of the neurotic, you understand the behavior. Such behavior patterns have to do with subconscious reenactments during periods of conflict of childhood rituals used as protection from fears, anxieties, bewilderments—that is, traumas. Any adult traumatic experience may pull out of the unconscious the protective rituals of childhood—altered into, or disguised as, apparently mature reactions. Repression and sublimation are ways of coping with neurosis. That much of Officer Weston's disturbed performance would emerge during his reassignment of duties 'to a desk' (that's in quotes)—putting him within view of his superior officers—reinforces the earlier pattern of the authoritarian father who— . . . Set into motion thereby is the— . . . the— . . . Set into motion are— . . . Aroused— . . . (N.T.M.: Adjust all this or delete; may be too technical?) Officer Weston's assuming the role of police officer may be said to— . . . (N.T.M.: Already used? Use later?) The ego resorts to strategies against disruption of its covert activities. Therefore, obsessional behavior— . . . (N.T. M.: Delete *all* of that?) "*Click*. . . . *Click*. "The manifestations of the unconscious may be compared to bodily functions. The contest between duty and desire is manifest in Officer Weston, echoing the syndrome of pleasure at war with punishment. (Delete or expand?) The adult is responsible and free. The child is irresponsible, thwarted in his freedom, deprived of the— . . . Deprivation is— . . . Clearly, deprivation is— . . . This may result in concealing— . . . Clearly, this may give rise to— . . . to— . . . to frustration. (Delete? Condense? . . . Expand?) (Paragraph:) PSYCHOLOGICAL OBSERVATIONS (all capitals and underline): The origin of Officer Weston's aroused sense of protectiveness toward children is at the core of his present disruptive pattern. After considerable probing by me, Officer Wetson—Wes*ton*—admitted that his father preferred his sister, two years younger than himself, to him. (Rephrase:) Officer Weston was two when his sister was born. Among his earliest and most persistent memories are those tinted—tainted—by the fact that (quote) 'my father made no bones about preferring my sister over me' (close quote). Officer Weston is resentful, although he tries to conceal this, that his mother did not (quote) 'put a stop to it' (close quote)—that is, the open partiality toward his sibling, which she could see clearly. The mother herself was apparently an aloof woman, given to drink, especially during a period when they were, in Officer Weston's words (quote), 'in a bad slump, real, real poor—but she kept drinking' (close quote). For a time, Officer Weston attempted to gain the respect of his father by being (quote) 'overly protective' (close quote) of his young sister. By imitating him, he would please his father—at the same time (quote) 'make up for' (close quote) his growing feeling of anger, resentment, and subsequent guilt toward his sister—the fact that she, too, was a child generated further feelings of ambivalence. Often he followed his father and his sister on their way to school, hiding along the way—(quote) 'becoming invisible' (close quote)—he was at once companion and friend and stalking adversary. Trying to disguise the pain it caused him, Officer Weston narrated an incident during which he walked into the bathroom when his mother was bathing his sister, then age eight, and he exhibited his penis. Clearly, this was a flaunting of his manhood to them—his asserting *his* sameness with his father and *their* difference. Although finding it amusing, the mother told his father, who punished him (quote) 'by sentencing me to solitary confinement in my room for three weekends' (close quote). With genuine pride, Officer Weston points out that he is not bitter at his father because, through him, he learned the 'discipline that made him a good soldier and a good officer' (quote from 'discipline' to 'good officer'). (N.T.M.: Did I make too much of sibling rivalry?) (Paragraph:) In a very real sense the adult Officer Weston had worked out his own trauma constructively. By becoming an officer, he himself became a symbol of authority his father had represented. (N.T.M.: Used before?) (Quote, and capital 'L') 'Like my father' (close quote) is a phrase he repeats often—and proudly. Through his commendable interest in youth activities, he not only accomplishes that role of father but compensates for his feelings of guilt involving his dislike for his sister—now married and the mother of twins. Paragraph. Officer Weston's views toward what he considers (quote) 'the perverted side of life' (close quote) stem from his background of concern for children. Prostitutes,

homosexuals, permissive parents, deviants from what he calls
(quote) 'the family unit' (close quote), he views as harmful in
direct proportion to the harm (change that last word to— . . .
leave a blank) they inflict directly or indirectly on children—by
exposure to (quote) 'their degenerate lifestyles' (close quote)
and by (quote) 'not reproducing to give a kid a chance at life.'
As a member of the vice detail, therefore, he became somewhat
overzealous, and on at least two occasions was reported for
having overreacted—once in the arrest of a black prostitute who
told him that she (quote) 'hustled to support myself and my
kids' (close quote) and another time when a homosexual who
made a sexual overture toward him turned out to be a family
man, with three children. In both instances, Officer Weston was
found to have acted with (quote) 'undue force' (close quote). He
was reprimanded—although, he points out, convictions resulted
in both arrests. (N.T.M.: Omit? Irrelevant?) (Paragraph:) We
come now to the afternoon of— . . . (Miss Burstyn, please get
the date for me; I have it here . . . somewhere . . . in my notes;
I think it's— . . . but I don't want to lose my train of thought in
this—. . .)." *Click. . . Click.* "(Miss Burstyn, I have lost my
train of thought, leave a few blank lines for me to fill.)
(Paragraph:) In both instances— . . . Oh, yes! On the afternoon
of blank, blank, blank, when Officer Weston received the Code
Nine-nine-nine signal, his anger was already aroused by the
suspicious man near the school grounds. Without in any way
discounting the officer's occasionally negative view of some
members of the black community, based on his exposure to
(quote) 'its worst elements' (close quote), what occurred was
subsequently seen by him symbolically in terms of his childhood.
I asked the officer to free-associate about recent events. Without
hesitation he chose to speak about the shooting. When he
learned the details of the situation—the teenagers, the tossed
evidence, Mrs. Lincoln's exhortation—Officer Katoff apparently filled him in immediately during those (quote) 'jumbled
moments' (close quote)— . . . When he— . . . It is clear that on
an unconscious level the fact that Mrs. Lincoln had exhorted, or
allowed, her male child (quote) 'to do bad' (close quote)—that
is, throw away evidence and run— . . . It is clear that that
evoked in him his mother's allowing his father to prefer his

sister. (N.T.M.: Adjust). So he shot at the woman who— . . . It is important to remember that Mrs. Lincoln—Mr. Lincoln—was (quote) 'looking on and allowing the bad behavior' (close quote; I'll adjust that later). By instructing the teenagers to elude rightful authority, Mr. Lincoln and Mrs. Lincoln— . . . (Start that again; my notes are a bit jumbled here:) It is very (underline 'very') clear that when Mr. Weston saw Mr. Lincoln (make that 'Mrs. Lincoln'), he— . . . that when he shot at Mrs. Lincoln, he— . . . Mr. and Mrs. Lincoln became, for him, *one* parent! (Miss Burstyn, leave a half page or more, I might have some more thoughts on all of that later.) (Paragraph:) Officer Weston affirms forcefully that he does not feel guilt about the shooting, although of course he regrets that a life had to be taken. In his words, it was (quote) 'a decision I can live with' (close quote). I find those statements accurate refections of his beliefs. It therefore becomes evident that his subsequently disruptive behavior in his official—and social—performances stems not from guilt over the shooting but from the evoked earlier traumas which until now he had been able to sublimate in his work. His present behavior results from transference, causing the disruption of his finely tuned defenses. (Paragraph:) PROGNOSIS (all capitals and underline): In these few therapeutic sessions Officer Weston has already achieved remarkable insight into the underlying causes of his recent behavior. Indeed, he stated as much to me. He has been twice cleared of wrongdoing during two grueling official investigations. He recognizes that his depression—affecting his work and his personal life—has its roots in childhood and not really in the present regrettable affair culminating in the death of Mrs. Lincoln. (Paragraph:) It is my strong opinion that, having faced that already, Officer Weston will become symptom-free within a reasonable period of time. Psychiatrically speaking, he has already begun the essential process of working through his problem. (Paragraph:) My prognosis is that the disruptive behavior will diminish dramatically, and that Officer Weston, after a brief period of adjustment, will resume his worthwhile performance as an officer of the Police Department. To that end, his staunch values—his sense of justice—must be reaffirmed. They have been shaken to their very foundations.

(Miss Burstyn, make three copies of this draft, I'll have to revise it substantially.)'' *Click.*

* * * * *

Officer Weston waited in his car. The shifting sun glared into his eyes. Out of the white blaze he saw the familiar car drive past him and park a block away on the opposite side of the street. Then the driver emerged.

He was medium-sized, younger than middle-age; he walked briskly and sat on the same bench where Officer Weston had first seen him, that afternoon. The man carried a magazine and pretended to read—but his attention was locked on the school hardly a block away.

Along the street, tall palm trees leaned away from the wind. Strawy leaves, the kind that hang limply from the bottom of the green-fanned trees, littered the lanes. Officer Weston saw one of the branches crashing down just ahead. For a moment he allowed his eyes to stray toward it, to pull away from the reflection, in his rearview mirror, of the man sitting on the bench.

The man on the bench set the magazine aside, his hand planted on it. Officer Weston looked across the street. School was out. Children moved in all directions along the gusty streets. They didn't walk or run—they seemed to push each other along, stagger, even fall, skip, bounce, hop, tangle on their own legs. Then they broke up into clusters, individuals. Several got into the cars of parents, others jaywalked to meet waiting, familiar adults, some paused at the crosswalks.

Three girls—perhaps nine, perhaps ten years old—moved in that jagged running, skipping, stumbling way toward the bench where the man sat, his hand pressed on the magazine. At the corner, one of the girls got into a car with a woman, the other turned into another block. The third one—dark-haired—shuffled playfully along the street, across it. On the bench, the man arranged himself rigidly.

Officer Weston's eyes were clouded with sweat. He mopped them with an already-soaked handkerchief. The man on the bench leaned forward.

Officer Weston opened the door of his car, stepped out into the heat and wind, and closed the door—loudly.

The man stood up from the bench and looked in horror at Officer Weston staring at him from across the street. Moments before the little girl would have passed the bench, he rushed away.

Abandoned, the magazine surrendered to the grasping wind. The man got into his car, not looking back.

Officer Weston saw the car back up into an intersection, and then drive off along the lanes of palm trees.

Back in his own car, Officer Weston made a U-turn in the same direction.

Alone, the dark-haired girl moved jauntily despite the wind. She kicked one of the dead yellow leaves away from her path. A rush of wind tugged at her legs. She pushed down her dress.

Officer Weston parked his car a few feet ahead. He slid over to the passenger side, and he unlocked the door. He arranged his rearview mirror. The little girl replaced the man who had sat on the bench. Officer Weston leaned back. He stretched his legs. His hands dropped between them. He undid the buttons of his pants. They opened on a hairy V. His hard, urgent cock pushed up.

Officer Weston felt cold excitement pierced by hot pain. His eyes focused as if through a red veil of steam on the dark-haired, light-complected little girl nearing his parked car.

Lost Angels: 13

He chose each one of us to go with him to Sister Woman, and the fourth one is— . . . "Orin, what is going to happen tomorrow?" Lisa woke startled. She sat up in her bed and looked at Orin.

Orin lay on the other bed. His eyes were already open, or they opened instantly. His hands were behind his head; his torso was bare—the first time he had slept without his undershirt since that night when he cried, that sexual night, Lisa realized. Opposite him, Jesse woke when she repeated her question.

Not *tomorrow*! Jesse knew, turning to give his full attention to Orin's answer. She thinks it's still yesterday-night. *Today's* Saturday!

Like a purplish scrim, the drawn curtains filtered the haze of beginning dawn. An edge of the wide window scorched orange by the rising sun threatened another day of ferocious heat. Reflections from the pool outside painted fiery waves on the ceiling.

Orin said, "I don't know."

But *today* is Saturday! Jesse almost said that aloud and he sat up in bed. Was it possible that Orin didn't really "know"! Cody *always* knew, *exactly*.

Jesse assuaged himself: Orin was talking about the part that depended vaguely on Sister Woman; there were several possibilities there—but *each* had a definite shape, a definite goal. Reassured, Jesse lay back, although the glow at the window extended like a luminous fan, announcing full morning. Before he closed his eyes, Jesse saw that Orin was shirtless and that Lisa—so beautiful, *so* very, very beautiful—was staring at Orin.

It's already tomorrow, Lisa realized, fully awake. As she

leaned back in bed, she wanted to hold back the dawn bleeding at the window, to will back the purple haze of an uncommitted day.

Jesse and Lisa woke again to the sound of water running in the bathroom. The door open, Orin was showering—a liquid shadow of flesh and reddish, water-darkened hair against the translucent curtain. Naked for moments, he emerged—the slender body defined. Surprised by the allowed nudity, Lisa and Jesse looked at the exposed form as he began to dress.

He had left the shower running, and it was as if that sound was washing away last night's unreality—morning continued to render the turbulent night unreal.

Lisa was about to close the door to take her shower. Orin said, "It's okay, Lisa." She showered behind the diaphanous curtain. She felt their gaze, welcomed it.

Jesse wished his eyes could part the curtain. Even through the translucence, her body glowed. For a moment Lisa, too, revealed her naked body, and then wrapped herself in a soft towel.

Jesse showered without even drawing the curtain, but he kept his back to the open door because he was hard.

Submerged for long—threatening and desired—the sensuality among them flowed into the exhilarated brightness bursting into the room as—like always before—the new day swept even further away the unreal, unwanted night. Now, neither Lisa nor Jesse were sure they wanted Orin to fulfill his promise to tell them "everything."

All three ready to leave for today's trek, at the door Lisa looked back at Pearl on a chair and almost ran to grab her, at least say good-bye—but she didn't.

They had breakfast at Denny's on Sunset nearby: eggs and bacon and hotcakes. The intimacy allowed earlier by their nakedness grew—they laughed, their arms would tangle as they reached for syrup, sugar, butter—and they would laugh; their bodies touched, they shifted legs under the table—and they laughed even more. Joining in their happy mood, the waitress told them it was "loads of fun to wait on people who didn't have a jag on."

"Well, I just *knew* we'd run into you again!" said the

jubilant woman they had seen yesterday at the Movieland Wax Museum. The hostess was seating her and her husband at a table just feet away from their booth.

"Well, hello!" Lisa tried to match the woman's dogged gaiety. "Mornin'," Jesse lengthened a drawl. "Mornin', ma'am; sir," Orin greeted courteously.

The woman's hairdo had barely been damaged by the wind, which had plucked it from its shield of spray only on one side. Her husband could not keep his eyes away from Lisa, who wore a ruffled white blouse, off her shoulders.

"Well, what do you recommend?" the cheerful woman asked the three, and the waitress. When she and her husband had ordered the Special Number Three with orange juice, she turned back to the booth. "Well, you know the way we just keep running into each other over and over, I wouldn't be surprised if we ran into you tomorrow at the Gathering of Souls."

Lisa and Jesse James looked quickly at Orin. With her words, the woman had dredged up what they had buried since the suspended interlude when Lisa woke up briefly this morning. His silver poised in midmovement, Orin stopped eating. He didn't look up.

"Well, you know, that's *really* why we're here," the exuberant woman went on, "for the Gathering of Souls and Sister Woman's fireworks display of miracles; and, well, you know, she's hinted of something *very* special."

Orin put down his silver, softly. He still didn't look up.

The woman continued her blissful gush. "Well, Lord, the *cures* that saintly woman has brought about, all those gifts to the Holy Spirit. Well, I just know hundreds of sinners will be slain in the Spirit of the Lamb," she went on ecstatically, and told them of "the little gift" they had just given themselves—"a new Chevrolet, especially for our drive to the Gathering of Souls tomorrow." She glowed with rapture. "Well, it's a two-tone blue car."

"You might just see us there." Orin finally looked at her.

"Well, that would be a joy—like a climax to our running into each other like this. Well, it can't be accidental. Well, it's like Sister Woman says, that there are no accidents under heaven!" She seemed beside herself with jubilation. Her flushed face erupted ino a series of smiles. Tiny utterances of happiness issued from her mouth. "Well, that would be just wonderful!—to run into you at the Silver Chapel on the Hill, for Sister Woman's Gathering of Souls, God love her and her blessed mission! Well, the way she actually extends salvation even to the *dead*— those who have died in sin!—through the intercession of the living! Well, I call *that* inspiring—and, well, no one else does it but Sister Woman."

"No one but her," Orin said somberly. He stood to leave. Then anger seemed to push out words: "That's what she *says*!"

The woman's laughter stopped. Her breathing came like panting. Then the bountiful good humor returned. "Well, this food is *delicious*!" she announced jubilantly over her plate.

As if feeling Lisa's troubled eyes on him, Orin looked at her—and he smiled. She smiled back at him, sexily but shyly. She and Jesse rose to leave with Orin.

Waving delightedly as the three left the restaurant, the happy woman chimed, "Well, good-bye—or rather, till we meet again."

Outside—and the wind was still for almost minutes—they saw a brand new dark and light blue Chevrolet with dealer's license plates.

"I bet that's their ole new car. Ugly," Jesse said, doubly proud of the classy Cadillac they'd be getting into. "You're hot as pistols," he told the Cadillac, and extended his words to Lisa. "That's what Cody said to that Verna when she walked out in a black negligy," he trumpeted his firm memory. He looked at Lisa—as sexy as that. "No," he was confused again, "he said *Verna*'d knock your eyes out—*he* was hot as pistols." The very last line of Cody's had hinted of lapping at the edge of his consciousness, but confusion shoved it back.

A motorcycle cop drove into the parking lot—all black sunglassed authority. Jesse got into the Cadillac quickly. Lisa had to climb over his long legs to sit in the middle. The cop looked at them through the menacing glasses. "What year is it?" He pointed to the car.

"Fifty-three," Orin answered, lowering the top.

"Beauty, real beauty." The cop looked at the car and Lisa.

Driving away, Orin said, "Relax, Jesse."

"Just got used to being nervous around cops," Jesse blurted,

" 'cause I was in the army—just a short time—underage! Kept going AWOL! Real restless! Kicked me out when they found out I was just a kid, and I had to go back to— . . .'' His sudden "confession" stunned him, even while he went on. "And when— . . .''

Orin stopped him. "Whatever happened in the past, that won't matter soon. Sister Woman promised. Wipe away all the tears." He said that happily.

"Aw*right*, kid!" Jesse said in the same mood.

Yes, Orin believed that! A fragment of last night's shattered darkness stung Lisa. And now Jesse seemed about to believe it, too! Reality stabbed through the hazy happiness of the day. "I want a flavor of the week!" Lisa rejected it all forcefully—and when they stopped at a red and white Baskin-Robbin's, she immediately began to devour the first of *two* double-scoop cones!

In the city on hot weekends, traffic is light in the afternoon; everyone has fled to the beaches early.

Orin, Jesse, and Lisa rode on Wilshire. "Let's, Orin!" Lisa said when they passed the famous La Brea Tar Pits. Taking the last delicious bite of her second cone, Lisa thought, It will all go on, like this, on and on and on.

"Yeah, let's!" Each time they had passed the park, Jesse had wanted to stop—but he didn't like being judged by a dismissed choice.

In an area of several blocks of green park, children played—there was the atmosphere of a fair—roaming clowns performing, people selling balloons like clusters of multicolored grapes; old people resting.

Among trees and shrubbery is a large pool of tar, millions of years old. Alive still, it bubbles in slow restlessness. Within it, a carefully reconstructed mastodon, a saber-toothed tiger, a giant bear stand petrified, a million years beyond their time.

As close as they could come to it from behind the wired fence that surrounds the pool, they watched the oily black surface of the tar, reflecting colors like a scummy rainbow.

"The animals were trapped in the pools!" Jesse learned from a placard nearby. "See," he explained, "they'd get stuck, and then pre-da-tors—one of *them*—would pounce on that animal, and they'd all sink into the tar, like quicksand. That's why *that* one— . . ." He pointed to a mastodon, entrapped, struggling against the dooming tars. ". . . —is fighting to get out. . . . "I wonder if he did," the awesome question struck him. He went on hurriedly, "And that's how scientists know what the animals looked like, from their bones."

And a small mastodon watched the sinking one in horror! Lisa felt sad—imagining the doomed struggle in the thickening trap.

Orin said, "Millions of years ago, and it was all forming." He reached up with one hand, feeling the rising wind.

In awe, Jesse James was silent. Millions of years—and here *they* were!

An incongruous modern building houses a museum there. "It contains the reconstructed skeletons of thousands of prehistoric birds and animals! From fossils!" Jesse read from his guidebook. Feeling Lisa's rapidly declining interest, he added, "And there's the skeleton of an Indian maiden!"

Lisa definitely did not want to go in.

They walked to the County Art Museum a long block away, a clean white structure of stairs and arches and stately square wings. Orin wanted to see the Modern wing. Lisa would have preferred the Old Masters—and Jesse didn't really care.

They stood before an enormous painting covering one whole wall. Colors collided with others as if hurled from the dark whirling center of the canvas.

Outside, the wind increased with the heat. They left the car top up. The radio was set on the news station. ". . . society. 'Audiences are *so* jaded,' Fred Haywood told me in an exclusive interview at the Polo Lounge," a woman's voice said. "Haywood has the job of arranging the entertainment for Rodeo Drive's International Gala Ball. He told me the challenge is to come up with an act that will excite the audience *after* the eight-course meal catered by the chef of Chez Toi. The exclusive black-tie affair will be limited to two hundred guests. Funds raised by the celebrity affair will go to the Orphaned Children's— . . ."

Jesse punched the country and Western station—sure of his

right to do so now—turning up the volume so they could hear the singer lament crushed dreams, and praise love sustained.

Orin turned off the radio. "The old woman, she had sinned grievously," he said. He faced straight ahead. He clenched the steering wheel tightly with both hands, but his voice was even. "All her life. Steeped in evil."

And so just like that, he was keeping last night's promise! Did he want to hear what was coming? Jesse wondered.

Seated between them, Lisa wished she were in back—to avoid the words.

"I was her eyes, read to her from her books—stories, everything. But only toward the last. The old woman said Sister Woman looked like a ghost, a messenger from beyond, because by then her eyesight was failing bad. Sister Woman—she spoke the most beautiful words you ever heard—and she spoke cruel ones, too—but you have to hear that, too, so you can choose whichever you want. She said she could wash away all the pain and all the sin. And even after death—if it was too late. The old woman, she listened—and I remember it all so clear. Sister Woman's words, they were like nothing you ever heard. Nothing *I* ever heard. Nothing the old woman had ever heard, either. So we wrote her. She wrote her first, in her great big letters— and then I wrote for her, what she told me. Wrote Sister Woman everything—all about the sins— . . ." He closed his eyes, held a long sigh, opened his eyes, repeated: "Sins, blackness, the sin; always, always failing, lower and lower until we almost touched hell."

We. . . . Jesse puzzled over Orin's word.

"Still alive and touching hell! And Sister Woman answered! She said she understood—everything. Understood everything!" Orin captured one word, softly—as if assuring himself: "Everything." Now he resumed in a cadenced, slow voice: "The old woman was dying, knew it; too late to save herself—in *this* life. Just in the next." He shook his head. A gentle smile touched his lips, then faded. "She got so thin I could lift her with one arm, almost. She's sitting in her bed, and she's saying, 'Orin, you underline that word *proof* in that letter; tell that Sister Woman we want *proof.*' " He paused, as if filtering memories.

"But she's not here and you are," Lisa said. She wanted to

hold him, shelter him—feeling his controlled pain, the mysterious hurt buried in his memories.

"Was she real, *real* old, Orin?" Jesse formed sad words.

"Fifty. Not quite that."

Jesse was jarred. He had thought of her as very, very old, the way Orin spoke.

Not yet fifty. Lisa, too, had imagined an old, old woman. The shifted reality confused, then disturbed her.

"The illness just got her," Orin seemed to answer their silent questions. "Long time a-coming, and then it just took over. But even then the sinning went on." His words erupted. "I stopped calling her my— . . . !" The rest choked. "But she stayed *so* beautiful." The gentleness returned. "Like a beautiful ghost."

Lisa looked at Orin's glazed eyes. Was the dead woman his mother?—the question floated on her consciousness. And the dark sin— . . . She pulled out of the disturbing currents, rejected the thoughts. No! The woman was just someone he had loved—loved strangely and powerfully. . . . A woman loved strangely. . . . Lisa's own troubled memories whirled. Even when she fled from her into the sheltering darkness of the cherished theaters, she was actually searching her, her mother, her mother's past, reflected in the silver black images of abandoned movie heroines, abandoned over and over and over, like her mother— that woman "who could have been a movie star." "I'm sorry," Lisa sighed into the wind.

Again Orin shook his head. "I think—I actually believe—the reason she cursed—her last words were curses!—was to make it real hard—*real* hard—on God. And Sister Woman. Challenging to the last moment!" He sighed an endless sigh. "So now Sister Woman has to prove to me that the blind woman is saved—out of the fires of hell. And then I can tell her— . . ."

Yes, like Cody talking to his dead Ma in the black wind. "How will she prove it?" Jesse asked quietly.

"She'll *have* to know how," Orin said, again as if the logic was obvious.

The aimless dream had found direction in a nightmare, and the nightmare could be ended only by waking—but if ended too abruptly, it might abandon Orin forever in its impenetrable darkness. And if Sister Woman did not give him the proof he needed, what?

The sun spilled long shadows as they drove past the glassy gravestone buildings of Century City.

"And if she doesn't give you proof, Orin?" Jesse knew he could ask questions now.

"She *will*." Orin's face clouded. The blue eyes deepened.

"But if— . . ." Jesse pursued just so far.

Orin's tone changed. "There's two wills. She wrote each one out by hand—by herself, so careful, each word. All legal. She checked over and over, made sure. I can destroy whichever one I want. Sister Woman knows that. Everything's waiting now. And it's up to her."

Jesse inhaled heat, which boiled in his body. He could hardly form the words: "How much money, Orin?"

"Million. More. Maybe two. Never thought to count it. Lots left for us," he smiled an important promise. Then he was somber. "When the old woman's at peace, really at peace, at last," he seemed to speak to himself, "then *I* will be at peace, too, from her life *and* her death—and I can let *her* rest from mine."

He had come to bury the dead woman—really bury her, in his mind—whatever she was to him, whoever she was. Lisa thought she heard hints of that now in the recurring echo of some of his haunting erratic words and lessons. To bury her. Was it the dead who reached out in anger to the living—or the living who didn't let go, in greater anger? . . . All the discarded awarenesses returned to Lisa now, jostling the dream of unperturbed aimlessness in this languorous city.

"There's a right time to die—and a wrong time," Orin's cadenced voice said. "Like if the best that's ever going to happen has already happened and nothing after will be that good; or if the worst is still to come and you couldn't take any more—then that's the right time; but some lives end before they're *finished,* and then others have to live for them, even die for them." The wind seemed to echo the rhythm of his words. "Depends."

Lisa thought of Maria.

Now he smiled the incongruous little-boy smile. "That explain just about all of it—like I promised?"

"And how do we figure in it, Orin, me and Lisa—with that Sister Woman?" Jesse asked firmly.

"Clear," Orin said simply. "Sister Woman said there would be four angels, four rebellious angels."

There it was again—the same illogical logic with which he delivered his lessons to them—allowing him to assert his fantastic reality to include them. And he *had* been able to lead them into the park, that deep night, led them to— . . . the fourth rebellious angel he had chosen, Lisa understood.

"Got to fulfill *our* side of it," Orin said, "so she'll have to fulfill hers. She wrote us back, lots of times. We read her letters, studied them, listened to every word in her sermons, me and the old woman did; and we understood. . . . The old woman would say, 'Orin, you mind now—can't let her have excuses. No excuses. Got to fulfill *our* side.' "

Our side. Jesse heard the sweet words. *"Our* side," he beamed aloud. Then with sudden anger he realized that Orin was including the man in the park! "What makes you so damn sure we'll go along with you, Orin—wherever the hell you're going?" His rage shocked him, and he glanced at Lisa for support.

"Don't have to," Orin answered easily. "Never did. Only if you want to. *You* decide. Don't have to do a thing a-*tall.*"

His shabby life till now; transformed. Jesse felt rejected by Orin's easy answer; his own question sounded mean, and it had left him abandoned. He felt frightened, a sense of loss. "I guess there's nothing wrong in wanting to know why that man in the park is so important to you—to *us,*" Jesse ordered his words carefully.

"Thought I did," Orin said. "Gotta be four lost angels."

Why four? Lisa wondered. Did *he* know?

"Talked to him, before I could even approach him, and— . . ."

"The mornings you were gone?" Jesse tried not to sulk.

"Yes. Told him about you; he had to see you to trust me," Orin continued, as if their questions, not his statements, might be strange.

That hot, hypnotized night in the park—when he pushed the

stone in signal. "And you went *looking* for him?" Lisa asked; said.

"Found him," Orin said. "Drew conclusions, studied it all from those news reports."

The same way he studied intricate structures, patterns. Lisa remembered him that afternoon at the Observatory, staring through the telescope, and then those boys set off firecrackers, like bullets.

"Half-looking, half *had*-to-happen," Orin said, " 'cause that's how things 'just happen.' Like I met you. Guess, yeah, I was looking."

Choosing *us* carefully, *finding* us. Like him—the man in the park. But *why* four! Why did that woman insist on *four*?

Jesse felt awed by coincidence which isn't.

"And if she can wash away the old woman's sins, she can wash away all our tears. All the guilt," Orin sighed. "All the horror we ran away from."

All the horror, Jesse James thought.

Guilt, Lisa heard. Horror. What if Sister Woman did give him what he wanted? What was the real test?

"And I saw four angels standing on the four corners of the earth," Orin recited last-night's echoed words. "These are they who come out of great tribulation and have washed their robes and made them white in the blood of the Lamb, but they shall hunger no more, neither thirst any more. For the Lamb which is in the midst of the throne shall feed them, and shall lead them unto living fountains of water, and God shall wipe away all tears from their eyes."

Jesse surrendered tension and anger. Four angels, he thought. Orin knew. *"Got* to be four," he said aloud.

Lisa looked fearfully at Orin and Jesse.

"Now we have to go to the park," Orin said. "Okay?"

Jesse nodded easily.

They would go with or without her, Lisa knew. And she *would* go with them. She loved them, and they loved her—and she—they—had to face what was out there, had to know what seemed and what was. That was the only possibility of pushing away the darkness looming over Orin—perhaps now over Jesse. "Yes," she said.

"Knew you'd see it," Orin said happily.

In the white desert, when Orin had stopped to pick him up, with Lisa so pretty already in the car—Jesse remembered the Cadillac like an apparition in the wavy unreality of sun and heat—as far back as then, Orin was collecting his "evidence," "fulfilling" his side! *Yes!*—he had rejected many others along the long highways, the many coffee shops and motels—choosing, searching for, him and Lisa! And so his determination to find and approach the man in the park made sense. Now Jesse did not feel threatened by that. He felt *special!*

It was late dusk when they reached the park. Vast parts of it were dark, shaded deep gray; others were still splashed by windy sunlight. They walked and ran into the heart of the greenness until they reached the naked rocks on which they stood that first time. Orin dashed halfway along the blackened burnt patch and toward the green mass. "It's Orin! And Lisa! And Jesse!" His voice mixed with the sounds of the wind.

The verdure remained sealed. Orin bolted across the bare stretch and plunged into the cove.

Perspiration melting like ice, Jesse gasped.

Lisa dashed against the ripping wind and toward the greenness that had swallowed Orin.

Inside the tangled enclosure of the cove—a shell of dried twigs, branches, vines, leaves—like the inside of a cave, the size of a room—inside, Lisa faced Orin—alone. Then Jesse was with them.

The enclosure was littered with empty cans of food, opened bottles, papers, a soiled sleeping bag, spilled iodine, a portion of a bandage. Sheltered from the wind, the cove contained a quivering stillness.

"He's gone," Orin said. There was amazement in his voice. "Said he wouldn't leave—*he promised!*" His voice veered toward franticness.

A part of the dangerous unreality had fled, Lisa thought gratefully.

In a carefully cleared space, a rifle lay.

"He *did* have a rifle." Orin's voice was puzzled. "He *lied*, said he didn't!" He frowned deeply.

Jesse leaned over the weapon. "Its an M-16," he identified

it. "Godamighty, you realize what he could've done with that? Could've sprayed the park in a second with— . . . Safety's on, though." He secured it doubly.

"He didn't *want* to hurt anyone," Lisa said adamantly.

Orin touched the rifle. Kneeling by it, he studied it, as if amazed by its simple complexity. Then he rolled it carefully in the green sleeping bag.

"Leave it, Orin," Lisa's strong voice said. "It's dangerous."

"Not with the safety," Jesse was proud of his knowledgability.

"Can't leave it," Orin said urgently. "Gotta take it away, 'cause now they're looking for where he was. If they find this, it'll be bad, real bad." He lowered his head. "And I have to tell Sister Woman I have proof there *were* four rebellious angels," he said. His voice slid toward panic. "Gotta have *my* side of the proof."

When they moved out of the cove, Lisa looked back at the sorrowing pines over the enclosure.

After Jesse and Lisa were in the car, Orin placed the wrapped rifle in the trunk.

"Drive out on the other side, Orin," Lisa said quietly, firmly, "Like on the first day we came here, remember?"

Jesse remembered, easily. Would it—could it—happen, finally? The mounting sensuality this morning— . . .

This side of the park was shaded purple. Light fell only in dusty slanted sheets. "Here," Lisa said.

It was the place where Jesse had almost challenged Orin in those moments of demanding sexuality that distant afternoon.

Orin parked on an isle of dirt off the main road. They got out.

This day's sensuality, released by Orin this morning with his nakedness and theirs—Lisa would use it. Eager—anxious—Jesse would help. She pointed to the trail, the path. They moved through it. Before the cove, Orin waited. For a moment, he looked puzzled—young, lost, innocent.

Lisa reached out and took his hand, leading him in—and pulling him away from the screaming ghost she felt sure his life had become a ritual to. Orin stared at her with eyes whose color melted into liquid blue.

Lisa's fingers slid down Orin's cheek, to the edge of his shoulder. She reached for his hand and placed it on the bare flesh over her low blouse. Answering her nod, Jesse's hand quickly coaxed the blouse lower, exposing a portion of one breast. His fingers touched the nipple. He thought, *It's happening!*

Orin's body trembled. He turned away. But Lisa held him, gently. His head lowered. "Help me!" Orin whispered. Lisa placed her lips on his. Jesse's hand cupped her exposed breast. Closing his eyes, Orin touched the other one, still covered. The blouse slipped down easily. Orin's tense hand—but not his lips—pulled away. Then his hand returned to the naked flesh. Jesse released Lisa's skirt, her panties, revealing the tinted softness between her legs, sequined in spurts of vagrant light. Then he connected his lips to hers on Orin's.

Lisa opened Orin's shirt. The two bare torsos pressed against hers, hands gliding. The three faces joined in moist lips, tasting flesh, perspiration—and Orin's tears?

Jesse lowered his hands. He turned Lisa's body more fully toward Orin's. Orin pulled back. Lisa touched the cool moisture on his face, soothing it, the other hand opening his pants. His cock, like Jesse's, was full and hard.

His arms enveloping the two bodies—and theirs his—the three mouths connected. Orin thrust into Lisa, and with a sigh of joy released from a sob of sorrow, he came—and Lisa felt the long, long orgasm. Jesse replaced him, his "Ah!" echoing Orin's and extending Lisa's, which had united the two. The three bodies held each other.

Then they separated slowly. They adjusted their clothes. Orin's head was bowed as he buttoned his pants, his shirt. Lisa and Jesse waited anxiously for his look. Orin turned away from them. Out of his wallet, he pulled a small paper, perhaps a photograph. He laid it on a rock near the opening of the cove. The wind carried away what he had placed there, as weightless as a soul. Turning, he smiled at them.

He had released a photograph, a constant presence, Lisa felt certain; and, along with the disappeared, mysterious man in the cove, that strange woman who beckoned nightly?—would he release *her* now? Yes, Lisa told herself. *Yes!*

As they descended in the car, an eerie smoky veil advanced on the darkened city.

They stopped to buy food. Outside the motel, they could taste ashes.

The closeness extended as they ate together at the familiar table. There was a shy embarrassment, but there was also a gentle, secure connection.

Then Orin looked at his watch.

No! Lisa saw him touch the television. Only for the news, she insisted. Only for the news!

Kenneth Manning's voice was excited: ". . . —estimated at least a week, more, living on canned food in the park. He gave himself up early this morning—or just wandered out into the area of the Observatory."

The picture on the screen showed the wrenched face of a man whose eyes were as colorless as the sweat that glistened on his cheeks, jaws, his exposed, skinny chest. He was wearing ripped combat clothes. His hands were handcuffed behind him. Police were leading him toward a black squad car.

The voice of another announcer, a man, was filling in the details. "Though unarmed when apprehended, the Viet Nam veteran who had escaped the hospital apparently thought he was back in combat in the jungle. We tried to get a statement." Several microphones were thrust before the terrified man ogled by eyes and cameras. The man's mouth opened. Screamed words spewed out: *"People burning!"* The police pushed him behind the blurred windows of their car, erasing the terrified face.

Now Eleanor Cavendish, in the studio, said, "We have a tape of Dr. Frederick Krug in his home in Beverly Hills. Dr. Krug is an authority on Viet Nam veterans who experience what are called 'flashbacks' and believe— . . ."

"I'm glad you took the rifle, Orin!" Lisa said fiercely. The image of the terrified veteran, handcuffed, remained. "Now they can't connect it to him."

On the screen, a man in his sixties, his head shaved totally, spoke authoritatively. "This is not an uncommon syndrome with soldiers. Even when they know they have fought justly, any criticism of war sets into motion a whole syndrome of unjustified guilt, not for the official killing, no matter how regrettable, but, more, for childhood guilts evoked— . . ."

Angrily, Orin turned off the sound.

"He wasn't going to use that rifle or he would have!" Lisa said.

"They'll take him back to the hospital," Jesse said sadly.

"But he'll run away again!" Lisa said.

"No," Orin said. "They won't let him."

The picture on the television screen had changed. It showed a building of astonishing architecture—slabs of silver plastic, dissected triangles, elaborate designs of angular geometry, all like a magnified, twisted snowflake. The camera pulled back on the enormous building to reveal rows and rows of pews, and, elevated and separated from them, a huge transparently silver platform behind which a radiance of plastic slabs burst into a giant fan.

Orin raised the sound: ". . . —thousands, a capacity sponsors believe will be exceeded tomorrow when one of the country's foremost evangelists and so-called faith-healers—known only as Sister Woman—will hold what is being billed as a 'Gathering of Souls in the Silver Chapel on the Hill.' The chapel was completed earlier this year at a cost of eighteen million dollars. Joining Sister Woman will be other major figures in the evangelical movement, now arriving from all over the country. The giant crusade will open tomorrow, and its sponsors predict countless miracles, cures, and spiritual manifestations known as 'slayings in the Spirit.' . . . Well, finally, folks!"—Eleanor Cavendish wiped her brow in emphasis—"it looks as if we may—*may*—be in for some relief from the Santa Ana heat, at last. Unfortunately, the winds have already fanned two major fires, threatening to link into one." The camera exposed a semicircle of fire like a blazing, broken crown.

Orin stood with his back angled to the screen.

"Tonight she's got to give us proof," he said.

And Lisa knew that what had occurred in the park was not an ending to the ritual, which must now unwind, fully.

Orin shifted channels.

Jesse looked in panic at Lisa. What would happen now!

Lisa remembered the two gentle heads that had leaned on her shoulders in the cove, in the park.

The blazing cross appeared on the screen. On her throne-

backed golden chair, Sister Woman sat alone, robed in white
satin woven through with golden veins of thread. Not even her
private breeze intruded. On her lap, her hands were slain birds
to be resurrected. The camera framed the delicate white features
of her face, as still as a photograph. Tears gleamed, tiny pieces
of melting ice on her dark lids.

Orin sat on the edge of the bed. Jesse and Lisa flanked him.

"Please," Orin pled to the figure on the screen. "Please say:
'I am here.' Say it, say it! *'I am here.'* Say it, Sister Woman,
please." He seemed to want his words to penetrate the screen,
the woman's mind. His exhortation assumed the rhythm of
prayer. "And then I'll know she's speaking through you, just
like she said she would, if you really did what you claim, and
all you have to say is, 'I am here,' that's *all* the proof I need,
she *told* me—and I'll hear her through you and I'll know she's
saved. And me."

Say it for him, Lisa pled silently. Jesse's hand was cold on
hers.

Sister Woman's red mouth opened. It formed four slow
whispers: "Awesome. Wondrous. Glorious. Terrifying." She
began tonight's sermon. "Awesome, wondrous, glorious, terrifying are— . . ."

Sister Woman: "Slain in the Spirit"

". . . —the fireworks of God!" The voice that had begun as a whisper soared to an exalted shout.

Palms out, fingers trembling, hands rose before her—men and women attempting to touch the radiance of her power. Young, old, they sat before her in arcs of ascending rows.

From her golden throne elevated by three concentric steps before the truncated cyclorama of sky, Sister Woman faced the television studio. Cameras on dollies swiveled to point at her like guns she commanded. Wires tangled in confused black and white veins. Microphones floated, lights on racks rose and drifted, a controlled constellation. Behind cameras, men advanced, retreated, adjusted angles.

Sister Woman's icy tears thawed. Her hands continued their deep slumber. "There are no accidents in heaven. In the divine order of things all is perfect, and God's perfect design is called 'salvation.' There is no substitute. The world began with fire when the flaming light of God ordered the chaos of night and the spirit poured forth resurrection. As it began, so will it end—in scorching flames of— . . ." She hurled the word, a bolt of judgment: ". . . —fire!" Her hands thrust out in sudden life, the satin sleeves sliced like merciless blades. In the filtered key light kept on her throughout so that she assumed an aura of ageless immutability, her long hair gleamed like white gold on pale, pale shoulders. For this sermon, her private breeze was stilled.

Nightly in incantatory tones and with configurations of her hands, Sister Woman mesmerized her vast following. They waited in early-forming lines outside the religious television station she ruled.

Now her voice hummed. "On the eve of this spring's Gathering of Souls at the Holy Silver Chapel on the Hill, in the season of renewal, let us speak of revelation— . . ." The soft chant broke violently. ". . . —and warn of . . . *doom*!" Her long pause extended the brutal threat, hinting of irrevocable finality. "And offer proof!"

Already her words carried an additional power! The Lord had armed her doubly against Satan. Tonight she would speak not only to her congregation in the studio and beyond, but to that doubting man who wanted *special* proof. Though he did not know what that youngman looked like, Brother Man tried to search the mass of faces in the studio, because, yes, it was possible that he might be out there, this moment, to receive his proof—*and she would give it to him!*—and if he was not here now, later perhaps, drawn by her magnetizing power—even *before* the Gathering of Souls! But refracted cylinders of colored lights obscured Brother Man's vision. He saw only the roaming shadows of hired guards. Even as pure a woman as *she*, was not immune to violence. And that youngman Orin— . . . The urgency of his calls. No!—he pulled his thoughts away from those *she* had rejected.

He looked at her. *An aristocrat among new, clowning evangelists!* Beyond the edge of encurvated artificial sky, Brother Man thought that with pride. No grotesquerie of halting voices for her—no stupid entertainment, no whining choruses. Those who flocked to Sister Woman came to hear of a real God, a real Satan; to hear powerful mysteries and secrets revealed; to sway in the song of His blessings, tremble in the fear of His wrath— all through *her*—and to hear of real angels battling every ferocious second for *their* souls.

In a prism of shadow etched by slabs of studio lights, the tall, slim form of Brother Man was clothed in the usual subdued, tailored suit. Although he would not go on camera tonight, he had been made up as usual, in his own dressing room; that was part of each night's treasured ritual. Then he would go to Sister Woman, cherishing the soft moments when, standing beside her, he shared her mirror, her reflection, and was blessed by her halo of silver lights.

"Fire rages in the city at this very moment, devouring canyons.

Ignited winds scour the earth.'' Sister Woman clasped her fingers before her eyes, to emphasize the horror of her privileged vision of damnation. "But that is as nothing compared with the rage of souls in the fires of doubt, courting the fires of damnation.'' When she delivered her sermons, her exalted sermons—not the lessons she gave most often, almost simply addressed, sitting facing Brother Man, who asked questions for her certain answers—no, when she truly preached, she tantalized with what seemed random themes at first, insinuating evocative words, at times breathing asides to a particular soul in dire need.

In the monitoring room, multiple screens fractured her image— one capturing her intact, a distant white-robed figure against the electric sky, another the abandoned hands, a third the colorless then suddenly black eyes. The director pointed an assertive finger at the framed shot of her widening eyes, a camera moved in on her face. A small, nervous man, a middle-aged cherub in checkered pants and white sweater, he orchestrated and choreographed lights and cameras—sky and clouds—with his own elaborate language of hands.

"For just as when the seventh seal on the Holy Scroll was broken by the Lamb,'' Sister Woman began to insinuate her fateful theme for tonight, "when the sun became black, the moon bled, the earth trembled, stars fell like torches—*and the earth was blinded!*—so we, too, will come to know that the day of wrath is come."

A sob erupted. A woman in the studio congregation reached for an invisible presence, and staggered into the aisle: *"I am born!"*

"She's slain in the spirit!'' a man in awe uttered Sister Woman's phrase, which described a state of grace wrenched out of spiritual struggle.

A sharp stab of the director's fingers at the screen on the monitor! The ready camera circling like a vulture pounced on the ghostly reconciliation. Within the stare of the camera's trap—the director had locked his fingers—an usher in a tuxedo mantled the crying woman, draping a white cape over her. The director's fingers sliced back toward an image of Sister Woman.

Although her sermon had just begun, off-camera, in a long

glassed booth, two dozen or more operators for the Mission of Souls held telephones to their ears, accepting offerings, love gifts, pledges to witness. The last few days' sermons, tinted with hints by Sister Woman of "something awesome" to be revealed tonight or at the Gathering of Souls—perhaps both days, in stages—had generated a nervous excitement, carried within the urgent ringing of telephones.

Her racked hands assumed the attitude of quiet prayer. She proffered hope: "And on the eve of the Gathering of Souls, let us remind of the eternal offer of salvation, yours to take, like sweet, ripe fruit from the sheltering tree of God." The blessing of a smile appeared on her reddened lips. Often—like now—she would stop for extended moments, lean back on her throne, eyes closed, as if private voices speaking *to* her might soon speak *through* her—or as if to receive divine inspiration. Then words might pour out. Now they devoured each other: *"Fire! can! scorch!"* Again the words slowed, were extended: "But . . . the same . . . fire . . . can . . . also . . . purify." The last word stretched, was held. Her whole body unclenched—arms, hands, fingers extended to their limits. *"Divine fire can purify even in hell!"*

There it was, her essential bold promise, what they came to hear. While others offered salvation, she threatened damnation—and then dared to extend the greatest reprieve—salvation within the very smoking flaming depths of hell. Conquering all the raging controversy it aroused, her message assuaged the guilt of the sinful living for the sinful dead.

"I am wallowing in the spirit!" a black woman quivered. She was draped in the white mantle. The moans of the audience rose, their hands toward Sister Woman in her painted heaven. "I am in the spirit!" A man was slain in the same powerful thrust. One of the ushers mantled him, too. The director made a decisive motion—rigid hand slicing his neck: No more manifestations of holy slayings on camera! Only exulting voice-overs would be captured by the roaming microphones now.

"Thus saith the Lord: Assemble yourselves, and come, gather like an army on the mountain." Sister Woman clenched one fist, raised. "Come, that ye may taste . . . salvation!" She cupped her hands into a chalice and drank airy benediction. "He is ready for combat!" her voice trumpeted.

"Reveal to us!"

"Let us see Him!"

Watching her reflected on flanking screens, Brother Man realized in constantly renewed wonder that through the miracle of television that same image was this very moment hurtling miles and miles to those who would wait into deep night—and journeying even farther in syndicated segments. Her spirit over electric airwaves was as ubiquitous as the spirit over troubled waters. She was where she belonged—on the throne she had earned from the moment years ago when she descended into hell to war against Satan—and screamed words he would remember forever, words she sometimes used to illuminate her sermons, words he often repeated—but only silently, to himself—to borrow strength out of the turbulent time of her fierce battle: *"Blood! White! Red! Black! And the pale rider!"* . . . *"Open the door of fire!"* . . . *"I am here!"* . . . *"Power over thee!"* . . . *"I am slain in the spirit, the Lamb protects me!"* . . . *"It is done! I am here!"* And out of that battle she had emerged triumphant, God's power flowing through her hands; and her growing congregation called the girl Sister Blessed until she became Sister Woman!

And that man from Massachusetts *dared* to demand *proof!*

"Yea, the water is troubled, evil dwells among us," Sister Woman bemoaned, her head bowed. "Sin reigns—fornication, avarice, greed, lust, adultery, pillage, abomination, pride, blasphemy, lust, envy, covetousness, idolatory, gluttony, sloth, incest!" At each sin, her hands clenched and unclenched, clenched and unclenched on the curved arms of the golden chair. "I am against thee, Satan! *Power over thee!*" With a slash of her hand, Sister Woman denounced the invisible demon.

Earlier today, they had walked along the hedged, shaded lanes of their guarded, vast estate, where they were born; they watched the glow of fire gathering miles away above them in these days of auguring wind. Sister Woman told Brother Man that tonight she would go on alone. Brother Man never questioned her wisdom. The Lord did not speak to him, although at times he was bold to think that he heard His sigh.

"Prepare to gather on the hill tomorrow," she told the cameras and the congregation in the studio, already swaying to her holy rhythms. "Come to the Gathering of Souls!" Her tones were soft. "And they *will* gather. For in a vision I have seen something awesome soon to come. Tonight? Tomorrow?" She shut her eyes as if to pull out of darkness more of that vision. Her words became a whisper, an intimate reminder. "And after these things have come to pass, I will see four lost angels at peace—and a woman, a woman at rest, at last—and many more souls!—for God shall wipe tears from their eyes and the former things will pass away."

Two weeks ago a letter arrived in the handwriting that had become familiar, signed by the name just as familiar: *Orin*. This letter announced the death of the woman in Massachusetts. It was only one in a series of letters that had commenced after a scandal-tabloid printed an article about Sister Woman's—their—mother and father; a lurid delving into deep wounds. The first letter from the woman in Massachusetts enclosed a sizable donation and began with the words *"You* know!" Then the letters—always containing a generous gift of love—were written for her by the youngman named Orin. . . . Soon after the announcement of the woman's death, there followed another letter; the youngman would trek to the city to bring the dead woman's true gift. *If!* Sister Woman told Brother Man Satan was preparing to wage battle. Through the sorrows of this man and the dead woman he was challenging her—again. She knew the signs. She would fight!

"The Book of *Revelation*, of what has come to pass and what is to come—the Book of Apocalypse—the last book of the Bible—the Book of John the Divine—to it, to him, to Jesus, who spoke through him—and left pages for us to write on, through his inspiration—to it, to him, let us turn tonight for proof . . . of promises."

Proof! Through the preceding days, Brother Man suffered with Sister Woman as she waited for revelation in the vined grotto of their sprawling mansion in the hills. The man Orin wanted proof that the departed soul was saved—she had insisted on it. Oh, Sister Woman had proof, of course; she conveyed it nightly to those who came to her in sorrowful need—and she

had conveyed it to the blind woman, assuaging her in letters—
"Yes, I know Satan," Sister Woman wrote her—during her last
turbulent days; but this man Orin demanded something definite,
unstated—which only he and the woman knew—in exchange
for a "great manifestation" of the dead woman's devotion.
Sister Woman had more than mystic powers, and she ascer-
tained the veracity of the letters; yes, the Lord guided her to the
truth of the woman, her life, her growing illness, the youngman—
and the truth of the black sins and of the accumulated fortune,
which would allow her to extend salvation to even more souls.
For that reason—and because of the woman's urgent need of
salvation, and the man's!—their souls in mortal danger—Sister
Woman accepted the challenge. Then the telephone calls came;
the man was in the city with others, for proof! When Brother
Man expressed fear, Sister Woman shook her head—there was
no danger. She waited for instructions from heaven. But the
vortex of wind muted the voice of divine direction, the hot earth
and its whirling elements conspired against it. They knew the
name of the powerful conspirator, a presence from their childhood.

Even as children, they had heard his sounds of blasphemy, of
madness *demanding* doom. In the cavernous house those growls
of Satan issued from their father and mother—while the somber
woman who came to take care of them, the only grandmother
they had, read to them from one book, the Book, the Holy
Book.

Someone had entered the studio!—a man; another? Past guards!
Brother Man knew the ruses Sister Woman's followers managed—
to enter once doors were locked. Tonight the invisible powerful
presence of that youngman shaded the service. The two figures
sat down.

"Proof?" In one movement Sister Woman's hand glided
from her heart to a Bible beside her, revealed now in a blazing
sword of light. The gold letters on black radiated as if kissed by
heaven.

Later, fleeing into hidden rooms, into coves in the wilting
gardens, the two children drowned the shrieks of madness by
screaming out the words of God the woman taught them. They
shouted them against the insanity sweeping the house now like
razing fire. The girl's shoulders trembled then—and, once, the

boy held her, to still the fear; he touched the tear-moistened face. "No!" she screamed and flung his arm away. She faced the house beyond the maze of gardens. *"No!"*

"But hear the words of *God!"* Sister Woman brought the Bible to her lap, her hands absorbing its power.

Then in the echoing house the howls of pain or laughter were throttled. There were two full days of silence. The solemn woman praised God and instructed the girl to go into the quieted room.

With her eyes closed, Sister Woman recited the invocation from the Book of *Revelation*, the most mysterious book of the Bible: " 'Grace be unto you, and peace . . . from Jesus Christ— who is the first begotten of the dead.' " She began to gather her proof.

The girl found her father and mother dead in the bed rancid with liquored vomit and among scattered deadly pills and broken hypodermic needles. When she saw the naked bodies, limbs entangled, she fainted—or so the boy thought.

" 'These things saith the first and the last, which was dead and is alive,' " Sister Woman continued to pick phrases from the strange book. She sat so straight, the folds of satin were like solid liquid.

For seven days and nights the girl thrashed in raging fever. Throughout, a doctor—or several—and aunts, uncles, close and distant strangers—and the somber woman—hovered about the dying child. The boy and the woman kept an unbroken vigil beside her. Desolately he whispered into her ears memorized words from their favorite book of threatened angels.

" 'For he who overcomes shall not be hurt by the second death.' Oh, hear it: 'The first begotten of the dead! Which was dead and is alive! The second death! Blessed and holy is he that hath part in the first resurrection! And the sea gave up the dead which were in it, and death'—*and hell!*—'delivered up the dead!' *Hell . . . delivered up . . . its dead!"*

On the first day of the girl's fever, she writhed in bed, screaming, *"No!"* over and over, her colorless eyes opening only to seal, as if to thwart unspeakable horrors flashing before her. On the second day her cries were pierced by clear words: *"Blood! White! Red! Black! And the pale rider!"* On the third day she was so peaceful, so silent, that the boy thought she was dead. Then she opened her eyes and demanded, *"Open the door of fire!"*

Behind the throne, twilight darkened her sky as clouds of gray light grappled in the simulated heaven. *"Blood! White! Red! Black! And the pale rider!"* Now with those words from the time of her fever, Sister Woman introduced into her sermon the four horsemen of the apocalypse, beginning the orchestrated narration that would bring her to the brutal crescendo of her startling promises: "And in heaven the Holy Scroll containing the mystery of life was sealed with seven seals, which only the Lamb was worthy to break. And on the breaking of the first four seals, the four horses of the apocalypse raged through the devastation of pillaged plains! Four riders! One on a white horse sent out to conquer in war, one on a red horse to bring strife and rob the earth of peace and cause men to kill, one on a black horse wreaking havoc and famine! And the pale rider on the gray horse—the pale horse of Death—was followed by *Hell!*" Now she roamed over the visions of that most hallucinated book of the Bible, rearranging its sequence into a pageant of her own, rechoreographing the violent events. Those who listened to her did not care, they came to hear *her* private truths, *her* revelations—and so the same book's warnings against adding to the words of prophecy did not extend to her inspired interpretations, buried holy truths which she unearthed—and it was that she gave them and wove a complex web of mysteries and secrets—to be felt, not understood—until she wanted to be understood, and was—lashing her meaning in scorched words.

On the fourth day of her fever, her eyes wide open but blind to those about her, even to the boy, the girl shouted, *"I am here!"*

The director made circles in the air. A cameraman seated on a movable contraption of steel stalked the throne.

In breaths that erupted into shouted ire—symphony of blessings, cacophony of curses—words and phrases that could flow like a river purling comfort in rivulets of surcease or flood wrath in waves of devastation; and with the turbulent dance of her hands, swirling in arcs, gliding like air, crashing like lightning, she evoked now from her throne fire, earthquakes, stalking death, plagues, wars, pestilence, the wrath of God in seven vials, blood, burnt earth, poisoned seas, blinded sun, darkened air, the voice of many waters, seven stars, and— . . . She wove these words slowly, clearly, words she wanted understood: ". . . —the punishment of the woman in purple and scarlet, dressed in gold and precious stones of sin—drunk, the mother of harlotries and blasphemies." In hypnotizing rhythms—and the congregation swayed, hummed—she described the Court of Heaven as if she were among the witnesses in white garments about the throne of God, and her hands formed the orbits of planets, earth, sun, stars, and then she destroyed her constellations. "And two more seals were broken releasing the sobbing martyrs and stirring the earth!" Now her voice became subdued, the colorless eyes deepened toward black in shadowed light. Even her satin robe was hushed as she approached the mystery of the seventh seal, as she prepared the cruel images to be clearly understood. Her face was like painted ice.

On the fifth day of her illness her brother saw her thrashing. She sat up and screamed, *"Power over thee!"* On the sixth day she gasped, *"I am slain in the spirit, the Lamb protects me!"*

In the studio, guards converged on . . .! No, just ushers silencing a woman attempting to speak in tongues. Brother Man looked at his sister, so serene on her throne. *She* was not afraid, and so to be apprehensive was to distrust her, and to him that was blasphemy. Wherever he was, that youngman Orin would soon praise her!

On the seventh day she woke him as he lay on the cot they allowed him in her room. *"It is done,"* she sighed and fell asleep. A few hours later, she woke again. Her face was cool. The fever was gone. *"It is done,"* the girl said. *"I am here."*

Against the cyclorama, Sister Woman waited, extending silence. A sphere of light enclosed her, separating her from darkness.

"Mother and Father were burning in hell," the girl told her brother and the woman who stood over her with the book. "I waged war with Satan for their souls. I have pulled them out of the bottomless pit. Now I must dedicate my life from here on to the Lord." The woman knelt, and so did Brother Man.

Her careful spell constructed to be smashed, Sister Woman still waited to crush it. The hypnotized would be awakened harshly, ready to grasp for God's salvation. *Now!* She shattered their trance: *"The seventh seal was broken, Heaven watched in awe and saw— . . ."* She flung her words at the moaning congregation: *". . . —Jesus—in hell!"*

In a torrent she unleashed the words that would conquer souls:

"Nailed to the cross, the sky a war of elements, Jesus looked up and pled for the living: Father, forgive them for they know not what they do! And in hell, flames scorched higher in rage at the radiance of his holy sacrifice! The damned writhed in boiling rivers of their loathsome sins! And the Lord looked down into hell! And he pled for the damned: Father, forgive them for they know *now* what they *did*! Between the Crucifixion and the Resurrection, Jesus descended into hell! *Open the door of fire!* He floated over the vile brimstone! And Satan roared out of the blaze: Thou art Lord of the saved in heaven, but I am Lord of the damned in hell! And Jesus saw the tinderwood of the fiery nation materialize as the evil Lord forced his slaves to perform each deadly sin before him in a pageant of corruption! And howled blasphemies damned Jesus and heaven! And limbs of fire formed writhing copulations! And lust roared out in panting curses and laughter! But out of the whine of evil ordered by the prince of darkness, out of the unclean laughter, the riot of lust, Jesus heard the sad, pleading whispers buried within the rising conflagration: Save us, O Lord of the Universe, save us who live in hell! And the Lord ascended to the throne of heaven and petitioned God for a second death of purgation, a new salvation— and it was granted! And bands of angels lunged into the pit! And heaven and hell warred on the raging battlefield of the abyss! And the Lord poured out his power, and one lost angel was freed! And the Lord extended his might, and another lost angel was set loose! And the Lord drew holy strength, and a third lost angel was released! And the Lord battled fiercely, and a fourth angel was unchained! Four angels freed! And then more released from burnt damnation! The sinful dead rose against the devil's deception of them! Those deceived into unrepenting, blinding sin struck in revenge for the heat of hell! *Oh, when the seventh seal was broken and heaven was stilled in awe, the souls of the dead damned to hell rose against Satan and were saved!''* In triumph, Sister Woman grasped for heaven.

Praise God! They are risen! Help them now, Jesus! Oh, beloved savior! Help us now! Bless you, Sister Woman, and the power of the Lord!

Sister Woman paused as the camera pulled back on a clearing sky. "And how did that come to pass?" Her black eyes were colorless again. "Because gathered about the cross of His martyrdom, the faithful *living* prayed and repented, stirring the power of angels, saints and martyrs, the warriors of God. It was the *living* who gave them that power! *You!*''

Only this afternoon in the grotto, the word had come. The wind inhaled, its howling abated. "The Lord has guided me at last," Sister Woman told Brother Man. "He has instructed me to deliver the same sermon that the lost woman and the lost youngman first responded to. He will imbue those past words with new ones, and in them will be his proof.'' They retreated to her viewing room draped in black, and they watched the tape of that sermon the man and the woman responded to. Brother Man saw Sister Woman's lips move in rehearsal of her own past words, and she added others aloud.

Yes! Jesus had surely whispered into her ear, Brother Man knew. Yes! At this very moment that man—wherever he was— would be receiving ineffable proof! Yes! And he and his great offering would cause all to marvel at the power and the glory of Sister Woman and the Lord. Yes! His eyes attempted to search the massed audience again. And again he could make out only the ominous shadows of guards moving along the aisles, pausing, moving.

Now Sister Woman leaned forward, speaking intimately to each listener. "After the death of someone loved—a mother! a father! a sister! a brother!—did you sob in anguish in the desert of your loss? Did you regret?—cry out, If only I *had*—! If only we had *not* . . .! If only I could shout into heaven or hell and be heard! If only I had another chance, more time, an inch of time, a few seconds more, a moment, a breath, a sigh, a sliver of a magic moment, a glimpse— . . .!'' She stopped. "Oh, hear the agonized screams of those in hell! Feel their pain as they walk on scorching stones! Hear them choke on bile and vile smoke!

Those you love tortured beyond imagination! Hear their howls of agony!''

"I hear them!''

"Please! Stop their pain!''

Moans of tortured ecstasy rose.

Within the twisting hysteria, a slender form moved urgently out of the dark shadows in back and into the penumbra of colored lights. Seeing it—but swept by Sister Woman's glory— Brother Man allowed no fear this time.

"If you could save them, all regrets would be swept away!'' Sister Woman pulled back the tide of accusing memories she had unleashed.

"Help them! Help us!''

"Tell us how!''

"How?'' she breathed softly. "Oh, with your tears shed in repentance for sins, with your purity, your trust, with acts of sacrifice, offers of love.'' Rivulets of words flowed. Her tears gleamed like diamonds, precious presents. The opened palms poured her abundant promises. "And *those* will quench the flames and blow like a cool sea breeze over the fires and soothe the captive souls—and allow the *second* death, the *new* resurrection, *salvation! and your own will be assured!*'' Other words rushed: "Just as your evil will fan the flames into fiercer heat torturing in unspeakable pain those you love!'' She leaned back, the battle fought. *"Choose!''*

"I have chosen!''

"I have purified, I am purified!''

Then a man's urgent voice screamed, *"You have given me proof, Sister Woman!''*

It was him! Brother Man knew. He saw only a dark shadow.

The slender form stood in the aisle.

Sister Woman rose from her throne.

The man did not walk toward her. Guards and ushers moved about him.

Brother Man advanced beyond the impeding lights.

Sister Woman remained standing, staring.

Brother Man knew what she must already have known: It was not him. It was an old man, trembling now in holy frenzy, mantled in the white robe. But tomorrow it *would* be that youngman Orin!

Standing, Sister Woman was tiny. She was a tiny, fragile woman. Now into the camera she sighed, "Oh, tomorrow! At the Gathering of Souls! Bring your gifts of love to God, your souls! Announce your presence and say, exultantly: *I am— . . .!*"

She stopped. She stared deeply into the camera. Her eyes were black, black. She waited, as if listening for urgent words.

She finished: ". . . —and say, I am slain in the spirit of your love, O Lord, for You have given me proof of the fireworks of God!"

Brother Man shut his eyes, blinded by her beauty.

Escorted by several guards, Sister Woman glided away from the studio, away from the sobs, the pleas, the grasping hands. Quickly, Brother Man covered the tiny form with a white satin cape. Although since the seven days of fever she had never perspired, after her sermons, her body quivered. Along halls and cubicles he led her to her dressing room. Guards remained outside.

Brother Man closed the door. Sister Woman sat on a white sofa. One large picture—of Jesus rising out of dark flames— hung on her walls.

The telephone rang.

Sister Woman held the receiver to her ear, she did not utter one word.

The voice at the other end of the line said, "Sister Woman, you are a disciple of Satan."

She closed her eyes.

The controlled voice of the man continued. "You warned that Satan deceives, in order to deceive more cunningly yourself. *You* are his deceiver. You gave no proof, you just added words to the sermon she drew false hope from. You lied. You gave me—and the blind woman— . . . You gave *me* no proof. She told me what the proof would be, Sister Woman, and then I would know you had reached her, the way you promised; I would know because she would speak to me through you when you would say, '*I am here.*' "

Seconds after he had hung up, Sister Woman kept the receiver at her ear. Her darkened eyes and red lips were abandoned in the drained face.

Brother Man took the telephone from her and placed it on its cradle.

Before her, darkness whirled. To stop it, she stood up, her frail body in forced control. She said harshly, "Something awesome will happen now! *Let it break loose!*"

Her small body sagged into the chair. A coldness rushed through every vein in her body. *An evil God? A holy Satan?*

She was perspiring! Brother Man saw in amazement. And trembling! Just like when the fever— . . .!

She felt the cold perspiration dotting her forehead, then running down her face, her neck, down her breasts, between her legs, into her body.

Brother Man reached out to stop the violent spasms. The cape slid off. His fingers touched the flesh at the top of her smooth, smooth shoulders. He closed his eyes.

She made a rasping sound as she pushed his hand away. Releasing her tense body, she leaned back. Then she said in the tiny voice of the child who had raged in fever for seven days, "I have been with Father and Mother in hell—I waged war with Satan for their souls. I pulled them out of the bottomless pit. If I had lost, we would be with them in hell. Four lost angels— Mommie and Daddie. And you and I, brother and sister like them."

Lost Angels: 14

"There ain't no God!" Orin yelled. His hand had remained on the telephone since he had hung up moments earlier—as if it might still speak to him, retract or add, revise. He looked at Lisa and Jesse James in amazement. "There's no God." This time he whispered it. The words were followed by two long gasped sighs. His blue eyes were the color of evening light, that dark. The face was so crowded with rage and surprise that Jesse took a disguised step away from him.

"She was lying, and the blind woman's really dead," Orin said in wonderment. Sorrow overwhelmed the other emotions flickering on his face. The thick eyebrows knotted,

As if, for the first time, death existed for him, though it had surrounded them in this city of gaudy dying. Gently, firmly, Lisa lifted his hand from the receiver. The hand was cold, so cold. She covered it with both her hands, to bring back the abandoning warmth.

Suddenly Orin laughed.

Jesse greeted the laughter eagerly, forcing his own. "You never were serious about that Sister Woman, were you! *Were you!*" He turned to Lisa for confirmation. "Orin was just joshing us all along, like he's always doing! And we believed him! We believed you, Orin!"

"That's right—a big joke!" Orin's laughter continued.

"It wasn't real," Lisa said softly. No warmth returned to the hand she held.

The television stared blinded. They had faced it for a timeless time throughout Sister Woman's angry sermon, waiting for the words she did not speak.

Still laughing, Jesse took another step away from Orin; this time he did not disguise his move.

Lisa formed laughter, forced laughter.

Jesse extended the straining howls. Now the three laughed and laughed and roared and laughed. They folded over on the bed. The infected laughter tumbled into hysteria. They fell back on the mattress. They held each other. The hollow laughter united them, protected them. The more they tried to stop it, the more the enraged laughter seized them. Lisa gasped, "Orin, you're crazy!"

The laughter faded into an echo. Orin stood.

Outside the wind abated as if the hot desert might be preparing to withdraw it, the sound they had grown used to. Dust scratched at the window. Lisa's last words echoed.

And he *had* been crazy—she had banished that thought, till now, now that the insanity *was* over. And it *was* over!—now that Sister Woman was buried in the gray glassy darkness of the television. And the spectral man in the park was gone, too. Both had existed for them only there, on that lifeless screen, Lisa realized. *Now the nightmare was over!*

Lisa stood next to Orin. "And *you're* crazy, too!" she tossed at Jesse, to diminish the impact of her earlier careless words.

Jesse jumped off the bed, and he swept his sinewy arms about Lisa's and Orin's waists—attempting to spin around with them. But his hands dropped away. The three bodies stood apart, as if abandoned by a slow centrifugal force.

"Got to get out of here!" Orin's gaze ricocheted from the dead television set. "Got to celebrate, 'cause it's *all* over!" he revised the urgency. "A drive, take a drive, to the ocean!"

"Yes!" Lisa agreed quickly. That seemed right—to go there, where the water would wash away the residue of the horror.

"Yeah!" Jesse greeted. Anything—anything!—to shove back the objectless panic bruising the laughter.

Orin was already at the door, Lisa grabbed Pearl, Jesse rushed outside.

Black wind in short anxious bursts that anticipated its dying—or perhaps only another momentary respite. Orin stared at an expiring vortex of dust.

Inside the indigo Cadillac, Jesse thought, *The money!* We'll just go on and on now, just like before! Better! Much better! He, Lisa, and Orin!

Los Angeles is a city that becomes deserted early. The daily frenetic activity—made possible by almost limitless sun and warmth, which nestles at the edge of the city, the beginning of the ocean—stops early, or moves inside. Only tight, scattered insomniac pockets remain for night figures to prowl within yellow-lit shadows.

Odd to be driving these empty streets, Lisa and Jesse realized in surprise. The pattern of their lives, drawn by Orin, had culminated nightly in their return to the motel to hear Sister Woman after a day of touring the city. That had all shifted as abruptly as the blades of slicing dust ahead.

Compressed within the car, their laughter seemed emptier. Stopped for long moments, it would erupt sporadically as the Cadillac glided smoothly onto the Santa Monica Freeway. Only isolated cars dashed along its lanes, lights like the tracers of bullets. Warm currents of wind swept into the car.

Off the freeway! They were on the wide Malibu Highway, driving along the wavy coastline, flanked on the right by precipitous cliffs, which slide into the ocean when the earth trembles or water floods; and on the left by the world of the ocean's darkness. They drove beyond the gray yellow lights of open cafés, through the canyons of Malibu, into deep darkness.

Orin shifted to the left into the paved road that circles Zuma Beach. Scattered here and there, were darkened cars, vans, wide deliberate distances between them.

Orin parked the car so that it blended into the shadows near bruised cliffs that rise up to end the road. They got out. "Over there." Orin pointed to craggy promontories, blacker than the ocean and the sky. Under the smoldering moon, livid white waves lapped over the beach.

The three moved along the warm sand and toward the dark outlines of jutting rocks—beyond the fallen silhouettes of couples on the beach. The night was so white the three cast deep shadows on the sand. The cliffs were farther than they had appeared.

When they reached them, rocks loomed before them. A broken path led through an opening to a small crescent of beach known as Pirate's Cove. Orin climbed the rocks, helping Lisa, held up by Jesse.

The whipped spill of waves mantling the shorelines had reduced the strip of sand. Above it, a huge, black cliff rose straight up. At the tip of the sandy clearing, rocks formed caves before bunching into boulders clutched by rabid crests of water.

They stood on the warm sand and against the tall cliff. There was a rare breath of coolness in the air, and within the sound of advancing water, an indistinct, insistent murmuring containing a million whispers. Hot wind plucked at the sand through breaks in the wall of rocks.

Orin raised his chin—as if in defiance of the roiling ocean; as if he were through hunting patterns within the chaos of forms and elements.

Following his gaze, Lisa saw in the night and water, whorls of darkness.

They moved toward the sheltered cave against the huge knots of rocks. Exhausted, Lisa slid onto the warm sand, Jesse lay next to her, and then Orin was on the other side. Their laughter had died somewhere in the night and along the beach.

Lisa felt coils of emotion unwinding as the two beloved bodies pressed against hers and she pressed against theirs.

Before Jesse fell asleep, he glanced at Orin. When they woke . . . Orin would announce new plans. . . . A new future. . . . And everything would be fine. . . . Fine. . . . Like Cody, always in control. . . . And Orin *was* like Cody, not him, Jesse, he faced that easily; he, Jesse was the loyal friend Cody never had . . . till now. The peaceful thoughts woke Jesse into a dreamy clarity. "I never was really mean," he said. "Just always figured I needed to be tough."

Before she fell asleep, Lisa realized she had left Pearl in the car, on the back seat. That was all right. She curved her body so that all three were closer. Muted here, the sound of the waves now promised peace. Lisa thought, It was always possible. It is possible.

Beyond the cave, the sounds of night conspired in hushed tones.

Day flooded the horizon of silver water and glaring sand. Erratic puffs of hot wind rose and died.

Lisa sat up. Roused by her abrupt movement, Jesse woke.
"Orin's gone!" Lisa said.

Jesse blinked at the blaze of morning, shimmering layers of
gray and silver and blue. They moved out of the cave. Wind
swooped, was slain, stilled like the wings of a dying bird.

Orin's footprints, beginning a diagonal toward the gnarled
rocks, had been erased by the slapping water. Jesse felt the pull
of terror.

They watched the water rush against the land and then retreat,
leaving a jagged wet pattern, returning to erase it, creating
another, quickly destroyed, and then another.

Jesse bounded toward the huge rocks at the end of the sandy
strip. Lisa followed. The craggy wall was so steep they had to
climb it by grasping protrusions of stone with their hands.
Beyond, they faced an expanse of savage scarred rocks swept
by water.

Orin sat many feet away, staring toward the ocean. His
shoulders were hunched, his hands in his pockets.

"Orin!" Lisa shouted.

He looked back at them. He stood. He waved. "I am here,"
he said. Then he made his way toward them, his body pressing
against the rocks, his feet anchored carefully to narrow cracks.
Lisa held out her hand, and he linked his to it.

"You scared us!" Lisa said.

"Went out there in the dark, had to see it," Orin said.

"See what?" Jesse longed for an easy answer.

"What there is," Orin said.

They moved down the rocks to the crescent of beach.

He *had* buried the blind woman at last—the way he had
buried the bird in the desert, suspecting it all perhaps as far back
as then, Lisa thought.

On the curved edge of the beach, they splashed water on their
faces, arms. They laughed easily now—not with last night's
hysteria. They touched playfully, intimately at times. They
moistened their own and each other's clothes, pressing them to
their bodies, letting the wind iron them that way, quickly in the
heat. They felt fresh as they climbed the rocks back to the main
part of the beach.

Early wanderers were there, coastline tramps with purple

brown faces, fishing poles, bundles; erecting lean-to's, making fires for cooking—before the sunbathers and tanned surfers invaded in tribes and drove them away.

The Cadillac waited for them. When they were all inside and Orin had started the motor, he got out, the car idling. Jesse turned back quickly; Lisa looked in the rearview mirror. Both saw the trunk of the car open, then close. Orin returned, and they rode back toward the highway.

"I am *real* hungry!" Orin announced. Jesse and Lisa echoed him, reflecting his easy mood.

Along the highway, weekend beach traffic, undaunted by the canyon fires and redirected from the areas where flames blocked the roads, was snarling early. At Alice's Restaurant, on stilts over the beach, they had breakfast. They ordered everything! —extending the natural laughter as they ate.

"Might as well use up some of that money, now that it's *all* ours," Orin said between bites of food.

Just like him! Just like *that*! Jesse looked at Orin in awe—and relief. he felt no greed, no—he had in the days earlier, for moments, yes; now he just felt relief that a future that included him and Lisa and Orin had been acknowledged. Jesse James had never been happier in his life!

Lisa felt the same happiness—and relief. The money had had no reality for her until now; it had belonged with that woman, who was gone. And now it merely made her feel peaceful, happy with Orin and Jesse. The tension was gone, left behind on those deserted rocks where Orin had sat, abandoning his nightmare, she felt sure as she looked at Orin. A calm new man was emerging, sane now. Sane now.

Orin left a bountiful tip. And when he paid, Jesse noticed, the wallet was *filled* with bills, no longer separated into days. That's what he'd gotten just now from the trunk.

Back on the highway, traffic increased with cars on their journey to the beaches. Hints of coolness nudged the heat. Traffic thickened, but the Cadillac was moving in lanes away from it, toward the freeway, away from the canyon fires, toward the city bathed in new light.

They were on the Santa Monica Freeway. Beyond, everywhere, palm trees bobbed out of the azure of a smogless morning.

Occasionally they still bent with the wind, but less so, resisting more easily. The rim of the distant fires seemed contained in a luminous band, its smoke blowing away from the city.

Jesse turned on the radio; it was set on the news station. ". . . —scandal when it was first bought and painted lime green," the voice of the announcer was saying. "Its garishly painted nude statues attracted crowds and notoriety. Its thirty-eight rooms have been vacant since a fire caused extensive damage. Now the mansion is being restored, beginning tomorrow."

Jesse shifted the dial. He knew he no longer had to bother to check Orin's expression for disapproval. Country and Western sounds filled the car. What's gone, what's left—wiped away by what's to come, the song accepted.

Look at him, so different in a good way, Lisa continued to study Orin, calm, smiling. She felt the soothing happiness, warm, close.

On their side of the freeway, traffic was even sparser now. On the opposite lane the mechanical crush increased. Soon it would peak in the minutes before noon.

The indigo Cadillac flowed along the freeway, toward a crystalline blue sky, toward palm trees increasingly serene, toward buildings cleansed by fresh wind pushing away the stagnant heat of days and nights.

Wide spaces between shooting cars, sparse traffic moves rapidly at this hour on Sundays in an area where all the freeways, or their extensions, converge, connecting all the sections of the city and its outskirts, and all its varied lives. Separated from the San Diego and the Long Beach freeways, the Santa Monica Freeway collides into the Harbor Freeway, which splits into the Hollywood and Santa Ana freeways—east and west, north and south—before it attaches itself to the Pasadena Freeway and rushing joins the San Bernardino Freeway in one direction and in the other the Golden State Freeway, which grasps the Ventura Freeway.

The beautiful indigo Cadillac entered that limbo of freeways now.

It was almost noon.

"This is where we were that afternoon!" Jesse recognized the area excitedly. He pointed to the thickly forested slope of hill he had climbed above the freeways.

"That's where we're going to throw the rifle," Orin said. "Take it apart, scatter the pieces so no one can find it."

With sadness, Jesse remembered the captured man in the park. Yes, it was *right* to undo the rifle this way.

Another welcome burial! Lisa accepted. Now, Orin was ordering the past insanity. It was over. How different today was from that other day.

Orin directed the car off the freeway. There it was, the weedy lot. Above freeways the silent trees loomed. Orin parked the car on the same street. They got out—Jesse shirtless and deep-tanned, Lisa golden and beautiful, Orin boyish and handsome. All laughing, they stood on the partition that separates the grassy decline into the freeways from the hill above.

Orin opened the trunk door of the car and he brought out the rifle. He undid the bedroll around it. The rifle was dark. Lisa took Pearl from the back seat.

Jesse looked at the rifle. "Easy to take it apart," he said to Orin. Now they would all throw its parts into the thick greenness above the traffic moving fast and uninterrupted below.

The rifle was so light Orin held it in one hand. He tilted his head, looking at the black weapon. He located the switch that would release the magazine.

When she gazed down into the freeway this time, Lisa felt no fear. The happiness that the past had contained would be retained. Only the nightmare was over—had not shaped, really. She felt Orin's peace, Jesse's, her own, as if the wind, increasingly cleansed now of sullied heat, were gathering the peace around them. She laughed happily. Orin and Jesse laughed joyously with her. They stood near the green grass and vines sprinkled with pale lavender flowers. Lisa looked at the doll in her hands. She studied it carefully.

"You think he intended to use the weapon, Orin?" Jesse pondered.

"Depends," Orin said.

That word. Lisa clutched Pearl suddenly to her.

Jesse laughed abruptly. "Down there! Look! Probably got a flat tire on their brand-new car!"

Just below, a dark and light blue Chevrolet, shiny in the noon sun, moved off the freeway onto its shoulder.

When she saw the blue-toned car come to a total stop, Lisa felt a resurgence of the heat. "You can't tell for sure from way up here, Jesse!" she said urgently. "It isn't them!"

"Who?" Orin asked casually, ready to release the black magazine.

"That funny woman we kept running into everywhere," Jesse answered, "and her husband who never said anything, remember?—she kept laughing all the time like she was having such a great time, said they just bought a new blue Chevrolet." He laughed again. "The one down there sure looks like the one we saw. They're probably on their way to that Gathering of Souls— . . ." He stopped.

Darkness captured Orin's face. *"No!"* he screamed. His thumb retreated from the release lever and his index finger touched the rifle's trigger.

Bullets sprayed the freeway below, Orin jerked the rifle away, it swirled in an arc, bullets spat into an extension of another freeway, he pulled the rifle up, a tracer among invisible bullets bolted out, an orange splinter of a fatal star twisting into an overpass beyond.

"No!" Lisa covered her eyes.

"No!" Jesse screamed.

"No," Orin barely whispered. He removed his finger from where it had released the safety, had barely touched the trigger. He looked down at the rifle as if only now discovering its horror. "No."

Below, in the freeway, metal, chrome, glass smashed above the shrieks of brakes. Human screams crashed against death. A car hurtled up a slope, another veered against it on its side— both contained in a blossom of swirling flames. The repeated sound of metal assaulting metal ground into a deafening roar. Untouched by the bullets, other cars collided into twisted iron sculpture. Two bodies spun out of the vortex of fire. Flames grasped another lane, another car. Out of bursting orange and red, a body ran along the freeway and fell under the spattering of shredded steel and glass. Beyond, in an extension of this freeway, more metal fused in hard jolts. Fire rose as if from the earth itself. On the overpass, which a tracer bullet seemed to have ignited, flames sprouted and raced in slender devouring lines. Running figures fell, others escaped into the grassy slopes. In broken cars, bodies froze, others rushed out, falling—rising or surrendering to springing death. In three separate limbs of the murdered freeways, triumphant fire spat flames. The recurring clashing of metal on metal, of horns blaring, choking, of glass bursting—and screams, screams—all extended the shrieking roar. Thick shreds of smoke shrouded the sky over wounded bodies and bleeding death, and bodies standing unhurt—all tossed out on the freeway as if by a raging, indifferent force.

Then the lanes seemed awesomely quiet. There was a strange hollow silence that contained its own roaring sounds.

Orin still looked down at the weapon that had unleashed the massive devastation.

Unbelieving, his ears deafened by the chain of eruptions, Jesse stared at him.

Lisa opened her eyes and looked at Orin. He seemed startled, terrified, confused. He still clung to the rifle, as if he could withdraw its destruction. Lisa felt a long, soundless scream implode within her—and him, and Jesse.

Orin shook his head as if to clear his mind, understand what had occurred.

Below, the two-toned blue Chevrolet moved away, untouched.

Smoke rose toward Orin, Jesse, Lisa. And soon distant sirens pierced the paralyzed roar.

Orin rubbed his eyes, as if to break a trance. One hand reached out, to touch Lisa's shoulder. As if that contact snapped the trance, he shouted loudly, to be heard, "Run away, Lisa!"

Lisa shook her head. "No!" she screamed and clutched the frayed doll.

"Yes, run away!" Jesse shouted just as loudly—knowing that she must and that Orin knew why. When he felt her body trembling, Jesse realized his arm, too, was embracing her.

"No, no, no, no, no!" Lisa yelled.

"Now!" Orin insisted. "Not much time! Now, Lisa! Run up into that hill!" he yelled, as if the force of his words would push her. "You've *got* to! You and Jesse!"

"You both come with me!" Lisa shouted. "You and Jesse
and— . . .!"

"Can't!" Orin cried. His eyes shifted across the street, toward the hill. "They'd follow all of us that way. I have to stay
here—with the rifle—draw them here while you and Jesse— . . ."

"No, no, no, no, no!"

"One of us has to escape, Lisa, and it has to be you." In a
deliberate, definite tone, Jesse altered Orin's exhortation.

"No!" Lisa screamed. *"No!"*

Orin's eyes searched the horizon. Still touching her shoulder,
he rushed words: "Throw the doll away, Lisa! Throw the doll
away! She's dead and you're alive!"

Lisa flung the doll into the smashed pit below.

"Now *live,* Lisa!" Orin yelled. He pushed her gently but
forcefully away.

At the same time that a part of her soul flung itself backward
to lock forever with Orin and Jesse, Lisa felt her body rushing
away, understanding that she could save them only by fleeing
from their deaths and with their lives—not by dying for them or
with them. Her body hurled itself beyond the edge of the
freeway, across the concrete separation, and into the forested
hill.

Watching her disappear into the thick, concealing coves of
tall trees and sprawled sheltering shadows, the rifle still in his
hand, Orin turned to Jesse. "You, too, Jesse! Run! Quick! Just
barely time enough!"

Jesse looked toward where Lisa had vanished—a moment
ago, minutes, already forever. He said silently, Run, Lisa, live!

Orin screamed, "Run, Jesse!"

No. Jesse looked at Orin and shook his head. No. He stood
next to Orin and waited.

And then sirens and the whir of helicopter blades gathered
distantly, and then surrounded them, and then enclosed them in
a narrowing swirl of lights. Out of the slashing sounds, whirling
lights, and gray, choking smoke, policemen in dark uniforms
and gas masks crouched.

"Run, Jesse!" Orin yelled. He waited for seconds, staring at
Jesse.

Jesse shook his head, decisively. No.

Orin nodded. Then he held the mysterious weapon with both his hands, and he raised it mutely over his head, directing fire to him from the crouching dark-uniformed figures. His body wrenched and then fell on the green earth. A circle of blood on his chest grew, finding its shape, the shape of a deadly liquid rose.

Only when he saw the body crumble on the vines and flowers did Jesse hear the bullets that had killed Orin. Jesse flung himself on the ground. With pain—but also with the triumph of his total loyalty— Jesse stared at the familiar face of his friend. He took the weapon from the hand that still touched it, stood up, and prepared to shout Cody's last words, remembered at last—*I made it, Ma! Top of the world!*—but still he could not form them, because in that eternal pinpoint of a moment Cody's meaning was replaced by his own. Sobbing, Jesse James whispered instead:

"I made it . . . Pa."

At that moment he saw or thought he saw the indigo Cadillac explode into a huge orchid of roiling black and white flames out of which bills of money flew from the car's rent trunk—money—or leaves—dark green leaves scattering in terror or freedom into the wind.

Jesse fired into the sun—a slash of cold white—shattering the white heat.

Pulled in many directions by stinging bullets, Jesse fell on Orin's body.

Within spilling shadows, under long green branches, Lisa heard the blast of shots. They forced her gaze back. Did she see or imagine—or feel—Orin and Jesse twisting into death? The shots ricocheted, trapped in her mind, killing Orin and Jesse over and over and over and over as she continued to climb. Weeds and brush and broken branches scratched at her legs, hands. Bloodied perspiration glued dark smoke and ashes to her face and body as she pulled herself up through tangles of thicket—resting for moments or longer, moving again, climbing, knowing—and only because shadows lengthened—that time was moving, too, had not even paused for death. Again she looked down through gaps between trees, as if she might yet discover the terror erased.

Flooding water and foam poured out of giant hoses below, far, far below. Steam hissed. Fumes wound grappling shadows of smoke into the wet heat, into stalled time.

Mandy Lang-Jones stood above the freeway and surveyed the stilled catastrophe as close as she could come. Rushing television crews had descended to record the spattered horror. Among wires of cameras, Mandy Lang-Jones tried to estimate the number of dead. Sparse Sunday traffic had allowed cars to escape past smoldering flames, probably keeping the deaths low. But it would still be a top national story for days, and the perfect hook for her series on mass killings!

Mandy mussed her hair, touched her face with ashes, moistened her eyelids with spit, and located her body so that millions of screens would frame her against the frozen holocaust and the glow of flames in the canyons. She faced electronic eyes. Her voice throbbed into the microphone: "This is Mandy Lang-Jones! I am standing at the site of one of the worst mass slaughters in recent times! The two snipers who fired into the freeways have been killed by police, who speculate they belonged to a splinter radical group! Beyond that, all that is known is that on this hot June day, an act of meaningless violence— . . ."

Beyond, the sound of sirens rose, fell, floated away with the whir of helicopters—farther, fading into crushed silence.

On the shadowed hill, the encompassing verdure, Lisa pulled her eyes away from the blurred terror and pushed her body against the stagnant heat. Gathering sorrow threatened to choke her. So quickly, Orin and Jesse were remembered images, echoes of words, cries and laughter!—beloved strangers whose voices were stilled now forever. *Forever!* So quickly and that sudden and *forever!* Protesting that sudden, mysterious, immutable silence, she screamed, and the screams tore from her body:

"*Orin! Jesse!*"

Trembling, she rested crying on soft earth. What had Orin fired at? The fatal trigger—pulled on purpose? Aimed at nothing, in panic, despair, sorrow, betrayal, lost hope? No! He had touched the trigger accidentally!

She grasped at twisted roots and pulled herself up through

gray shadows. Orin and Jesse were dead. And so was Pearl Chavez.

Lisa climbed toward streaks of sky barely tinged by distant, dying flames.

A dark silhouette on the crest of a hill, she stood above black ruins, blackened stones, and she felt the blessing of a cool breeze. Wiping away sweat and tears streaked with blood, she heard the indistinct murmuring of lingering wind, whispered curses left among the dark green pines. She listened intently, determined to drain out of the secret sounds those she needed in order to live. She heard them!—in the brushed leaves; thought she heard echoes of Orin's and Jesse's exhortation: *Live, Lisa!*

Even as branded horrors singed her mind, she clung to the sounds she had dredged out of the dead wind. She *forced* the merest breath of hope, and she thrust it against the memories of this season of heat and blood and fire.

END

Epilogue

Killed in the slaughter on the freeways in Los Angeles were: Manuel Gomez, Barbara Ann Leighton (also known as Amber Haze), Alana Freeman Stephens, Michelangelo Valenti (also known as Mick Vale), Debby Weston, William "Billy" Young, and an unidentified teenage male bearing the designation "Stud" tattooed on his upper left arm.

Among the wounded were: David Howard Clinton and Hester Washington.

Among those on the freeway at the time but unhurt were: James Huston, Norris Weston, and an unidentified woman of about fifty, probably a derelict who had wandered on foot into the freeway.